THE DOOR AT
THE CROSSROADS

THE DOOR AT THE CROSSROADS

ZETTA ELLIOTT

Rosetta
Press

The characters and events portrayed in this book are fictitious. Any similarity to real persons, living or dead, is coincidental and not intended by the author.

Cover design by Deasy Suryani
Interior design by Deasy Suryani
Front cover photographs: Shutterstock, Weeksville Society
Back cover illustration: Shutterstock
Author photo: © Valerie Caesar

ISBN-13: 978-1515392163
ISBN-10: 1515392163

Judah

1.

I may be a killer, but I am not my father.

Genna

2.

I am awake. I am alive. But the dream — the nightmare — isn't over. I am here, in the twenty-first century. But it's happening all over again.

It is September 11, 2001, and New York City is under attack. The fires that burned in 1863 are burning once again. There is chaos in the streets, and people are dying. It isn't happening to me, but it is happening all around me. People are fleeing Manhattan, their faces blank with disbelief and powdered white with ash. Nothing has changed — not the hatred, not the killing. I have traveled more than a hundred years, and nothing has changed. Except this time I am alone. This time Judah isn't here.

Judah

3.

Reverend Garnet says to start at the beginning so that's what I'm trying to do. But how can I tell my story when my past is the future and my present is the past?

My father killed my mother. I saw him do it with my own eyes when I was just a little kid. And I always swore I'd never be like him—until I got here. It's still Brooklyn, but it's 1863. The country's at war with itself. I've been trapped in this world for less than a year and I've already killed two men. *Two men*. Both of them White.

I never wanted this to happen. I didn't ask to be sent back in time. But I'm here now and the girl I love—the one person I thought I couldn't live without—went and left me. Again.

Genna's *there* in the future and I'm *here* in the past—alone.

Reverend Garnet says to write it all down. He says my account must be complete—if I leave anything out, folks will think I'm making all this up. But no one could dream up the things I've seen and done.

Reverend Garnet says, "You will be a witness, Judah. You must testify on behalf of those who cannot speak for themselves." He says I'll feel better if I stand up and testify—not in a court of law, but in the court of public opinion. He says people won't judge me if I make them understand it was self-defense. But I'm not sure I can convince a room full of strangers when I can't even convince myself.

Judah

4.

It was a warm night in June — 2001. I was drumming in the park with some friends when my phone went off.

"Judah — it's me. You got to come over here, man. Like, *now*."

Samuel's my cousin. He works as a security guard at the botanic garden and he's usually real laid back. But that night I could tell that something was wrong. I left the drumming circle and walked deeper into the park so I could hear better. "You at work?" I asked.

"Yeah, son. We got a wedding reception here tonight and things are getting out of hand. This fool — Sikes — he's new on the job and this is his first time doing a night gig."

Sometimes it takes a while for my cousin to cut to the chase. My palms were still pulsing and I wanted to get back to my drum. "Samuel — what's any of this got to do with me?"

He sighed and lowered his voice. "Genna came by earlier. You know she ain't supposed to be in here at night but things got a little hectic and she got past me, son."

I stopped walking and tried to imagine what could have driven Genna into the garden so late at night. Her family lives in a building across the street and her mom's real strict, so if Genna was on her own there must be trouble at home. "Is she okay?" I asked.

Samuel didn't respond right away, which made me think he was holding back. My voice got louder and harder than I wanted it to be. "Samuel—what's going on?"

"I don't know, Judah. Your girl—she looked kinda upset, a'ight? And then Sikes—he went out on patrol in the cart and…

"AND?"

Samuel practically hissed into the phone. "Son—that fool discharged his *weapon*! He's here right now filling out the paperwork. His partner says he got spooked and shot at a rabbit, but…"

"But—*what*?"

"I'm trying to tell you, son. *Genna's still out there*. I'm on the desk and I ain't seen her come by. And there ain't no other way outta here, Judah."

I meant to say, "I'm on my way," but my heart started to pound and nothing came out of my mouth. I snapped the phone shut, left my drum with Peter, and raced over to the garden.

It wasn't easy, but Samuel managed to get me past all the guests in their tuxedos and fancy dresses. I was a mess—my t-shirt was soaked with sweat and I tried to act calm but panic moved my limbs in ways I've never moved before. I raced through the shadowy garden and it felt like I was swimming at the bottom of the sea—the night air was like dark, cool water. I was actually shivering by the time I reached the fountain, and right away I could tell something was wrong. I'd been there a dozen times before—Genna and I used to meet there after school. She always kept loose change in her pocket so she could make a wish. The first time we kissed was on the bench that circles the fountain. It's made of stone and the curve makes sound travel fast—people can communicate even if they're sitting far apart. They call it the whispering bench.

I didn't want to believe anything bad had happened to Genna, but something just didn't feel right. The cool air felt…electric, almost. There was no one in sight and everything looked silver in the moonlight—the grass, the water, the flat stones on the ground—everything gleamed like it was covered in a thin coating of frost.

A sudden breeze made my skin tingle. Then I heard a voice so I spun around but there was no one there. *Don't leave me…* The words hung in the air like a leaf slowly sinking to the bottom of the fountain.

"Genna?"

As soon as I called her name a cloud passed over the moon and everything went dark. It's always peaceful in the garden but usually you can still hear the noise of cars speeding down the parkway. Yet in that moment, it felt like all sound had been sucked out of the garden. I'd never heard that kind of silence in the city before.

I was just about to head back to the visitor center when something on the ground caught my eye. It had an orange glow even though it was so dark out I could barely see my hand in front of my face. I figured it must be a penny but when I bent down to pick it up, I discovered instead a coin-sized drop of blood. I walked over to the fountain and dipped my fingers into the water to rinse the blood away. And that's the last thing I remember doing. A streak of lightning tore open the night sky and when I opened my eyes again, I wasn't in the botanic garden any more. I was *here* — still in Brooklyn — but in a whole other century.

Genna

5.

I wake up alone in Mama's queen-sized bed. The clock on the dresser tells me I have slept past noon. The bedroom door is closed, but I can hear the television coming from the living room. I crawl out of bed and realize I am still wearing the clothes I had on yesterday. Yesterday. A day ago I was in another century. I reach up under my t-shirt and feel for the scars on my back. They're still there. But I am here now, in this world. I'm back where I belong. I'm home. Then why do I feel so alone?

I make up the bed, then sit on the edge and look at my reflection in the mirror. I remember how months ago I would sit here at night in front of the dresser and twist the little buds of hair so that my locks would grow. Judah's aunt locked my hair before school let out. That was late June, and now it's September—less than three months have passed. But when I went back to 1863, it was winter—Christmas eve. I stayed in that Brooklyn from December to July, and my locks grew all that time. Seven months.

I look in the mirror and finger my locks. They were tiny buds when I left but now they are four inches long. I open one of Mama's drawers and take out a scarf to cover my head. Then I realize I don't have to hide my locks anymore. I roll the scarf and make it into a headband instead, pushing my hair back off my face. The mirror assures me that I look like a regular teenager, except for the dark circles under my eyes. I look normal, but I know that I'm not. Judah knew, too—even before we went back in time. Judah always knew I was different.

Thinking of Judah makes me feel hollow inside. My stomach is empty, and I can't remember the last time I ate. But what I feel for Judah is a different kind of hunger. I look at the phone on the bedside table and consider calling Judah's aunt. Right now I would give anything just to hear his voice. But I know if I call, Judah won't be there. His Aunt Marcia will answer the phone, and what could I tell her? What will I tell my own mother when she asks me where I've been?

In the living room Mama is talking to someone on the phone. I hear her voice through the walls, and the sound of her footsteps as she walks across the room. My back stiffens as she approaches the bedroom, but Mama goes past the door and turns off the TV instead. I sigh with relief and tell myself to relax. She's my mother. What am I afraid of?

"I don't know, Louise, I didn't ask her. She just got back last night, and she fell asleep almost right away. She looks fine, on the outside, at least. No, I didn't—Louise, I just told you I didn't get a chance to ask her anything! She was tired and upset, so I just put her to bed. And now we have to deal with all this. Lord, help us...I just turned off the TV. I know I can't hide it from her, Louise, but it doesn't have to be the first thing she sees when she wakes up. Some homecoming that would be—"

Mama stops talking when she sees me standing in the open doorway. "I'll call you back, Louise." Mama clicks off the cordless phone and rushes over to me. "Hey, baby, how do you feel? Did you sleep okay?"

I nod and lose myself in my mother's embrace. Mama still smells and feels the same. We hold onto each other for a real long time. Then Tyjuan tries to get in on the action by squeezing himself between our legs.

Mama laughs and scoops Tyjuan up in her arms. "Okay, little man, she's all yours." Mama hands my little brother over to me and heads for the kitchen. "You must be hungry. Let me get you some breakfast. Pancakes and eggs okay?"

I smile and nod at Mama before she disappears into the kitchen. Then

I look at the beautiful little boy I am holding in my arms. Before I can even take a real good look at Tyjuan, my eyes fill up with tears. I carry him over to the sofa and sit down so I can get a hold of myself.

"Hey, there, baby brother. Do you remember me?"

Tyjuan laughs and hoists himself up so he is standing on my lap. He tugs at my locks and I bury my face in his plump, warm body. I am home. *I am home.* My tears keep falling, but I start to laugh as well. My fingers remember all of Tyjuan's tickle spots, and soon he is squealing with joy.

Mama sticks her head around the corner to see what's going on. Her eyes start to shine as well, but before any tears can fall there is a loud knock at the door. "I wonder who that could be?"

Mama answers the door, and for just a moment I hear a familiar voice. It is Mrs. Charles, our neighbor who lives at the front of the building. "Is it true? Is she back? Did you see them fall? What a day, sweet Jesus — everything happening all at once..."

I peek around the corner just in time to see Mama push Mrs. Charles back out into the hall. She pulls the front door shut behind her, and whispers so I can't hear. I look around the living room, suddenly aware that something isn't right. Sirens are wailing outside, but that's not unusual. Then I remember what I heard of Mama's phone conversation with her best friend, Louise. I reach for the remote just as Mama comes back into the living room.

"Mrs. Charles says, 'Welcome home.' She wanted to come in, but I told her to come back after you'd eaten your breakfast — " Mama stops talking as I turn the television on.

"Oh, baby, you don't want to see that right now..." Mama gently tries to take the remote from me.

"Don't, Mama," I say quietly, and sit transfixed in front of the screen.

Mama sighs and takes Tyjuan from me instead. "There's nothing but bad news on TV today. Seems like the whole world's turned upside down." Tyjuan wants to come back to me, but Mama won't let go. She nervously bounces him up and down on her hip, her eyes swinging from my face to the TV.

I sit on the edge of the sofa—my spine stiff and tingling with that familiar electric sensation—and tune out everything but the matter-of-fact voice of the newscaster. I just sit there, unable to speak, unable to move, unable to take my eyes away from the images of chaos on the screen. No. *No no no no no.* This isn't happening. This can't be happening. Then I look at the screen more closely. I look up at the clock on the wall and realize it has happened already. The Twin Towers have fallen. New York City is under attack.

Suddenly there is another loud knock at the door. Mama jumps and carries Tyjuan over to the door to see who's there. This time the voices refuse to be kept out in the hall. Mrs. Charles pushes her way into the apartment, followed closely by Louise.

I am perched on the edge of the sofa like a bird about to take flight. My back is damp with sweat and growing hotter by the moment. I don't want anyone to touch me, but Mrs. Charles is coming at me with her arms open wide.

"Genna, baby! You alright? Let me take a look at you—"

"What's that smell?" Louise puts her hand on Mrs. Charles' shoulder, and both women turn to Mama.

"Oh, Lord, I forgot about the pancakes!"

Mama's arms are full of Tyjuan who's still fussing and reaching for me, so Louise and Mrs. Charles push past her and all three squeeze into the kitchen. The smoke alarm starts going off, and Tyjuan's screaming real loud now. Mrs. Charles props the front door open with a chair to air the place out, and Louise throws what's left of my breakfast into the sink.

"Girl, you trying to burn Brooklyn down, too? There ain't a fire truck to be found out there, so you better watch what you leave on the stove."

Mama's doing three things at once—apologizing to her friends, trying to soothe Tyjuan, and using her free hand to swat at the smoke alarm with the broom. "I don't know where my head's at this morning. I was just trying to make a nice breakfast for Genna. Louise, get the eggs out of the fridge—there should be enough left for an omelet. Is there any bread? We could make French toast. Lord, what a day..."

Mrs. Charles takes the broom from Mama and smacks the fire alarm good and hard. It stops beeping and things start to calm down. "Take a seat and make that child hush, Lorene."

Mama does as she's told, but catches a glimpse of me before I can take flight. "Genna? Genna!"

I ignore Mama, dart through the open door, and head straight for the roof. On my way upstairs I notice that nothing about this building has changed. The hallway is still littered with trash, the floors are sticky and unswept. But this morning no one is hanging out in the hall. People are inside their apartments, huddled around the television watching our city fall apart.

I take the stairs two at a time and soon I reach the top floor. The stairs leading to the roof are rigged with an alarm, but it almost never works. I dash up the steps quickly, just in case the alarm goes off, and open the door at the top which is, as always, unlocked. I push it open and stumble breathless onto the roof.

Startled pigeons squawk and scramble out of my way. I wait a moment for my eyes to adjust to the bright sunlight, then I turn north. There, in the cloudless blue sky, I see the proof I dreaded but needed to see. New York City is burning. A huge, black plume of smoke is spreading across the sky. Nothing has changed. More than a hundred years ago— or was it really just one day?—I stood with Martha on the roof of the Brants' house, watching the draft riots destroy Manhattan. It was 1863 and nighttime then; it is 2001 and broad daylight now. But nothing has changed.

I look down into the back alley. It's still filled with reeking garbage and howling cats. Slowly I walk across the sticky tar roof to the front of the building. The streets below are filled with the sounds of chaos—sirens scream endlessly, frantic parents drag their confused children home from school, others gather in loose knots to discuss the tragedy.

I close my eyes and try to shut out the noise, the smell, the images of destruction. But inside my mind the dream will not die. It plays over and over again—each scene flowing into the next—the horde of hateful faces chasing us on the night of the riot, people white with ash stumbling through the streets of lower Manhattan, Judah firing the gun over and over until the black-haired man falls dead, bodies plunging from the towers like wingless birds to avoid being roasted alive…

I open my eyes. Nothing has changed. The sirens are still screaming, and the air is tainted with the smell of death. I step up onto the ledge and stand very still, balancing myself between the roof and the air, the present and the past. Will this nightmare ever be over? I can make it end. I can put out the fires, silence the sirens, erase the dark history once and for all.

"Genna?"

Mama's voice pulls me back an inch. I can tell from her voice that she is still at the back of the building, which means she hasn't seen me yet. One step forward and I will be gone. One step back and I will be trapped in this world. What did Judah used to call it? *Babylon.*

"Genna?" Mama's voice is louder now, more desperate. If she sees me this way…

And what would Judah say? If he knew I was thinking of giving up instead of fighting, instead of finding a way back to him? Judah never gave up on me.

I lean back and my feet land on the roof with a thud. Mama follows the commotion made by the pigeons and finds me sitting on the warm tar.

"Genna, baby, are you okay?"

Mama is still holding Tyjuan in her arms. He sees me and shrieks with delight. Mama tries to hold onto him, but my baby brother is determined to come to me. Mama finally gives up and sets him down on the roof. My knees are pulled up close to my chest, but Tyjuan toddles over to me and forces his way onto my lap anyway.

Within seconds Tyjuan becomes a soft, warm, brown blur. Through my tears I smile at his gurgling baby talk, the familiar touch of his little fingers in my ears, my mouth, my hair. I hold onto Tyjuan and think of the baby boy I left in another century. I wonder who is holding Henry now.

"Genna, are you okay?" Mama kneels down to wipe the tears from my face. "I know it's awful, baby. I'm so sorry it had to happen on your first day back. I'm sorry it happened at all. I don't know what this world's coming to…" Mama stops talking and looks at me with desperate, frightened eyes. We are alone on the roof, but her voice drops to a whisper. "You're going to stay with us, aren't you, baby? Promise me you won't leave again."

I try, but I can't look at my mother. I don't want to hurt her, but I also don't want to lie. Instead I look at Tyjuan and wonder if he and Mama will be enough to keep me in this world. Suddenly I feel incredibly tired, like a bird that has been circling in the sky, searching for a safe place to land. In the distance, the black cloud of smoke is smearing across the blue sky. Mama puts her arms around us and tries to keep our family together as the city goes up in smoke.

Judah

6.

My body is on fire. The air around me is cold but there are flames burning beneath my skin. The grey sky pities me and sends down thick clumps of snow to smother the flames. I close my eyes and let the snowflakes wrap me in a soothing white blanket.

Judah

7.

"Lester, you see what I see?"

I blink and look for a face as ugly as that voice, but all I can see is a sky so white it blinds. I try to sit up but a sharp pain in my side makes me groan and my head falls back with a thud. I hear a second voice.

"What is it, Charlie—some kinda bear? Lemme get my gun!"

Bear? Gun? I have the impulse to run but not the energy. My body lies like lead on the cold, hard ground. I know that I am outside and I know that I'm in trouble, but I don't know anything else. I try to raise my arm but it feels like there's a magnet pulling me into the frozen earth. I shiver and try to speak: *help!*

A soundless puff of frost slips between my lips. I cannot hear my own voice but I hear the soft crunch of snow as the two men approach. I say a quick prayer and open my eyes. Two White men are standing over me. There is no trace of compassion in their eyes.

"Well, well, well." The bigger one scans my body with appraising eyes and then hauls off and kicks me in the ribs.

This time I hear myself cry out in pain but my limbs are still too heavy to lift. I want to curl into a ball. I want to jump up and put my fist in this White man's face. But all I can do is press my lips together so they don't know how much pain I'm in.

"He sick?" The leaner man steps back, suddenly afraid I might have some sort of contagious disease.

"Naw. He ain't sick—just wore out from running. The gal was the same way, remember?"

Gal? Are they talking about Genna? Is she here? I close my eyes and try to calm my mind so I can think clearly. If these men have found Genna, then they can take me to her. But if they haven't found Genna, I need to be careful about what I reveal. Could she be hiding nearby?

With a grunt, the stocky one squats down and points a fat finger in my face before leering at me. "You're ours now, boy!" Then he turns to his friend and says, "Looks like it's gonna be a merry Christmas after all, Lester." Their laughter sends clouds of frost into the sky.

Christmas? I close my eyes once more and try to make sense of these strange clues. I'm hurt. I'm outside. It is cold, but how could it be Christmas already? Have I been in some sort of coma for six months?

Charlie stops chuckling and his foul, liquored breath hovers over my face. I open my eyes and see the black stubble on his unshaved face and smell the stench of his unwashed clothes. Something about this man doesn't seem right. Maybe he and Lester are a couple of homeless guys— maybe they'll just take my money, my phone, and my shoes, and then leave me alone.

Charlie rubs his hands together and I think now he's going to roll me. But instead he gets this evil gleam in his eye and says, "Another runaway. I knew it! I knew that gal couldn't have run off by herself. And we ain't gonna make the same mistake twice—this time we're selling this buck ourselves 'stead of turning him in and letting some other dumb nigger walk off with our reward."

This time I keep my eyes open wide so I know for sure that I am awake. Was I dreaming, or did this White man just say *nigger*? He thinks I'm a *runaway* and there's only one word that goes after runaway—*slave*.

I try to stay calm but inside I am like a pot that's about to boil over. I try to turn onto my side but my body won't obey, and all I can manage is to turn my head. A steaming stream of vomit pours out of my mouth and spatters onto Charlie's boots. He jumps back, curses, and kicks me again, which only unleashes another stream of vomit.

"Goddamn nigger!" Charlie tosses fresh snow onto his boots and tries to brush the slime away.

Lester comes around the other side and peers at me from a safe distance. "Look at his hair! I ain't never seen hair like that on a nigger before. Have you, Charlie?"

Charlie stops fussing with his boots and pins his angry eyes on me. "Hmph. Not round these parts. He must be one o' them African niggers — straight off the boat! Here — check his teeth."

Lester pulls back, alarmed. "What for?"

"I hear Africans got sharp, pointy teeth — they're savages, you know. So go on — check his teeth."

Lester pulls back even further, obviously afraid. "You check 'em."

Charlie gives a hollow, nervous laugh. "Shame on you, Lester. You mean to tell me you're scared of a dumb ape? Why, he's so weak he can't even move." Charlie kicks me lightly in the leg and once again I am unable to will my body to respond.

When Lester still doesn't look convinced, Charlie starts hopping up and down, tickling his armpits in his best performance of a monkey. Lester frowns, swallows hard, and cautiously extends the tip of his rifle toward my jaw.

Charlie lunges forward and bats the gun away from my face. "You damn fool! What're you trying to do — blow his head off?"

"You told me to check his teeth!" cries Lester.

"With your hand, you idiot, not with your gun!" Charlie pauses a moment. "Here — help me sit him up. And put that gun down before you blow out whatever brains you got."

Lester does as he's told and the two men reach down to grab me by the shoulders. As they pull me into a sitting position, I glance at the gun lying just a few feet away on the ground. I've never fired a gun like that before, and I can't even feel my fingers right now, but I know I have to try to do *something*—soon. I can't explain what's happening to me, but I can tell this situation's only going to go from bad to worse.

Once they've got me propped up, Charlie reaches in to tug at my lips, then surprises me by slapping me across the face. When I cry out, more from surprise than pain, Charlie peers inside my mouth and proclaims, "He's got teeth like a horse! Buyers like that in a slave."

"So he ain't from Africa after all," Lester concludes with a note of disappointment in his voice.

"Might be," says Charlie, like he's some kind of expert. "What's that?"

Lester jumps up, panicked. "What's what?"

Charlie tightens his grip on my shoulder to stop me from falling back onto the ground. "There—under his arm. There's blood on his shirt."

Lester draws near and lifts up my thin, stained shirt. I look down and try to see the wound that suddenly starts throbbing with pain.

"I think he's been stabbed, Charlie." Lester lifts my shirt some more so that Charlie can take a look. I shiver as the winter wind presses against my bare skin. Charlie roughly pokes the skin under my left arm. I wince but try not to cry out.

An oily grin spreads across Charlie's fat face. "That ain't no knife wound—that's a brand. Fresh, too. I told you he was from Africa. Fresh off the boat, I'll bet."

Lester lets go of my shirt and looks at me with something like awe. "I thought they wasn't bringing 'em over from Africa no more."

Charlie grunts. "They ain't allowed to, according to the law. But you know well as me that there's a way around every law in the book. He musta been smuggled in."

"How'd he get way out here in the ash dump?" Lester asks.

"I don't know and I don't care. Let's get him cleaned up and take him down to the docks. I know a fella who'll take him off our hands for a fair price."

"We gotta clean him?" Lester frowns and I wonder about the last time *he* took a bath.

"Make him look decent, that's all. That woolly mop's gotta go. You got your hunting knife?"

"Sure." Lester tugs up his pant leg and pulls a large knife from a holster strapped to his ankle.

"Well, what are you waiting for? Cut it off!"

The throbbing in my side quickens and I feel something—a faint tingle—stirring in my legs. They *cannot* cut my locks. I won't let them cut my locks. It's forbidden!

Lester grabs a hunk of my hair and screws his face up with disgust. "All of it?"

"Sure," Charlie says. "Sampson had all his strength in his hair, right? We'll have less trouble with this nigger once he learns who's boss." Lester still looks uncertain but Charlie goads him on. "Go on, Lester. Start cutting. I'll hold him."

Lester grabs hold of my hair, tugs my head back, and starts sawing at my roots with the blade of his knife. I try to summon whatever strength I can find to resist but manage to revive only my voice. My limbs still refuse to move. "No—stop!"

I try to twist my head away from the blade but Charlie just gets behind me and wraps his fat arm around my neck. With the air squeezed out of my throat, I press my eyes shut so the tears of rage don't spill out.

Lester hacks away at my hair—locks I have grown for half my life. When he is done, he tosses it aside like it's trash. "What you want me to do with all this wool, Charlie?"

"Leave it here," he says, removing his arm from around my neck. Defeated, I slump forward and hang my shorn head in shame. Charlie takes up a thick lock of my hair and uses it to wipe his vomit-stained boot. "This stuff'll make a nice warm bed for some poor critter. Come on, Lester—help me get him up. It'll be dark soon."

Lester tucks his knife back in its sheath. He grabs one of my arms and

Charlie grabs the other. As they heave me up off the ground, I seize the opportunity to strike back the only way I can. I suck up all the saliva in my mouth and hurl it into Lester's face. Stunned, he wipes my spit from his cheek and then curls those same fingers into a fist and slams it into my face. I feel a tooth loosen somewhere along my jaw but still manage to pull back my head and ram it into Lester's face.

He lets go of me and tries to stem the flow of blood. "He broke my nose!"

I collapse in a heap on the ground and enjoy a brief moment of satisfaction as I watch the blood gush down Lester's pale face.

Then Charlie barks at me, "Animal!" He picks up Lester's rifle and brings the butt down hard on my head. I lose consciousness with a half-formed curse hanging on the tip of my tongue.

Genna

8.

"Here, baby, I brought you some clean towels…"

Mama's breath goes back into her mouth, thin and sharp as a blade. She is staring at the scars on my back, not wanting to believe they are real. I could look my mother in the eye simply by facing the mirror. But instead I wrap the towel around my body and keep my eyes on the water swirling down the drain.

Mama reaches out and touches my bare shoulder. Her fingertips are cold and I jump in spite of myself.

"Who did this to you?"

I have been back nearly a week, and Mama has been patient with me. I have put off answering her questions. I have kept my other life buried deep inside of me. The chaos of 9/11 makes it easy to change the subject. But I always knew I couldn't hide the truth from her forever. The scars on my body won't let me keep the past a secret.

"Genna, who did this to you?"

I shiver as cool air slips inside the open door. "I can't tell you, Mama." It's the truth, but Mama doesn't understand.

"Why not?" Mama pushes the knife back out of her mouth. It is aimed right at me, but I know who Mama really wants to hurt.

"You wouldn't believe me, Mama. You wouldn't understand."

Mama stares at me for a long time, her eyes hard and unforgiving.

Then she sits down on the toilet lid and sighs heavily. "Genna, baby, this world ain't what it used to be. People are flying airplanes into skyscrapers. A week ago I would never have believed that could happen, but now I know different. Try me, Genna. *Please*. I need to know what's happened to you."

I sit down on the edge of the tub and stare at my bare toes. Mama reaches out and touches my locks. "Your hair has grown so quickly."

My mother touches my locks so gently, with such tender admiration, that I start to cry. Mama puts her hands on my shoulders and pulls me onto her lap. I am too old and too big to be held like this, but I let Mama rock me just like she used to when I was a little girl.

"You don't have to hide anything from me anymore, Genna. I didn't do right by you, I know that. And I'm so sorry, baby. But we've got to be honest with each other from now on. 'Cause I can't lose you again. And I can't keep you safe unless you trust me. Okay?" Mama brushes the tears from my eyes and I nod silently. Then she takes a deep breath and says, "It wasn't that boy, was it? That Rasta?"

I jump up off Mama's lap. "No! Mama—how could you think that? Judah would never hurt me. He saved me—he saved my life, Mama!"

"Okay, baby, calm down. Please, Genna—I had to ask. He went missing about the same time as you—we all figured you were together, but I didn't know if you'd gone willingly. I thought maybe he forced you to—"

"Judah didn't force me to do anything!"

"Okay, okay, I believe you, baby. Whatever you say. Just tell me who hurt you like that."

I don't want to get too close to Mama, so I press myself into the corner by the sink. I don't know how to tell this story, but I am so tired of holding it in. And Mama's right—what happened on Tuesday proves that just about anything's possible. I take a deep breath and decide to just say everything at once, even if it doesn't make sense.

"I went back in time, Mama. To 1863. I went to the garden that night after you — after we had that fight. And I made a wish in the fountain, and I got sent back in time. Judah came to the garden looking for me, and he got sent back, too, but we couldn't find each other for a long while. We were slaves, Mama. And I don't know who beat me like that, but Judah got whipped, too. It happened all the time back then because Black people weren't real people, we were property. White folks owned us, and they could treat us any old way. I was lucky — I met good people who helped me. And then I found Judah and the riots started and then I got shot and that sent me back here."

For a long time Mama doesn't say anything. She just looks at me with that crease between her eyes. Mama looks at me like I am a stranger, like I am some alien from outer space. Mama looks at me as if I'm crazy, but I can tell she is fighting something inside herself. She knows I am not a stranger or an alien — I am her daughter. And I am not lying. Something inside her knows that I am telling the truth. But how could this be true?

Mama presses her eyes shut. Then she opens her eyes and shrugs helplessly. "I don't know what to say, Genna."

I pull the towel tighter around me to help me hold onto the truth. Mama gets up from the toilet, takes off her robe, and offers it to me. I take it from her and put it on. It is the same old, thin robe Mama has always worn, but right now having it on makes me feel warmer than standing in the sun. Mama gives me a small, silent smile. Then she leaves the bathroom and goes into the kitchen. I hear her filling up the kettle with water. Then I hear the clicking of the burner and the soft whoosh as the flame leaps up. I avoid the mirror hanging over the sink and follow Mama into the kitchen.

She is sitting at the table, her face buried in her hands. I stand in the doorway for a long while, not sure what to say or do. When the water is about to boil, I go over to the stove and turn off the gas before the kettle starts its shrill whistle. Then I pull out a chair and sit down next to Mama. I put my hand on her arm but she doesn't respond. Mama is weeping quietly behind her hands.

"Don't cry, Mama. Please, don't cry. I'm okay now. I'm back. It's going to be okay now."

Mama pulls her hands away from her face and looks at me. This is the first lie I have told. We both know it's not going to be okay.

"I'm so sorry, Genna. I'm sorry that I hit you that night. I'm sorry I didn't go after you when you ran out of the house. It's all my fault..."

"It's nobody's fault, Mama, it just happened. I don't know why, but it did." I get up and tear a paper towel off the roll. I hand it to Mama so she can dry her eyes, and then I start making us both a cup of tea. I can feel Mama's eyes on my back. Her robe is threadbare, but I know she is wondering what other scars are hidden underneath.

"What was it like — being there — in the past?"

Mama's throat is hoarse and dry. I hand her a mug of mint tea and sit down across from her. "Brooklyn was so different, Mama. I could hardly believe my eyes."

"Tell me about it." Mama sips her tea and waits for me to speak.

I decide to start at the beginning, with being found in the ash dump by two White men, Lester and Charlie, then being rescued by Sam who took me to Weeksville. Mama listens to me with the slightest smile, like she is a child and I am telling her a bedtime story. Whenever I stop, she asks me questions and urges me to go on. I hardly have a chance to drink my tea, and it is cold by the time I tell Mama about the draft riots and the terrifying night I got sent back to this century.

When I stop talking, Mama keeps on watching me with that strange smile on her lips. I lower my eyes and wonder if I was wrong to tell her the truth. I didn't tell Mama the entire story, but I feel as if I have more room inside now. In a strange way, talking about Mattie, Martha, and Judah makes them seem not so far away.

Mama pushes her empty mug aside and gently touches my arm. "You must miss them, your friends. It sounds like you never got to say goodbye."

I blink fast and fight back the tears that gather in my eyes. "I'll see them again someday." I realize too late that this is the wrong thing to say. The skin creases between Mama's eyes again and her voice becomes sharp with panic.

"What do you mean, 'see them again'? You can't see them again, they're gone—*you're* gone! You're here, where you belong."

Mama pauses and waits for me to agree with her, but I can't. I avoid her eyes. I don't want to see how afraid she is, and I don't want her to see how determined I am to go back.

"You stay out of that garden, you hear me? Genna?" Mama waits for me to answer, but I still don't say a word. She softens her voice and tries again. "Genna, baby, I need you. You and Tyjuan, you're all I've got left. And it's not safe anymore—we don't know what's going to happen next. We've got to stay together. Right?"

Mama's eyes are pleading with me, and her fingers are wrapped tight around my arm. I nod but keep my eyes on the cold tea at the bottom of my mug. Mama needs more of an assurance than this, but there is nothing more I can offer.

"It's over, Genna. This terrible thing that happened to you—it's over. There's nothing you can do now. Just leave it alone, please. Let's just try to go back to the way things were."

Mama knows as well as I do that things won't ever be the same. But then I think, maybe this is Mama's dream, maybe I should accept hers the way she has tried to accept mine. My story may not make sense to her, but Mama isn't trying to convince me that it isn't real. So I just smile at Mama the best I can, and inside I tell myself that what happened to me isn't over—not for good, not yet.

Judah

9.

When I open my eyes again, the first thing I notice is the rattling of rough wooden boards beneath my body. I can feel the movement of whatever vehicle Charlie and Lester are driving. I try to move my arms and manage to bring my hands up to my face. My wrists are bound together with rope but I am grateful that at least my limbs are working again. I reach up and touch what's left of my hair—nothing more than short, ragged tufts. Then I press my face into my open palms and ask Jah for the strength I'll need to survive in this strange new world. I don't know where I am, or how I got here, or why. All I know is who I am, so that's what I hold onto. That's the one thing they can't take away from me.

I press my heels into the rumbling boards and shift onto my back. A canvas tarp is stretched over me, blocking out the sky, which seems to have darkened since we left the ash dump. Judging from the sounds and the rocky ride, my best guess is that I'm in the back of a wagon. The pain in my side is still throbbing. What did Charlie call it? A *brand*. My ancestors were branded before and sometimes after they were sold into slavery. I think I'd remember if somebody held me down and pressed a red-hot iron into my side. If it hurts this bad now, it must have hurt like hell then. Charlie and Lester think I'm African—and a fugitive. Unless this is the craziest dream I've ever had, that has to mean I'm no longer in the twenty-first century.

My head aches from too many unanswered questions — and from the blow Charlie gave me that knocked me out. My tongue feels thick in my dry mouth, and one of my molars seems to be hanging by a thread. My belly rumbles with hunger and I try to remember the last meal I ate. Time doesn't have any real meaning any more. I try to focus on the one thing that hasn't changed despite this weird time warp: I have to find Genna.

Finally the wagon rolls to a stop. I lie still and strain to hear the men who plan to sell me.

"It sure is cold tonight." Whiny, nasal voice — Lester.

"That's a good thing," says Charlie. "Folks are less likely to be out and about. We don't need a bunch of folks stickin' their noses in our business."

"True. So what do we do now?"

"He up yet?"

Lester swings his rifle like a bat and whacks me through the canvas. I curse and try to kick back at him, though my legs are still weak.

"Yep. He's up."

Charlie chuckles. The wagon bounces as he jumps down from the driver's seat. "You wait here and I'll go get our man. I bet he's over at the tavern."

"I'll come with you then," says Lester, hopping off the wagon. "We can have a drink to warm ourselves and seal the deal."

"And who's going to watch *him*?" Charlie asks, annoyed. "You got to stay here and keep an eye on this nigger. We lost one already and I don't aim to lose this one, too."

Lester grumbles but Charlie's the one calling the shots. "Just shut up and lay low for a minute. I'll bring him over, we'll show him the goods, and then you and me'll go get a drink. Alright?"

"Alright. Just don't leave me standing out here all night, Charlie. I'm half froze already!"

As Charlie's heavy footsteps recede, I lie still and try to come up with a plan. In the distance I can hear the sound of sloppy singing — the tavern.

Charlie and the slave trader are there, so I need to go in the opposite direction but my wrists and ankles are bound with rope. I won't be able to run unless I somehow get Lester to untie me.

"Hey!" No response. I raise my voice and try again. "HEY!"

Lester jabs at me with the butt of his rifle. "Shut up, or I'll give you something to holler about."

"I gotta go."

Lester draws closer to the back of the wagon. "What?"

"I need to use the toilet." I think a moment—do they have toilets in this world? "I'm sick. You want me to soil myself—and the wagon?"

Lester hesitates, then flips back a corner of the canvas tarp. I look up and see his nervous face framed by the starry night sky. I can tell he's trying to decide what Charlie would want him to do. Finally Lester shakes his head and says, "Hold it."

"I can't," I say with a groan. I shut my eyes for a moment and pull my knees up to my chest as if I'm suffering from cramps. "I don't feel so good. I think I might throw up again."

Lester makes a sound of disgust and pulls back. I watch him as he looks around for somewhere he can take me to relieve myself. I hope he's dumb enough to fall for this. I couldn't overpower two men, but I can definitely take this one.

"Guess you'll just have to clean me up before you sell me then." I turn my face away as if I'm about to puke.

Lester flings back the tarp. "I'll be damned if I'm going to clean up your mess. Get up!"

I rush to obey but my hope crashes as quickly as it soared when Charlie's voice cuts through the cold night air.

"What are you doing, Lester? We gotta go." The wagon lurches as the heavy man hauls himself up onto the seat. The horses neigh and shift as Charlie grabs the reigns.

"Where we going?" asks Lester, turning the tarp back down.

"To the warehouse. Now quit jabbering with that nigger and get up here."

As always, Lester does as he's told. The wagon eases forward but stops after only a minute or two. The two men jump down and come around to the back. Charlie yanks back the tarp and glares at me. "Get up, nigger."

I pretend to be weaker than I am and take my time trying to sit up so I can get a sense of my surroundings. We are in some kind of warehouse. Huge wooden crates and barrels are stacked all around. A soft orange light comes from one corner of the building. I assume that's where the sale is going to take place. I look out the open door at the empty cobblestone street. Then a man wearing a cap rolls the wide warehouse door back into place, cutting off that route of escape. He disappears into the shadows before I can see his face. There is a regular, rectangular door built into the larger warehouse door. I squint in the dim light and see that the smaller door is sealed with a bolt on the inside. Right now that's the only exit I can see.

"Hurry up!" Charlie hisses at me and grabs one of my ankles. For the first time I notice that I am not wearing shoes. Charlie turns to Lester. "Gimme your knife."

Lester obeys and I smother the excitement I feel inside as Charlie cuts the rope binding my feet together. I follow Charlie's command and ease myself off the wagon and onto the ground without help. I hold up my hands hoping he'll cut that rope, too, but Charlie gives the knife back to Lester and starts to inspect me instead. He roughly brushes at my clothes, and accuses Lester of doing a bad job cutting my hair. "You made him look too wild!"

Before Lester can defend himself, a stern voice drifts over from the lit corner of the warehouse.

"I'm waiting, gentlemen."

Charlie straightens his own clothes and puts the oily grin back on his face. He grabs one of my arms and nods at Lester to do the same. I glance at the bolted door and let myself be led over to a broad wooden desk. An oil lamp rests on one corner and another White man is seated in a chair with his feet propped up on the desk. The gold buttons on his coat catch the light but the man's eyes are flat and dark.

"So. What have we here?"

"Runaway, Captain," says Charlie. "We found him just a few hours ago and came straight to you. Figured a man in your line of work would know what he's worth."

The man surveys me from head to toe. I shiver in spite of myself but manage to look him in the eye. "Where are you from, boy?"

I hesitate, wondering whether it's best to say Brooklyn or Jamaica. Then I see Charlie getting ready to answer for me, so I blurt out, "I'm from New York."

"Liar!" yells Charlie.

"It's true!" I insist loudly. "I live in Brooklyn—and I'm not a slave. I'm FREE!"

"Gag him," says the slave trader in a calm voice.

The man in the cap emerges from the shadows and pulls a kerchief from his coat pocket. Lester and Charlie tighten their grip on my arms while the man in the cap rolls up the kerchief. It's not until he passes in front of me that I realize he's not White. For just a moment he lifts his head so that I can see his eyes and in the flickering lamplight I see that he's Black like me. Light-skinned, but definitely Black.

I'm not naïve enough to think that every Black man I meet is my brother. This man works for a White slave trader, so there's not much chance he'll help me escape. Still—if he knew I was being kidnapped. If he knew Genna needed me...

Charlie jabs me in the ribs, and when I cry out in pain, the man slips the gag into my mouth and ties it tightly behind my head. Without a word, he disappears into the shadows once more.

Charlie clears his throat and continues. "He ain't from New York— he's African. Had hair like snakes all down his back when we found him.

He's even got a fresh brand on his side. Look!" Lester yanks up my shirt and I wince as Charlie lifts my left arm to reveal the oozing wound.

The man behind the desk narrows his eyes and frowns. "Looks infected."

Charlie realizes his mistake and pulls my shirt back down. He won't get a good price for damaged goods. "Nothing a little brine won't cure. He's got good teeth, and you can see he's big and strong—come feel his muscles, if you like."

"No need for that," he says with obvious disdain.

Lester suddenly pipes up. "He had a gal with him but she got away."

The captain smiles, amused. "You mean the two of you couldn't handle her?"

"Oh, we handled her alright." Charlie nudges Lester and gives a sly wink to the captain. My blood surges with rage. If either of those bastards laid a hand on Genna—

Lester rushes to explain. "But we ran into trouble when this nosy old nigger—Sam Jenkins—claimed he knew her. Said she wasn't a runaway when you could tell clear as day she'd been running!"

Sam Jenkins. I memorize the name of this Black man who tried to help Genna.

Charlie coughs and spits a wad of phlegm just a few inches from my bare feet. "That old fool claimed she was from Weeksville and the police captain took his word over ours! A White man's word don't count for much in this town these days."

Weeksville. I store that place in my memory too. I tense the muscles in my legs and feel certain my strength has come back. My hands are still bound and there are four of them, but I'm fast and I've studied jujitsu for years. If I catch them by surprise, I might make it to the door and unlatch the bolt before they realize what's happening. If Genna's caught up in this crazy world too, then Weeksville's the first place I have to go to try and find her.

I'm so busy plotting my escape that I almost miss the next clue that the White men carelessly drop. The man in the fancy coat swings his booted feet off the desk and says, "Well, don't you worry, gentlemen. Down in Dixie a healthy young buck like this will fetch two or three times the price of a wench—unless she was fair. Those near-white gals sell for over a thousand dollars sometimes."

"This gal was dark as pitch," Lester says. "Not bad looking, though."

Charlie gives his friend a playful slap. "You sweet on that nigger wench, Lester?"

"Naw! I just wish we'd brung her here instead of the police station. It don't pay to try and do the right thing."

"No, it doesn't," says the captain. "Well, let's get down to business. I've got a ship sailing for Norfolk tonight." He reaches inside his coat and pulls out a leather wallet. "I'm prepared to take that spirited buck off your hands and for your trouble, I'll give you one hundred dollars."

Lester drops my arm and greedily reaches for the bills but Charlie swats his hand away. "Just a minute now, Captain. A moment ago you said this here buck will sell for a high price down south."

"Ah, but as I'm sure you've noticed, we aren't 'down south' yet. You carried him five miles, gentlemen. I must carry him across the Mason-Dixon line. My risk—not to mention my expense—is considerable. I think ten percent is a reasonable finder's fee. Of course, if you feel you can do better elsewhere, then by all means…"

Lester darts his eyes at Charlie, hoping he'll accept the bills that are already within reach. Charlie looks miserable but he nods at Lester and the transaction is complete. As they count their money, I take a step back—out of the circle of yellow light cast by the lamp. The captain is using a quill pen to write something in a book. I glance over at the bolted door. This is my chance. I take another step into the shadows, then spin and run straight into what feels like a wall. I stagger back and realize it's the man with the cap. He's not much taller than me, but twice as broad. Before I can move he clamps a damp kerchief over my face. I press against his chest with my bound hands but within seconds I am on my knees.

"What's that?" asks Charlie.

I search for the door that leads out to the cobblestone street but each breath I take brings me closer to the floor.

"Chloroform," says the man at the desk. "He won't wake until after we've set sail. Considering the circumstances, it's best to get him on board with as little fuss as possible. Ned here will look as though he's simply helping a fellow sailor who's had too much to drink."

"You're a clever man, Captain."

"I am a man of business, gentleman. Efficiency maximizes profit."

The words of these White men swirl like water in my ears. I cling to the only two words that matter: *Genna...Weeksville...*

The yellow light of the oil lamp spins away from me like a shooting star. I close my eyes and gently slip under the surface of a deep, black sea.

Judah

10.

My locks weigh upon my face like a prickly woolen blanket. Still groggy from the drug, I bring my bound hands up to flick my hair aside and realize—remember—that my locks are gone. I close my eyes and try to string together the events that roll across my mind like scattered beads. I am lying still in the dark but my stomach lurches with every heave of the ship. *The ship.* I am at sea. Scenes from the past twenty-four hours flash against my eyelids. Something brushes against my face again and this time I nearly catch the rat before it scurries away.

I feel a hard surface nearby and push myself up so that the crate is at my back. Above me, the small squares of a grate allow light to penetrate the dark hold of the ship. I can hear the crew moving overhead and the steady chugging of the steam engine. Not far from me is a bucket filled with my own waste. The kerchief that used to gag me now hangs uselessly around my neck. I am packed in here with the scavenging rats and the rest of the cargo from the warehouse—just another commodity to be shipped and sold.

The rat returns and tries to nibble at the rough skin on the soles of my feet. I send it flying with a swift kick, and for the first time feel the weight of the iron shackles that circle my ankles. Between them hangs a heavy, rusted chain no more than two feet long. My wrists are still bound with rope but somehow seeing myself in chains makes the truth harder to deny. I am a slave and I am on a ship that is sailing south—to the South where Black people are bought and sold and whipped and worked to death. And all of it's legal—until when? I pull my knees up to my chest and try to remember everything I ever learned about slavery in school—which isn't much.

"Hungry?"

I jump and shift a bit so I can see around the corner of the crate. A ladder is centered in a square shaft of white light. I didn't hear anyone coming below deck but then the ship is full of sounds that are new to me. A cheerful whistle weaves between the stacked crates and barrels bound together with creaking ropes. I recognize the tune almost immediately: "Good King Wenceslas." But it isn't—could it really be—*Christmas*?

Finally the Black man in the strange cap appears bearing another wooden bucket in one hand and a metal mug in the other. What did the captain call him? Ned.

My stomach groans as savory steam rises from the mug. Ned sets the bucket down and pulls what looks like a stale cracker from his shirt pocket. I force myself to look away and silently vow not to take anything from this Black man. This *traitor*.

Ned checks the contents of my slop bucket and holds the mug out to me. "Best put something in your belly while you can."

I ignore him but he knows I'm hungry and won't be refused. "Go on. Got to keep your strength up."

The rat emerge from the shadows, ready to seize whatever crumbs I might toss its way. Another spasm of hunger tugs at my gut. I won't be able to escape and get back to Genna if I'm faint with hunger. I tell myself that taking food from this sellout will help me and eventually hurt him.

I feel no guilt as I reach out and wrap my hands around the metal mug. It is half-filled with warm yellow broth. For just a moment I think of my granny's fish tea and the stories she used to tell of her grandmother's life on a sugar estate in Jamaica. The slaves were freed but given no land and so most wound up cutting cane for their former masters just as they had before Emancipation.

Ned leans against a stack of crates and watches me. "Where you really from?"

This time I don't hesitate. "Jamaica," I say, wondering if it will help or hurt me to reveal my accent.

He grunts with interest. "Think we got a fella from Barbados on board."

"A slave?" I ask bitterly.

"A sailor," he replies, looking straight into my eyes. "Like me."

"You're free?"

"Bought myself eight years ago and got the papers to prove it." He squats, reaches inside his jacket, and pulls out a creased, yellowing piece of paper. He unfolds it carefully and holds it out to me. It says, in fancy script, that Ned Lowell has been "manumitted."

"You're a free man and this is the only job you could get—working for a slave trader?"

Ned folds up his free papers and puts them back in his pocket. "Captain Hogan was the one who owned me!" he says with a wry smile. "Brought me on board when I was a boy, taught me the ropes."

"Shouldn't your name be Logan, too, then?"

Ned shrugs and the smile on his face disappears. "Lowell was the name of the White man who owned my folks. Figured I'd keep it—in case anybody's looking for me."

For just a moment I look at this grown man and see the frightened child he must once have been. My sympathy doesn't last long, though. How could someone who was torn away from his own family sell other people into slavery?

"Captain Logan ain't a slaver—not no more. Not since they strung up Captain Gordon last year."

"Gordon? What'd he do?"

"Same thing a whole lotta folks do—shipped slaves from Africa to Cuba, heading for Brazil. Half of 'em was children." He pauses to shake his head. "Bad business, slaving. But there's too much money in it to keep men away. Gordon took a chance but he got caught, and Lincoln decided to make an example of him. The *Sally Ann*'s just a cutter used to carry goods up and down the coast—from Providence all the way down to the West Indies. Trade was good before the war. But the Anaconda is squeezing us out."

"Anaconda—like the snake?"

"Yep. The Union navy's got the coast wrapped up tight. Most southern ports are closed now—unless you can slip through the blockades. Big money if you make it, but if you don't..." Ned lowers his voice and goes on. "The captain's luck hasn't been so good lately. And when his luck turns...sometimes the captain takes on extra cargo."

I scowl and suck my teeth with disgust. Not "extra cargo"—*human* cargo. Ned rushes on. "Only when he's got debts to pay and he doesn't do it as much as before, what with the war and all. Truth be told, I was kinda surprised the captain agreed to take you on." Ned pauses and settles himself more comfortably on his heels. "Might be he don't plan to sell you at all," he says with a meaningful look.

I shift my feet so that the chain rattles accusingly. "What you mean?"

He coughs and offers me the cracker again. "It's not so bad if you soak it for a while." He points at my mug.

I accept the hard cracker, dip it into what's left of the broth, and repeat my question. "What do you mean he might not sell me?"

Ned shrugs. "Make yourself useful. Be willing to learn. Don't give him no trouble. If you show you can get along with the rest of the crew, could be he'll let you work it off."

"Work what off?"

"Your purchase price."

I remember the bills he gave to Charlie and Lester. "A hundred dollars?"

He chuckles. "No, son. You're worth closer to a thousand."

"But the captain knows I'm free."

Ned tips his capped head back and rests it against the crates. "Can you prove it? You got no papers, nobody White to vouch for you. And you're sick as a dog out at sea."

I take another sip of broth and stare at the white mush gathering at the bottom of the mug as the cracker dissolves. How long would it take for me to earn a thousand dollars as a sailor? First I'd have to earn the captain's trust and pretend I don't mind being a slave. What if I try to get along and he sells me anyway? Why should I trust a man who's already proven he's scum? And why should I pay anyone anything when I *know* I'm free? Somehow Ned reads my mind.

"Ain't no use asking why. Life ain't fair—not for a Negro." He pauses and lets his words sink in. "You done?" I nod and Ned rises, takes the mug from me, and sets it on top of a nearby barrel. "This gonna hurt."

My body stiffens and I glance around for a weapon. "What?"

He nods at the bloodstain on my shirt. "Gotta stop the infection. Captain's orders. We can do it lying down or standing up—your call. There's a joist over there."

I follow his gaze to a hook high up in one of the beams. "What do I have to do?"

"Just take your shirt off and hold on."

I stand and try to pull the filthy shirt over my head but the rough cloth is stuck to the wound in my side. I look down and see that the yellow pus has hardened into a crust that seals the cloth to my skin.

"Need a hand?" Ned asks.

I shake my head, close my eyes and quickly yank the shirt free. The scab of pus and blood rips off and fresh blood trickles out of the sore. I shuffle over to the beam, lift my hands up, and let the rope around my wrists loop over the joist. My heels are lifted off the deck but I balance on the balls of my feet and press my forehead into the wooden beam to steady myself.

Ned takes up a bucket filled with salty water. "Ready?"

I take a deep breath, close my eyes and nod. Ned aims the bucket at my left side and sloshes the brine against my skin. I grind a moan between my teeth until all sounds of pain disappear.

"Okay, once more," Ned says before pouring the rest of the water onto the sizzling wound.

My knees give out this time and I hang by my wrists for several moments, breathing hard. After a while I feel Ned's hand on my shoulder.

"Think you can stand?" I nod and accept his help unlooping my wrists from the hook in the beam. I lean forward and rest my elbows on my knees. The wound hurts even worse than before.

Ned pats me on the back. "Let's see if you can get your sea legs up on deck. Fresh air be good for you. Soon as you're dry, I'll put a bandage on and get you a clean shirt."

"Thanks," I whisper.

"Don't got to thank me none," he replies in an upbeat voice. "Just following Captain's orders."

I look up at Ned and wonder why his voice has changed. Then I look past his shoulder and see the captain standing midway down the ladder that leads below deck.

"Took it like a man, did he?"

"Yes, sir."

The captain nods wordlessly before turning and climbing back up on deck. Ned glances at me to see if I understand what just happened. I guess I'm supposed to care that I made a good impression on that White man. But right now, with this salt eating a hole in my side, I couldn't care less.

Genna

11.

Judah isn't dead. I don't know that for sure, but it feels like it's true, so that's what I keep telling myself. And that means I'm one of the lucky ones. There are so many people grieving in the city right now. Little kids have lost their parents, husbands have lost their wives — in just one hour thousands of families were torn apart. It seems like everyone lost someone on 9/11, which means I'm not the only one hurting right now. And like I said already, Judah isn't dead, he's just somewhere I can't go. I don't have to wait to find his name on a list, and I don't have to wear black to his funeral. I know that I'm lucky, but it doesn't make me feel any better. It just makes me feel even more alone.

For the families of victims of 9/11, there's a hotline you can call if you need to talk to someone. Psychologists are donating their time to help people deal with the disaster. A lot of the people who were lucky enough to make it out of the Twin Towers alive are suffering from PTSD — post-traumatic stress disorder. I read about it in those old psychology books Hannah gave me. It used to be something only veterans got — soldiers went to war and came back shell-shocked, thinking and sometimes acting like the battle was still going on.

But you don't have to go to war to have symptoms of PTSD. Anyone who's lived through a traumatic experience can have flashbacks. It happens to people who survived plane crashes or really bad car accidents, and to women who've been raped. It's like whatever happened to you isn't over, it keeps playing like a movie inside your head and you feel just as scared and helpless and out of control as when it actually happened. Sometimes, when I go to sleep at night, the draft riots come back to me. I wake up covered in sweat, and my legs ache from running on those hard paving stones. I try not to cry out and wake everyone up, but you can't always control what you do in your sleep. I sleep on the sofa in the living room now, but I know Mama hears me sometimes.

They've stopped looking for survivors at Ground Zero. Now they're mostly just sifting through the ash, collecting whatever body parts they can find so family members will have something to bury. Some piece of flesh or bone to tell them that the person they loved really is gone and won't be coming back.

I don't have a single piece of Judah. Not a lock of his hair, not a ring, or a sweater that still smells like him. All I have are my memories, and they're mostly bad. I remember the lash marks that criss-crossed his back after he'd been whipped in the South. I remember the long, heavy dreadlocks they cut from his head. I remember the way too much pride and too much pain turned Judah's eyes to stone, even when he looked at me. And I remember that night when we ran through the streets of Brooklyn — back in 1863 — trying to escape a mob that wanted us dead.

I remember everything — Mrs. Brant's icy blue eyes, Nannie's upside down smile, and the way Martha looked when I gave her that parcel of food to share with her hungry family. I remember the smell of little Henry's milky breath, and Mattie's too-bright eyes watching me as I twisted my locks at night. I remember it all, and maybe that's why some days I feel like I'm still there. I know I'm here, in this Brooklyn. I know that it's 2001, and I know that my country is about to go to war. But sometimes it feels like I'm still there, and sometimes — most times — I wish that were true.

But until I can figure out a way to go back, I have to act as if I'm a part of this world. I'm reading all the history books I can get my hands on. That's the only way for me to stay close to Judah, to know what's going on in his world. The draft riots did end eventually—the Union army turned around and came back to New York City, and they fired on the mob just like they fired on Confederate soldiers days before at Gettysburg. The city rulers fixed it so that poor men could get out of fighting the same way rich men could, and by the end of 1863, New York City began drafting Black men to fight for the Union Army.

Time goes faster in Judah's world—I have to remember that. It was early July when I left him, but it's already September here. Only two and a half months passed in this Brooklyn while we were trapped in that other world, even though we were there for almost half a year. I don't know why time would speed up like that, and math isn't my strongest subject, but I think I've got the conversion right—four days in Judah's world equals one day in mine.

That means if I've been back a little more than a week, then it's already August in 1863. Judah might still be getting ready to leave for Liberia, or he might have left Brooklyn for Canada or some other state—thousands of Blacks left the city after the riots. I don't blame them. But I hope Judah decided to stay put. Otherwise I won't know how to find him once I get back. And I *am* going back. I don't know how, but I'm going to find a way. I've traveled through time twice now—I made it there and I made it back here. I didn't have any control over when or how I went, but that doesn't mean I can't figure out how to do it again. I'll go back, find Judah, and bring him back to this world. Or maybe I'll just stay there with him.

In a way, I don't belong here anymore. It's funny because that's how I used to feel before all of this happened. I used to stand in front of the fountain and wish that I had different clothes and a different home and a different body—I wanted to be someone else. Then I got sent back, and for a while I *was* someone else. And now that I'm home, now that I'm here in the twenty-first century, I feel so out of place. I'm still me, but nothing about my life feels right. The city seems strange, even though I've lived here all my life. Everything looks the same but feels different—even the garden. Things in this world seem hard—there's so much concrete and steel—and everything's stacked on top of everything else. I actually miss the wide, open fields around Weeksville. I miss the quiet at night, and the stars that all these electric lights blot out of the sky.

In this Brooklyn things happen too quickly, everyone's in a rush, nobody looks at anyone else—or if they do, it's with suspicion. The whole city's locked down, and weighed down with grief. But there's also anger bubbling beneath all that fear and sorrow and shock, and I don't want to be here when that rage reaches the surface. Most people just want answers, but more than a few want vengeance. All I want is to be with Judah and to be safe.

For so long I yearned to be here, to be surrounded by my own people. Yet even though almost all the faces I see every day are black or brown, nobody seems to recognize me. It's the same with Mama—I missed her so much while I was gone, but now that I'm back, I almost feel like I'm invisible. It's like I'm standing behind a cardboard cut-out of myself. And Mama knows the real me is hiding somewhere, but she doesn't want to look too close. She can't bear to find out who I've become.

A couple days after I got back Mama took me over to my old high school. She talked to my guidance counselor, Mrs. Freeman, and made up some corny excuse for why I was late registering for my classes. Not that it really mattered—things have been pretty chaotic since 9/11. I got my timetable for the eleventh grade—it's okay, I picked most of those classes last spring—but I don't go to school all the time. I go some days, and other days I just stay home or else I head to the library. Mama wanted to stay home to be there for me and Tyjuan, but she can't afford to right now. She's got to work a shift and a half every day, and that means leaving real early in the morning and getting home late at night. Mama's working overtime to pay that lawyer she hired, and she's got to pay him every last dime, even though he didn't get Rico off.

Mama thinks being back in school is good for me. I guess she figures I won't think about the past so much if I fill up my time with classes and homework and all the other things teenagers do. She even said I could get a part-time job if I want. I haven't decided yet whether I'm going to call Hannah or not. I wouldn't mind babysitting her little boy again—after all, I've got plenty of experience. I spent the past six months taking care of the Brants' baby boy, but I can't exactly put that on my resume. Besides, I don't want to start anything I can't finish. Kids drop out of school all the time, so I don't think anyone would notice if I just stopped going to class. But I don't want Hannah counting on me when I know I'm not planning on sticking around.

Mama—well, I haven't figured that one out yet. I don't want to upset her, and I know she's trying hard to prove that she trusts me. But every time I go out, I can feel Mama's eyes digging like hooks into my back, and I know she's worried one of these days I'm going to walk out that door and never come back—just like the other members of our family.

I feel bad about that, but at least I know that if I go—when I go— Mama won't be alone. She'll still have Tyjuan. And maybe, just maybe, once I find Judah I'll come back. All I know for sure right now is that the only time I felt like I belonged in this world was when I was with Judah. And being here without him just feels wrong. When I was lost deep in the past, he kept searching for me—he never gave up. He found me and he found a way for us to be together. Now it's my turn to make things right.

Judah

12.

I think about Genna every day. They say absence makes the heart grow fonder, and I guess it's true because each day we're apart only makes me love her more. I never said it out loud when we were together, but I hope she knew from the poems I gave her and the plans I shared just how much she meant to me. Sometimes at night when they chain me below deck, I lie awake and try to write haiku in my mind. I count out the syllables and turn them into words of hope.

love is the anchor
that links my heart to yours so
the sea can't part us

Seems like Ned was telling me the truth. Life's not so bad on this ship. I do what I'm told and follow the rules, and in return they take the chains off me and let me up on deck during the day. I soon learn that sailors don't care what color you are so long as you do your share of the work. A few days of scrubbing the deck on my hands and knees earns their respect. They share their food with me, give me some old sacks to use as bedding—one White sailor even gives me his old clothes after he buys a new set onshore. It's strange at first to see these White and Black men drinking and laughing and getting along. I actually start to believe that maybe I can become one of them—maybe even sail all the way down to Jamaica and see my homeland.

When the captain finally says I can go onshore with Ned and two of the others, I am too excited to be cautious. Norfolk is in Union hands and we're dropping off supplies and mail for the troops. Ned doesn't look at me as we row to shore. When we reach the dock, we unload the boat and the others talk about going for a drink at a nearby tavern. I am eager to look around. It's a mild day, the sun is shining. I think I can trust my new friends.

But Ned says, "We ain't done yet." There's an edge in his voice but I don't think anything of it. He sends Jim and Caleb to pick up some supplies the captain wants, and then Ned tells me to follow him. We walk into town without talking. When we reach a church with a tall white spire I see a Black man sitting in a wagon on the other side of the street. He nods at us but doesn't get down.

"Captain needs someone to collect a package from Mr. Ferguson," Ned says. He nods at the man in the wagon and explains, "Caesar will run you over there. I got a few things to do myself. Think you can find your way back?"

Ned looks at me and I can tell he's trying to say something with his eyes. But I read him wrong. I think this is just another test—a way to earn the captain's trust. So I just say, "Sure," before climbing up and taking a seat next to Caesar.

"This is a Union town," Ned says without looking me in the eye. "Anyone asks, you tell them you're from Virginia—understand? Not Jamaica, not New York. Virginia."

I don't understand but I nod as if I do. Only when it's too late do I realize that the Emancipation Proclamation has gone into effect. Any fugitive slave from a state within the Confederacy is now free—if he or she can make it to the north or seek protection from the Union army. That's why Ned told me to act like I was from Virginia. I guess in a backward sort of way he was trying to help me out.

But I don't figure that out until all chance of freedom is gone. The wagon pulls off and Ned disappears around the corner of the church. There are Union soldiers everywhere but I keep my eyes on the buildings that line the street, memorizing our route. I want to make sure I can find my way back to the docks. When the wagon stops I hop down and follow Caesar around the red brick house to the back door. We go inside and I stupidly obey when he tells me to go down into the cellar to get the package for Captain Hogan. Then the door closes behind me, I hear the bolt slide into place, and I realize what a fool I've been.

A slave trader comes to collect me in the middle of the night. The streets are empty then—not a Union soldier in sight. By the time the sun rises the next day, I am back in chains, packed like cattle with twenty other slaves on a train heading south.

Judah

13.

I pound on the cellar door for at least an hour. I pretend the hard wooden door is my own thick skull. How could I have been so stupid? When my fist starts to ache, I sit down on the dusty stairs and try to come up with a plan. I'm in Norfolk, Virginia. It's January 1863. How can I get back to Brooklyn? If I find a Union soldier, I can say I'm a runaway. But what happens next? Do they make you serve in the army? I saw a movie once about those Black soldiers from Massachusetts. Almost all of them died in a battle in South Carolina. They were brave, but most of them wound up dead—buried in a mass grave by Confederate soldiers. I don't want to be a slave but I also don't want to die in this world. If Genna's in Weeksville, then that's where I need to be. But if I do run, can I find my way north alone? How do I find the folks working on the Underground Railroad? Has it ground to a halt now that Lincoln has issued his proclamation?

I think so long and hard that my head starts to ache. When the door finally opens, the sun has set and I know that the *Sally Ann* is probably long gone. An old Black woman with a head of small, silver plaits stands in the doorway glaring down at me. She holds a candle in one hand and a plate of food in the other. I see the steam rising from the plate and my stomach rumbles with hunger.

"You act right, you can sit 'n eat at the table. But if you gon' act the fool, you can stay down there and eat with the mice."

This woman looks like somebody's grandmother but she's got a voice like a prison guard. I'll never escape if I stay down here in this damp cellar. I need to look around, ask questions, and come up with a plan. I stand and wipe my hands on my pants. "Yes, ma'am," I say, looking up at her with innocent eyes.

She sees straight through my act. Her voice hardens. "I mean it, boy. You try 'n run, it only gon' make this mess worse. Massa Ferguson ain't a mean man but he don't take no sass. He a good shot and he got the best huntin' dogs in all o' Virginny. You run, you dead. Understand?"

I lower my eyes and try to sound humble — defeated. "I understand. Got nowhere *to* run now. I sure would appreciate some food, though."

This time my words convince her to trust me. She steps aside, giving me enough room to squeeze through the cellar door and step into the dim, warm kitchen. She sets the plate on a small wooden table and nods at me to take a seat. I pull out the chair and fold my hands to say a quick prayer of thanks before digging into the plate of chicken and rice.

She watches me for a moment and then asks, "You know the Lord?"

I make sure not to speak while there's food in my mouth. I can tell that manners impress her. "Yes, ma'am." Before I take another mouthful of food I add, "I'm Judah."

Despite the dim light I see her mouth twitch. She looks like she wishes I hadn't told her my name. I'm hoping she'll sit down, open up, and help me find a way out of this new dilemma. But the old woman just presses her lips together and holds the candle up so I can see my food.

"Well, Judah, you just keep on prayin' and trustin' in Him. You in a spot of trouble right now, but trouble don't last always."

When I'm done eating, she leads me to the study. An elegantly dressed, white-haired White man is sitting by the fire, reading. He glances up at me, says, "Thank you, Minnah," and then goes back to his book. The old woman curtsies and then leaves me standing there in the doorway. The dog lying at its master's feet lifts its head and growls at me. I imagine this dog chasing me through the woods. I flex my fingers and wonder if I could strangle this dog—snap its neck to save my own.

Ferguson acts like I'm not even there. If I step back into the dark hallway, would he notice? If I make a break for it, how far could I get? Minnah couldn't stop me but she said there were other dogs. And what about Caesar, the slave who drove me out here—would he take my side or would he act like an Uncle Tom?

I don't know what to do so I just stand there feeling like a fool. The room is filled with books. One entire wall is lined with bookshelves and stacks of books cover the desk and much of the floor. Ferguson finally finishes the chapter he's reading, closes his book, and looks up at me. In the flickering orange light it's hard to tell how old he is. He wears spectacles and the fancy clothes of a gentleman but he doesn't look frail. He looks like a man who could put up a good fight.

Ferguson removes his glasses and says, "Come here, boy."

His voice is not unkind but I don't appreciate being called out of my name. Still, I know he expects me to act like a slave so I do as I'm told and step closer to the fire. The dog growls more loudly and crouches as if it's about to pounce on me.

Ferguson strokes the dog's head. "Hush, Artemis." The dog obeys and settles quietly at its master's feet. Ferguson looks at me and almost smiles. "You have been deceived."

"Many times," I say, keeping my eyes on the dancing flames.

"Captain Hogan did order some books from me," Ferguson says. He pauses and waves a hand at the piles of books arranged around the room. "But the captain, as I'm sure you know, is a gambling man—and he has a terrible poker face. You, on the other hand, are quite inscrutable."

Ferguson waits to see if his big word will get a rise out of me. Inscrutable means he can't tell what I'm thinking or feeling. I plan to keep it that way.

"Bring me those books," he says with another careless wave of his hand.

I move over to the desk and scan the stacks of leather-bound books.

"Which ones?"

"You will address me as 'sir' or 'Master.'"

I curse him under my breath but finally say, "Which books do you want, sir?"

"Bring me the classics—something by Homer."

I don't stop to think—I haven't learned to do that yet. I scan the spines of the books. The titles are printed in gold that flashes in the firelight. I find *The Iliad* and *The Odyssey* by Homer. I pull out the two books and take them over to Ferguson.

He glances at the titles but doesn't take the books from me. Instead he looks into my face with a cunning smirk. "Hogan told me you were a smart nigger. Who taught you to read, boy?"

I look at the floor and say nothing. Frederick Douglass taught himself to read and write. Should I say I did the same? Slave owners think education makes a slave "unmanageable," which is why it's illegal to teach a slave how to read and write. If I tell the truth and say I learned in school, this White man won't believe me. So I just keep my eyes on the rug.

Ferguson sighs. "You've been ruined, I'm afraid. I've no use for a slave who doesn't know his place. A few years out in the fields should cure you. What's your name, boy?"

"Judah."

He looks at me and I remember to add, "Sir."

"Minnah gave you something to eat?"

"Yes, sir."

"Good." Ferguson reaches for a small bell on a nearby table. He rings it and within seconds I hear footsteps coming down the hallway.

"Show our guest to his room, Caesar."

"Yessuh," the slave replies with a slight bow. He nods at me and I turn to follow him but Ferguson's voice pulls me back.

"Get some rest, Judah. You have a long journey ahead of you." He sets the spectacles back on the bridge of his nose, opens his book, and starts reading again.

Caesar is just as tight-lipped as Minnah. He ignores my questions and leads me outside to the carriage house. As we cross the yard, half a dozen dogs emerge from the shadows and clamor for Caesar's attention. They whimper and whine when he shuts them out of the carriage house. At the back is a small bedroom. A rug made of woven rags covers the floor and a rusty, cast iron bed is pushed up against the bare white wall. Caesar takes a thin quilt off the bed and makes up a pallet on the floor.

"You take the bed," he says when I move to lie down on the quilt. I object, wanting to be close to the door, but Caesar sneers and says, "You the *guest*. 'Sides, you be sleepin' rough 'fore long."

I take off my shoes and stretch out on the narrow bed, which creaks and groans with every move I make. Caesar lies on the floor watching me with wary, sleepless eyes. If by some miracle I manage to get out of this room, I'll never get past all the dogs sleeping just outside the carriage house door. Running is out of the question. All I can do now is wait.

I turn on my side so I am facing the wall. I close my eyes and try to conjure an image of Genna. It's springtime and we are in the botanic garden. The pink petals of cherry blossoms fall down on us like snow. Genna smiles and reaches up to brush the petals out of my locks. I slide my arm around her waist and pull her closer. I kiss her soft, smiling lips…

I open my eyes and remind myself that *that* Brooklyn no longer exists. Even if I make it out of the South and find Genna somehow, nothing will be the way it used to be. I close my eyes again and try to imagine Genna as she might look now—in *this* world. I think of the baby locks sprouting from her scalp. Is she oiling them each night like my aunt showed her? Or did they hold her down and cut them off? The thought of Genna alone, needing me, not knowing where I am, makes me shake with rage. The bed creaks beneath my body and I force myself to be still.

The yelping dogs wake me moments before my new "owner" enters the room, a lantern held above his head.

"Get up, boy," he orders in a low, gruff voice. Caesar stands behind the slave trader, his face void of sympathy.

I swing my legs over the edge of the bed and reach for my shoes.

"Leave 'em," says the stout, bearded White man. "You need to be taken down a notch. Some fool's spoiled you, but I don't molly-coddle my niggers. You're gonna learn your place with me, boy. Now," he pushes the barrel of his gun into my shoulder, "let's go."

As soon as I step away from the bed Caesar grabs my shoes and holds them to his chest like a prized possession. The shoes on his feet are better than my hand-me-downs, but I guess that's not the point. I turn and walk out of the carriage house without bothering to say goodbye. Farewells are only for people who care.

Genna

14.

"Alright, class, settle down. Today we will be learning about the Civil War. Take out your textbooks and turn to page 317..."

Mr. Collins' voice is drowned out as thirty of us unzip our book bags and heave our U.S. History textbooks onto our desks. As soon as the commotion dies down, Mr. Collins turns out the lights and switches on the overhead projector.

In the dark, Mr. Collins becomes someone else. Instead of a short, bald, middle-aged White man, our history teacher turns into an actor in a play. He waves his hands all over the place, and paces back and forth. He talks with a phony accent, like that'll make us forget he's just an ordinary guy from New Jersey.

The overhead light shines on his face like a spotlight, and Mr. Collins begins his performance. "You will be tested on the contents of chapters four through seven at the end of next week, so I strongly recommend that you take careful notes." A collective groan goes around the class. Mr. Collins waits for it to subside, then continues with his routine. "This material is particularly relevant to your generation, I think. For example, the United States is currently debating whether or not to attack Afghanistan. How many of you believe our nation ought to go to war?"

I look around the darkened classroom. Nearly all the hands are up in the air. One girl wearing a pretty blue head scarf sinks down in her seat.

Mr. Collins smiles grimly beneath his shaggy grey moustache. "I see. And how many of you would be willing to don a uniform, pick up a gun, and defend your country?"

Just as many hands go up. Mr. Collins knits his bushy eyebrows together. "Hmm, interesting. Do we have any conscientious objectors? Miss Colon—I didn't see you raise your hand."

I blink and look at Mr. Collins, unable to hide my surprise. Then I look around the classroom and realize all eyes are on me, and some don't look too friendly.

Mr. Collins clasps his hands behind his back and slowly begins to pace in front of the class. "Do you believe this country ought to go to war, Miss Colon?"

"I—I don't know," I say quietly.

"You don't know!" Mr. Collins' voice booms across the darkened room. "Well, class, let's help Miss Colon make up her mind. Who can give me one reason for going to war?"

Several hands go up this time, but Malcolm doesn't wait to be called on. "Payback! We ought to bomb them twice as hard as they bombed us. We got to send a message to Osama bin Laden—let all them terrorists know they fucked with the wrong country!"

"Curb your enthusiasm, Mr. Donaldson, and watch your language, please." Mr. Collins' eyes gleam with anticipation. "I see one major flaw in your rationale, and that is, that 'they' didn't bomb us, did they?"

"What you talking about, man? They turned airplanes into bombs. They attacked us on our own soil."

"True. Mr. Donaldson has made a valid point. But terrorism is a very tricky phenomenon. Throughout history, war has been fought on the battlefield—or in the sky, or at sea—by organized, armed, and trained military personnel. There were rules of engagement, you knew who your enemy was. But times have changed, ladies and gentlemen. The old rules no longer apply. If we bomb Afghanistan, we risk killing innocent civilians."

"So what?" Malcolm spits out. "Thousands of innocent American civilians died on 9/11. And we know who our enemy is—Osama and al Qaeda. The Taliban's letting them hide in their country, so the whole country's got to go. Like I said, it's time for payback."

Mr. Collins examines Malcolm as if he were a bit of mold growing on some cheese. Then he strokes his moustache and returns to me. "What do you think, Miss Colon? Is the U.S. justified in going to war?"

I clear my throat and try to say something that won't get me into trouble. "Sometimes you have to fight to defend your rights, but…"

"But what? Speak up, Miss Colon."

"I don't know. It just seems like people use war as an excuse to do some pretty terrible things. And it affects everyone differently—rich people stay safe, and poor people end up dead. During the Civil War, for example—rich men could pay for someone else to take their place, but poor men couldn't afford to buy a substitute. And that led to the draft riots of 1863."

I stop there, worried my classmates will think I'm showing off. Mr. Collins stands still for a moment and stares at me with his eyebrows raised high above his eyes. "Well, it is gratifying to know that at least one student has bothered to do the assigned reading for today." Then he starts pacing again. "Let us consider Miss Colon's proposition. Who would suffer most if the United States declared war against Afghanistan?"

"The terrorists!" says Malcolm.

"The people of Afghanistan!" cries someone else.

"Women and children!"

"American taxpayers!"

"Blacks and Latinos, that's who."

Mr. Collins stops pacing again and looks for the person who gave the last response. "Blacks and Latinos? Why would they suffer if the nation went to war?"

I look across the room and find Peter, Judah's friend, staring Mr. Collins down. "Because there are a whole lot of Blacks and Latinos in the

Armed Forces. My cousin's in the Marines, and my whole family's proud of him. But Genna's right—war hurts poor people the most, 'cause they're the ones who join up hoping for a chance to travel, or to get money for college, or even just to have a job. But then they end up dying in Gettysburg or Viet Nam or Kuwait—wherever the rich politicians send them."

"I see. Mr. Raymond has raised a valid point, and one not unrelated to the draft riots mentioned previously by Miss Colon. Should soldiers be required to fight for a cause in which they do not believe, or from which they may not benefit?"

Sharae, one of the most popular girls at our school, surprises everyone by firing the first response. "Everybody benefits from freedom and democracy. It don't matter what color you are—everybody bleeds red."

Malcolm nods at Sharae and then tries to impress her with his macho routine. "That's what I'm talking about! When it comes to war and defending your country, the only color that matters is red, white, and blue. You're either for the flag, or against it. Simple as that."

I don't want to take on Malcolm by myself, but somebody's got to tell the truth. I take a deep breath and join the fray. "Actually, it's not always that simple. Black men had to petition the government for the right to fight in the Civil War—here in New York City they weren't allowed to enlist until the end of 1863. The Union army needed soldiers, but they didn't want Black men to have guns. And then poor Whites got so angry about the draft that they attacked and killed innocent African Americans—women, children, and men. They didn't want to fight a war to end slavery because they didn't want slavery to end."

"Why not?"

I am already nervous so when Malcolm turns around and asks me that question, I almost choke. Peter jumps in and helps me out. "They were afraid that if the slaves were freed, there'd be more competition for jobs. You don't have to pay a slave, but you do have to pay a free man. And so long as there were slaves in the country, even poor Whites had somebody to look down on."

Malcolm sucks his teeth. "Man, all that's ancient history. Why can't we go back to current events, the stuff that's happening now? I'm tired of hearing about Black folks always getting beat down."

"You won't hear about it if you read this textbook." I look around the classroom to see who said that, but all eyes are on me. Those words came out of my mouth.

Mr. Collins mashes his eyebrows together and marches over to me. "Somehow I suspect Mr. Donaldson very rarely reads his textbook, Miss Colon. You, on the other hand, seem very familiar with the contents. Are you saying you find this five-hundred page book lacking in some respect?"

I shrug and try to pull myself together. Why did I say that out loud? "It's got five hundred pages and it weighs five hundred pounds, but it doesn't say a whole lot about African Americans, or anyone else who's not White."

"I think you'll find, Miss Colon, that the chapters we are covering this week have quite a bit to say about African Americans."

Mr. Collins doesn't even look at me when he says this. He's too busy strutting around the room. I feel my cheeks starting to burn.

"Sure—the section on slavery. But what about free Blacks who were living in the North—in places like Philadelphia, Boston, or New York? Even Brooklyn was its own city back then, and the third largest in the country. What about places like Weeksville—does anyone in here even know about Weeksville?" I pause and look around the room. "Of course not, 'cause it's not in the book. Weeksville was an all-Black community in Brooklyn. That's where a lot of the refugees went for safety. During the riots Black people had to get out of Manhattan 'cause the mob was burning things down and lynching any Black person they could find—"

"I think 'lynching' is a bit extreme, Miss Colon. African Americans were 'attacked,' certainly, and one or two were 'murdered,' perhaps. But not 'lynched.'"

"Lynching is when a mob of people kills somebody who hasn't

legally been convicted of any crime. Black people were lynched during the draft riots, Mr. Collins. They were hanged from lampposts in broad daylight, in the middle of the street."

"Really. And may I ask what evidence you have of this?"

"Evidence? Thousands of people died in the World Trade Center attack. The only proof we've got is their ashes, but you believe that happened, don't you?"

"Clearly, there are distinct differences between the two historical moments—"

"So? Just because CNN wasn't there to cover the draft riots, doesn't mean I'm making it up. Bodies that are set on fire or dumped in a river don't always make the six o'clock news—or these crappy history books you make us read." I slam my textbook shut and shove it off my desk. It lands with a loud thud on the floor. "But that doesn't mean it didn't happen."

"Yeah, she's right." Malcolm shoves his book off his desk, too, and several people around him do the same.

Mr. Collins' white neck begins to turn red. The flush creeps up his throat and onto his face. "Alright, class, calm down. Obviously it was more difficult to document atrocities that were committed in the nineteenth century."

"That doesn't mean they didn't happen."

"No, it doesn't. But you can't present a hypothesis without offering substantiation, Miss Colon." Mr. Collins pauses to enjoy the murmur of confusion caused by his big words. The redness leaves his face and he smiles smugly before continuing. "You say the murder of innocent African Americans isn't recorded in our history books. Then how, may I ask, do you know that it happened?"

Because it almost happened to me. My spine tingles as I sink back into my seat. "I read other books, and I found stuff on the internet."

"Really? Then you won't mind providing us with the titles and authors of those books, or the websites where this 'stuff" is published."

"Isn't that your job?" asks Peter. Mr. Collins glares at the people who snicker.

"I don't have that information, but I can get it," I tell him. "And even if it wasn't on the internet or in any book, I'd still know that it happened."

"How?"

"I just know." I say the words sullenly, not wanting to admit defeat.

Mr. Collins sees me slumped down in my seat. His eyes sparkle as a mean little smile twists his lips. "You 'just know.' Perhaps you're blessed with psychic abilities, Miss Colon, but the rest of us require something more concrete. At the very least you owe some sort of documentation for this outlandish claim: newspaper articles, first-hand accounts—"

Suddenly a shock goes through my body and I am flung out of my seat. "I don't owe you anything! I WAS THERE! Okay? That's how I know. *I was there!*"

My angry words, hurled so unexpectedly, wipe the sarcastic smile from Mr. Collins' face. I stand at my desk, my spine stiff and straight and sizzling with electricity. There is total silence in the classroom. Soundlessness swirls around me like ice cold water. It rises quickly from my ankles to my knees and keeps on swelling. I can feel the silence swallowing me up, and I can feel myself starting to tremble. I grab my bag off the floor, shove my books inside, and plunge out of the room.

In the hall I pause for a moment, not sure whether I should clear out my locker and leave for good. My heart is racing, and I have only taken a few steps down the hall when the classroom door opens behind me. I jump and look over my shoulder—it's Peter.

"Genna, hold up—"

Suddenly I am hearing another voice but it is not in the hallway, it is inside my head, and this voice is telling me to leave. I turn around and walk as quickly as I can towards the stairwell.

Peter calls my name again, but when I ignore him, he comes after me. I rush towards the red exit sign and push open the door to the stairwell. I can hear Peter's sneakered feet thudding along the hall as he breaks into a run.

"Genna, wait—" Peter grabs my shoulder, but I shake him off and keep heading down the stairs. Peter is determined. He reaches for me again, and this time manages to pull my book bag off my shoulder. The contents spill out of the unzipped bag, forcing me to turn back.

Peter bends down to help me. His face is close to mine, but I refuse to look at him. "Where's Judah?"

Peter says this so softly, so gently, fresh tears spring to my eyes. I pretend I didn't hear him and keep shoving loose pens and papers into my bag.

Peter stops helping and stands over me. "You know where he is. I know you do."

"You don't know anything," I say angrily as I reach for a loose handout.

Peter pins the paper beneath his foot and glares down at me. "I know you know. Tell me where he is."

I tug at the handout. "Get off, Peter."

"Tell me where Judah is."

I let go of the handout and stand up so that Peter can look into my face. "If I knew, don't you think I'd be there with him?"

Peter stares at me for a moment, then stoops down to pick up my handout. I brush away my tears, take it from him, and heave my book bag onto my shoulder once more. Peter sinks down onto the steps with a silent nod. There's nothing more that I can say, so I turn and go down the stairs alone.

I head outside without my jacket and let the autumn air cool my body and my temper. The crisp wind blows right through my shirt, and before long I am shivering. I fold my arms across my chest and walk quickly, trying to leave behind Mr. Collins, my stunned classmates, and my accidental admission.

I am halfway up the block before I remember that I have an appointment to see Mrs. Freeman that afternoon. My watch tells me it's not yet noon. I'll just calm down, get something to eat, and then go back at two o'clock. Mr. Collins probably won't bother to report the incident to the principal. After all, it's not like I threw anything at him, or picked a fight with another student. Those are things Rico used to do. I'm Genna Colon, the quiet girl who sits in the corner of the classroom, does her homework, minds her business, and gets good grades. So I mouthed off to a teacher. So I walked out of class. So I told them all that I'd witnessed something that happened almost a hundred and fifty years ago. It's no big deal. That's what I keep telling myself as I walk down the street. It's no big deal.

Judah

15.

None of us has shoes. The iron shackles rub the skin off our ankles and our feet bleed, blister, and swell as we trudge mile after mile. At first you feel every sharp stone in the road but after a few days your soles grow tough and you learn to grit your teeth to numb the pain. There are eight of us — seven men and one pregnant woman.

The slave trader, McAvoy, has a heart of stone and a mouth full of rotten black teeth. He's also got two men helping him out — Gus is White and Dabney's Black. All three are on horseback and by my count they've got seven guns: four pistols and three rifles. Knives, too, 'cause I've seen them skinning rabbits sometimes for their supper. We get boiled corn mush — one serving in the morning and another at night. That's it and yet they expect us to walk at least twenty miles a day. That poor sister — they put her in the middle of the coffle and in her condition, she mostly gets dragged along. I can tell that the men ahead of her are trying to go slow but Gus has a wooden club and he makes sure the coffle moves at a pretty fast clip — slow down and he'll crack your skull open.

Our feet are shackled and so are our wrists. A length of chain runs between us, linking us like prisoners on a chain gang. But we don't sing. We don't even speak to one another. By the time we stop for the night, we're almost too tired to eat the handful of mush they ladle into our filthy palms. We sleep together, eat together, shit together. Only the woman gets a few hours off the chain and we all know what they're doing to her each night. She comes back crying every time, and we all pretend to be asleep so we don't choke on our rage. We dream of being free and making those bastards pay for everything they've done to her—all the things we are powerless to prevent. Then we wake up the next morning, force down some more mush, and drag ourselves down the dusty road.

Once in a while the coffle stops at a plantation to see if they've got any slaves for sale. It's the middle of the war but folks down here still think they can win. They see us coming and sometimes the little White kids will trail along or throw stones at us. I look at these White folks and in their eyes I see how sure they are that things will always be this way. But I know that the war will be over in a couple of years and they won't be able to buy and sell us anymore. They won't be the masters of anyone. They'll be broke. Their cities and homes will be burned to the ground. They'll be losers. I try to remind myself of that when little blonde kids are spitting at me and calling me a filthy nigger.

When it becomes clear that having a pregnant woman on the coffle is slowing us down, McAvoy finds a buyer, which isn't hard to do. Her swollen belly proves she'll make a good breeder. Buy one slave woman and every child she births—every child that lives—is another slave you own for life. I watch that sister go and hope the folks who own her now are decent people. I think of the baby inside of her and know that he or she will be born a slave but will grow up free.

Four of us are sold somewhere in North Carolina. Another slave trader buys me from McAvoy but after money changes hands I hear my new owner muttering about the shape we're in. McAvoy takes his shackles and chains with him when he goes, but we are still bound to one another with rope. Every bone in my body is tired and my feet are so torn up I don't think I can walk another mile. All thoughts of running have vanished. I haven't given up on freedom but right now all I can do is bide my time and wait until my strength is restored.

The new trader, Beardsley, leads us to the edge of town and ties us in a gated pen that smells like it recently held animals. He orders a Black boy to bring us a bucket of soapy water and tells us to wash up. Then an old Black woman comes around and hands out bowls filled with hot rice and gravy. This simple, delicious meal nearly brings us to tears and against our will we feel grateful to this new White man who treats us almost like human beings. But we are still his property and deep down we know that his attention to our needs is just a way of protecting his investment.

When the sun has almost set, a train whistle blows in the distance and before long the steam engine chugs into view. Beardsley leads us out of the pen and over to the track. The train slows and as the caboose nears, Beardsley unties us so that we can climb into the moving car, which is already full of Black men and women. Then the door is closed and locked, leaving us packed into the wooden train car like a herd of cattle.

And that's how we spend the night—standing and dozing like cows being shipped to the slaughterhouse. There are small, barred windows high up the sides of the car but the heat makes us too weak and lethargic to scale the walls of the lurching train. Each time the train stops, about a dozen men and women are led out and sold right off the station platform. As the herd thins, those of us who are left spread out. I sit on the dusty floor and try to imagine where the next transaction will land me.

"Smell that?"

There's no toilet on this train. We hold it as long as we can but as the hours pass, folks get desperate and go in the bucket that sits in one corner of the car. One of us empties it every time the train stops but it fills up fast and stuff sloshes onto the floor as the train rocks along the tracks. It feels like it's over a hundred degrees in here. I know what I smell and it ain't pretty.

I turn and look at the man standing a few feet away from me. His face is turned up to one of the barred windows. Shafts of yellow sunlight break against his skin, which shines with sweat. He closes his eyes and takes a deep breath like he's standing in a rose garden instead of a stinking shit box.

"Ahhh!" He sighs and his body relaxes with what seems like relief. "Taste that salt air! We near the sea now!"

The sea? My heart jumps in my chest and I pull myself up off the floor. I wait for a smooth stretch of track and then leap at the bars in the high window but the train sways and I land with a thud against the wall of the car. The man comes over, spreads his feet apart to steady himself, and laces his fingers together to form a foothold for me. I put a hand on his shoulder and hoist myself up, hoping to get a glimpse of the Atlantic — and all the boats that can carry me back home. South to Jamaica or north to New York.

"What you see?" asks a woman from the far corner of the train car. Her sister was sold at the last station and her voice is hoarse from hours of weeping.

I know by now not to be fooled by appearances but my first glimpse of Charleston *almost* makes me smile. I see houses the color of sorbet — pink, yellow, mint green. Colors from the Caribbean. The palmettos and humid air remind me just how far south I am now. Before I can find practical words for the grieving woman, the man hoisting me up says, "Charleston. We's in Charleston, South Carolina!"

By the time the train pulls into the station there are just twenty of us left. Beardsley breaks us up into lots — eight are handed over to a broker, and the rest are left in a prison just a few blocks away to be sold later. A fat White man with a cigar in his mouth looks us over as his own slave puts the shackles on once more. Then he heaves himself up into a buggy and we trot after him through the busy town.

Our chains drag loudly against the cobblestones, but no one seems to pay us any attention. White ladies in fancy dresses flick open their fans and watch us with curiosity or disgust. Most men ignore us, though I see a few appraising us with their eyes and one asks when the auction will be held. Black men and women — some with metal badges pinned to their clothes — try to capture the attention of Whites by calling out the wares they hope to sell. Red flags flutter outside buildings where slave auctions are already underway.

We finally arrive at Ryan's Mart, an enclosed slave market in downtown Charleston. The fat man climbs down from his buggy and leads us through a low, dark room and out into a sunny courtyard. "Get them sorted, Sampson," he says before walking off with another White man to discuss tomorrow's sale.

His slave leads us into a four-storey brick building that has bars on the ground-floor windows. The cells inside would be cool if they weren't so cramped. Our shackles are removed but there's hardly any room to stretch our limbs, and we do what we can to respect the privacy of others. A couple with a small child is seated on the floor. The woman is trying to talk to a solitary boy but he's got his palms pressed against his face. He's muttering something that doesn't sound like English to me. I wonder if he's from the Sea Islands. Black folks out there speak Gullah, which is English mixed with words brought over from West Africa.

"What's wrong with him?" I ask when the woman finally gives up and turns back to her own little girl.

"Poor thing's seen too much already, I reckon. He just don't wanna see no more. We been here two days and he ain't had a single bite to eat."

I can't say I blame him. How any child survives in this world, I don't know. I look over at the little girl clasped in her mother's arm. Her father reaches over and gently strokes his daughter's cheek. By this time tomorrow, she may be sold away from them forever. Money will change hands and their child will become the property of someone else.

I find a place to sit on the other side of the frightened boy. I try tickling him and pulling away his hands but he starts to scream so I leave him alone for a while. When dinnertime rolls around, they bring us bowls of rice and mashed yam. I try to get the boy to eat but he stubbornly refuses, and judging by the smell, he's soiled himself more than once. The woman looks over at him and shakes her head sadly.

"He's gonna end up in the dead house if he keeps that up."

I'm sure I must have heard her wrong. "The 'dead house'?"

She nods and tilts her head toward the barred window. "When a slave's too sick to sell, they put him in the dead house to get better or..." She shrugs and holds her daughter even closer.

Can a child really will himself to die? I decide then and there that I won't let that happen. When night falls the boy curls up on the floor with his hands still pressed up against his face as if sleep isn't enough to shield him from this sick reality. I look at that little kid rocking himself back and forth, and it's all I can do not to start bawling myself.

I silently slide along the wall until the top of his head touches my thigh. I wish he would let me hold him in my arms but for now I'm content just to be within reach. I hope he knows he's still got people who care about him. After a while he stops rocking and falls asleep. But when morning comes his nightmare—*our* nightmare—will start all over again.

An hour before the auction we're led out of the holding cell to stand in the courtyard so buyers can get a sneak peak at the merchandise. The fat broker with the cigar conducts his own inspection first—squeezing the men's muscles and the women's breasts, daring us to object. We know as well as he does that no decent person will buy a slave that acts or even looks rebellious.

The folks around me have all been sold before and they're hoping to be purchased by a "good" master. They've been slaves all their lives—they're shape-shifters, changing into whatever they think the Whites around them want. But I refuse to wear a mask. Whoever dares to buy me will know just what kind of slave they're getting—the running kind.

The broker waddles over and tells the man next to me to lift his arms up. While the man is reaching for the sky, the broker sticks his hand between the man's legs to weigh his genitals. With a sick grin on his face, the broker turns to me. I do as I'm told and raise my arms but keep my eyes locked on his. Chomping down on his cigar, the broker puts one sweaty palm on my left bicep and then rams his other fist into my belly.

"Better learn your place, boy. I aim to make a tidy sum offa you and

I won't get squat for no uppity nigger. Don't you ever look a White man in the eye. You hear me?"

I can't answer because I am gasping for air. He leaves me doubled over and saunters over to the couple with the little girl. He nods approvingly at the woman's neatly braided hair and tidy appearance. Her husband lowers his eyes and bows at the fat man.

"Suh, we sho' would 'preciate it if'n you could find us a new massa 'n a good home. I ain't got no tools right now, but I can earn a dollar a day with my badge."

The fat man sweeps his sleazy eyes over the woman and plucks the cigar from his mouth. "What's yer name, honey?"

"Susannah, suh. This here's my Thomas and our little girl's name is Tillie."

In his oily voice he says, "I got some fine folks comin' to see y'all. You be sure to make a good impression, you hear? I'm hopin' we can fix you up with a private sale."

The couple beams with gratitude. No auction block *and* the chance for their little family to stay together. Thomas looks like he's ready to kiss the broker's feet, despite the way the fat bastard's looking at his wife. "Yes, suh, we will. Thank you, suh! Thank you!"

After a while the wide wooden door barring one end of the courtyard rolls aside and White people flood the place, eager to inspect us but anxious not to appear in too much of a rush to mingle with slaves. I pull back until I feel the brick wall against my back and watch as white fingers prod at black bodies and pry mouths open to look at teeth.

There is one White woman in the group. With her fancy blue dress and matching parasol she looks like she's going to a garden party, not a slave auction. A young man strolls beside her, his attention drawn to the half-naked "bucks" expected to be sold as field slaves. The woman tilts her frilly parasol so that she can survey the lot of slaves for sale. She turns to speak to her brother and becomes annoyed when she realizes he's no longer at her side.

"Why are you over there? I need a *girl*, Louis. Leave the studs alone and come with me."

I watch as the young White man blushes and then hurries back to his sister. She notices the young mother holding her child and points in her direction. "That one might do. She looks clean enough, at least. You—yes, you, gal. Can you sew?"

Susannah steps forward and remembers to curtsy before responding. "Yes, missus. I did all the sewing for Missus and Miss Harlow over at Oak Lane."

"Harlow?" The White woman's eyes narrow and I see the fear in Susannah's eyes before she drops her chin and stares at the ground, wondering if she's said something wrong. "I attended Claudia Harlow's wedding last month. You're the wench who worked on her trousseau?"

"Yes, Missus."

"That gown was exquisite."

Susannah drops her eyes and barely nods, knowing this is not meant as a compliment to her.

"The silk came from France, did it not?"

"Yes, Missus. Massa Harlow sent for it special."

I wonder if that fancy wedding is the reason Thomas and Susannah are up for sale. The White woman's eyes roam over Susannah's body, settling on the little girl shyly burrowing into her mother's neck. "Who minds the child while you work?"

"Oh, she don't need no mindin', Missus. She a real good baby, real quiet—don't make no fuss, none at all." The tremor in Susannah's voice reveals her fear of losing her only child. "Tillie already picks up thread and scraps off the floor. Won't be long 'fore she can do simple stitches. I gon' teach her just like my mammy taught me. She be a help to you, Missus, a real help."

The White woman stares at the child and frowns. But her desire for a gown as fine as Claudia Harlow's must outweigh her distaste for the child because she sighs and says, "Well. I suppose you'll do. Where's that horrid man? Find him and pay him, Louis, so we can conclude our business and be done with this place."

Thomas speaks up but keeps his eyes lowered and his voice respectful. "Need a blacksmith, Missus? I do fine ironwork. Real fine."

I am so absorbed in this scene that I forget I am also up for sale. A rough hand grabs my shoulder, pulls me off the wall, and spins me around to reveal my bare back.

The broker wipes his palm across my shoulders and down my spine. I clench my fists and fight the urge to bury my fist in his fat gut. "See? Not a mark on him. This young buck's a prime field hand. Worth a pretty penny. Why, in a year or two you can buy him a gal or rent him out as a stud."

I turn around and glare at the broker. He shoves me back against the wall and grabs Thomas by the arm. "This one here's just as strong and he's got a nice, easy disposition."

A tall, thin man with reddish hair takes his eyes off me and turns to Thomas. Then he glances at Susannah, sees her distress and says, "I've no use for a blacksmith. I need a strong hand to work on my farm."

"A smithy's strong—just look at his arm." The broker grabs Thomas' right arm and pushes up the sleeve of his shirt to reveal his muscles. "Hammer or hoe—don't make no difference. And I guarantee this buck here won't give you no trouble."

The man scoffs at the broker's sales pitch. "Until he runs off looking for that wench."

I take a closer look at him then. Something in the red-headed man's stiff movements tells me he's trying to hide something—his inexperience maybe. He isn't as well-dressed as the White woman and her brother, though he sounds more educated than the broker. If he's a first-time slave owner, that could work to my advantage. He isn't completely gullible, but if this red-headed man took me out to his farm it wouldn't be hard to run away. I see my chance and take it. I step forward and say, "A man like Thomas can't do field work."

The White people are stunned to hear me speak but only the broker's face turns red with rage. He pulls the cigar from his mouth and puts the lit end an inch from my eye. "Shut yer trap, boy. Ain't nothin' in yer wooly head that these folks wanna hear."

Thomas turns back to the White woman, desperate to win her favor. "I do ironwork, Missus. Gates and fences and fancy railings and such. I can make your house the finest house in all of Charleston."

"Our house already *is* the finest in Charleston." She waves her hand dismissively and says, "I haven't any need for a blacksmith."

"You could hire him out," I say with my eyes on the ground.

The White woman doesn't even acknowledge me, which probably saves me from getting another punch in the gut from the broker. The woman simply looks from Thomas to Susannah. Her eyes fall at last on the child nestled in the arms of her future seamstress. "What can you earn in a day?" she asks finally.

Hope lights up Thomas' face. "With steady work, more than a dollar, Missus."

The White woman nods, and with a wave of her gloved hand says to the broker, "I suppose I'll take both of them."

Susannah's so terrified that she dares to touch the woman's sleeve. "What about Tillie, Missus?"

The woman sighs impatiently and brushes Susannah's fingerprints off her sleeve. "I suppose she'd better come along." Then she turns and says, "See to the bill, Louis."

"Since when do you want a blacksmith?" her brother asks as he pulls a large leather billfold from inside his jacket.

She pulls him aside and says, "Really, Louis, sometimes I despair of you. It's the wife I need, but keeping the husband close means I'm sure to own several more slaves before long."

Her brother chuckles as he sifts through the bills in his wallet. "And what will *you* do with a bunch of pickaninnies?"

"Why, sell them, of course." Then she laughs and swats his arm

playfully with her parasol. "How stupid you are, Louis. Now go and pay
the man. We must do our part for the Confederacy and show those horrid
Yankees that our way of life has not changed."

Susannah and Thomas collapse into each other's arms. I almost smile
until I look up and find the red-headed man's eyes on me again.

"You say you're used to farm work?"

"Yes, sir. I've worked in the fields since I was a boy." I used to help
my Pappy grow onions back in Jamaica but that was ten years ago. All I
really did was pull weeds, but right now I'm going to tell this green White
man whatever he needs to hear.

"Where's your kinfolk?"

I take a moment to consider what this question means. Kinfolk? Why
would a White man care about my family? I almost say, "New York," but
then change my mind and say, "They're in Jamaica."

"Jamaica? That's a long way from Charleston."

He's trying to hide his emotions but I can tell that he's pleased to
know I'm on my own. "Yes, sir. I left when I was a boy."

The red-headed man nods and seems satisfied—even relieved—by
my answer. I guess he figures I won't run if I don't have a family to run
back to. How can he not realize that freedom means more than anything
else—even family? Then I remember what he said about Thomas running
off to be with Susannah and I know he's right to be asking about kin.

Eventually the broker herds all the White folks out of the courtyard
and tells those of us not sold privately to form a line. Then he leads us into
the building where the auctioneer is waiting.

I am not the first to be sold but my cheeks burn with rage and shame
as I watch the others climb up on the platform and wait to be sold to
the highest bidder. I think of "mock auctions" held at my high school to
raise money for school dances or new football uniforms and I wonder
how anyone could bid on another human being. Several of the buyers
are passing an open flask between them and lewd remarks are shouted
out about various body parts. The fat broker eggs the crowd on, turning

the sale into a carnival game. Sometimes even the slaves laugh, eager to please the men with money who hold their fate in their drunken hands.

When it's my turn I follow two other shirtless men up onto the wooden platform. I look out at the sea of white faces and steel myself against the urge to flee. I'd rather be back in the cell—even back on the coffle—than on the auction block. I've never felt so humiliated. A voice in the crowd urges us to fight one another to prove our strength. I glance at the two other men and step back, unwilling to play such a degrading game.

Just when I think things can't get any worse, the broker calls out, "And now, gentlemen, for your entertainment I present Little Nigger Ned!" And he thrusts the traumatized boy from the cell up onto the stage. The crowd goes wild.

Little Man's on the brink—I can tell. When the auctioneer urges men to start bidding, the kid just loses it. He presses his hands into his face, starts moaning, and rocks from one foot to the other. The fat broker tries to get him to dance but the boy eludes his grasp and starts to howl instead. I try to get him to come to me but there's too much noise—the crowd seems to like nothing better than to watch this little boy lose his mind from fear and grief.

He dodges the white hands reaching for him and runs in circles, coming dangerously close to the edge of the stage. I want to reach out— wrap this child in my arms and take him back to his mother, wherever she may be. But I'm a slave. I can't even help myself. And these White folks are standing there in their fancy clothes, howling with laughter. Howling like wolves.

Then it happens. Dizzy and terrified, the boy runs straight off the edge of the stage and lands with a terrible thud on the hard floor. A collective gasp goes up from the crowd but then the laughter starts all over again. I've had enough. I push my way past the other two slaves and hop off the stage. I have to push a few White men aside to reach the boy, which infuriates the broker. He screams at me to get back on stage but I pretend I can't hear him.

I turn the boy over. There's a gash on his head and he's moaning softly, but his eyes are open and seem to be fixed on mine.

"I got you, Little Man," I whisper as I gather the boy in my arms. His limbs hang limply and I wonder if any of his bones are broken. The next thought in my head is, who will buy this kid now? I stand there holding the boy, waiting — hoping — fearing that someone will claim him.

Just then the auctioneer calls out, "Sold!" Then the broker comes over, his arm wrapped around the shoulder of the red-headed man.

"This young buck will make a fine hand, Wallis. And because I've got such a soft heart, I'm gonna throw in the pickaninny for free!"

Wallis throws off the broker's arm and doesn't bother to hide his disgust. "I don't want the boy. Just him." He steps toward me and I see he has a length of rope in his hand. He's ready to tie my hands and lead me away but right now my hands are full. I steal a glance at my new owner's face and see he's looking at the boy with something like pity.

"But I'm givin' him to you — no charge! In a couple of years, that boy will be a half hand. Why, he can clear weeds and fetch things for you now."

"He looks half dead," Wallis says.

"Aw, you just watch — after I give that lil' nigger a shot of bourbon, he'll be right as rain!"

The broker stuffs the cigar stump back in his mouth and pulls a silver flask from a pocket inside his coat.

Wallis swats the flask away and glares at the fat man with obvious disdain. "Where's the boy's mother?"

"Dead — small pox. Wiped out a dozen slaves on the Fullerton place but the boy survived. He's charmed, I tell you."

"He's touched. Ran right off the stage."

"He was just scared," I say, daring to look Wallis in the eye. I tack on a soft "sir" so he won't think I'm being uppity.

"Can he walk?"

I try to lower the boy to the ground so he can test his legs, but the child suddenly clings to me and threatens to start wailing again.

Wallis presses his lips together and shakes his head. I'm about to beg for the boy but before I can open my mouth the White man loops the rope back up and says, "Bring him then." He pushes his way through the raucous crowd and I follow him with the heartbroken boy in my arms.

Genna

16.

"Well, well, well. Looks like Dorothy found her way back from Oz."

The smile I had carefully pasted on my face slides right off as soon as I hear Toshi's voice. A good-looking, twenty-something man laughs nervously, and then reaches out and pulls me into the apartment.

"Hey, c'mon in. It's Genna, right? I'm Troy." He offers me his hand, and I realize this is the first time we've ever met. Toshi's boyfriend is a complete stranger to me, yet he is doing more than my own sister to make me feel welcome right now.

"You hungry? We're just having lunch. Go on in and sit down—go on." Troy gives me a gentle shove and I step into the kitchen. Toshi looks at me but keeps on chewing her food. They are having fried chicken from a takeout place. The kitchen table is covered with Styrofoam containers holding greasy French fries, coleslaw, and macaroni salad. Toshi's plate is stacked high, but she reaches for the cardboard bucket and adds another piece of chicken to her plate. As always, she pulls the crispy skin off with her fingers and eats that first.

Looking at Toshi eating that way I can't help but think of a cow. I don't say this out loud, of course. But I still feel bad when Troy hands me a plate and says, "You better get some quick, Genna—my baby's got a real big appetite now that she's eating for two."

Somehow I manage not to drop the plate, but I can't keep my mouth from falling open. Toshi sucks the grease off her fingers and pushes her chair back from the table so I can see her belly.

"Just three more months to go," says Troy with obvious pride.

I'm trying, but I still can't think of anything to say. How long have I been gone? The last time I saw Toshi was near the end of June—she wasn't showing then. It's almost October now. She must have known… did Mama know, too? Is that why she threw Toshi out? Suddenly things start falling into place. I drop into an empty chair at the table. Troy starts piling food onto my plate.

"Sorry, baby," he says to Toshi. "I thought she knew."

"Don't worry about it," says Toshi. "My little sister's just playing innocent. She's real good at that."

"Toshi, I swear, I didn't know. Nobody told me…" Toshi just keeps on eating her food like I'm not even there. "Congratulations," I tell her anyway. Then I turn to Troy. He looks a little uncomfortable right now, but every time his eyes fall on Toshi's belly, he starts to smile.

"Congratulations, Troy. That's real exciting—hey, I'm going to be an aunt!" This fact really does get me excited. In fact, it's the best news I've had since I got back.

Toshi checks me out for a minute, then tries to act nice by passing me a box filled with doughy biscuits. I take one and notice a diamond ring flashing on her finger. "You're married!" I exclaim.

Troy laughs out loud this time, and Toshi grins, too. "Engaged. Mama didn't tell you nothin'?"

I shake my head and bite into a piece of fried chicken. In a way, this feels like a family reunion—the ones you see in commercials on TV. Our family's far from perfect, but right now things feel pretty good. I keep my head down and focus on my food. I'm going to be an aunt, I think to myself. Toshi's baby will be able to play with Tyjuan.

Things get awkward again once the food is gone. I'm not sure what to say to Toshi or Troy, so I stand up and start clearing the table. I figure doing the dishes will keep me busy for a while, but Troy has something else in mind.

"Don't worry about it, Genna. Just sit down and relax, I'll take care of the dishes. You and Toshi got a lot of catching up to do."

I look at Troy like he must be some new kind of man, offering to clean up like that. Toshi sees the surprise in my face and smiles smugly at me. I sit back down at the table and try not to look as awkward as I feel.

"Shouldn't you be in school?" Toshi asks sarcastically.

I shrug and watch tiny bubbles float towards the ceiling. Troy is using way too much dish soap, but at least the dishes he places on the rack look clean. Whenever Rico washed dishes — which wasn't very often — I'd always have to wash them over again 'cause they'd be covered with crusty bits of food. Now I sit and watch the dishes drip themselves dry so I don't have to look at Toshi.

"Genna the truant — that's a first. Wait a minute, what am I saying? You were MIA all summer long. Where you been?"

I shrug again and start to wonder why I bothered coming here. Some things never change. It's been more than a hundred years since I've seen my sister, but nothing between us has changed.

"Mama know you're cutting class?"

I shake my head and try not to cop an attitude. Like I'd tell Mama about something like that. Like I need permission to do what I want.

"Somebody mess with you?"

This time I look over at my sister. Toshi's six months pregnant but right now she's got that look on her face like she's ready to fight somebody. And not because they pissed her off, but because they messed with me. Toshi never had my back before. Maybe she has changed after all.

"This teacher got me heated, that's all."

"Which one?"

"Mr. Collins. He teaches History."

"I know him. Short little shit with bushy eyebrows and beady eyes, right?"

I nod and find myself smiling at my sister.

Toshi's face is still serious. "You curse him out?"

I laugh out loud this time, and almost wish I had thrown the textbook at Mr. Collins after all. Toshi would have been impressed. "Naw, I just yelled at him and walked out."

"Hmph. Good for you. I guess you're a Colon after all."

Troy looks at me over his shoulder. "Uh oh. I hope not. Your sister's got one mean temper."

Toshi throws a gooey piece of macaroni at Troy. He ducks, but it sticks to his designer tracksuit anyway. While Troy cleans himself up with the dishrag, Toshi turns back to me. "He mess with you again, you let me know."

"He won't."

This time Toshi smiles at me. She thinks I mean that I can handle myself—and I can—but that's not what I mean. Mr. Collins won't mess with me again because I won't be going back to his class.

"School seems like a waste of time these days," I say. "There's so much going on, and yet they expect us to act like everything's normal."

Toshi rubs her hand over her belly. "I never thought I'd be saying this, but school's a good place for you to be right now, Gen. Folks who ain't got someplace to be end up causing all kinds of trouble these days." Toshi flicks her eyes at Troy. Troy looks at his feet.

"What kind of trouble?" I ask.

"A few days ago somebody broke into the deli at the corner. Looted it, then lit the place up."

I stare at Toshi in disbelief, my mouth open and filling with air. I remember all the times I shopped at that deli, the way the man behind the counter used to smile at me. "But they're Yemeni."

"What?"

"The storeowners—they're from Yemen. It says so right on the awning."

Toshi just shrugs. "Well, there ain't no awning no more."

"Yemen? Ain't that where that ship got blown up?" asks Troy.

Toshi cuts me off before I can reply. "Don't matter where they from—they're A-rabs."

"You shouldn't say it like that," I mumble with my eyes on the floor.

"Why not?" she asks. "A-rab, towelhead, terrorist—it's all the same to me."

Troy coughs uncomfortably but clearly knows it isn't wise to disagree with Toshi. I stare at the white roach powder piled in the narrow space between the fridge and the cupboard. "You know, not that long ago it was *us* they were hating. It was *our* homes they burned down—*our* stores."

Toshi says nothing so Troy jumps in. "Aw, c'mon now, that ain't right. Brothers is just feeling patriotic, is all. You can't compare them to the KKK."

"Why not? What's the difference?" I ask angrily.

Troy looks at Toshi as if to say, "Is she for real?" Then he digs his hands out of his pockets and frowns at me. "The difference is for once, the Black man ain't public enemy number one in this city. The cops are so busy acting like heroes and looking out for terrorists they ain't got time to be hassling me. That's the difference." Troy reaches back into his pocket and pulls out a pack of cigarettes.

"Don't you light up in here." Toshi points her eyes at Troy, and he quickly pulls the cigarette from between his lips.

"Sorry, baby, I forgot. Want me to go out in the hall?"

"Naw, just open a window or something."

Troy nods and obediently goes into the living room. With some effort, the window slides up and cool air drifts into the kitchen mixed with the faint scent of tobacco. Soon we hear Troy's voice talking to someone on the phone. It sounds like he's setting up an appointment. I'm not sure if I really want to know, but I can't think of anything else to say right now, so I decide to ask anyway. "What does Troy do?"

Toshi avoids my eyes and says Troy runs his own delivery company. "Like UPS?" I ask.

Toshi doesn't answer. She just squirms around in her seat and rubs her hand over her belly. "Damn, this kid's really getting down today. Want to feel?"

I nod eagerly, and reach out my hand. Toshi takes it and puts it on the side of her belly. She keeps her hand pressed over mine, and together we feel the baby kicking inside of her.

"That's a left jab," says Troy, sticking his head around the doorway. He stubs his cigarette out in a glass ashtray then sets it on the counter. "My boy's gonna be a prizefighter—the next heavyweight champion of the world!"

Toshi just chuckles and shakes her head. "You going out? Bring me back some crab legs and French fries—and don't forget the hot sauce this time."

"Crab legs? Where'm I supposed to get crab legs? Never mind, anything for my baby." Troy leans down and kisses the top of Toshi's head. Then he leans farther down and gently kisses her belly. "See you later, Champ. You be here when I get back, Genna?"

I glance at Toshi and shrug, not sure how long she'll let me stay.

Troy leans against the counter and all the playfulness goes out of his face. "Your sister won't admit it, but she could use a little company these days. Having a baby's no joke, and I'm here for her all the way, she knows that. But your Mama's cut her off, and I don't mean no disrespect, but it ain't right for Toshi to be going through this alone. So you come by whenever you want, Genna—check on Li'l Mama when I'm not here."

Toshi rolls her eyes but her sly smile tells me she appreciates her fiancé's concern. "I don't need nobody checking up on me, Troy. 'Sides, Genna's got school to go to, and I'm sure Mama's told her to stay far away from me—just in case what I've got is catching." Toshi winks at Troy, and this time he shrugs and pushes himself off the counter.

"You welcome anytime, Genna. And you can crash here too if things get hectic at home. We got a extra key around here somewhere. See if you can find it for her before she goes home, baby." Troy nods at me, blows a kiss to Toshi, and goes out of the apartment with his cell phone pressed against his ear.

"You really having a boy?"

Toshi pushes her chair back and hefts her feet up onto the opposite seat. "Troy thinks so."

"That's what the doctor said?"

"One thing I know for sure, little sister, is that every man wants a son. The doctor said it was too early to be sure, but he thinks I'm having a girl. I told Troy it might be a boy, so he wouldn't get any ideas about stepping out on us..."

"Troy doesn't seem like that kind of guy. What are you going to do once he finds out the truth?"

"Once the baby's born, I won't have to worry about a thing. That baby girl will have Troy wrapped around her little finger. For now, what he don't know won't hurt him."

I nod so Toshi will think I understand. Then I ask, "Do you think Papi would have stayed if we'd been boys?"

Toshi's eyes go cold. "Who knows. Papi was a foreigner—he already had a way out. But I know you didn't come over here to talk about Papi. So what's up? Mama send you over here to spy on me?"

I shake my head and lean my elbows on the table. I wish Toshi and I were close, like real sisters. Then she wouldn't act all suspicious, and I wouldn't feel so unwelcome. I want to talk to my big sister, but I don't know where to begin.

"I hear she was pretty torn up after you left. First she found out her precious son's shit really does stink, then I lived up to her worst expectations by getting knocked up. Then you ran off with that Rasta— what's his name?"

"Judah."

"Right. So what happened? You two break up?"

"Sort of," I say quietly.

"Hmph. What's that mean—he cheat on you?"

I shake my head quickly, and Toshi laughs. "A man ain't nothing but a man, Genna. No matter how slick they talk or how righteous they pretend to be."

"Judah and me, we made a promise to stay together. But then I came back here, and..." I let my words trail off, unsure what else to say.

"And what? Now you want to get back together?"

I nod and Toshi shakes her head like she's heard it all before. "That's the nature of the beast, Genna. The grass is always greener, and you only want what you can't have. You're still young, so it's hard for you to understand. He was your first, right?"

I know Toshi's talking about sex, but I nod anyway. Then I change my mind and decide to tell her the truth. After all, I'm not ashamed of anything that has or hasn't happened between me and Judah. "Not like how you mean, but it's my first time being...in love."

"Yeah, well, don't believe the hype. I've been around the block a few times, and I can tell you love ain't no fairy tale. A woman's got to be realistic about love, otherwise she'll end up getting played. Take Troy — he's a good guy, we love each other, and I think he'll do right by me and the baby. But underneath it all, he's just a man. It won't surprise me if I wake up one day and he's gone."

I listen to Toshi and remember something I read once in a psychology book. "Maybe you feel that way because Papi walked out on us."

Toshi rolls her eyes at me. "I feel that way because most men don't know how to stay put. If they stand still too long, their feet start to itch, next thing you know — they're outta there. 'Cross the street, 'cross the country — they just keep on moving, making babies along the way. That's one thing I can say about Troy — he handles his business. Most brothers his age have two, three kids by now. But not Troy — this is his first, at least that I know of, and believe me, I did my homework to make sure. But back to this boy — what's his name?"

"Judah."

"Right. What makes you think he's still waiting for you? I hate to break it to you, Gen, but he's probably moved on by now. After all, *you* left *him*, right?"

I nod and from out of nowhere tears start trickling down my face. "But I didn't mean to—I didn't want to go."

"So why did you?"

There is nothing I can tell Toshi that will make any sense, so I just shrug and wipe my face with my sleeve.

Toshi hands me a napkin that's got ketchup smeared on one side. "You thinking 'bout going back?"

I flip the napkin over and blow my nose. "I don't know. You think I should?"

Toshi swings her feet off the chair and pulls herself up to the table. She twists the diamond ring on her finger then surprises me by reaching out and touching my arm. "Real love ain't something you find every day, Gen. But only you know how you really feel. If you just have a crush on this boy, I say, wait it out—you'll get over him in a month or two. But if it's for real, if you really love this boy, then you got to throw the dice. Maybe he's still waiting for you, maybe he's not. But you did make a promise, and even if we ain't got nothing else in common, us Colon women keep our word. Right?"

I smile a little despite my tears and nod at my big sister.

"You tell Mama 'bout any of this?"

"A little."

"Well, keep it that way. The less she knows 'bout your business, the better. And Troy's right—you ever need someplace to stay, you come here. I think I saw that spare key on the dresser—wait here, I'll go get it."

Toshi heaves herself up off the chair. I suck up my courage and grab my sister's hand as she walks by. I don't look up, just in case Toshi's disgusted and not just surprised. "Thanks, Toshi," I whisper into her palm.

Toshi pulls her hand out of mine and wraps her arm around my shoulders instead. "No problem, little sister. I never was any good in school, but I'm still good for something. You ever need advice, or just a break from Mama, you come to me. Okay?"

I nod and somehow find the nerve to rest my head against Toshi's belly. My sister holds me close for a moment, and we both feel the baby moving inside of her.

"This kid's really moving around today."

"Maybe she's going to be a dancer," I suggest, remembering Toshi's wild performances in front of the TV.

"Naw, I think Troy's right. She's a fighter."

Toshi smiles at me before leaving the kitchen. I try to smile back, but inside I'm hoping Toshi's right. My little niece will need to be a fighter if she's going to survive in this world.

Judah

17.

I do as I'm told and follow this man named Wallis out of the slave market and into the street. He leads me over to a wagon and unlatches the back. I watch as he tosses the rope in and then rearranges some sacks to make a sort of bed for the boy. "Lay him down."

I try to untangle myself but the boy whimpers and refuses to let go. "C'mon, Little Man," I whisper in his ear. "It's time to go. You have to get in the wagon." I try to pull him off me but the boy panics and grabs two fistfuls of my hair. I cast a nervous glance at Wallis, fearing he'll change his mind and make me leave the kid behind.

But the White man just sighs and says, "Well, you best get in with him, then." Wallis gives me a leg up and I manage to climb into the wagon with the boy's arms still clasped around my neck. I shift around and try to get comfortable amidst the sacks, barrels, and crates.

Wallis looks at me but doesn't close the wagon flap. After several seconds pass, he finally speaks. "Give me your hands."

I lean forward and hold my hands up so my new owner can loop the rope around my wrists. He avoids my eyes while doing this but I look in his face and see something I haven't seen yet in a White man— embarrassment. He ties a loose knot and then closes the wagon flap before going around to check on his horse.

I sink back against the stacked sacks and wonder how this journey will end. Wallis climbs up and settles himself on the front seat. I jump when something nudges my shoulder. I turn and see Wallis is offering me a canteen.

"Thirsty?"

I am, but I'm not sure if I am supposed to share a White man's canteen. I glance around the busy street but no one seems to be shocked by his gesture. I reach up over my shoulder and grasp the canteen between my bound hands. I take a quick sip and pass it back to Wallis but he refuses to take it from me.

"Go on. Drink your fill. We got a long ride ahead."

I take another swig before handing it back to him with a nod of thanks. The boy squirms but then spreads out and settles against my chest. I watch his eyes close and hope he's falling asleep and not losing consciousness. I think of all the medical shows I've seen on TV — does he have a concussion? Swelling of the brain? Should I try to keep him awake?

As the wagon lurches forward, the boy's head drops heavily against my neck. I close my eyes and say a silent prayer for us both. When we leave the noise of the city behind, I hear Wallis humming a familiar tune. After searching my memory for a moment I come up with the song: "Abide with Me." My granny used to sing that song while she was washing clothes in the yard and we sometimes sang it in the Methodist church on Sunday mornings. Frederick Douglass said that the worst slaveholders were the ones who called themselves Christians and believed they had a God-given right to buy, sell, and beat their slaves. I hope Wallis doesn't prove Douglass right.

I watch the landscape change as we head west and try to make a map in my head. I figure the best way to escape is probably by heading back to the coast. The swampy lowlands will make it hard for dogs to track me and I may be able to get passage — or stow away — on a boat heading back to New York. As the wagon bumps along the dirt road I think of all the stories I've heard about runaway slaves. Those who could read and write sometimes forged a pass and signed their master's name so they had proof they were allowed to be off the plantation. An enslaved woman who was light-skinned dressed up as a White man and pretended her dark-skinned husband was her valet. Another man had himself nailed inside a wooden crate and shipped north. But most fugitives simply ran on foot and sought help from sympathizers along the way. That's probably what I'll have to do. Like most fugitive slaves I won't have a map or a compass. I'll have nothing but the North Star and the compass in my heart to guide me toward freedom.

The sun has set by the time the wagon turns off the main road and finally rolls to a stop next to an old barn. The air has cooled considerably but with the boy's body draped over me like a blanket, I've stayed warm. It's hard to see much in the darkness but candles lit in the windows reveal a modest house made of wood on a low hill in the distance. A door opens and a swinging light comes toward us. I squint in the darkness and realize it's not a firefly but an older Black woman holding up a lantern. When she gets close to the wagon Wallis says, "Evening, Alma. How's your mistress?"

"She be glad to see you, Marse. We was spectin' you hours ago."

"Yes, well the auction wasn't quite as…orderly as I'd imagined. Is supper ready?"

"Yessuh, but Missus wouldn't eat a bite till you reached home."

"Tell her I'll be up just as soon as I get these two settled for the night."

"Yessuh."

It's hard to tell just how old Alma is but when she peers into the wagon it's clear she's not happy to see me or the boy. Wallis comes around to the back of the wagon and helps me climb down. My bound hands make it easy to keep the boy close. He slept almost the entire way but woke as soon as the wagon wheels stopped turning. He no longer clings to me but seems content to rest quietly in my arms. My stomach rumbles with hunger and I hope his calmer mood means he'll eat something—if we get fed.

"These supplies can stay in the wagon till morning," Wallis says and

I realize it will be my job to do all the heavy lifting from now on. Wallis closes the wagon up again and gestures for me to follow him into the barn. Alma's already heading back up the hill but Wallis calls over his shoulder, "Alma, bring two plates out to the barn once you've seen to your mistress, please."

"Yessuh, Marse," she replies without turning around.

Wallis opens the barn door and reaches for another lantern hanging inside on a nail. He takes a box of matches from his pants pocket and strikes one to light the wick. A soft orange glow chases away some of the shadows in the cavernous barn. Little Man wriggles in my arms so I set him down and his curiosity draws him inside. Despite the sad history that brought him here, he hasn't yet learned to be afraid of new beginnings.

Wallis leads us to a far corner and says, "I thought you could sleep here for now. Just until we have a chance to build something more permanent." Wallis coughs to clear the apologetic tone from his voice and holds the lantern up to show a stall that's been swept clean. A lumpy corn-husk mattress rests on the floor and beside it is an overturned crate that serves as a sort of table. There's also an empty bucket that I assume is meant to serve as a chamber pot.

"I planned for one, not two. I guess the boy can stay in the house with Alma during the day. My wife's good with children. Has he got a name?"

I watch as the boy crawls across the mattress and plants himself in the far corner of the stall. He looks up at me and doesn't smile, but it's still hard to believe he's the same traumatized kid I met in the cell the day before. Eventually I remember to answer Wallis' question. "He hasn't spoken yet. Maybe he'll open up tomorrow. He's had a rough day."

"We all have," Wallis says with a weary grin.

I turn away so he won't see the rage flashing in my eyes. What hardship did this White man experience today? He left his house with enough money to buy one slave and came home with two people that he legally owns for life. And a hot meal is waiting for him—cooked by the *other* slave he owns for life.

Perhaps Wallis senses my mood because he suddenly sets the lantern on the crate and takes up a length of chain that's coiled on the floor.

"This is just temporary...but necessary, I'm afraid. Wouldn't want you disappearing in the night." One end of the chain is attached to an iron loop embedded in a wooden post. The other end is attached to an iron cuff that Wallis fits around my ankle. I watch as he fumbles with the lock before pocketing the key. To run, I'll have to work the iron loop out of that wooden post. Or I'll have to wait until Wallis' trusts me enough not to chain me up like a dog each night.

"If there's anything else you need," he says, "just let Alma know. She'll be out with your supper before long. Until then, just—uh—make yourself comfortable and I'll see you in the morning."

I nod and watch as Wallis rushes for the barn door. He meets Alma coming in with two steaming bowls and waits outside as she delivers our supper without saying a word. Wallis doesn't close the door as she exits the barn and I strain my ears to hear his instructions to Alma. His head seems to be spinning with all the considerations of a first-time slave owner. He can't seem to decide whether he should treat us like guests or like animals.

"Alma, see if you can find an old shirt for Judah to wear. And the boy's got a bad cut on his head—be sure to clean it and bind it with some cloth, please. He needs a bath, too, but that can wait till tomorrow."

"He young, Marse. Too young." Alma's voice isn't defiant but it still sounds like she's reprimanding her owner.

"The boy?" Wallis asks. "I couldn't leave him there. Just give him time to settle in."

From the corner of my eye I can see Alma shaking her head. I keep spooning food into my mouth and pretend to have no interest in their conversation. Little Man is using his fingers to shove the savory pieces of meat into his mouth. I tell him to slow down but I'm shoveling my food in, too. Alma gave us generous portions of rice and some sort of stew with okra and carrots. I can't tell if the meat is pork and at this point, I don't honestly care. I can't follow a vegetarian diet if I want to survive in this world. Once I'm free, I'll do a cleanse and return to livity.

"Missus said you was gonna get a man to help you out in the field, not no young pup."

Wallis teases her. "Were you hoping for a husband, Alma?"

She chuckles and says, "You know my courtin' days is over, Marse."

"With your cooking I'm sure you can win over any man, young or old."

I feel Alma watching me as I try to help the boy get some of the rice inside his mouth instead of dropping it all over the bed we'll be sleeping on tonight. Her voice loses its playfulness. "He too young, Marse—and strong. Boy like that won't think twice 'bout runnin' off."

Wallis tries to sound firm. "He won't run. I'll see to that."

Alma isn't convinced—and neither am I. "You got to watch him close, Marse. Keep an eye on him all the time. Missus said you was gonna buy a older slave—one whose runnin' days was behind him."

Wallis sighs, clearly done being lectured by his cook. "I did the best I could with what I had, Alma. Now if you'll excuse me, I'll go see Mrs. Wallis and tell her about my day. Please see that they've got what they need for the night."

'Yessuh."

Alma mutters something neither Wallis nor I can hear, and then sticks her head in the barn and calls out, "Y'all done eatin'?"

"Yes, ma'am." I stack the bowls and hand them to Alma. "Thank you," I say as she takes the empty bowls from my hand. "That's the best food I've had in a long time."

Compliments and courtesy usually work with elders but Alma isn't impressed. She just gives me the evil eye and walks off muttering to herself.

I test the length of chain and carry the bucket as far from our bed as I can. Then I relieve myself and try to get the boy to do the same. Neither one of us smells that fresh but there's no way to wash up or change clothes so we get ready for bed. The boy claims the far corner of the stall and watches me as I kneel to pray.

Alma comes back to the barn with a wool blanket and an old shirt. When she sees me on my knees she waits until I finish and then says, "I hope you thanked the good Lord for givin' you such a good master, boy." Then she tosses the shirt and blanket on the bed.

I look at her to see if she's serious. "My name's Judah," I say with as much respect as I can muster after such an exhausting day.

Alma must hear the edge in my voice because she launches into the lecture Wallis cut short earlier. "Marse don't know slaves like I do. He a good man but he too soft-hearted. Lord only knows what we gonna do with this child. Marse say his head ain't right."

"He'll be fine. I'll look after him."

"You will, huh? And just when do you think you gon' have time to look after a half-wit? You here to *work*, boy. Nothin' else."

"I'm just saying you don't have to worry about him."

"I ain't worried 'bout no lil' boy—I'm worried 'bout *you*. Marse ain't got money to throw away and he spent just 'bout every penny he got buyin' you. If you run, he's sunk—along with me and the missus, and she's already ailin'. Marse don't come from money like the missus do. But her Pa cut her off without a red cent on account o' her marryin' for love. Lord Jesus, I don't know why I'm tellin' you alla this."

Neither do I. I'd really like to get some sleep but this woman seems determined to lay down the law—as she sees it. I read about slaves who act like it's their job to protect the property and even the reputation of the family that owns them. But I don't need this old woman to tell me how grateful I should be. I didn't ask to be bought like a cow or a pig. And I'm not about to give up my freedom just to help some White man climb the social ladder. Wallis seems decent and he's treated me better than any other White man I've met in this world. But I don't owe him a thing—not my gratitude, not my loyalty.

"I better get some rest," I tell her, hoping she'll take the hint and leave me alone. "Mr. Wallis wants to fix the roof on this barn tomorrow."

She squints her eyes at me and says, "Mister? He ain't 'mister' to you, boy. He's your *master*. I don't know where you come from, but 'round here you better know your place. Whether you like it or not, you a slave."

I lie down on the lumpy mattress and pull the blanket over me. "Goodnight, ma'am." I close my eyes and wait for her to leave but she stands over me a while longer.

I stifle a groan when she starts talking again. "You just remember what I told you. We done had enough trouble 'round here, what with Missus losin' the baby and all. The Wallises is good people, far as White folks go. I ain't never had no reason to complain. Just give 'em a chance, boy. That's all I'm askin'."

Finally she leaves, taking with her the orange glow from the lantern. I open my eyes to the blackness and look up at the stars winking at me through the holes in the barn roof. *Give them a chance.* She can't seriously believe life with a "good" master is better than being free. Only a person who's never known freedom could think something like that.

Little Man turns in his sleep and reaches out until his tiny hand presses against my chest. He murmurs something I can't understand and then grows still. I wonder if tomorrow he'll tell me his name. If not, Wallis may choose a name for him—Caesar or Adonis, an ironic name meant to mock and demean. I look at the boy in the dim starlight and see a tiny fish lost in the deep blue sea. If he can't tell me his name, I think I'll call him Jonah. Because the prophet Jonah was swallowed by the beast in the sea but, against all odds, he lived to testify.

When I try to pry the boy's fingers loose he latches onto my hand instead. Though my body is weary, I feel something stirring inside. For weeks I have worked to make my heart numb but this boy reminds me that I am alive. With him, I can be my true self—no mask, no deceit. But Wallis bought me because I told him I had no kin. I leave the boy's fingers wrapped around mine but inside I close the door of my heart. It's not only chains that bind you. It's love.

Judah

18.

I wait ten days before I run. For a week and a half I do everything Wallis asks me to do without a complaint. Together we fix the roof on the barn, we uproot four trees and clear rocks from his fields, and we repair the fence that separates his land from his neighbor's. For the first couple of days Jonah haunts me like my shadow. If he can't see me, he starts to wail and if he can get close to me, he wraps an arm around my leg to keep me close. This continues until Alma manages to lure the boy up to the kitchen with a hot buttered biscuit smeared with plum jam. I tell them his name is Jonah but Alma keeps calling him "Lil' Joe" so that's the name that sticks.

Alma also insists on finding work for Joe to do. He can't be more than five years old but she's determined to make him "earn his keep." At midday she brings a bucket of water out to the field and sends Joe over with a tin cup. Most of the water has splashed on the ground by the time he reaches us but the job makes him feel important. He gathers sticks for kindling and picks small stones out of the soil that Wallis hopes will soon grow cotton.

Mrs. Wallis hasn't left the house for weeks according to Alma, and when she does step outside she's thin and pale as a ghost. But the sound of Joe's laughter as he chases a butterfly draws her out to the garden behind their house. Once or twice I've even seen her sitting on the front porch in a rocker, holding the boy on her lap. I haven't been inside their house but Alma likes to boast about how Wallis used to be a schoolteacher. That would explain why he doesn't seem to know much about farming. If there are books around I hope Mrs. Wallis will use some of her free time to teach Joe how to read. Give him something he can use once he's no longer their property.

After a few days, things are going so well that Wallis starts to whistle while we work. When the sun sets and we quit for the day, he tells me I'm a good worker—like that's some kind of compliment. I always smile and say, "Thank you, sir," knowing that this is just a performance. I am anything but a good slave. Wallis is glad to be getting a solid return on his investment, and it looks like the fat broker in Charleston was right—Joe is already useful and will only take on more tasks as he grows. But I have other plans.

While we're out in the field I keep adding details to the map in my mind. I act like I am eager to fix the roof of the barn, but really I just want to get a good look at the land. From the top of the barn I can see where the forests are and which roads lead east and north. Those are my two options. Those roads will lead me home.

My act has fooled Wallis but Alma's still not convinced. One day she brings lunch out to the field earlier than usual. Wallis tells her to set the metal pails down under a nearby tree but Alma lingers next to me instead. She waits until Wallis crosses the field and then starts interrogating me.

"So. When you leavin'?"

I flinch and cast a quick look over to where Wallis is standing. Then I push the shovel I'm holding deep into the rocky soil and avoid Alma's eyes. "What you mean?"

She grunts. "You thinkin' 'bout runnin.' I can tell." Not a question this time. Just a fact.

"What makes you think that?" I ask innocently.

"I seen how you been pushin' that boy away. Actin' like you don't care when I know you do. You gone already."

I shrug and keep on digging. It's risky, but I drop my act and tell her the truth. "Can't take him with me."

"No. But you could stay. Stead of breakin' his lil' heart again. Marse ain't so bad. I seen plenty worse. If'n his wife's daddy owned you and you was fool enough to run, he's hunt you down, let the dogs tear you to pieces, and leave you swingin' in the breeze. Food for the crows."

I'm sure Alma has seen some terrible things in her life, but I am not Joe. Her tales don't frighten me. "I'm not supposed to be here," I tell her. "I wasn't born a slave."

Alma just scoffs at that. "Maybe not. But you a slave now. Marse done paid a small fortune for you. He ain't like them rich planters got more slaves 'n they can count. Marse a fair man but he can't afford to let you walk off again. You all he's got."

"What about you?"

"I cook and clean, help the missus when she's ailin'. But I can't build no barn or plow no field. My hard workin' days is behind me now. 'Fore long I be headin' to Glory." She closes her eyes and starts to sing an old spiritual I've heard before:

> *Steal away, steal away, steal away home.*
> *I ain't got long to stay here.*

I ain't got long to stay here either, but I don't tell Alma that. Religion is a drug for her. It numbs her to the pain and teaches her to wait for her reward after her life is over. But I am not numb. I feel every indignity and I won't turn the other cheek. I spit into the dirt and say, "You steal away to Jesus if you want. I got somebody else waiting for me."

For the first time, Alma's eyes show genuine interest in me. She digs her fist into her hip and almost smiles. "A gal?"

I just nod, not wanting to open that box right now.

Alma sighs and for just a moment she looks like a younger woman—a woman who remembers how it feels to love someone without fear. "You sure she's waitin' on you? Folks move on, you know. 'Sides, Marse pro'ly get you a woman in a year or two. You could settle down, start a family.

Give Joe a li'l brother or sister."

I keep my eyes on the ground so Alma can't see them blaze with rage. "And give Wallis another slave to own? I don't think so. I'm no stud."

Alma's eyes shine and her voice sharpens with mockery. "You a man, though. What you gonna do? Cozy up to that cow?" She laughs and walks over to the tree where she deposits the pails containing our lunch. On her way back to the house she keeps that smirk on her face but her eyes send a warning: *I'm watching you, boy.*

Alma's eyes are on me all the time—until the sun goes down. She sleeps on the floor in the house so she can be close by if her mistress needs her during the night. I sleep in the barn with Joe, beyond the reach of Alma's prying eyes.

I save a small portion of my supper for three days and manage to get Joe to steal a couple of extra biscuits from the kitchen for me. When Wallis isn't looking, I scoop up a large, bent nail from the barn floor while we're fixing the roof. It's not as sharp as a knife but it will pierce human skin or the hide of any animal that might happen to attack me. Traveling with a "pass" written by my master would provide extra insurance, but there's no way I can slip inside the house and get my hands on a quill, ink, and a piece of paper. So I bundle the little I have in the filthy shirt I was wearing when Wallis bought me at the auction, and then tie the sleeves around my waist. I want to wait for a full moon but impatience makes me settle for a half. I need enough light to see my way through the night but I don't want--and can't afford—to be seen by anyone else.

I have lived in the country before but the absolute blackness of the night still unnerves me. I stand at the barn door and wait for the last candle to go out inside the Wallis home. Without a watch, I can only guess the time but folks turn in early here in the country. I figure it is just past nine, which means I will have eight hours before anyone stirs and discovers I'm gone. Eight hours to put as much distance as possible between myself and this farm.

Alma was right—Wallis hasn't mistreated me so far and maybe he never would. She likes to say he's got "a tender heart," and maybe that's true. When I split my big toe open on a sharp stone out in the fields, Wallis went into his house and came out with an old pair of shoes for me to wear. The soles are worn through in a couple of spots, but those same shoes will speed my journey tonight. No amount of kindness can make up for the fact that he *owns* me. This place will never be home. Home is where you're free, where people love you for who you are and not for what you can do for them. Home is wherever Genna is.

I take deep breaths and will my heart to slow but it refuses to obey. I give up and instead try to channel my adrenaline so that I can focus on what lies ahead. I glance back over my shoulder and search the shadows for the little boy I am leaving behind. In the dark I can't make out his body, but I can hear his faint breath as Joe continues to sleep peacefully in the stall we once shared. From now on he will sleep alone, unless Alma takes him up to the house. I feel a flicker of guilt and wonder if Joe will remember how I cared for him or if he'll remember me as just another person who disappeared without saying goodbye.

My clothes are damp with sweat and I shiver as a cool night breeze blows through the open barn door. I can't look back anymore. From this point on, I will only look ahead. I face the night, take a deep breath, and step out of the barn. My only witness is the night sky full of mute stars, white but too distant to harm me. I creep away from the Wallis homestead, careful not to wake the dog sleeping in the yard. I cross the fields I recently cleared, climb the fence I helped to repair, and plunge into the woods. I become a fugitive. I run toward freedom. I run for my life.

Almost immediately, tree branches claw at my face and the sweat on my skin mingles with blood. I wish I had a machete to slash at whatever blocks my way but I have only my hands to clear a path. I hear small animals scurrying away as I thrash and claw my way through the woods like a wild beast. The road is just a few yards away but I don't dare walk out in the open in case I encounter White men on patrol. I am the prey they hope to capture. I belong to Wallis but there will be a reward if they restore his stolen property.

I have already decided that if Wallis wants me back, they will have to kill me. *Give me liberty or give me death.* I am too breathless to laugh, but what did "the Founding Fathers" ever know about the desperate desire for freedom? Only the man who has been unjustly enslaved knows what freedom is really worth.

I try to hold onto these noble ideas as the night wears on and my legs grow heavy with fatigue. Travelling from Charleston to the farm took hours in Wallis' wagon. For a moment I curse myself for not stealing his horse. But could a slave ride his master's horse down the road in the middle of the night without raising the alarm? I tell myself it is better to be hidden in the woods, even if the journey takes twice as long. Once I near the coast, the land will become marshy. I will let the swamp swallow me and keep me safe from the dogs, patrollers, and anyone else on my trail.

My mind races faster than my legs and the night becomes a blur. One moment I am thinking of Wallis, hoping he is still fast asleep. The next moment I am thinking of Genna, her soft voice circling the stone bench in the garden to whisper a love poem in my ear. Then I am back in the woods, falling and stumbling and drowning in the darkness.

I run until my lungs feel like they will burst. Then I stop at a stream to wet my feet so the dogs won't catch my scent. I drink just enough water to wet my throat but not enough to make me cramp when I start running again. I scramble up a steep embankment and nearly reach the top before losing my balance and tumbling back into the ravine. My head hits a stone and I catch one last glimpse of the half moon above before surrendering to a blackness deeper than the night.

Genna

19.

Turns out mouthing off to Mr. Collins is a big deal after all. When I get home, Mama's leaned up against the kitchen counter, her arms folded tight across her chest. I take a look at Mama's face and figure if she asks me, I'll just tell her the truth. I've never caused any trouble at school before, and she always taught us to stand up for what we believe. Plus Mr. Collins is White. I figure that fact alone will keep Mama from taking his side.

"Sit down, Genna."

I do as I'm told. It's quiet in the apartment, which means Mama hasn't yet picked up Tyjuan from Mrs. Dominguez.

"Where you been, Genna? And please don't lie—your guidance counselor called me at work. I know what happened in school today."

For just a second I worry that maybe Mrs. Freeman's mad that I blew off our appointment. Then I remember what I've decided about school, and I figure it doesn't matter anyway. "What did she say?"

"We'll get to that in a minute. Right now I want to know where you've been all afternoon."

"I—I went by Toshi's place."

Mama's eyebrows go up in surprise. I can tell she wants to raise her voice too, but Mama's trying hard not to lose her cool. She's worried if she gets angry with me, I'll leave. Walk out that door and disappear like I did the last time we had a fight.

I don't want to get a lecture on teenage pregnancy, so I decide to change the topic. "Where did you think I went, Mama?"

She sighs heavily and lets her arms drop to her side. "I didn't know —maybe the garden. It isn't like you to skip school or talk back to a teacher."

"He asked for it, Mama. He tried to tell the class that Black folks didn't die in the draft riots — weren't lynched and tortured — but they were!"

Mama wants to be proud of me for knowing the real deal about U.S. history. But something heavy is tugging at the corners of her mouth. "What else did you say, Genna?"

I lean back and pull my thoughts together. This is what it's really about. This is the big deal. Not slamming my textbook on the floor, or yelling at Mr. Collins, or skipping school. It's because I told the truth. It's because my secret slipped out.

I shrug and turn my eyes toward the potted herbs struggling to grow on the windowsill. "I was there, Mama. I saw what happened."

Mama doesn't say anything for a long time. I sit on the hard wooden chair, wishing I was back at Toshi's place, wishing I could go upstairs, get Tyjuan, and take him over to the garden. Right now I wish I could just disappear, be anywhere but here.

Finally Mama clears her throat. She inches along the counter towards the door, ready to block my exit in case I try to leave. "Mrs. Freeman thinks it would be a good idea if you talked to somebody, Genna."

I suppress the urge to roll my eyes. Copping attitude won't help right now. "Like who?"

"Someone who can help you understand why you're so — interested in the past."

I think for a moment and then let myself smile once I've figured it out. "You want me to see a shrink?"

Mama raises her voice so I can hear her over my laughter. My reaction is only making things worse — I sound crazy even to myself--but I can't seem to stop.

"Mrs. Freeman recommended that you see a psychologist. I think this would be a great opportunity, Genna. You could ask this woman all kinds of questions about her training and what her job is like. After all, you'd like to become a therapist someday, right?"

I finally stop cackling and think about what this means. When I finally look at Mama, I don't say a word but I make sure she sees the betrayal in my eyes. She sold me out. My own mother sold me out. I wonder what she told Mrs. Freeman, and what Mrs. Freeman told Mama to make her agree to send me to a shrink.

"She's a Black woman, Genna. Her name's Dr. Fitzpatrick. She's very busy these days, because of 9/11 and everything, but Mrs. Freeman felt certain she'd be able to get us an appointment. I think we should go, Genna. I want you to get some help."

"I don't need help, Mama."

"I think you do, baby. I love you, and I know you believe that you really did go back in time. And I've seen your back—I've seen all the marks on your body. And the way you describe everything, it seems so real, even to me—"

"But you still think I'm making it up." I say it flatly, like the hard, heavy truth that it is.

Mama sighs. "I think maybe you're confused, Genna. I know you *think* it's real, but sometimes our minds play tricks on us..."

"There's nothing wrong with my mind, Mama."

"Maybe not, maybe it's something else. But you're different, Genna. You haven't been the same since you got back. You don't seem interested in school, in your future. It's like you're here, but not here. This doctor could help you feel like your old self again."

"What if I don't want that, Mama? What if I like my new self? You want me to go back to being the person I was before. But that person's gone, Mama, and she's never coming back. There's just me—*this* me. Are you embarrassed? Are you worried people are going to talk about you because you've got a son in jail, a daughter who's pregnant, and another kid who's lost her mind?"

"I'm not ashamed of none of my kids. I love my children—all of them—no matter what!"

"Are you sure, Mama? You go upstate to visit Rico once a week, but you've never gone to visit Toshi—and she's just a couple blocks away."

"This isn't about Toshi, Genna, it's about you."

"Well, I'm making it about Toshi, Mama. You want me to go see a shrink? I want you to go see Toshi."

Mama screws up her lips to keep all her anger inside. I look in Mama's eyes and I can tell exactly what she's thinking: *I'm the parent, you're the child*. But I'm not a child anymore, and if Mama wants me to do something for her, she's got to do something for me. I fold my arms across my chest and wait for Mama to make up her mind.

I don't want to talk to a psychologist, but I figure it can't hurt. I know what happened to me, and I know there's nothing wrong with my mind. Besides, if going to see a shrink once makes things better between Mama and Toshi, then I figure it's worthwhile. Toshi needs Mama right now, and Mama's going to need someone else to hold onto, 'cause I won't be here long. Of course, I'm not going to tell her that I've decided to go back to the nineteenth century. Toshi's right—the less Mama knows about my business, the better.

"So do we have a deal?"

Mama unscrews her mouth and frowns at me. "How do you know your sister even wants to see me?"

I look at my mother and realize she's scared. She's afraid if she goes over there, Toshi won't let her in. I felt the same way when I stopped by this afternoon. I could lie to Mama, but I figure it's better to tell her the truth. "I *don't* know, Mama. But there's only one way to find out."

Mama sighs and pulls a chair back from the table. She sinks down in it and holds her head in her hands. "I just want things to be right again, Genna. That's all I want. I just want to make things right."

I slide my chair over so I can put my arm around Mama. "Sometimes making things right means admitting you were wrong."

Mama looks at me and I can tell she's hoping that that's exactly what

I'll do — go see this shrink and realize I was wrong, that I never really went into the past, never witnessed the riots, never left Judah behind.

If that's what Mama needs to believe, that's alright with me. Because I know it really happened. And I know I'm going back.

Judah

20.

I wake to the sound of dogs barking in the distance. With difficulty and a streak of pain that momentarily blinds me, I manage to right myself and gather my bearings. My heads throbs and my body is stiff from fatigue and the awkward position in which I spent the night. The barking grows louder as the tracking party approaches and my heart sinks within my chest.

"Here, Pa! He's over here!"

I fumble with the shirt tied around my waist until my fingers wrap around the rusty nail. I want to plunge it into my chest—choose death after failing to find liberty—but I am too weary to summon the courage for suicide. Instead I grab hold of a heavy branch and prepare myself to at least kill the dog before it sinks its teeth into my flesh. But before the hound can reach me, a man calls it off and the dog turns back, whimpering.

It's a boy—not a man--who reaches me first. I refuse to look away as he sneers down at me, his doughy, pink face flushed with excitement. The boy holds a rifle across his lap but he doesn't even bother to aim it at me. He knows I am no longer a threat. I want to spring up, grab the rifle, and smash it into his smug, pink face. But I cannot afford to lash out now. Whatever lies ahead—and I know it will be brutal—I tell myself I must survive. Surrender now, survive, and run again.

I try to convince myself that this failure can be turned into a lesson. I have not found freedom this time, but I have learned something valuable about the journey—and about myself. I close my eyes and say a silent prayer as fatigue and resignation weigh my body to the ground. I turn my face into the soft moss on the tree trunk and let the humiliation of this defeat harden my resolve.

This baby-faced boy has earned his first reward as a slave catcher. He's almost giddy as his father—Wallis' closest neighbor, Caleb Horton— instructs him to tie my wrists with rope. Then the boy mounts his horse and drags me through the brush and over to the road that leads back to Wallis' farm. They can see that I am injured but my limp only amuses them and gives Horton an excuse to whip me as often as he likes. I hobble along the dirt road, stumbling so often that I am dragged behind the boy's horse for the first mile. Then the joke wears thin and the father dismounts, smashes his fist into my face, and heaves me over the back of his son's horse like a sack of potatoes. My bound hands hang before me, ready to catch the tears of shame I won't let fall.

When we reach the farm, I avoid eye contact with everyone and say nothing as Wallis' neighbor—who is too poor to own any slaves himself— describes the hunt in great detail and with enough profanity to embarrass the former schoolteacher. Charles Horton is too coarse for Wallis' refined wife who coughs once or twice before excusing herself and going back inside the house. Alma follows to tend to her mistress, though it's clear she'd rather stay outside and glare at me.

I don't know how much money changes hands but I can tell Wallis is anxious to end the transaction and be rid of a man he relies upon but considers his inferior. Horton isn't ready to go, however, and doesn't hide his disappointment while complaining that I was too lazy to even put up a fight when they found me in the woods. I barely have the strength to stand and sway unsteadily with my head hanging forward, not caring if these White men believe I am defeated or ashamed. Wallis says little through it all, but makes sure to express his gratitude to his neighbor for tracking me down and bringing me back in one piece.

"Make 'im pay for it," Horton advises him as he and his son mount their horses and prepare to head home. "Fifty lashes, or a couple o' toes — maybe both. So he knows not to run again. I could teach that boy a lesson he won't soon forget."

Wallis' neighborly courtesy starts to thin. "That won't be necessary. I sure do appreciate your help tracking him down, but I can handle it from here."

"Suit yourself," Horton replies with obvious disdain for Wallis and maybe a tinge of regret. A poor White man who's looked down on by his neighbors probably likes nothing better than grinding slaves into the dirt.

Finally Horton realizes he has worn out his welcome. "We best be gettin' back. C'mon, Jeb."

I expect the conversation to end there but then Horton's fat hand suddenly reaches down and grabs hold of my hair. He yanks my head back so that both he and Wallis can see my face. I keep my eyes turned downward and refuse to flinch even as Horton's spit lands on my cheek.

"I'll be seein' you, boy," he hisses in my ear before roughly shoving my head forward. I stumble but manage to keep my balance. I won't go down on my knees before this trash ever again.

Horton wheels his horse around and trots off with his son but not before calling out one last piece of advice, "Watch that boy — night and day. He's a hard-headed nigger and that kind always tries again."

Wallis waits for the two riders to disappear from sight, then he tugs at the rope and I follow him into the barn. He walks slowly, wearily, as if he's the one who has been running all night. I have shamed him in front of his neighbors and know his punishment of me will have to prove to everyone that he is not weak — that he is the master and I am the slave. I have had time to prepare myself for what's to come and have accepted all the possibilities. By the end of this day I may lose an ear, some toes, or the skin off my back. Perhaps Wallis will brand me — burn an R into my face so that people forever see me as a failed runaway. I have been branded before. I can take that kind of pain. And I will wear that R like a badge of honor.

But without help, it will be difficult to brand me. As the only other man on the farm, it would be easiest for Wallis to whip me but to my surprise, he leaves the whip hanging from the nail on the barn wall and instead chains me to the post like the first day I arrived from Charleston. He says nothing and seems as determined as I am to avoid eye contact. I glance at his face as he works and can only see grim determination. Once I am securely chained to the post, Wallis saddles his horse and leads her out of the barn.

Alma is waiting for him. As he mounts, I hear her pleading with Wallis to whip me—or send for the overseer from his father-in-law's plantation. I'm surprised she doesn't offer to beat me herself. I'm sure nothing would give her greater satisfaction than to punish the ungrateful slave who has wronged her kind master by daring to claim his own freedom. Harriet Tubman once said she could have freed a thousand more people if they'd just realized they were slaves. Alma is the kind of scared, hopelessly ignorant slave that Tubman was talking about. If Jesus himself rolled up in a chariot and offered to take her away, she'd hesitate.

Wallis says nothing to Alma other than giving her instructions to leave me without food or water for the rest of the day.

Before the sun sets, Wallis returns from his father-in-law's plantation with a special iron collar for me to wear. It has spokes that stick out from my neck and turn up toward my face. Each spoke has a bell at the end, which means every move I make sets the bells jangling. From now on, Wallis and everyone else on the farm will know where I am every minute of every day. My feet are shackled as well but Wallis leaves my hands free during the day so I can work.

I would rather be whipped than wear this collar. Sleep is almost impossible and so I stumble through each day like a zombie. Joe runs from the monster I have become. He hides behind Alma's skirt until I shuffle off to the sound of rattling chains and sour bells. Shame makes me hide my eyes from everyone, and I swallow my words so my voice won't reveal my determination to run again. I soon get used to hearing more than I can see. I wait for Wallis to whip me but the beating never comes. Instead he slips into the barn late one night and says, "You can read, Judah, can't you?"

I nod even though it's clear he's not really asking a question. The bells jingle and my eyes fall back to the straw scattered loosely on the barn floor. I am a slave and I can read, which is illegal. He was once a schoolteacher but now he's slaveholder. Education improves a man but ruins a slave. What happens next stuns me more than any blow.

"My wife thought you might like to have this." Wallis takes his hand out of his pocket and holds out a small, leather-bound book. A bible. "She finds comfort in the Word and thought you might, too."

I try to speak but my throat has closed. I raise my shackled hands and take the precious book in my hands. My heartbeat pounds in my ears as I struggle to make sense of this moment.

"Take good care of it," Wallis advises me before turning to go.

I clutch the book in one hand and use the back of my other hand to swipe at the lone tear sliding down my face. I clear my throat and speak for the first time in days. "Please thank your wife for me," I say in a ragged voice. Then I add, "Sir."

Wallis nods and then heads back up to the house. I turn the bible over in my hands. My calloused fingers feel too rough to turn the delicate pages of verse — verses I have not read for months. I sit on my pallet and turn to Exodus:

Wherefore say unto the children of Israel, I am the LORD, and I will bring you out from under the burdens of the Egyptians, and I will rid you out of their bondage, and I will redeem you with a stretched out arm, and with great judgments. (6:6)

I read until night settles over the farm and my eyes can no longer see the words on the translucent white page. I close the bible, press it to my lips, and then wedge myself into a corner of the stall. I have learned to sleep upright but tonight my sobs set the bells tinkling. For the first time I wish Joe were beside me once again. I ache for someone to hold and so wrap my arms around myself and imagine Genna is here to hush me and wipe away my tears.

Another week of playing the penitent slave and Wallis, shamefaced, takes the jangling collar off my neck. I play the obedient, grateful slave for two more weeks. I hum hymns and spirituals as I work with Wallis out in the field. As soon as he stops chaining me up at night, I run again. I leave his wife's bible behind.

I make it much farther this time, spending a night, a day, and another night on the run. I know I am near the coast because the ground in the woods has become soft and moist, making it easy to hide my scent from the dogs. During the day I allow myself a few anxious hours of rest. I burrow into the marshy earth, covering my weary body with branches, leaves, and pads of moss torn from fallen logs. I become part of the earth, lying so still that insects and animals crawl over and around me without fear. I shut my eyes and think of the maroons—runaway slaves who found freedom in the mountains of Jamaica—and feel my ancestors guiding me toward freedom. But on the second day of my journey that fragile dream is shattered by the sound of howling in the distance.

The baby-faced boy has followed his brothers off to war, so for this hunt Horton invites his brother-in-law to split the reward for tracking me down. The terrain won't support horses so I climb a dead tree and watch as the two White men approach on foot, rifles ready, a length of rope looped over their shoulders. I fear that rope more than any snake in this swamp. Has Wallis given them permission to shoot me on sight? I tell myself that even as a repeat runaway I am still too valuable to kill. For a poor man like Horton, this is sport. But for Wallis, this is business. He expects to own me and my labor—plus my children and *their* labor—forever. I am the wealth he will leave to his heirs if his wife is able to bear him a child.

This time, I give Horton the fight he was hoping for the last time I ran away. When they are directly beneath me, I lunge from the tree like a lion, knocking both men to the ground. I crush the hound's skull with one swing of a heavy branch. Stunned and winded, Horton struggles to stand but then falls to his knees when the rock I hurl connects with his forehead. Before Horton's wiry brother-in-law can reach for his gun, I pin him to the marshy ground and cut off his cries for help by squeezing the air out of his throat.

We are deep in the woods. I could kill both of these White men and no one would ever know. A smile creeps across my face as I watch his head slowly sink into the swampy soil. I would have killed him if Horton hadn't crept up behind me. With one vicious swing of his rifle butt he knocks two of my molars out before dragging me off his brother-in-law. They tie my feet and hands with the rope they brought. Then they take turns cursing and kicking the shit out of me before hauling me back to Wallis, bruised, battered, and bloody.

I am barely conscious by the time Horton dumps me at Wallis' feet, but I hear him say, "Should a let me whup 'im the first time he run off. Told you he'd try again. You got all them books in your house, but you don't know niggers like I do."

Alma has hardened her heart against me but the sight of my broken body lying in a heap in the barn still draws a gasp of horror from her. She tends to my wounds as best she can, her lips pressed together in a thin line as she peels away what's left of my stained, tattered clothes. If she thinks I deserved the beating for running away again, she keeps her opinion to herself. Her hands move the wet cloth over my wounds with a touch that is efficient and not without tenderness.

Shamed once more, Wallis swallows his pride and asks his father-in-law for advice. The next day the old man rides over himself. I listen from my pallet in the barn. Wallis has chained me to the post once more, though

I am too weak to stand right now. I was spared the iron collar this time, and if I twist my head I can see what's happening outside through a crack in the barn wall.

Wallis' father-in-law doesn't bother to get down from his wagon. He doesn't even look at Wallis. The old man just stares straight ahead and says, "You can't break that nigger, send him to someone who can." Then he nods at the Black men sitting in the back of his wagon. "Jack, Cuffy, and Will are yours for the week. You should be able to get this place in working order by then."

Upon hearing their names, the three enslaved men climb down from the wagon and stand before the two White men, their eyes downcast.

Humbled, Wallis takes off his hat and tries to look his father-in-law in the eye. "Thank you, sir," he says quietly but with respect.

The old man spits into the dirt near Wallis' feet. "Don't want your thanks. I want you to take care of my little girl. Make her happy. Give her what she needs."

"That's what I aim to do, sir."

Wallis' father-in-law grunts, then turns his wagon around and rides out of the yard. Wallis stares after him until one of the men says, "We best get to work, suh." It's a suggestion but the enslaved man turns his voice up at the end so that it sounds like a question. So that Wallis knows *he* knows who's in charge.

Wallis nods and the men gather the tools they need from the barn, avoiding eye contact with me. Wallis stands before me for a long while saying nothing. Then he mutters, "You've left me no choice, boy." And I know my fate is sealed.

Judah

21.

Hezekiah Morgan earns money and the respect of his wealthier, slave-owning neighbors by "breaking" slaves. Horton might have earned a living the same way but he takes too much pleasure in inflicting pain. A slave breaker has to know—and respect—the limits of pain. It's a skill to break a man's spirit without breaking his body. When a slave becomes too hard to manage, his owner will threaten to send him to Morgan—and sometimes just the threat is enough to correct the slave's behavior. But for unmanageable slaves—for men who insist they are men and not animals or pieces of property—Morgan is one step above a death sentence. It's said that if Morgan can't break a slave's will and make him obedient, then the slave isn't worth owning.

Alma makes sure I understand this before she slips a warm hoecake into my bound hands. Joe's nowhere to be seen and I'm glad. He doesn't need to see me chained in the back of the wagon, being driven away by a stone-faced White man. I don't feel good about leaving him behind, but I know Alma will take care of him. But she'll be lying if she tells him that I'll be back soon. Because no matter what lies ahead, I know I'm not coming back.

Wallis says nothing as we prepare to leave the farm, but I can tell by the way his shoulders slump that he doesn't want to do this. He is an educated White man with a conscience—maybe even a good heart—but he can't afford to lose his investment, and he can't afford to lose face. He wants to prove to his father-in-law and men like Horton that he's not soft on slaves. He wants to be one of them. So he chains my feet and hands, loads me into the wagon, and drives me across the border into Georgia.

Morgan owns a small farm that he runs using slave labor. Troublemakers are left at his doorstep and he literally whips them into shape. Before Wallis even has time to turn his wagon around and get back on the road, Morgan rips my shirt off and orders a passing slave to tie me to a wooden post in the middle of the yard.

When he sets down the load of firewood he's carrying, I catch a glimpse of the slave's bare back. It's covered with lash marks that haven't yet healed. He looks at me with dead eyes that tell me his spirit has already surrendered. He has become the slave his owner wants him to be. Morgan has used the lash to make him believe he is a beast, not a man. This slave moves like a zombie as he comes toward me with arms outstretched, and for just a moment I feel like I am looking in a mirror. Is this my future?

No. I say the word out loud but this scene from a horror movie continues to play. Morgan snatches his whip off a fence rail and snaps it several times. I blink and wonder if my eyes are really seeing blood spraying from the whip as it whistles through the air. No doubt it gets plenty of use. I look around the yard and see a girl about my age standing in the doorway of a small cabin. For a moment our eyes meet and then she disappears inside without saying a word. Without trying to help me. I swat away the grabbing hands of the zombie slave but then he lunges at me, grabs hold of my arm, and tries to lead me over to the whipping post.

"Don't," I say calmly, though my heart is racing. Up close he is more like a rabid dog than a mindless zombie. I realize I can't reason with him, so I try to pry his fingers off my arm. "Stop—you don't have to do this. We can be free—both of us!" I hope to see a flicker of desire in the man's eyes, but there is nothing in his black eyes besides fear.

I manage to wrench my arm free and pull away, but then another bare-chested slave appears from inside the barn. Without even waiting for orders from Morgan, he rushes over and helps the other slave drag me to the post. I am younger than these men and ready to fight them both, but then a third slave appears and together these three Black men tie my wrists with rope before hanging me from a hook at the top of the wooden post.

There are *four* of us and just *one* White man. We could seize our freedom if we just worked together, but these men are no longer men. They don't see me as their brother. *I* am the mirror they need to shatter. I am an ugly reminder of the men they used to be. The whip will open my back and not theirs if they do Morgan's bidding, so that's what they do.

My toes barely touch the ground but I try to remain upright as I wait for the first lash to land on my bare back. I focus my eyes on the post and realize the wood has not been chewed up by the whip—but by teeth.

"For the next two months, boy, you're mine." I can't see Morgan but I hear him lash the air, testing out the whip. He's about ten feet behind me and doesn't need to shout but his performance isn't only for my benefit. "I hear you're a educated nigger," he says with contempt. "Too smart for your own damn good. Well, I'm here to teach you how to be what the good Lord made you—a slave. Consider this the first lesson."

Morgan cracks the whip in the air once more and then sends it tearing across my back. My body slams into the post and I grunt but manage not to scream. The next blow feels like fire and by the fifth one I can feel the blood trickling down my back. I have bitten through my lower lip to keep from crying out, and the metallic tang of blood fills my mouth.

Morgan pauses and calls out, "Count, nigger. You can count, can't you? Smart nigger like you can prob'ly count to a hundred." There is another pause and then a fierce lash sends my teeth into the soft wood of the post.

"I'm talkin' to you, nigger. You answer me when I'm talkin' to you."
Another lash. Then another. And another.

I can no longer balance on my toes and dangle from the hook like a piece of meat at the butcher's. Morgan comes close and hisses in my ear, "*Yessuh*. That's how you answer when I'm talkin' to you, boy. Understand?

Yessuh."

When I refuse to answer, he hauls off and punches me in the side. I groan and try to muster the strength to kick him at least, but my body is no longer mine to command. Morgan walks away, cracks the whip in the air, and starts again.

"Count, nigger."

Another lash slices into my back like a razor.

"Count, nigger!"

Almost against my will the words leave my mouth. "Yessuh."

Morgan pauses and addresses the other slaves who stand watching in silence, witnesses who will never testify. "Did you hear somethin,' boys? We can't hear you, nigger. Speak up!"

I do as I am told and am rewarded with another lash across my bloody back.

"Now count!" Morgan barks.

I do as I am told but by thirty, my voice is gone. Morgan calls the lashes out himself. I black out more than once and then come to as each new lash flays the skin off my back.

Morgan whips me until his arm tires. Then he calls for water and I manage to lift my head enough to see the girl from the cabin bringing a bucket of water across the yard. She steals a glance at me and in her shining eyes I see the words she's too terrified to say: *Just hold on.*

Once Morgan has quenched his thirst, he sends the girl back to a house on the far side of the yard. Then he takes up the whip and asks one of the other slaves to remind him where he left off. When Morgan reaches fifty he comes close and grabs hold of my hair. Pulling my head back so I can see him, he says, "You will learn to be a slave, boy. You'll learn it and you'll like it." I see him nod at someone I can't see and then he lets go of my head. It falls forward and for a moment my eyes focus on the streams of my own blood that flow from the base of the whipping post. The rope around my wrists bites into my skin as I hang from the post like a stone.

"Hold on, son. You gon' be alright. Just hold on."

The kindness in the man's voice brings tears to my eyes. But I barely have strength to scream as he splashes a bucket of brine across my back. I lose consciousness and sink into oblivion.

When I come to I am lying on my stomach on the ground in a small, hot, dark room. There are no words for the pain I feel. I can't turn my head or move my little finger without screaming in agony. A soft voice comes out of the darkness, startling me.

"Hush, now. If you woke me, you might wake Massa, too. And you can't take another whuppin' right now. Just be still."

Genna's face floats through the darkness. I blink my tears away and try to focus. It's the girl I saw earlier. "Where am I?"

"Sick house," she says simply. When I close my eyes again, she says, "Might as well work on these feet since I'm up. All the men that come here have feet like yours. Tore up, swole up. Price you pay for runnin.'"

I stifle a moan as her hands gently lift my left foot and rub in some type of strong-smelling salve. I want to see her face again but I have to wait until she inches her way around the small shed. She is careful not to brush my limbs with her bare feet—and her feet are all I can see because I can't lift my head.

"That hurt?" she asks.

I can't shake my head but she carefully sets my foot down. "I just let you rest then. Mama be in later to see to your back."

"Don't go," I whisper.

"What's that?" she asks, squatting down near my face.

I lick my lips and taste the salt of tears and sweat. My bottom lip is shredded and raw. "Please don't go."

The girl carefully seats herself on the ground and gently strokes my hair. Tears slip out from under my closed eyelids and land on the scratchy wool blanket. "Judah," I say, wishing I could offer her my hand. Wishing I could tell her how much her kindness means to me after so much cruelty.

"Judah," she says in a voice that sounds like a smile. "I'm Jonetta. How 'bout I sing you a song, Judah?"

For the rest of the night I weep silently while Jonetta sings. In the morning I wake to a different pair of feet circling me. When the woman sees that my eyes are open she says, "Name's Mary. Just came to see if you hungry."

I can barely remember eating the hoecake Alma gave me before Wallis took me away. How much time has passed? Hours? Days? Time seems to stand still in this dark shed, and the pain feels like it will never end.

Mary's bigger than Jonetta and not as careful. The rough hem of her skirt scrapes my bare skin as she moves around the shed. "Can you eat?" she asks impatiently. "You won't get but two days to heal 'fore he puts you to work, so better eat while you can."

I manage to nod. Mary leaves and moments later Jonetta arrives with a bowl of steaming cornmeal porridge. She kneels by my head and patiently ladles it into my mouth, wiping my mouth with her apron when necessary. She tells me about Mary and Jack, the elderly couple who have raised her as their own. Morgan bought her mother when she was already with child, but his plans for his new "breeder" fell apart when the young woman died in childbirth. Morgan had already purchased Jack and Mary for a song due to their age, and he earned their gratitude by allowing them to remain together.

"They're loyal," I say with a voice that hides my contempt.

Jonetta scrapes the last of the porridge from the wooden bowl and shrugs. "They're old. They been together a mighty long time. If one of 'em makes trouble, Morgan'll whup 'em or sell 'em off."

When Jonetta offers me one more spoonful of porridge, I turn my face away. It doesn't look like I'll find any allies here.

Jonetta sighs and leans back against the wall of the shed. "Jack and Mary know their place—and so do I. You gon' have to learn yours, too, else he'll take it out o' your hide."

I am allowed one more day of rest and then, as Mary predicted, Morgan demands that I join the other slaves out in the field. I can barely stand and my wounds bleed freely throughout the day. If I am slow completing a task, Morgan hits me with whatever is close at hand—a hoe, a broom, a hammer. By the end of the week I have lost another tooth and my left eye is sealed shut. If I don't leave here soon, I know I will kill Morgan—or die trying.

I try to talk to the other enslaved men but they avoid me like the plague. In fact, I'm pretty sure one of them is a snitch. His name is Elijah—or that's what they call him—and the fine lines carved into his cheeks tell me he's from Africa. Of the three, I expected this man to be my ally—to want freedom as much as I do. Jack just chuckles when I call Elijah a traitor.

"You lookin' in the wrong place, boy. Scars on the face ain't the ones that count—not when they neat 'n tidy like that. Now, the scars *you* got gon' tell everybody what a handful you is."

He's right. If the skin on my back ever heals, the scars will serve as proof that I am—or once was—unmanageable. Morgan is determined to break me and my body can't take much more of his abuse. What I need is time to heal but I know I will have to act quickly if an opportunity to run appears.

Since the enslaved men won't talk to me, whenever I see Mary or Jonetta I try to find out about the surrounding area. The road Wallis took traveled southeast, which means I am closer to the coast than before. The dense trees surrounding Morgan's property make it hard to get my bearings, so I ask Jonetta to tell me about the neighboring plantations. I think Jonetta likes talking to me, and she's probably glad to have someone her age around the place. Jack and Mary have mostly learned to hold their tongues, and they have each other so they don't look for opportunities to talk with me. But Jonetta does. She shies away from some subjects but I use whatever charm I can muster to get her to open up with me. I don't want to cause any trouble for her and I hope she's not sweet on me, because I can't stay here. Not for two more weeks, not for two more days.

"Who lives over there?" I ask one evening as the sun sinks below the trees.

"That's Sweet Fields, Massa Cullen's plantation. He got close to a hundred slaves. Treats 'em well, I hear. Some of 'em even got shoes."

Jonetta puts one foot over the other and tugs at her skirt so that it falls a bit lower. She doesn't need to hide her feet from me. Mine are too disgusting to touch even with the homemade salve she gives me to rub on the soles at night.

"He grows cotton?"

She nods and looks down at the basket she's weaving. "And women."

"Women?" I can tell by the look on her face that this is one of those subjects Jonetta wants me to know about but would rather not dwell on. But I can't just leave it alone. "He grows women?" I ask in a playful tone, though I suspect she's not pulling my leg.

"I only been out there one time, but I know he got a row of cabins separate from the quarters where the field hands sleep. Those cabins are for Massa' Cullen's fancy women."

"His 'fancy women'? They're free?"

Jonetta shakes her head quickly. I wish she would just cut to the chase but whatever's going on over at 'Sweet Fields' makes her frightened or ashamed — or both.

"They slaves like the rest of us." She turns the basket as she carefully braids the dried reeds. "Massa Cullen and his boys...they partial to yella gals."

Yella. Yellow. Here in the South there are plenty of names for mixed-race people: mulattoes, quadroons, octoroons. Yella, high yella, meriny. I'm not sure what to say about Cullen and his "boys." White men aren't the only ones who like light-skinned Black women. Plenty of Black men feel that way, too. Jonetta must think I'm one of those men because she's looking at me out of the side of her eye. I shrug and say, "Yeah?" like it's no big deal.

"Yeah. When the baby comes, Massa sends it down to the quarters to be raised by one of the grannies. Then, once she's grown...he sends her back."

I frown. Jonetta has skipped over a chapter in this story. A White slave owner and his sons like light-skinned women. So they rape them. Or breed them. Or both? I glance at Jonetta and then take up one of her discarded reeds. I twine it around my finger so she knows I'm not studying her. "Back where?"

She sighs impatiently. "To the cabins. To work."

I've seen White men travelling up and down the road at all times of day — and night. Now I know why.

Jonetta goes on. "The real light ones he can sell for a good price when a trader comes callin,' but Massa Cullen don't hardly ever let 'em go. He likes to show 'em off to his friends. Mary say Massa Cullen take more pride in his women than his racing horses. He lets his friends use them gals too."

Use. I want to ask Jonetta what she means, but something in the weak line of her mouth tells me this is as far as she's willing to go. But there's one thing I have to know.

"Is Morgan one of Cullen's 'friends'?" I ask quietly.

She nods.

I stare at the tree line and try to imagine the horror of working in a brothel with your own daughter or sister or mother. And the man raping you could be your father. If Cullen makes his neighbors pay, the women surely don't see a dime. He's a pimp breeding his own whores. But they're not whores. They're just women — and girls — trapped in a nightmare that can't end soon enough.

Jonetta surprises me by going on. "Mary told me her old massa was that way. She used herbs to keep herself from gettin' big. It's a tea you drink to bring the blood on. She showed me how to make it when I was just a girl."

I frown. I understand why a woman might not want to live with proof of her rape. But if Mary taught Jonetta how to get rid of an unwanted baby, then she must have believed Jonetta was at risk. I feel my muscles grown tense, which tightens the raw skin on my back. I bite back the pain and try to find the right words. "Does Morgan—I mean, has he ever…"

Jonetta quickly shakes her head and my muscles relax. What if she had nodded instead? What if she's lying because she's ashamed?

I have to get out of here. Before I forget what it means to be a man. Before I start to feel something more than brotherly concern for Jonetta. Before Morgan's cruelty pushes me too far.

On Saturday one of the broken slaves gets picked up by his owner. On Monday two more satisfied customers drive away after collecting their "new and improved" property. I watch the wagons rolling down the drive and know this is my chance. If I run now, Morgan will have no one to call for help except Jack, Mary, and Jonetta. Jonetta wouldn't try to stop me, Mary's getting on in years, and I think Jack is tired of doing this White man's dirty work.

We are digging holes for a new fence. My back burns and bleeds under the blazing sun. Jack glances up and tells me to take a quick break while Morgan's eyes aren't on us. "Catch your breath but be ready to start up again soon's I say 'go.'"

I nod and try not to bend over—that only pulls the muscles in my back and makes the pain worse. I know it's risky but I need to say the words out loud. "I'm leaving."

Jack doesn't look me in the eye. He just blows a long stream of air out his mouth. It's a silent whistle that only I can hear.

"You ain't in no kinda shape to be runnin' right now, son."

He's right, but it's now or never. "I can't wait. Morgan will probably get new slaves in a day or two," I explain. "I have to go while he hasn't got help."

"He got me," Jack says.

I lean on the shovel and try to read the message in Jack's eyes. "You saying you'd try to stop me?"

Jack's gaze roams across the field until it reaches the cabin where he lives with Mary and Jonetta. "I got a family. You run off and I *don't* try to stop you, what you think Massa gon' do to me? You his bread and butter. You run and he lose more'n his money. Lose his reputation as the best slave breaker in the county. He might sell Mary or Jonetta to make up the loss — or sell me just for spite."

I never thought about that. I stare at the hole I'm digging and weigh my options. I'm so deep in my own thoughts that I don't react in time to Jack's whispered, "Go!"

Morgan storms at us, his eyes trained on me. "You lazy nigger!" He snatches the shovel out of my hands and swings it at my head. I try to dodge the blow but the tip of the shovel still catches the back of my head. I fall to the ground and feel the dirt and gravel scratching at my raw back.

"Wah di bloodclaat?" Without thinking I spew every curse I can think of at Morgan. My Jamaican accent returns in full force, shocking the White man as much as my defiance. "Dutty stinking Babylon boy! Eediat bwoy! Dutty jankcrow....fiyah fi yuh fassyhole!"

Morgan's face turns red with fury. "What did you say? Speak English, you animal!"

Morgan bends down and slams his fist into the side of my head. For a moment, I actually see stars. I try to get up, but he punches me in the face and this time I fall back into blackness. I come to when I feel myself being dragged across the yard. Morgan has me by the heel and the stones on the ground rip at my bare back. He's hauling me back to the whipping post in the center of the yard.

Panic and pain force me to turn onto my side and I claw at the dirt with my fingers to slow our progress. When Morgan feels me resisting, he turns and gets ready to strike me again, but this time I thrust my foot into his stomach, knocking him back. Then I press my palms into the ground and swing my legs around like the brothers I used to see doing capoeira in Prospect Park. That move catches Morgan off guard. I knock his feet out from under him and in an instant, our roles are reversed: *I* am standing over *him*.

I see the terror in Morgan's eyes and feel the corners of my mouth twitching as I fight the urge to smile. His rifle is several feet away, leaning against the barn door. The whip so often clutched in his hand is dangling like a dead snake from a distant fence rail. Neither the gun or the whip will help Morgan now — and he knows it.

In desperation, Morgan scans the yard for help. When he spots Jack, his cold blue eyes light up. "Jack! Jack! Come get this nigger."

I can see Jack out of the corner of my eye. He is still standing by the fence Morgan told us to fix. He has a hammer in his hand, but Jack isn't swinging it any more. He is frozen. Waiting to see just what I can do.

Morgan's mutt starts barking and then I hear Mary's voice and the dog suddenly grows silent. This is my chance.

The hope fades from Morgan's eyes. His voice cracks with terror. "Jack! Goddamn, you — get this nigger offa me or I swear to God, I'll tear your hide open! I'll whup you and your wife!"

Jack still doesn't move and that's when Morgan really starts to panic. He tries to flip over and lunge for his gun, but I grab him by the waist and haul him up off the ground. I hurl Morgan aside and calmly walk over to the barn. I grab the rifle and stand before him, surprised by my own strength and by how easy it was to take control.

Morgan starts cursing me again so I take three quick steps and ram the butt of the gun into his face, hoping to knock out a few of *his* teeth. Morgan falls back but quickly drags himself back up, not wanting to lose sight of me. He wipes the blood from his mouth and tries to reason with me.

"Now, boy — put that gun down. I know I been hard on you, but this ain't the way to put things right. You wanna go home? I'll send you back to Wallis first thing tomorrow. Just hand me the gun…"

Morgan's voice grows thin and small. It is like listening to a mouse. I laugh and toss the gun aside. I have never felt this strong before. I haven't smoked in months yet I am higher than I have ever been. "Get up," I order.

Morgan gets to his feet. He is trembling but I don't know if it's from fear or rage. "You're dead, nigger," he hisses before lunging at me.

I grab his shoulders and spin, throwing him to the ground once more. Morgan flips onto his back and tries to scramble backward like a crab but I pounce and pin him in place with my knees. His hands reach for my throat but I am faster. I have no fear. A sense of calm blankets my body like velvet. My movements are smooth and deliberate, not frantic.

My fingers close around Morgan's stubbly throat and squeeze until his fingernails stop clawing at my face and his arms fall limply to the ground. I hold on until I feel Jack's hand on my shoulder. "Let go, son."

I do as I'm told and loosen my fingers. I stop pressing my knees into Morgan's dead body and stand up—like a man.

The dog wobbles over, whimpering softly. I can't see a wound on its body, but Mary's done something to weaken the fierce animal. It sniffs around its dead owner and then starts howling with grief.

Jack picks up the rifle and without hesitation shoots the dog dead. "Four less feet for you to run from," he says with a grim smile.

I nod and look off across the field. Beyond lies a dense line of trees. I am ready to run but I pull his eyes back to Jack's face. I owe him a debt I don't really know how to pay. "You all could come with me," I say, knowing full well that Jack and Mary won't run.

The old man shakes his grey head and swings his eyes over to where Mary is standing in front of the house they share. "We too old. This your chance, boy. Best take it while you can."

I stare at Morgan's body and try to piece together a future that is better and not worse for Jack and Mary. "What will you do?" I ask.

"Wait here," he says simply. "Morgan has a sister up north. Married to a Quaker, I hear. Guess we belong to her now."

Flies are gathering over the corpses already. Jack swats them away and starts unbuttoning his sweat-soaked shirt. It's old and worn but better than the burlap sacks Morgan gave to the rest of us to wear—not that we could wear anything with our backs torn by the whip. Jack's shirt has been cleaned and mended by loving hands. I glance at his back and feel a brief pang of envy at the smooth skin there.

Jack holds his shirt out to me. "Put it on. It'll stick but you can't run with your back open like that."

I was totally in control just a moment ago but now I am grateful to be following orders. My throat tightens but I force myself to speak the feeling in my heart. "I owe you my life."

Jack shakes his head. "Don't owe me nothin'. You took a chance, and now you got a chance now—a chance I never had. I hope you make it, son."

I want to say something more but suddenly a door slams shut and Jonetta flies across the yard with a sack of food for me. Before she even reaches me the words tumble out of her mouth.

"Take me with you, Judah! I know the woods—and I can run fast as any man."

Jack turns away to hide the hurt in his eyes. I know he doesn't want his adopted daughter to go, but I also know he won't stand in her way. Wearily he walks over to Mary who is already holding another shirt in her hands. I look at them and think about the life they built together—held together with hope and love and luck. What will happen to this family if Morgan's sister *isn't* married to a Quaker—or if she'd rather sell her inherited property and pocket the money? What if they're put on the auction block and Morgan's neighbor buys Jonetta?

I think about Cullen's cabins filled with "yella" women, White men traveling up and down the road with coins jingling in their pockets. What if one of them rapes Jonetta? What if her lighter-skinned daughter grows up and takes her place with the others? I can't leave her to that kind of future. But then I remind myself that that won't happen because the war won't last that long.

"You don't have to run," I tell her. Jonetta's face falls as the faith she placed in me slips away. "Freedom's coming," I assure her. "Just wait for it—try to wait just a couple more years."

"You ain't waitin'," she says defiantly.

"I just killed a man. You don't have to run but I do. The war will end soon—I promise."

"How you know that?"

I can't tell her the truth so I say, "I had a vision—I saw the future in a dream."

Jonetta gives a short, bitter laugh. "A slave can't see past the end of each day."

"I'm not a slave."

Jonetta weighs me with her eyes. "You different, alright. Knew that soon as I laid eyes on you."

For a moment we stand in the yard unable to speak, unwilling to move. Then I remember the body of the White man I killed is lying just a few feet away and realize I have to go. "I'm sorry, Jonetta," I say with all the kindness I can muster. "I can't take you with me. Jack and Mary are good people—you're better off with them."

Jonetta drops her eyes and lets go of her dream of freedom as she passes the sack of food to me. "Go north 'til you reach the river," she says as if I asked her for directions. "Get your feet good and wet 'fore you head east." Her tear-filled eyes find mine. "I hope you make it, Judah."

I reach out and touch her cheek. "I will. But pray for me just the same."

Jonetta manages a weak smile and shakes a few tears loose by nodding at me. I wave to Mary and Jack, and then walk real casual-like to the far end of the field. No point drawing attention to myself by running. Jack will also take his time notifying the neighbors. He will tell them that a slave has killed Massa Morgan, that it happened while he was out in the fields. Mary will tell them I shot the dog before heading west. Through her tears, Jonetta will tell the posse that I have yellow skin and a scar on my left cheek. All three will lie to buy me a little more time. I will owe them a debt I can never repay.

Genna

22.

"Genna? I'm Dr. Fitzpatrick. It's nice to finally meet you. Please, come in."

I head towards the open door with Mama right behind me, but Dr. Fitzpatrick stops her before she can follow me inside. "You can wait for Genna out here, Mrs. Colon," she says politely.

Mama looks surprised, then worried. Her fingers tighten around mine.

"It's ok," I tell her, and ease my fingers free.

Mama clutches the straps of her pocketbook instead and smiles nervously. "Alright, doctor, if you think that's best. I'll be right here if you need me, baby."

I smile at Mama but wish she would stop treating me like a child.

Dr. Fitzpatrick gently closes the door to her office. Unlike the fluorescent glare of the waiting room, the doctor's office is filled with soft, golden light. There is a green suede sofa against the wall and two comfortable looking leather chairs in front of her desk. Dr. Fitzpatrick tells me to sit down in one of them, so I do. I watch her as she takes a pen and notepad off her desk. I try not to look surprised when she comes over and sits down in the leather chair across from mine.

Dr. Fitzpatrick swivels the chair so she is facing me. "Is it okay if I sit here?"

Having so little space between us kind of freaks me out. But I turn my chair as well and try to act real blasé. "Whatever."

I'm not really sure how this is supposed to work, if I'm supposed to start telling her my problems or if she's supposed to ask me a question first. I look around the room so I don't have to look at Dr. Fitzpatrick. There are two purple cushions resting at either end of the sofa. They are covered with looping gold thread, silver sequins, and lots of little round mirrors. A large mirror with a gold frame hangs above the sofa, and the golden light comes from two table lamps that have crinkly white paper shades.

My eyes finally rest on the doctor's wide wooden desk. From where I am sitting, I can only see the backs of three framed photographs. The only thing visible on her desk is a gold plate with her name on it. I stare at it for a while, knowing Dr. Fitzpatrick is watching me. The doctor is a big woman, almost as tall as me, with short, curly bronze hair and ginger-colored skin. Her face is soft and plump like the leather chairs we are sitting in.

Dr. Fitzpatrick seems serious, but relaxed. "You look like you're far away," she says finally. "What are you thinking about, Genna?"

"Your name."

"Really? What about my name?"

"It's Irish, right?"

"Yes, it is."

"But you're not Irish."

Dr. Fitzpatrick smiles like I just said something funny. "Well, no. I'm African American."

"Is your husband Irish?"

"I'm not married. What's interesting about my name, Genna?"

"Nothing," I say quickly, with a shrug. Then I change my mind and decide it's probably safe to tell her what I really think. "It's just strange that you have an Irish name even though you're Black."

"Why is that strange, Genna?"

"Well, a long time ago Black people and Irish people didn't always get along. During the Civil War, there were riots over the draft, and Irish mobs killed a whole lot of African Americans."

"So you think Irish people hate Black people?"

"That's not what I said."

"I'm sorry, maybe I misunderstood."

I don't like it when people twist my words around. For just a moment I think of Martha, my Irish friend, and Willem, the Black boy she loved. The mob killed Willem during the riots, and they would have killed Martha, too, even though she was one of their own. But I can't explain all of this to Dr. Fitzpatrick, so I come up with something else to say instead. "I was just saying that it's funny, you having an Irish last name. I mean, it's not funny, really. Your family might have been owned by someone named Fitzpatrick. It might be your slave name."

Now it is the doctor's turn to act like she's not surprised. "It's true that some African Americans kept the names of their owners after Emancipation. Others made up new names, or chose to take the names of people they respected, like Washington or Lincoln. My family's a bit different. My great-great-grandfather was an Irishman. He fell in love with and married my great-great-grandmother, who was Black, and that's why I have an Irish surname."

The doctor looks like she's waiting for me to say something, so I say, "oh" and hope that she'll move on.

"You sound as though you know a whole lot about history, Genna. Is that your favorite subject?"

I think of Mr. Collins and his beady little eyes. "No," I say quickly and a bit too loud. "I just like learning about the past."

"Why? What makes the past so interesting?"

"I don't know. You have to know where you come from in order to figure out where you're going. And some people think if you don't learn from the past, you'll repeat it."

"Would that be good or bad?"

"For African Americans it wouldn't be so great. A lot of terrible things happened to us in the past."

"Like what? Can you give me an example?"

"Sure. Like slavery—and segregation. Stuff like that."

"I see. Did anything positive ever happen in the past?"

I don't answer right away. I wait a moment and try to figure out where this is leading. The doctor's trying to get something out of me, but I'm not sure what it is.

"I guess," I say cautiously. "I mean, Black people had it rough for a real long time, but they still survived. They invented things, educated themselves, and tried to keep their families together. They fought for their rights."

"We've come a long way, haven't we?"

"All the way from Africa," I say drily.

"Yes, that's true, but what I meant was—"

"I know what you meant."

Dr. Fitzpatrick looks at me for a moment, then writes something down on her notepad. I'm not trying to disrespect this woman, but I need her to know that I don't want to be here.

When the doctor's done taking notes, she adjusts her glasses and looks at me. "Don't you think we've made progress, Genna? As a people?"

I shrug and sink further down in the peanut butter-colored armchair.

"Your guidance counselor tells me you want to become a psychiatrist some day. You couldn't have done that a hundred years ago. It would have been very difficult, at least, for a young Black woman like yourself."

The doctor waits for me to respond, then sits back and crosses her legs. "What do you think about the world we live in, Genna?"

"What do you mean?"

"Well, let's start with the United States. Do you think things are better than they used to be?"

"Not really, no."

"Why not?"

"Why not? People hate us so much they flew airplanes into the World Trade Center and the Pentagon! Thousands of innocent people died. You call that better?"

"Why do you think those attacks happened, Genna?"

I keep my voice calm and low this time. "Like I said, because people hate us."

"Do you think that's fair?"

"Of course, it's not fair. Life's not fair. But shit happens, right? You're in the wrong place at the wrong time—you're in the wrong body, or the wrong city, or the wrong building—and suddenly you wind up dead."

"Do you think that could happen to you?"

It almost did. These are the first words that enter my mind, but I'm careful to keep them inside. To the doctor I say, "Sure, why not?"

"And how does that make you feel, knowing something terrible could happen to you at any moment?"

I watch the doctor closely and decide it isn't safe to answer this question. She waits for about a minute, then puts the cap on her pen and sets her notepad on the little round table next to her chair.

"You know, Genna, it's perfectly natural for you to feel angry, even scared because of what happened on 9/11. A lot of people feel that way even people much older than you."

"So?"

"So, I think it's important to be honest with yourself and with others about how you really feel."

"I know how I feel. I know *exactly* how I feel."

"Do you, Genna? How do you feel right now?"

"Right now?"

"Right now."

"I feel like I'm wasting my time."

"Why do you think you're wasting your time, Genna?"

"Because there's nothing wrong with me. You just said yourself that lots of people feel the way I do."

"So you do feel angry and afraid?"

"Sometimes."

"What do you do when you feel that way, Genna?"

"Nothing. What can I do? Everyone expects us to act like nothing's changed. We're just supposed to get up each morning and go to school and do our homework like none of this ever happened. Like thousands of people didn't die a couple of miles away from here. Like we can't still *smell it*."

"Sometimes it is difficult to carry on with our lives. Is that why you've stopped going to school?"

I fold my arms across my chest and sigh like I'm getting bored. "What's the point?"

"The point is, we survived. Lots of innocent people lost their lives, you're right. But we didn't, and it's important for us to keep on living, Genna. I feel sad and discouraged sometimes, but I get up each morning and come to work."

"That's because this is your job. You get paid to help other people. I don't get paid to go to school. No one even cares whether I'm there or not."

"Your mother cares. Your teachers and your guidance counselor care."

I roll my eyes and look for my reflection in the tiny round mirrors sewn onto the sofa cushions. Dr. Fitzpatrick tilts her head to the side as if she's listening to something that's far away. "Don't you believe that, Genna?"

I don't want her to think that I think my mother doesn't care about me. I know that the people she's talking about want to help me, but they don't know how. Still, I'm not trying to blame anyone else for my problems, so I just say, "They don't understand."

"What don't they understand?"

"I'm different. I'm not the same person I was before."

"Before what, Genna?"

I look at Dr. Fitzpatrick but I don't say a word.

"Your mother told me you ran away from home this summer. Is that true?"

"Sort of." I wonder what else Mama told her.

"Where did you go?"

Once again I keep my mouth shut, but this time I look away. I try to keep my heart closed but I feel it opening just the same. A single tear slides down my cheek.

"Did things happen to you while you were gone, Genna? Things that made you feel angry or afraid?"

I keep my arms locked around me. I suck in my bottom lip and try to keep myself together.

"Can you tell me what happened, Genna?"

I shake my head, and two tears drip off my chin. Inside I almost wish that I could tell Dr. Fitzpatrick what really happened. I wish I had one person in this world who would listen to me and truly understand.

"Why not?"

"You wouldn't believe me."

"How do you know that, Genna?"

"Because you're a stranger, and my own mother doesn't believe me. Plus you're a shrink—you'll just think I'm hallucinating or schizophrenic or something like that. If I tell you the truth, you'll probably lock me up in an insane asylum or put me on medication. And there's nothing wrong with me. I'm not crazy."

"I don't think you're crazy, Genna. But you're right, I am a stranger—at least, we don't know one another very well yet. But I'd like to get to know you, Genna. Do you know the difference between a psychologist and a psychiatrist?"

This question catches me off guard, but luckily I know the answer. "Only a psychiatrist can prescribe medication."

"That's right. I'm a psychologist, Genna. I won't be putting you on any medication. I don't think you need it, anyway."

I don't want to, but I look straight into Dr. Fitzpatrick's eyes so I can see if she's for real. She looks like she means it. But I'm not ready to trust her yet.

"Your mother's waiting outside, right?"

I nod, and wonder what Mama's been doing all this time.

"She raised you and your siblings on her own, right?" I nod again and wonder what that's got to do with anything. "Your mother must be a pretty strong woman. I don't think she'd let anyone lock you up in an insane asylum. Do you?"

Mama's already got one of her kids behind bars. I know she wouldn't let anyone take me away. I shake my head and reach for the tissue box on Dr. Fitzpatrick's desk.

"It's going to take time for you to trust me, Genna, but I'm hoping that you'll try. I think you have an interesting story to tell, and I'd really like to hear it. Why don't we talk again next week? Would that be okay with you?"

I look at Dr. Fitzpatrick and part of me thinks, what's the use? But another part of me would really like to have someone I could talk to. I don't have to tell her everything. And if I agree to keep coming, maybe everyone else will lay off me for a while.

Dr. Fitzpatrick slides to the edge of her seat. Our knees are almost touching. "Will you come back and see me, Genna?"

Inside I am telling myself, it's ok, this is your choice, it's totally up to you. When I look at it that way, coming back one more time doesn't seem so bad. It'll make Mama happy, and it'll get me out of school again. "I guess," is all I say, but it earns me a big smile from Dr. Fitzpatrick. She gets up and I realize it's time to go.

"Ready?" she asks me.

Dr. Fitzpatrick opens the door. Mama jumps up and the magazine she was reading slides off her lap and onto the floor. As Mama stoops to pick it up, Dr. Fitzpatrick puts her hand on my shoulder. "I'll see you next week, Genna." Then she slips inside her office and gently closes the door.

Judah

23.

He sees me. I know he does.

I have been resting here for less than an hour, too exhausted to go any farther. Can he hear me breathing? Even without scanning the woods, it's clear he can tell that I'm here. He could expose me, raise the alarm, turn me in, and claim the reward. But he doesn't. Instead he gets down from his wagon and folds back the tarp to reveal an empty bed. There's enough room for me to climb in and lie flat on my stomach. With the tarp pulled over me, no one would know I was there. If he's on this road, he's heading north. I have run as far as I can. I can stay here and risk being caught while I give my weary body the rest it needs. Or I can step out of the shadows and see if this man will help a filthy runaway. I have lived like a wild animal for days. I don't need a mirror to know how bad I look. I can smell the blood, and sweat, and filth on my skin. Why should this man help me?

I try to pull back, withdraw into the woods until he disappears from view. But something about this middle-aged man has me mesmerized. From this distance, it's hard to say but...he doesn't look White. I cling to that fact as I scan his light brown skin and long black hair that reaches past his shoulders. There are a few grey streaks and his straight hair hangs loose, not in a braid. He could be Native American or a mulatto with "good hair." Most White farmers can't afford slaves. They spend all day out in the field—some burn and become "rednecks," some tan until their skin turns bronze. But this man isn't White. I'm sure of it. He's got blood in his veins that could make him my ally.

I watch as he calmly pulls a pipe from his shirt pocket and scrapes out the bowl with a pocketknife. He packs it with fresh tobacco from a small pouch he keeps in the back pocket of his pants. Then a match flares and pungent smoke wafts toward me as the man puffs on the pipe to get it going. Suddenly—without ever looking my way—he says, "You comin'?"

My ears fill with the sound of my heart pounding in my chest. He could be a conductor on the Underground Railroad. He could be my savior. Or he could betray me and turn me over to the sheriff. The penalty for killing a White man in the South is death—not a quick execution, but a long, bloody spectacle that other slaves will be forced to watch.

I try to see his eyes but the brim of his hat hides the one feature that will let me know whether or not I can trust this man. I swallow hard and step out of the woods and into the shade. I stand in knee-high grass, hoping he can't see that my legs are trembling. I can't run any more.

He nods at me and says, "Best be on our way."

I quickly wade through the sea of grass that separates me from the man in the road. As I climb into the back of his wagon, he says—once again without looking at me—"There's food and drink in that sack in the corner."

I nod in silent thanks and stretch out on the hard wooden boards, careful not to lie on my back. The man pulls the tarp over the wagon once more, leaving me in darkness. I hear him tying the tarp down. "Quiet as you can," he says before slapping the side of the wagon and climbing up into the driver's seat.

As the wagon rolls forward, I feel a sudden surge of panic that almost causes me to leap up and run again. But my aching muscles refuse to respond and soon the panic subsides. I lie still on the rattling boards, my limbs like lead. I am so hungry that my stomach knots at the smell of fresh bread in the sack near my head. I reach for it but only take a few swigs of water from the canteen I find inside.

Above me, the man hums a tune I can't recognize. Occasionally I hear him greet a passing rider but the wagon doesn't stop. The rocking motion combined with endless days and nights of frantic running make it hard not to surrender to sleep. But I still need to be vigilant. I know nothing about this man and yet I've placed my life in his hands. Up close he didn't look Black or even mixed-race, yet I thought all the Indians were forced to move west decades ago. Which ones were forced to walk the Trail of Tears? Which ones held African Americans as slaves? Was it the Cherokee or the Choctaw—the Seminoles? I can barely remember the handful of lessons about American Indians from the social studies classes I took a lifetime ago. Nothing I learned in school prepared me for the life I'm living now.

I wake when the wagon comes to a halt. I feel the man hop down from the driver's seat and before long the tarp is peeled back to reveal a sea of stars overhead.

"Where are we?" I ask as I struggle to sit up. My limbs are stiff and my muscles complain when I force them back into action. It's hard to see in the dark but we seem to have stopped by a river.

He nods at the black water rippling just a few feet away "That there's the Harbor River."

Safe harbor, I hope.

The man reaches into the wagon and pulls out the untouched sack of food. He hands it to me and says, "Union camp's not far from here. That's your next stop. Wait by the water's edge until you see a man in a boat. He'll have a lantern and a hat like mine. Pro'bly be whistlin.'"

That's the most he's said to me so far, but he hasn't painted much of a profile. I try to get a little more information from this reserved man. "Will he be colored, or White, or—" I stop myself before I say "like you."

The man pulls the tarp back over his wagon and lifts one corner of his mouth in a half smile. "He'll be a friend," he says, looking me in the eye for the first time. "Like me."

What I see in the man's dark eyes makes me feel ashamed for having mistrusted him. In the end, it doesn't matter which side of the color line he's on. This mysterious friend has brought me one step closer to freedom.

He leaves me at the river's edge before I can offer him my hand. "Thank you," is all I manage to say before the nameless man climbs back into the driver's seat of his wagon and disappears into the night.

The whistling man doesn't say much either. When he spots me rising cautiously from the reeds where I'd been waiting, he just tips his hat and holds out his hand to help me board the boat. Then he pulls his pole free from the muddy river bottom and pushes us into deeper water where the current carries us along.

"Union Army's plannin' a raid," he says with his eyes turned up at the stars.

I examine his face in the orange glow of the small lantern. There's no question he's Black, but I can only guess at his age. Is he a free man? Does he own this boat? How long has he been smuggling slaves to freedom? I smother those questions and abide by the need-to-know code that leaves both of us anonymous. Instead I just ask, "When?"

He just shrugs and says, "Gon' leave you by the mouth of the Combahee. Just lay low till you see them Yanks comin' up the river. When you see 'em, start hollerin.' Them Yanks be happy to see yuh. Slave today, contraband tomorrow. Next they'll make a soldier out o' yuh."

I want to ask him about the Confederate soldiers. Where will *they* be? Are they really going to let a bunch of Union soldiers just sail upstream without putting up a fight? I sit low in the pontoon between sacks of rice and wonder what the price will be for seeking sanctuary with the Union army. Will I be free to make my way back to New York? I want no part of this — or any — war. I already know what it's like to fight for my freedom, and I know how this war will end. My top priority now is to stay alive, and to find my way back to Brooklyn. Back to Genna.

That long night in the marsh is just about the loneliest of my life. I have never been this close to freedom — not in this world. What if I'm captured by Confederate soldiers before the Yankees reach me? What if I'm bitten by a poisonous snake and I die alone, in agony, with no one to comfort or mourn me? The possibilities for disaster seem endless. I try to quiet my mind by soundlessly reciting all the psalms I know by heart.

When morning comes, I hear a woman's voice calling us to freedom — singing an upbeat song about the glorious Union and the land Uncle Sam will give to the freedmen. I wade out to get a better look at the Black woman standing on the deck of the gunboat. Even from a distance her face looks familiar. In my world, that other Brooklyn, I have seen Harriet Tubman's face on t-shirts, and posters, and occasionally in a history textbook. They called her "Moses" because she led so many enslaved people out of bondage to freedom in the north. I knew she served as a scout and spy for the Union Army, but I didn't expect to see her leading the raid up the Combahee.

Harriet's presence on the deck lures the others out of hiding. I look around me and see that I did not spend the night alone after all. Dozens of frightened fugitives wade in the water, following Harriet's voice. At first some seem unsure of the lone White officer and the many Black soldiers in their Union uniforms, but I don't hesitate at all. I swim out and grab hold of a rope thrown overboard by a smiling Black soldier.

"Welcome aboard, brother," he says with genuine joy. I manage to keep smiling even as he slaps me on the back, sending pain spiraling through my body. I do what I can to help haul other swimmers out of the river.

After being betrayed by the men at Morgan's farm, I am overwhelmed by the sight of so many Black people selflessly helping one another. *This* is what we can do when we work together as one. I am not the only one with tears in my eyes. I am not the only one laughing with joy that cannot be contained. I am not the only one praising God for fulfilling His promise of deliverance.

As we move up the river, small boats are sent ashore. They quickly fill with slaves who ignore the overseers' threats as they abandon the rice fields and make their way to the riverside. Many carry chickens, pigs, sacks of rice and flour — anything that will strip the Whites who owned them of the fruits of *their* labor. The small boats fill quickly and yet the people just keep coming. The soldiers promise to return but the people fear they will be left behind and cling to the already full boats. The soldiers are forced to beat them back with the oars, but they are true to their word. The boats go back again and again until every last man, woman, and child has been saved. More than seven hundred of us leave slavery behind that day. That's what we think, at least. That's what we hope.

Judah

24.

Moses leads us to freedom. But freedom turns out to be a dismal, muddy camp on the outskirts of Beaufort. That night I huddle with the rest of the contraband around a campfire made with wood we have gathered ourselves. It's a good thing folks picked the plantations clean earlier today because it's clear the army isn't going to provide us with anything to eat — not unless we enlist, which most men seem ready to do. There is some grumbling, but no one complains. This is our first taste of freedom. This is what it means to take care of ourselves.

My refusal to enlist makes me unpopular with the other men. It doesn't matter to them that I was not born in the South as they were. It doesn't matter that I have someone waiting for me back in New York. All they see when they look at me is a coward — a disgrace to the colored race. I mostly take the insults, cold shoulders, and stray elbows without fighting back. All I want is to find a way out of the South. But one night a former slave named Hosea has too much to drink and won't let me walk away.

"We got *women* who ain't afraid to fight, but this boy can't wait to turn tail and run. Them Yanks come all the way down here to set us free. Now they need our help to finish the job and all you want to do is go up there. You worse than the damn Rebs!" He stops to take another drink from the bottle they've been passing around. "Maybe we ought to see if

Moses got a dress you can borrow—hey, boy? Maybe puttin' on a pretty frock gon' help you find your nerve."

He chuckles and some of the other men join in. They've been drinking and clowning around for a few hours, so I just let it go. But then Hosea raises his voice and says, "Looks like them crackers got you whupped, boy."

I know I should keep my mouth shut. I know this man is baiting me. I know he's probably just tired of being barked at all day by Union soldiers who claim they want to end slavery but want nothing to do with former slaves. Some of *them* are worse than the damn Rebs. I know all this but I'm tired, too, and can't muster the strength tonight to turn the other cheek. The words just seem to spill out, though I keep my Jamaican accent hidden. Right now I don't need one more thing to mark me as an outsider.

"I ain't afraid of nobody," I say quietly. When the older man hears the threat in my voice, his eyes stop smiling though his lips keep on grinning like a clown.

Hosea makes an exaggerated display of fear, which earns him more laughs from the other men. "That so? You sure look scared to me, runnin' around here lookin' for everything you can do—except fight."

The cluster of men around the campfire grows quiet. Their bodies tense, ready to jump up and avoid the blows that are sure to start flying.

I laugh in order to reassure the men that I'm not about to lose my cool. "Matter of fact, the last cracker that tried to whup me never whupped nobody ever again." To my ears, I sound like one of them. Another performance for another hostile audience.

For just a moment, Hosea looks genuinely nervous. But then I laugh at the flicker of fear in his eyes and he regains his courage.

"That so?" Hosea rises and hands the bottle of liquor to the man next to him. His voice gets low as well. "And we just supposed to take your word for it?"

I pull myself to my feet but force myself to grin so that my movements don't appear menacing. I brush the dust from my pants, shove my hands in my pockets, and then take a step back so it's clear I'm ready to walk away. "Tell me something, Hosea. Why you so ready to fight me? Why don't you save your strength for those crackers you hate so much?"

Hosea takes another step forward, unwilling to let me leave. "'Cause you're a coward—and a disgrace. Massa Lincoln finally give us guns to let us prove we're true men. And what do you do? Spit in the president's face."

Truth is, the Yankees only just started giving us guns. For most of the war they've used freed slaves as laborers and there's still a whole lot of work to do. I have no problem digging a ditch or unloading a ship if that's what it takes to get me out of here. But first I have to deal with Hosea. I silently flip through my options and decide to act like a penitent son.

"I'm sorry to disappoint you, Hosea. I really am. I wish I could be the man you want me to be, but I got someone waiting for me back home. She needs me, so that's where I got to go."

A few of the men around the fire nod in sympathy and I think my performance might actually work. Hosea lurches toward me but he's unsteady from too much liquor and his friends have to stop him from falling over. He angrily shoves them away, cursing at them now instead of me. "All o' y'all niggers are spineless. Don't know *nothin'* 'bout loyalty."

The other men grumble and leave him to stagger around the campfire toward me. I decide not to take another step and wait to see if he will make it over to where I am standing without tumbling into the fire. "Is that what you are, Hosea? A loyal slave?"

That stops him in his tracks. "I ain't a slave no more and neither is you. But you still act like a slave, lookin' around for the meanest kind o' work to do—shovellin' shit 'n moppin' up their blood. *Their* blood—blood they spilled to set you 'n yours free."

On my first day of "freedom" I went into Beaufort to see if I could find some work that didn't involve me shouldering a gun and saluting a White man. I'd heard the hospital needed men so I went over to the grand house that now serves as a place to care for soldiers. Most of them were dying of disease and not from battle wounds. I did odd jobs around the place but most of the time I did have a mop in my hand. And it wasn't blood I was cleaning up—it was vomit and diarrhea and every other foul-smelling fluid that comes out of a body that's burning up with fever.

I'm not sure how Hosea knows about my day at the hospital—and it was just one day because I never went back. Hosea is trying to shame me and for a moment my cheeks do burn, though I am far away from the campfire. A small voice in my head tells me I should walk away, that he's drunk and just blowing off steam. But I can't keep the bitterness from seeping out of my mouth.

"We wouldn't need to be set free if they hadn't put us in chains to begin with! Tell me, Hosea—what's this country done for me that I should be so grateful? Why should I shed *more* of my blood for White folks who don't even think I'm human? They think we're animals and that's how they treat us. Well, I don't need to take no more orders from these crackers. I can make up my own mind and I'm going north."

Hosea is still a few feet away from me, but he takes a swing or loses his balance and his fist connects with one of the other men. That man pushes Hosea so hard that he tumbles backward and falls into another man, knocking him down. I leave the campfire knowing at least some of the men gathered there agree with me.

The next day I go down to the docks at Port Royal and offer to help unload the ships. I don't have time to ask about wages. I take a moment to look around and see who's in charge, and as soon as the White captain sees me standing "idle" he starts hollering at me like I already work for him. Like I'm his slave.

"You there—boy! Don't just stand there—get these crates on board."

I quickly grab hold of a crate but before the White man turns away I hear him say to his friend, "Lazy niggers. Won't work unless you hold a gun to their head. And here we are, dying in droves to set them free. Worthless ingrates, every last one of them!"

I follow the other Black men loading goods onto the ship and with every trip I look for corners below deck that could conceal a stowaway. I learn from the other workers on the dock that this ship, the *Morning Glory*, will leave this evening on its way back up the coast to Wilmington. I make sure I am the last to carry a crate up the gangway and onto the ship. I linger in the shadows until the other men go above deck and then I fit myself between two stacks of crates and pray they've been secured so I don't get crushed once the ship sets sail.

In Wilmington I wait until men appear to unload the ship. Then I slip out from my hiding place and join the other workers as they carry crates off the ship. For a couple of days I stay on the docks, waiting for another chance to slip on board a ship that's heading north. But when I hear they need help on the railroad, I head over there instead. This time I don't wait for orders. I see other Black men carrying wounded soldiers to a train that will take them north so they can either convalesce or die surrounded by loved ones. When the train is nearly full of groaning, bandaged men, I creep inside and hide myself by lying between two pallets. The train pulls away and eventually we leave the South behind.

For days I ride in a stuffy car packed with sick men, so it's no wonder I arrive in New York with a fever myself. I manage to make my way to the waterfront where I can take a ferry to Brooklyn. But there's trouble on the docks and I run into a bunch of dockworkers jumping every Negro they can catch—and with a fever, I'm not quick enough to outrun them. To my surprise, an Irish cop pulls them off me, swinging his club without mercy. Two more cops drag me over to the ferry and their presence gets me on board without a ticket. Somehow I get to Weeksville but by the time I open my eyes, I'm not sure where or who I am. Genna hovers over me like an angel of mercy, pouring cold water into my parched mouth. When she calls my name, that's when I know that I am finally home.

Genna

25.

At the library I find a map that shows me where Weeksville used to be. I walk into the heart of Crown Heights but I am so busy keeping an eye on the projects that I don't even notice a break in the block. I turn my head, expecting to see an empty lot, but instead I see a tidy green lawn that stretches to the far end of the block. Who has a lawn in Brooklyn? And how come this fenced-in lot hasn't been filled with trash? I stop walking and look up at a dingy wood-frame house with a porch.

You don't see many wood houses in this neighborhood—we've got brownstones and apartment buildings and that's about it. Lots of concrete, lots of stone. I look ahead to the neatly mowed lawn stretching beyond the tall chain link fence and force myself to take a step forward. What I see takes my breath away. What I see is what's left of Weeksville.

One hand flies up to cover my mouth, to stop the scream sliding up my throat. My other hand swings up and latches onto the fence, and for a moment I hang by my fingers because my knees have given out. I know these houses. I have been here before.

In an instant I lose the impulse to scream and instead a sob slips through my lips. I press my feet into the hard concrete and press my face into the chain link fence. The steel wires scratch my cheeks and as tears spill down my face, I taste the trace of blood and salt and metal on my tongue. Judah is still part of this world. That world, I mean. He could be in this place in that time. 1863.

I can't let go, and I can't step back. I all but lunge at the small wooden houses as if hurling myself through this fence will somehow send me back to him. A wave of heat surges up my spine and quickly spreads throughout my body. When the tingling warmth reaches my fingertips, I lean back and pull. The mesh fence yields before the weight of my body; it billows but doesn't budge. I am about to pull again, harder this time, when suddenly I hear a voice. It's warbled, like a song from the bottom of the sea. *You gon' find her?*

My head spins around to face the projects, but they are strangely silent and still. Another voice, like a rumble of thunder, draws my gaze back to the Hunterfly houses.

I can't...

My heart pounds like a drum. I know these houses and I know that growling voice: Judah!

The air beyond the fence wavers like heat rising off asphalt in August. I blink hard to bring the scene back into focus, but the soupiness persists. Then voices return, clearer this time.

> *You gon' find her?*
> *I can't...*
> *Why not?*
> *I don't know how.*
> *Well — you gon' try?*

I hold my breath and try to think. Who speaks with that blend of slur and sass? A girl from the South...Mattie!

Another wave of heat surges up my spine and the air beyond the fence starts to shimmer once more. Through the fence I see people walking along a dusty road. A man on a horse tips his hat at a woman wrapped in a knit shawl. All of them wear old-fashioned clothes — the same clothes I wore when I went back in time. There is a whole other world beyond this fence. A world I know.

My fingers claw at the links, conducting heat from my spine, through my fingertips, and into the cold cords of steel. I look down the block, searching for a way in. A tall steel post roots the fence in the concrete sidewalk. The gates beyond the post are bound together with chain and a padlock. The heat within me surges, swelling the blood in my veins. A message pulses through my muscles: PULL.

"Young lady! Excuse me, young lady!"

The woman's voice rings out like a bell and in an instant the other world vanishes. Not slowly, like water going down a drain. I blink and the dirt road, the man on the horse, Mattie's and Judah's voices are gone.

"No...no!" Just as quickly my voice turns from a whisper into a howl. "NO!"

I can see the Black woman crossing the yard, but my senses strain to restore the scene she just destroyed.

"I'm afraid we're closed. You'll have to come back another day." As she gets closer, something about me wipes the smile off her face. She peers at me through the fence. "Are you alright?"

The look I give her makes her glad there is a fence between us. She backs up and retraces the steps that brought her out of the wooden house farthest from the street. I glare at her as she retreats, my aching fingers balled into fists. I was close. So close...

When I get home, I sink into the sofa and let my spine dissolve into the soft, stained cushions. Everything within me feels different. I am like a stream of lava slowing, stiffening, turning into rock. But time is fluid—I know that now.

"What happened to your face?"

Mama's worried voice snaps my bones back in place. I sit up and touch my cheek, then look at my fingertips and give in to the urge to lick the bloody tears that have caked on my skin.

"Don't do that!" Mama slaps my hand away from my mouth and hustles into the bathroom, muttering under her breath. She returns with a bottle of alcohol and some cotton balls. I brace myself for the sting. "You been fighting, Genna?"

"No!" Since when do I get into fights? Mama always thinks the worst of me. I tell myself that's why I have to keep lying to her. "I fell," I say with a sullen slump against the couch.

"Oh yeah? Looks to me like you fell into some other girl's nails."

I get up and look at myself in the mirror on the wall. "It must have been the fence..."

Mama sighs impatiently. "What fence?"

"I tripped on a crack in the pavement and fell into this wire fence. I must have scratched my face."

Mama won't let herself sigh again. She pinches her lips together and looks at me, hard. "You got to be more careful out there, Genna."

I nod and sit back down on the sofa so Mama can finish cleaning my face. I wince as the alcohol seeps into my scratched skin. Then I think about the shimmering world beyond that chain link fence and force myself not to smile.

Judah

26.

I am nothing like my father. I would never kill the mother of my child. Not over a rumor, a handful of words hissed by tongues soaked in too much rum. My father never came around much, but one night he took up his machete and took my mother's life. They say I watched it happen but all I remember is the crazed look in my father's bloodshot eyes. I thought he would kill me, too, but instead he went up the mountain and took his own life. My aunt says when they found him he still stank of rum. He's a duppy now, haunting the roots of the silk cotton tree. But I am alive.

I can live with what I've done. I wasn't drunk—just desperate to live. And it was my life or theirs, so I chose. I won't shed any more tears over what I've done. But some days I do miss the boy I used to be. There's no such thing as a teenager in this world. You're either a boy or a man. And I'm not a boy any more.

Losing Genna made me feel just like a kid again. Some magnet somewhere suddenly pulled her away from me, and there was nothing I could do. One second she was in my arms and the next moment she was gone. I had nothing left to hold onto, just the memory of that night—how scared and desperate we had been to outrun the mob. And then, when we thought we were safe, that evil cracker shoved a knife into Genna's back, and she fell against the fountain. I killed him—fired the pistol over and over until I was sure he was dead. And then I reached for Genna—

there was a beautiful black rose in the middle of her back — a small flower blossoming blood. I turned her over, and tried to get help, but before anything else could happen — before I could even say goodbye — she was gone. And I was left there at the fountain with nothing — no explanation, no hope of ever seeing Genna again, and nothing left in this world to love.

I sat on the edge of the fountain, too numb to cry and too tired to think of a way to send myself back too. There were no more bullets in the pistol, and I wasn't so sure I wanted to go back. Genna and I were planning to leave this country — together — but now everything had changed.

Men were arriving with stretchers to carry the wounded and dead rioters away. I sat there by the fountain until one of the Metropolitan police officers came over and put his hand on my shoulder. "What is it, son?" he asked. "Are you hurt?"

I looked up at him and saw that his pale face was flushed yet grim with concern. He was a White man, but I could tell he didn't hate me. He didn't want me dead. He wanted to help, but there was nothing he could do. I shook my head and got up from the fountain. I looked around the plaza to get my bearings, then started down the road that led to Weeksville.

I already knew how it felt to lose someone you love. It's like having a knife shoved deep into your heart, except you don't die. You never die from missing someone. You just walk around, bleeding inside, until your heart scabs up and gets tough. Then it hurts just a little bit less when the next person walks out of your life.

My Aunt Marcia used to say being Black was about a whole lot more than the color of your skin. She said being Black meant looking at the world with your eyes wide open all the time. She also said not everybody who looked like me would see me for who I am. And she was right about that. When I started high school, a lot of kids came up to me just because of my dreadlocks. They figured since I was Rastafari I probably sat around drinking rum, listening to reggae, and smoking weed all day.

I do smoke a little herb, but not like they think — it's not for fun, and it's not so I can block out what's going on around me. Ganja is a part of our faith, it's a tool we use to get closer to Jah—it's what helps us keep our eyes open wide. Because if your eyes aren't open wide—if you even blink at the wrong moment—you could lose your life. That's what it means to be an African in this country, whether it's 1863 or 2001.

Having your eyes wide open also helps you see people for who they really are. Take Genna. I knew the first time I saw her that she wasn't like other girls. Genna was quiet, and kept to herself most of the time, but I could tell she had something going on inside. Most girls, they got a lot going on *outside*—lots of lip gloss and flashy jewelry and clothes that show you just what they have to offer. But Genna, she didn't give anything away. And that mattered to me.

In a way, I don't think Genna knew how special she was. I guess maybe because no one had ever told her. But once she really started to see herself, once she stopped hiding underneath those scarves, I think she started to see the person I always saw whenever I looked at her—not the person I wanted her to be, but the person she really was.

The world we live in tells us it's not okay to just be yourself. All the movies and magazines and music videos say it's better to be like someone else. Genna chose to be herself and I chose to love her for it. But she didn't choose me. She didn't choose to build a life in this world with me. After everything I did to find my way back to her, she left me.

In this world, I have to keep my eyes open *all* the time. It's hard to sleep even, because you never know what's going to happen next. Once you've survived a riot—once you've been chained and whipped and sold from one place to another—you see the world differently. And once you've killed two men, you see yourself differently, too.

I haven't looked in a mirror in a real long time, but I know I'm not the same person I used to be. And not just because they took my locks. Aunt Marcia always used to say it's what's *inside* your head that matters most. And that's what worries me. My hair will grow and lock again. But I don't know if I'll ever be okay on the inside.

I keep my eyes open as wide as I can. And that means I see a whole lot of ugliness in this world. I see my people living without shelter in the woods around Weeksville, cold, alone, and afraid that mobs of Whites are going to come after them again. I see grown men who can't even look me in the eye because they don't feel like men any more. I see children who never laugh or play. They just stay close to their parents—if they've got any left—and wait for the next bad thing to happen. And me, I'm just praying something good happens next. Because if there's another riot or if anyone tries to steal me again, *it's over*—I'll end this nightmare once and for all. There won't be a way to go back. Not to the future, not to Genna. Not to the Judah I used to be.

Genna

27.

I go to school most of the time these days, just to keep Mama off my back. She and Mrs. Freeman agreed to let me drop Mr. Collins's class, so long as I agreed to make up the credits by doing summer school. I go to the garden on my lunch hour sometimes, but mostly I spend my days at the public library. They've got a special room there filled with old books and maps that show you how Brooklyn used to look. It's not the same as being back in 1863, but it's as close as I can get—for now.

Today I am in the youth wing of the library waiting to use the computers. A pretty brown-skinned girl with a long scarf over her hair comes up and stands next to me.

"Hey," she says with a smile.

"Hey."

I try to smile but I don't think I know this girl so I'm not sure why she's talking to me.

"It's Genna, right? I'm Rashidah. I'm in your U.S. History class."

"Oh, right." I smile and wonder what she thinks about the scene I caused the last time I went to Mr. Collins's class.

Rashidah tugs at the straps of her bookbag. She looks uncomfortable and I secretly hope she'll give up and walk away. I don't really have time to be making new friends in this world.

"I haven't seen you lately. Did you drop the class?" she asks.

When I nod she says, "Lucky you. It's *so* boring. The only exciting thing that ever happened in that class was when you stood up to Mr. Collins. I really respected you for doing that."

"Really? Thanks." I smile more easily this time, and Rashidah seems to relax a bit, too.

"Our first essay's due next week," she tells me. "I was thinking about writing on the draft riots. Know any good books I could check out?"

I laugh and put down my heavy bag. "You can take a look at these, but I'm afraid I've already checked them out myself."

"Are you writing a research paper for another class?" Rashidah asks.

I open my mouth, but the words I need don't come out. I close my mouth, then open it and try again. "I'm doing research but...not for a paper."

"Really? What's it for then?"

The truth is, I'm trying to find out what happened after the riots so I know what Judah might be going through. But I can't tell Rashidah the truth. So I just shrug and try to act nonchalant. "I'm just curious."

Rashidah doesn't look at me like I'm crazy so I stop trying to act cool and decide to just tell her the truth. "It's for this project I'm working on, but it's not for school."

Rashidah looks like she wants to hear more about my project, but I don't offer any details. She glances at the clipboard with the sign-up sheet. "Are you waiting for a computer?"

"Yeah. I just wanted to check something online, but they're booked solid today. Looks like I'm going to be here a while."

Rashidah nods and I think maybe now she's going to leave me alone. Instead she takes a deep breath and says, "You know, I have a computer at home. Why don't you come to my place? Maybe while you're online I can take a look at some of your books."

"For real?"

"Sure. Unless you really want to wait two hours just to get online for twenty minutes."

I turn and look at the clipboard on the librarian's desk. There are at least six names before mine. Then I look down at all the books in my bag. What will I say if Rashidah asks about my special project? I try to come up with a story in my head so I'll be ready just in case she asks.

But right now Rashidah is still waiting for me to accept her offer. She bites her lip and hefts her bookbag, which looks like it's already full of books.

"You know what? It's okay, I can go to another branch and look for my own books." She smiles a little and starts to walk away.

I step in front of Rashidah so she can't leave. "No, no—I don't mind. We can share these. It's just that my mom—she's kind of…"

"Strict? My folks are, too." Rashidah reaches into her pocket and pulls out a cell phone. "You can call and check first, if you want. Make sure it's okay."

I take the phone from Rashidah and punch in my phone number, even though I know Mama won't be home yet. I leave a message on the machine, telling her I'm studying with a friend. Then I hang up and smile at Rashidah as I give her back her cell phone. I hope she doesn't mind that I called her my friend.

On the way to her place we stop at a bodega to pick up some snacks. As we're leaving the store, a couple of boys try to talk to us.

"Hey, shorty, what's up?"

A chunky kid wearing a Yankees cap puckers his lips at me. His partner, skinny and tall, lets his hand slide down to his crotch.

Rashidah and I exchange glances and then burst out laughing as we walk away.

"Puh-lease—they must be thirteen years old!" I say.

"And who's *he* calling 'shorty'?" Rashidah asks with maximum attitude.

We're so busy laughing and eating our chips that we don't realize the boys have followed us.

"You laughin' at me, you fuckin' terrorist? What you got under that rag, huh? A bomb?"

The heavy kid's hand reaches out lightning quick and grabs at the scarf on Rashidah's head.

"Ouch!"

The scarf is pinned to another band of cloth on Rashdah's head and it doesn't come off easily. I try to help Rashidah, but the kid's wiry partner gets in my way.

"Leave her alone!" I shout.

The scarf finally comes off and the heavy kid waves it in my face before throwing it on the ground.

"Ain't nobody talkin' to you, bitch." He takes a step closer to Rashidah, an ugly sneer on his face. "What are you, one of them *Mooslems* from Africa? Go back where you came from, bitch. This is America! Home of the brave!"

"She *is* African—and so am I." For just a moment I wish Judah were here so he could hear me talk that way. He'd be proud of me, but Judah's not here right now. I need to handle this fool myself

"You're nothing but a coward," I tell him. "Why don't you go back to whatever cave you crawled out of and leave us alone."

The wiry kid holds his hand over his mouth and laughs at his friend. "Oh, snap, son! You gonna let her diss you like that?"

Determined to save face, the heavy kid directs all his anger at me now. He's a couple of inches shorter than me but solidly built and probably has no problem hitting a girl. I feel my back lighting up as my fury builds, but I'm not sure what I should do next. The last time I took on two guys at once was in 1863, and Paul Easterly showed up to save me. Since 9/11 the city's been crawling with cops, but I don't see a single one right now. The kid sees me hesitate and gets in my face.

"What'd you call me, bitch? You callin' *me* a coward?"

Suddenly his friend stops snickering and tries to pull him away from me. "Yo, man, chill—chill!"

Both boys look past me to a person coming up the block. Rashidah and I turn around at the same time to see who they're looking at. To my surprise, it's not a cop. It's Troy.

"Hey, Genna. What's up?" Troy casually twists the cap off the brown-bagged bottle he just purchased inside the bodega. "You alright?"

Troy saunters in between us and the two boys so that his body forms a kind of wall. His back is to me and Rashidah so I have to talk over his shoulder.

"These jerks were messing with us — they took Rashidah's headscarf."

Troy nods and takes a long swig from the bottle. "Give it back," he says simply.

The wiry kid glances at his friend, then picks the scarf up off the ground and hands it to Troy. Troy takes it from him, shakes it out gently, and passes it back to Rashidah. "Now apologize."

The heavy kid laughs nervously. "We was just playin', man. Ain't no big deal."

"It's a big deal if I say it is. This here's my little sister." Troy nods his head back at me. "I see either of you punks messing with her or her friend again, won't be no problem — no problem at all."

Troy extends his arms as if tempting the boys to frisk him. Rashidah and I can only see Troy from behind, but we both see the change in the boys' faces when their eyes reach Troy's waist.

"Understand?"

The edge in Troy's voice sends a chill up my spine. Both boys keep their eyes lowered to hide their fear. They nod at Troy, then turn and try to walk away without looking as humiliated as they feel. Troy waits until they reach the end of the block before turning to face us.

"They mess with you again — you come to me."

I know I should be thanking Troy right now, but I cut my eyes at him instead. When Rashidah goes over to a store window to adjust her headscarf, I say, "Why? 'Brothers is just feeling patriotic, is all.'"

Troy takes another sip from the bottle and rolls his lips together.

"That's a low blow, Genna. But I guess I had it coming, right? Why don't you take your friend home—better yet, take her over to our place. It's getting dark but I'll be home in a little while. I can give you both a lift."

I glance at Troy's waist but he pulls at his jacket so I can't see the gun. I look down the block and tell him, "We don't need a lift."

Rashidah comes back over, her eyes red from crying. "How do I look?" she asks.

"Fine," I tell her, linking my arm through hers. "Come on. Let's go home."

As we talk away, Troy calls out, "So now you think you can handle yourself, huh? Your head's too hard, Genna. You're just like your sister."

I look over my shoulder and say, "That's right. I *can* handle myself. Bye, Troy." I tighten my hold on Rashidah's arm and we head down the block.

When we reach her building Rashidah smoothes down her headscarf and wipes her eyes once more. "Do I look okay?"

I lie and tell her, "You look fine."

Rashidah's trying hard to act normal, but she's been trembling for the past ten minutes. I wonder if she has been attacked before. Wearing hijab makes her a target in the streets and at school. I wonder if I would have the courage to wear a headscarf in New York City right now.

"Maybe we should get together some other time," I say so she doesn't have to invite me in. "Here, take these." I unzip my bookbag and give her half the books I checked out on the draft riots. "You look through those ones, and I'll just use these other books for now."

"Are you sure? What about your project?" Rashidah asks as she takes the books from me.

"What I'm looking for probably isn't going to be in any book." I smile at Rashidah and wonder what to say next. Even though those boys attacked us, for some reason I feel guilty. "I'm really sorry about what happened, Rashidah."

She tries to smile at me but the pain in her eyes is clear. "It's ok. I mean, it's not your fault. It's been like that for a while now."

"It's not right," I tell her and then say it again like Rashidah needs me to tell her what she already knows. "My number's in your cell phone—when you're done with the books, just give me a call. Okay?"

"Okay. Bye, Genna."

I wave as Rashidah heads into her apartment building and then head for home. Without meaning to, I find myself at the garden. It has closed for the day, but I go up to the black iron gate anyway. I grip the rails and try to peer through the leaves, through the darkness to the fountain beyond.

So many things are wrong in this world. If I stayed, maybe I could do something to make things right. Maybe Rashidah and I could become friends. Maybe we could start a campaign at school to fight Islamophobia. But I don't really go to school any more, and I wouldn't be a loyal friend if I left Rashidah behind when she needs me to have her back. The truth is, the only person I'm loyal to is Judah.

I squint in the darkness for any trace of the ghosts that signaled the portal was about to open that night in June. But there's nothing in the garden besides shadows right now. It's almost October and the door that led me to Weeksville is still sealed.

I heft my bookbag onto my other shoulder. I gave Rashidah half of my books about the draft riots because I have other books that I need to read. Books that will teach me how to work magic. Books that will bring Judah back to me.

Genna

28.

"I thought you might want this." Mama sets a colorful prayer card on the kitchen table next to my bowl of cereal. "Your grandmother sent it from Panama last summer."

"You told Abuela I was...gone?"

Mama slides Tyjuan into his high chair and sets a bowl of cereal with no milk on his tray. I smile at my baby brother as he shoves a fistful of cornflakes into his mouth.

"I knew it was a long shot," says Mama, "but I thought maybe— somehow—you went looking for your father."

I do want to visit Panama someday. The annual parade is coming up in October. Every year I go and admire the girls wearing their perfectly pleated polleras, knowing that even if I wore the exact same dress I'd still feel like I don't belong.

I pick up the stiff, laminated card. On the front is a picture of the Virgin Mary. She is wearing a flowing blue robe. Baby Jesus is on her lap and two angels hover overhead. All have rosy pink cheeks and shiny gold halos. I flip the card over and read the "Hail Mary" prayer. I'm sure my abuela said dozens of these for me. I look at the blond-haired, blue-eyed Mary and wonder how Mama felt about receiving this gift.

"Did you pray for me while I was gone, Mama?"

"Of course, I did. But not to her," Mama says, nodding at the white

Mary. "I lit candles." Mama opens the fridge and pokes her head inside. "I even went to see a psychic."

My mouth falls open in amazement. "A psychic?"

Mama takes out a jug of orange juice and closes the door with a shrug. "I needed answers. The police were no help." Mama nods at the prayer card. "If you looked like her, every cop in the country would be looking for you. But when Black girls go missing..."

Mama doesn't have to finish that sentence. I know what she means. Some girls are missed more than others. I wait for Mama to pour herself a drink before asking my next question. "What did the psychic tell you?"

"Nothing I didn't already know." Mama takes a sip of juice and looks into her glass instead of looking at me. "That you left because you felt betrayed. That you were with a boy." She pauses and lifts her eyes to meet mine. "That your heart would lead you home." For just a moment all three of us are silent. "It sounded corny at the time, but..." Mama reaches out her hand to stroke my cheek. "Here you are."

"Here I am." I'm not sure my smile is convincing so I stuff a spoonful of cereal into my mouth and avoid Mama's eyes. Fortunately, Tyjuan distracts Mama long enough for me to swallow my guilt.

Mama yawns and drains her glass of juice. "I'm beat. Can you drop Tyjuan at Mrs. Dominguez's before you leave for school?"

"Sure, Mama."

"I don't know how I ever managed without you, Genna."

But you *did*, Mama, I say to myself. You did manage without me. And before long, you'll have to do it again.

After planting a kiss on my forehead and Tyjuan's, Mama heads into the bedroom and closes the door. I push my breakfast away and instead watch Tyjuan playing with his cereal. So far he hasn't turned his bowl upside down, but I know that moment's coming. He's already got mashed cornflakes all over his face and t-shirt. I'm not worried about being late for class, though, because I'm not going to school today. I can't. I have work to do.

I clean Tyjuan up and drop him off at the babysitter's. Mama will pick him up later, after she's had a chance to get some sleep. Then I'll come home from school, Mama will make dinner, and I'll watch Tyjuan while Mama goes to work. This is the routine we have settled into. Soon Toshi will have to take my place. She and Mama seem to be getting along—at least they're speaking to each other again. Mama still doesn't think much of Troy. I figure if things don't work out, Toshi and the baby can move back in with us. With Mama and Tyjuan, I mean. By that time, I'll be gone.

Turns out the books I got from the library aren't much help, but they're all I've got to go on. I'm not trying to cast a spell or put a hex on anybody, and I'm not trying to ward off the evil eye or get rich quick. Judah loves me already so I don't need a love potion. None of these books tells me how to travel through time, but I figure making a lucky charm or taking a special bath can't hurt.

I need to go to a botánica, but I don't want to go to the one in my neighborhood. I pass by it all the time, but I never see anybody inside. They've got two displays—one window's full of statues of saints covered in plastic, and the other one's got nothing but brooms made of straw. I know those aren't the kind of brooms witches fly on, but they creep me out just the same. Slaves used to "jump the broom" when they got married, but I don't know what else brooms are used for—besides sweeping up. There's another botánica farther down Nostrand and that's where I'm heading today. Not much chance anyone I know will see me shopping there.

On the train I flip through the book of spells I got from the library. Hoodoo, voodoo—all of this is new to me. I never really thought much about magic before—why would I? Magic is something you see on TV—a White guy waves a magic wand and pulls a rabbit out of a hat. Or he wriggles out of a straight jacket while holding his breath underwater. Magic belongs with clowns at the circus, or in a castle in England. People who use magic don't look like me. If I lived in an old mansion, maybe I'd find a magic closet and walk into another world. But I don't. I live in

Brooklyn.

I look at the list of items I need to get from the botánica. I know it will take more than this to tear a hole in time, but doing something feels better than doing nothing at all. When I come up from the train I know exactly where I'm going. I don't come over this way too often, but I have memorized the address of the botanica and don't have to waste time looking around. The only problem is, the name on the storefront doesn't match the name I found in the phonebook. I can't quite pronounce the words on the sign, either, but I know I'm in the right place. The window display is full of statues of saints and when I open the door, the smell of incense wafts over me.

A bell on the doorknob announces my arrival. Two Black women — one on either side of the counter — finish their conversation before turning to look at me. I smile and try not to look as nervous as I feel. The woman behind the counter doesn't smile back, but the other woman seated on a chair next to a shelf of candles nods and says hello.

I pull out my list even though I have memorized everything that's written on it. For some reason, I want them to know that I am not just some curious passerby. I am here with a purpose, but the shelves are crammed with so many things I hardly know where to begin. There are glass bottles of perfume and plastic bottles of honey. Bowls made of gourds are stacked precariously on a stool. Boxes on the floor hold dozens of paper bags filled with what I assume are herbs. I can hear a bird cheeping softly, but I can't find the birdcage where it is kept. Strings of colored beads dangle from nails and on the highest shelf just below the ceiling are dozens and dozens of saints. To my surprise, not all of them are White.

I am so busy gazing up at a Black Madonna that I don't hear the woman behind the counter talking to me. Finally her friend tugs at my sleeve. "You need help, yes?"

I nod and show her my list. She gets up from the folding chair and easily pulls things off different shelves. Nothing she hands me has a price tag on it but before long I've got everything I need. On my way over to the cash register I accidentally kick a box on the floor. I look down and realize this is where the cheeping is coming from. A chicken ducks its head under a flap of cardboard.

"Sorry," I say as I set everything on the glass countertop. I have never seen a live chicken before, but I try to act like it's no big deal. The woman behind the counter puts on her coat and walks away, gesturing for her friend to ring up my purchase instead. She passes me on her way to the front door and leans in to get a closer look at my face. I wonder if my cut has started bleeding again. The smile I was ready to offer her dissolves into discomfort.

"You know who that is?" she asks me, nodding to a statue above.

I glance up at the Black Madonna and for the first time notice the two red lines painted on her cheek. "Mary?" I say uncertainly.

She nods and then draws two fingers across her own cheek. "Ezili Dantò." The bell on the door handle jangles loudly as she goes out into the street without saying another word.

Now behind the counter, the other woman smiles at me and says, "You ever hear of Dantò?"

When I shake my head, she pulls a colorful picture from a manila envelope. She slides it across the counter so I can read the words printed across the bottom. Mater Salvatoris. The brown-skinned, brown-eyed woman holds a baby with one arm; her other hand seems to point to her heart. Both wear jeweled gold crowns and both are circled by a halo of stars. Suddenly self-conscious, I reach up and touch the scratches on my own face. "Why does she have those scars?" I ask quietly.

"Dantò—she fight. She is poor, but proud—and strong. Nobody mess with Dantò." The woman chuckles softly and puts my things into a paper bag.

I look up at the blue-robed woman with the serene brown face. I wonder if my abuela has ever seen a Mary like this. "How much for the statue?" I ask.

The woman thinks a moment and says, "Sixty. The small one I give you for twenty-five."

I don't have that much money to spend. The woman looks at me and then reaches into another manila envelope. She pulls out a dozen keychain-sized pictures of saints and sifts through them until she finds one of Mater Salvatoris.

"How much for that?" I ask, sure I can afford such a small copy.

She waves her hand as if to say, "Don't worry about it," and slips it inside the bag along with the rest of my purchases. I pay the woman, thank her for her help, and carefully step around the cardboard box to avoid upsetting the chicken. Outside I take the picture of the brown-skinned Mary out of the bag and put it in my pocket. It's good to have things that are small and portable. After all, I can't take a big statue with me when I go back in time.

I jump when a voice hisses in my ear. "Genna!"

Peter stands in front of me, his face grim and tight. He doesn't say "hey" and he doesn't smile. He just glares at me and asks, "Where's Judah?"

"What?"

"You heard me. Where is he?"

I don't say anything right away. I look at Peter and I know how much he must miss Judah. The two of them were best friends. "I don't know where he is, Peter." It's easier — kinder — to lie. I turn to go but Peter surprises me by grabbing my arm.

"You're lying. I want the truth, Genna."

We are on a crowded street in the heart of Brooklyn but panic grips me the same way it did when I found myself all alone on the docks back in 1863. I fought two grown men then and I am ready to fight Peter now.

"Let go of me!" I manage to wrench my arm free but Peter isn't ready to let go. He reaches for me again and this time captures one of my hands.

I scan the sidewalk for someone who will help me, but people just walk on by. This scene isn't new to them — or me. I am tired of being the one who always needs to be rescued, and I am tired of men thinking they can mess with me. In my mind I am tired but in my body I am mad. I can feel something inside of me turning—sliding—shifting—and in a flash I go from being panicked to being pissed. I lock my eyes on Peter and hold my breath as my spine starts to tingle and my blood starts to boil.

I can tell by the look on Peter's face that he knows something's happening inside of me. I close my eyes and feel the skin around my scratched cheeks tighten as my lips curl up into a smile.

"What the—ow!" Peter flings my hand away and cradles his singed fingers.

I open my eyes and fill my lungs with cool October air. Peter looks at me like I am someone he's never seen before. I can tell that things between us have changed. Peter may not be afraid of me, but he won't be grabbing me anytime soon.

"How did you do that?"

"Do what?" I ask without waiting for an answer. I dart across the street and head for the green globes of the subway station up ahead. But as the heat drains from my body, so does much of my strength. I can't walk fast enough to avoid Peter and it's not long before he catches up with me. He doesn't try to touch me this time but he does block my way. I try to go around him and nearly fall into the crates of fruit set out in front of a market.

Peter instinctively reaches out to help me, but at the same moment we realize that's not a good idea. "Maybe you should sit down," he suggests.

All I want is to get back home, but right now I don't even have enough strength to make it to the end of the block. Peter points to an empty milk crate. I nod, which makes me dizzy, but manage to sit down without toppling over.

Peter squats down and watches me. His eyes are filled with curiosity and concern. "You alright?" he asks.

I shrug off my book bag and search inside for a bottle of water. After a few sips I start to feel a bit better. The dizziness passes and I feel my bones clicking back into place. I start to feel solid once more but now my limbs feel like they're made of lead.

Peter looks at my hands, seemingly amazed that they haven't melted the plastic bottle. "Your skin—it felt like it was on fire."

I take another sip of water and think of what to say. "You shouldn't have grabbed me like that. I told you to let go."

Peter flicks open the bag from the botánica and peers inside. "You going to tell me what's going on?"

I sigh and then shiver in my sweat dampened clothes. "I can't."

"Why not?"

"Because you wouldn't understand." I finally look Peter in the eye so he knows I'm being real with him.

"I been watching you, Genna. I know something's going on. You used to be a straight-A student—now you hardly ever go to school. You hooked up with my best friend last spring—you two were glued to each other. Now you're here and he's not. When's the last time you saw Judah?"

I roll my lips together and try to decide if this is a question I can afford to answer. "September," I say finally. "The day before 9/11."

Peter frowns. "Was he alright? Is he in some kind of trouble?"

I hope not. "I don't know, Peter." He sucks his teeth, and I realize I need to end this conversation. "For real, Peter—I don't know." I gather my bags, take a deep breath, and pull myself to my feet. Peter stands as well, his face sour as the limes stacked just a few feet away. "Please don't ask me anything else." I try to edge past him, but suddenly the dizziness returns and I wind up falling into Peter instead. This time he catches me without hesitation, without harm.

"Come on. We better get you home." Peter grabs my bags and wraps his arm around my shoulder. As soon as we near the curb, a passing gypsy cab slows and honks at us. Peter lifts his chin and the cab pulls up to the curb. I open the door and crumple into the soft leather back seat. Peter has to give me a shove to remind me to slide over so he can squeeze in, too.

After giving the driver my cross streets, Peter resumes his

interrogation but his voice seems softer in the dark interior of the cab. "Listen, Genna. If you tell me what happened last summer, maybe I can help you out. I know people, and my uncle—he's got connections, too."

The scene outside the window blurs as my eyes fill with tears. I am so, so tired. "I'm sorry, Peter," I whisper, "but I can't."

Peter gazes out the opposite window but I know his attention is focused on me, not the street. "What did you mean that day—in history class—when you said you were there?"

My throat feels like it's closing. That always happens when I refuse to let myself cry. I cough a bit and try to restore my voice even though this is a question I don't know how to answer. "I—I didn't mean it like that. I was just upset, and it came out wrong—"

Peter sighs and I can tell he's tired too. Tired of not knowing the truth. He turns away from the window and looks at me. "Quit lying, Genna. Judah's in trouble, isn't he? And you're trying to find a way to help him. Well, you can't do it alone—you know that, I know that. What happened that night in the garden? I know Judah went there looking for you."

Looking into Peter's eyes is like looking into a mirror. He cares about Judah, too. I tip my head back against the leather headrest. Tears slide past my ears. "I went to the wishing fountain."

"And?"

I take a deep breath. "You really want to know?" Peter nods solemnly, so I take a deep breath and go on.

"And...these ghosts came out of the bushes."

"Ghosts." Peter says the word like he wants to make sure he heard me right. Not like he thinks I'm crazy. I chew the inside of my lip and nod once. Peter stares at me, hard. "And what about Judah—did he see them, too?"

I shrug and close my eyes. "I don't know. He must have got there after—after I'd been sent back."

"Sent back where? Home?"

I shake my head wearily. This is the moment. Do I dare tell him the truth—the whole truth?

Just then the driver pulls over and looks at us in the rear view mirror. "We're here," I say and quickly gather up my belongings.

Peter shifts so he can reach the wallet in his back pocket, and I seize my chance to slip out of the cab. My building is farther down the block and I head toward it as fast as I can. Behind me, I hear the car door slam but I don't hear Peter running after me. I turn around and see him standing by the curb, a hurt look on his face.

It's time, I think to myself. Mama's probably still sleeping, but school's not out yet. I can't just show up in the middle of the day—especially not with a boy. If Judah's cousin, Samuel, is working the security desk, he might let us into the garden. I call out, "You coming, or what?" Peter catches up and follows me over to the garden.

We don't say anything to one another until we reach the whispering bench. I force myself to look Peter in the eye as I tell him my story.

"I came here last June—alone. I snuck in late at night and when I saw those ghosts, I was terrified." I stop and try to figure out what's going through Peter's mind. But Peter's wearing his poker face, so I decide I'd better just go on.

"I made a wish and got sent back to Brooklyn. But not this Brooklyn. I went back in time, Peter. To 1863."

Peter doesn't laugh at me. He doesn't even blink. He just stares at me for a real long time, then he lets all his breath out in a long, low whistle. "And Judah went back with you?"

I nod and watch the wind chase fallen leaves around the fountain. "It took a long time for us to find each other, though. He was captured by slave catchers and taken to the deep South. He had to run for his life— more than once." I stop and remember the night Judah told me he'd killed a man. "It wasn't easy, but he made it back to Brooklyn. I found him in Weeksville. We were going to go away together..."

For the first time, Peter looks confused. "Go away? Where?"

"Liberia. Judah wanted us to go to Africa. I was going to go with him, but then during the draft riots I got stabbed just as I made another wish."

"And that's what sent you back here?"

"I think so."

"And Judah's still there."

I nod and press my lips together so I won't start to cry again.

Peter takes a deep breath and then blows the air out in a sharp whistle. "This is deep—real deep. What are you going to do?"

"Go back. I have to. And—I want to. It's hard being in this world—I feel so out of place, like nobody understands me. Only Judah knows how I feel, and he's not here. He's there."

"So what—you can just, like, make a wish and move through time?"

I shake my head and stare at the fountain that has disappointed me over and over again. "I've been here just about every day since I got back. I've tried everything I can think of, but...I don't know. I think I must need...something different. Something new."

Peter nudges my bag full of candles, herbs, and scented oils. "That's what this stuff is for?" When I nod, Peter reaches into the bag and pulls out the packet containing the special bath herbs. "I wondered what you were doing in Paradi."

"What?"

"Paradi—the botánica where you bought all this stuff."

"I thought that place was called Paradise."

"It is. Or 'paradi' in Kreyol."

"Kreyol?"

Peter nods. "That place is owned by Haitians, though plenty of Dominincans shop there, too."

I look at Peter as if we're meeting for the first time. "Are you—I mean, I never knew...you're Haitian?"

"Yeah. So?"

There's an edge in Peter's voice so I tread carefully. "It's just— you don't have a French name. Peter Raymond doesn't sound French to me."

Peter relaxes and even smiles at me. "Your name isn't what makes you Haitian. There are plenty of Haitians who have Russian or even Polish names."

"Really? I didn't know that." I pause, then decide it's safe to go on. I can't afford to miss out on this opportunity. "I've been reading these books I got from the library. Some of them talk about Haiti…" I reach into my book bag and pull out the book of spells. Peter looks at the cover and busts out laughing. Warm blood flushes my face but this time it's because I am embarrassed. "I — I'm looking for…"

"'Black magic,'" Peter says with a sneer. "Right?"

"No!"

I take a moment and wonder why calling magic "black" makes it seem dirty or sinister. "I just need a way to make it happen again. I have to go back in time — "

"And you think you can just light some candles and cast a spell? This book is a load of crap."

"How can you say that? You haven't even read it."

"I don't have to — I know what you Americans think about 'voodoo.'" Peter makes a sound of disgust. "It's Vodou. VO — DOU."

I listen to how Peter pronounces the word, with the hard O and emphasis on the second syllable. I make a mental note to say it like he does from now on. But then Peter sucks his teeth and goes on.

"Americans are so stupid. To you, 'voodoo' means nothing more than sticking a bunch of pins into a stupid doll. You believe everything you see in the movies."

I cut my eyes at Peter and suddenly realize why he and Judah are such good friends: they both love to look down on Americans. "Well, how are we supposed to find out more if everything you do is such a big secret?"

Peter practically snarls at me. "Just because you're American doesn't mean you get to know everything! You weren't interested in my culture before. You're only curious now because you need something. Vodou is a religion, Genna. It's not something you play around with whenever you're desperate or bored."

I look away, ashamed. He's got me there. And maybe if I had my own religion, my own culture, I wouldn't have to look so hard for the magic I need. "I didn't mean any disrespect, Peter — for real."

It takes a minute for Peter to cool down. "I didn't mean to take your head off. I guess I'm just used to playing defense when it comes to my culture. Kids at school made fun of me because I couldn't speak English when I first got here. They called me 'dirty' and asked me when I 'got off the boat,' like that's the only way Haitians could come to this country. And half of them were immigrants, too!"

I never said anything like that to anyone, but I feel guilty just the same because I've definitely heard other kids saying stuff like that. Even though it makes no sense, Black kids can be really cruel — even to kids who look just like them. Judah used to get teased because of his locks, Rashidah gets harassed because she's Muslim. Light-skinned versus dark-skinned. Dominicans versus Puerto Ricans. And the African kids — forget about it. Everyone's got a put down for everyone else. That's just how it is in the 'hood.

Peter goes on. "Haiti was the first Black republic in the world, but no one ever talks about that. American kids don't know their own history, so why should they know about mine?"

I think of beady-eyed Mr. Collins and wonder if he knows anything about Haitian history. If he does, he sure never taught us about it.

I figure I've blown it with Peter but he surprises me by saying, "Listen — if you're serious about this..."

"I am!" I cry, startling several starlings drinking at the fountain. Then I pull myself together and say, "I've never been so serious about anything in my whole life."

Peter's face looks like he's fighting something inside himself. Finally he says, "Maybe you should talk to my uncle."

"Because he's got 'connections'?"

Peter battles something inside himself once more, and then looks straight at me and says, "Because he's a oungan."

"A—what?"

Peter lifts his chin to show his pride. "My uncle's a Vodou priest."

Judah

29.

Since the riots, a lot of folks are camping out in the woods, staying out of sight until they figure out what to do next. Some folks are heading to Canada, others are thinking about heading west. Me, I don't really have a destination. For now, I just need to find a job and keep a roof over my head. Be still long enough to find the compass that points toward home.

Weeksville's not a very big place, but people here got real big hearts. They see or hear of a Black person in trouble, and they'll do whatever they can to help. Soon as I reach the outskirts of Weeksville, this lady calls to me from her front porch and asks if I want something to eat. I haven't eaten since noon the day before, so I'm feeling pretty empty inside. Plus I spent the night in the woods. It wasn't easy getting to Weeksville after the riot, not when I was trying to keep off the road. Hard to see where you're going when it's pitch black outside, and there are no street lamps to light the way. So I went into the brush and found a fallen tree to rest by—moss and dead leaves made the ground soft enough to sleep on, but none of us got any rest last night. I wasn't alone, but I didn't exactly have company either. I could just tell there were people around me—Black people running from the chaos downtown. We didn't speak to each other, and we didn't dare light a fire to keep ourselves warm. We just huddled there in the dark, waiting for daylight to come. Soon as the sky turned a little bit grey, I got up and got moving.

"You hungry, son?"

The sun is high in the sky by now, so I put my hand up to shield my eyes. I'm not sure, but it looks like a White woman. A tall White woman with a broom, sweeping the dust off her front porch. But this is Weeksville, and as far as I know, no White people live around here. I squint my eyes and try to get a closer look at her face. There are some Black people who can "pass" for White. In Jamaica we had people like that, too. I guess I must seem either deaf or stupid, because the woman sets her broom against the wall of the house and comes down the steps toward me.

"I got biscuits just come out the oven. And hot coffee, too." She reaches the fence that separates her yard from the road, and puts her hand on the gate latch. "Surely you have time for a quick bite to eat." She pauses and I realize she is as curious about me as I am about her. Her grey eyes sweep over me quickly. "You got people here, or you just passing through?"

Before I can answer, she opens the gate and waits for me to enter the yard. I take a quick look at my rumpled clothes and try to brush off some of the dirt and twigs that stuck to me overnight.

"Never mind that," she says, and puts a hand on my arm to pull me inside. She closes the gate and then points to the right side of her house. "There's a pump back there. You can wash up while I get your breakfast ready. You slept in the woods last night."

This is an observation and not a question. I can tell by the flat sound of her voice, and the way she turns and goes up the front steps without waiting for a reply. But I answer her just the same. "Yes, ma'am."

She turns on the porch and looks at me then. I'm not sure why she stares at me like that, but I start to feel kind of ashamed. Despite her grey eyes, thin lips, and pale skin, something tells me this woman is one of us. But Black or White, I don't like taking charity from anyone.

"We're not that formal around here. My name is Corina Claxton, but most folks call me Cora. What's your name?"

"Judah."

"Judah." She says it softly, like she is remembering something or someone else. "Go on and wash up, Judah. I'll bring your food out in a minute."

Once again, she doesn't wait for a reply. I say "thank you" to her back as she goes in the front door. Then I go behind the house and try to clean myself up at the pump.

I am still washing the sweat and grime off my face and hands when the back door opens. I blink the cold water out of my eyes and accept a cloth from a younger, browner, shyer version of the woman I met out front. I thank her for the cloth, and use it to dry myself off. The girl tries not to stare at me, but she is clearly as curious as her mother. Though she's tall, I figure the girl can't be more than thirteen or fourteen years old.

"Is Mrs. Claxton your mother?"

She nods quickly, then takes back the cloth and runs inside the house. I stand by the back door and wait. The yard is tidy, and looks as though it has been swept clean, like the front porch. An outhouse stands in one corner of the yard, and a large shed stands in the other. Through its open door I can see carpentry tools hanging on the wall of the shed, but no one is working there now. I notice an axe and several hunks of wood a few feet away from the house. When Mrs. Claxton appears with my breakfast, I offer to chop the wood for her.

"That's Felix's job," she tells me before handing me a plate that holds three buttered biscuits, a hunk of cheese, and several slices of ham. Her daughter stands beside her holding a tin mug filled with steaming black coffee. "Get something in your belly first. Then you can worry about that wood."

"Yes, ma'am." I take the plate from her and bite into the first hot biscuit. I try not to wolf down my food, but those biscuits taste so good! I'm tempted to eat the ham, too, but instead explain that I don't eat pork. Mrs. Claxton and her daughter stand right there and watch me eat. Every so often the mother nudges her daughter, and the girl offers me the mug of coffee. I take a sip, thank her, and then hand her back the mug. We continue this way until all the cheese and biscuits are gone.

I wipe the crumbs from my mouth and thank Mrs. Claxton for the food. For the first time, she smiles at me. "You're welcome, Judah. This is my daughter, Megda. Felix is her twin brother, but he's made himself scarce right now. Mr. Claxton went into town, but he should be back before too long."

I say hello to Megda, then I nod at the wood. "Can I chop that for you now?"

"Give your belly a moment to settle. Were you coming from Manhattan?"

"No, ma'am. Brooklyn. Downtown."

She frowns and looks away from me. "I hear there was trouble last night."

"Yes, ma'am." I think about Genna and the knife slides a bit deeper into my heart.

Mrs. Claxton watches me closely with her strange grey eyes. "You came to Weeksville alone?"

"Yes, ma'am."

She stares at me a moment longer, then drops her eyes, saddened but satisfied. "But you weren't alone last night." Again, she says this as though she already knows it to be true. This time I look away, and hope I won't have to answer any more questions. My fingers start to itch, and I look over at the axe, wishing I had something to do—somewhere to pour the anger I feel bubbling inside of me.

Mrs. Claxton hands the plate and mug to her daughter, who takes the dishes and goes inside. Then she looks at me and wipes her hands on her apron as if to say, "We're done with that conversation." I quietly smother a sigh of relief and take a step towards the woodpile.

"Do as much as you like," Mrs. Claxton says before opening the back door of her house. "If you get tired, there's a pallet in that shed over there. Get some rest before you move on."

I nod and grab hold of the axe. I set the first hunk of wood on the old tree stump and swing the axe high above my head. Then I take a deep breath and bring it down with all the strength I have. Mrs. Claxton watches the two halves fall to the ground, then turns and goes inside.

I keep going until all the wood by the shed has been chopped. Then I carry it over to the back door, and stack the smaller pieces along the wall. Mrs. Claxton sends Megda out with a mug of water. I drink it thirstily, and realize my shirt is soaked through with sweat.

"Want some soap?" Megda is trying to be polite, but I know she is trying to tell me that I need to wash up again. "I think you're about the same size as Felix. Mama?" Megda dashes inside and gets her mother's permission before returning with a bar of soap and a dry cloth. "Here, use these. I'll get you a clean shirt to put on once you're done bathing."

Mrs. Claxton comes back out and smiles approvingly at her daughter. To me she says, "Here, give me that shirt. I can put it to soak with the other clothes. You can come back for it tomorrow."

I pause and look around the yard. There is nowhere to change except the outhouse. Mrs. Claxton only laughs at me. "Boy, please. Don't tell me you're shy? Hurry up and give me that filthy shirt so you can get yourself cleaned up." She holds her hand out and waits for me to pass her my shirt.

I keep my eyes on the ground and slowly undo the buttons. Then I peel the shirt off and give it to her. I hope she will turn and go inside, but instead she watches me walk over to the water pump. Mrs. Claxton doesn't make a sound when she sees the scars, but I can feel her piercing grey eyes on my back. I splash water on my chest and arms and rub the bar of soap into a lather.

Mrs. Claxton finally senses my embarrassment and looks away. She stands by the door, her back turned to give me some privacy. "You didn't start off in Brooklyn then."

I rub the soap over my upper body, and then use the tin cup I drank out of to pour clean water over myself. "No, ma'am." I pick up the cloth Megda gave me and dry myself off. The hot summer sun beats down on my back, drying the ridged skin there.

"Well. If you need a place to stay, you're welcome to stop here for a while, Judah. You don't have to run any more."

I want to be polite and agree with Mrs. Claxton, but we both know there are still a lot of things for Black people to run from in this country.

"Will this do, Mama?" Megda appears at the back door holding one of her brother's shirts. Mrs. Claxton takes the shirt and shoos her daughter back inside. She hands it to me, then turns around again so I can dress in private.

"The person you lost last night—" Mrs. Claxton pauses to see if I will finish her sentence.

Without any hesitation, I slip back into the old lie Genna and I had used before. "My sister."

Mrs. Claxton nods once and checks to see that I am dressed before turning around to face me. "She wasn't hurt? I mean, I hope she..."

"We got separated during the riot. I thought I might find her here." I don't like lying to Mrs. Claxton, so I am relieved when a loud voice interrupts our conversation.

"Felix!"

A tall, dark-skinned man hollers angrily as he opens the front gate and strides across the yard. Megda hears her father's voice and slips back outside to stand next to her mother.

"He's not here, Lionel." Mrs. Claxton looks happy to see her husband, but she also anticipates his angry response.

"Well, where is that blasted boy? That son of yours has a knack for disappearing whenever there's work to be done."

"Come inside and sit down, Lionel, there's a fresh pot of coffee on the stove. I'm sure Felix will turn up before long."

"I can't stay, Cora. We need to clear a camp in the woods. Can't leave those poor folks out there with no shelter at night but the stars. Who's this?"

Before Mrs. Claxton can respond, I step forward and introduce myself. "My name is Judah. I'll help set up the camp." Mr. Claxton looks at me like I just insulted him. I take a step back and try again. "I mean, I'd like to help any way I can." I glance at Mrs. Claxton and add, "Sir."

Mr. Claxton's face relaxes a bit, but he still looks mighty stern. He sizes me up and practically barks, "Well, can you swing an axe?"

To my surprise, Megda pipes up. "He just chopped all that wood, Papa."

Mr. Claxton surveys the work I have done and seems satisfied. His face doesn't soften, but his voice becomes more civil. "Come with me, then, if you've a mind to. We can use all the hands we can get." He goes to the shed, takes another axe down from the wall and hands it to me. He turns briefly to his wife before heading out of the yard. "When that boy shows up, you tell him to wait here for me. I'll deal with him when I get back."

Mrs. Claxton nods solemnly, then she and Megda follow us to the front gate and watch us walk away down the road.

Judah

30.

I've been living with the Claxtons for nearly a month now. They're good people, and they treat me like I'm part of their family. Mrs. Claxton is especially nice to me. She says I remind her of her twin brother. I look at Mrs. Claxton, and she's practically White—except for the littlest bit of curl at the roots of her brown hair. I look into her grey eyes, and I don't see myself. But Mrs. Claxton says she and her brother were "twins on the inside" and like night and day on the outside, so maybe I do look like him. Her kids, Felix and Megda, are the exact opposite. They look identical, except Felix has his mother's grey eyes, and Megda's are brown like her father's. Megda is sweet, and quiet, and shy, but Felix—that boy's a mess. His mother says, "Felix doesn't wait for trouble to come, he brews it up himself." Mrs. Claxton always laughs when she says things like that, but I can tell she wishes Felix would straighten himself out.

That might be one reason why they asked me to stick around. I think Mr. and Mrs. Claxton are hoping I'll be a good influence on their son. Mrs. Claxton's always nagging Felix about doing his chores and helping his father out back. Mr. Claxton's a master carpenter—he can make anything out of wood. But Mr. Claxton is also no joke—I wouldn't cross him if he were my dad. "Spare the rod, spoil the child"—that's what he believes. But Felix doesn't seem to care. He gets the strap at least once a week, but it doesn't seem to do any good. Back home we used to say, "You don't listen, you'll feel." Felix is definitely hard of hearing.

In some ways, Mrs. Claxton reminds me of my Aunt Marcia. She's kind of strict and she doesn't smile all that often, but she sure knows what she believes. She can quote the Bible from back to front, and I think she likes that I know a little Scripture, too. I haven't told anyone that I'm Rastafari. I'm trying to let my locks grow back, and that means my hair doesn't look so neat. I can wear a cap when I'm working outdoors, but inside it's hats off. Mrs. Claxton offered to cut my hair for me, but I told her I needed to let it grow.

"You're a nice-looking boy, Judah. No need to have all that hair on your head. If you let it grow much longer, you won't ever get a comb through it." I just smile and keep on making up my bed out in the tool shed. The Claxtons told me I could share a room with Felix, but I prefer being on my own.

Mrs. Claxton watches me lay out the blankets, then pushes me out of the way and remakes the bed herself. "There. You sure you're comfortable out here?"

"Yes, ma'am. I appreciate you and Mr. Claxton letting me stay on a while."

"Well, we enjoy having you here, Judah. You're so industrious and well-mannered. And Lionel certainly appreciates all the help you've given him this month. He always hoped Felix would take an interest in his trade, but Felix isn't one for working with his hands."

I want to tell Mrs. Claxton that Felix isn't one for working, period. Every day he comes out back and tells me how he's going to run away and join the Union Army. Somehow he got his hands on an old hunting rifle, and Felix goes out in the woods firing at anything that moves. I told Felix he ought to finish up with school and then learn a trade — if not carpentry, then something else. Joining the army won't get him nothing but killed.

Mrs. Claxton watches me. I know she knows I'm keeping something in. But like my Aunt Marcia, Mrs. Claxton doesn't try to make me talk. She knows I'll say what I have to say when I'm ready.

"You must think about her a lot, your sister."

I didn't expect to talk about Genna tonight. My heart speeds up a bit, but I just sit down on the pallet and nod once.

"Maybe that's why you don't want to cut your hair. Are you worried she might not recognize you?"

Genna would know me no matter what. She found me before, when I was dying of fever. She recognized me then, even though my locks were gone. I can't tell Mrs. Claxton these things, but I have to tell her something.

"Where I come from, people don't cut their hair."

Mrs. Claxton narrows her eyes and frowns at me. "Ever?" she finally asks.

I shake my head and wonder if it's wise to share this with her. But I feel like I can't be my whole self unless I'm honest about who I am. "It says in Leviticus that men should never cut their hair. Where I come from, there are people called Rastafarians. I'm one of those people."

"Rastafarian? Is that—are you—*African*?"

"Yes, ma'am. I was born in Jamaica, but my people are from Africa. There are Rastafarians all over the world, but one day we will return to Zion—Africa, the land of our fathers." I pause and try to decide what else it's safe to say. "When I came to America, they cut my dreadlocks—I had long hair, it hung like ropes down my back—but they cut it all off. They said I was a heathen. An animal."

Mrs. Claxton glances at the bible I keep next to my bed. The African Civilization Society has crates of bibles ready to send to Africa, but lately they've been giving them out to the folks who had to flee Manhattan during the riots. I asked for one, and I usually read it at night before the sun goes down.

"You're not a heathen, Judah. Those monsters who walk around pretending to love God—they're the real heathens. One day it'll all be set to rights. One day…" Mrs. Claxton wraps her shawl around her shoulders and stares off into space. She does that a lot when she's talking to me. I wonder about her story—the things she must keep inside. She mentions her brother once in a while, but she never says where he is or why they aren't together. I appreciate that Mrs. Claxton never tries to make me talk, so I try to do the same for her. I figure if she wants to tell me something, she will.

"You're a devoted brother, Judah. I'm sure you'll find your sister someday soon. Our people are still so frightened, there's so much confusion in the city right now—in the entire country, really. But you mustn't blame yourself for what happened. I know you did everything you could to keep her with you."

Did I? I would have done anything for Genna. But in the end, what I did wasn't enough. She left me anyway.

Mrs. Claxton's voice grows quiet as the last rays of sunlight streak the sky red. "You remind me of my brother, Judah. I'm sure I've told you that before."

I nod, and Mrs. Claxton goes on. In the dim evening light, she looks younger and smaller, like a girl her daughter's age.

"His name was Anthony. He was a lot like you—strong-willed, and independent, but loving and kind. Our father—our master—told our mother he would free her when he died. But she made him promise instead to set her children free. He agreed, but then just before he died he changed his mind and said only one of us could leave. I wanted Anthony to go, but Mama said it was best for me to leave instead. Anthony said he was already planning to run away, and that he'd wait until I reached the North, then he'd come and join me. Then we'd work and save enough money to buy Mama so our whole family could be free." Mrs. Claxton stopped and looked down at me. Her eyes were dry, but very dark.

"I know he must be dead by now. It's been eighteen years since I left Georgia. If he were alive, Anthony would have found me by now."

I look up at Mrs. Claxton and wonder what I should say. She's probably right. Her brother probably is dead. As much as I've seen of the cruelty of this world, I doubt Anthony ever made it out of the South. But then I remember: *I* made it. It wasn't easy, and there was a price to pay.

But in the end, I found Genna. It was worth it, in the end.

"The one thing I know about this world, Mrs. Claxton, is that anything's possible. Your brother could still be out there. He could be somewhere waiting for you, the same way I'm here waiting for Genna. Don't give up on him, Mrs. Claxton. Don't give up hope—not yet."

I say this to Mrs. Claxton, but I also say it to myself. I have been living here in Weeksville for almost a month. And in that time I have kept myself busy—I've helped build a camp for the refugees from Manhattan, and I've helped distribute blankets and food to the others who come here for help. I've also become a kind of apprentice to Mr. Claxton. He's teaching me how to make furniture using the tools in his shop. But I haven't done anything yet to find a way back to Genna. And maybe I'm a fool to wait for her to come back to me. Maybe Genna's moved on with her life—and maybe I need to move on with mine.

Mrs. Claxton reaches out and gently touches the coarse, uncombed tufts of my hair. She opens her mouth to say something, but then closes her lips and just smiles at me instead. The last bit of sunlight has left the sky. It is too dark to read now, so I pull back the covers and get ready for bed.

Mrs. Claxton turns to go. "I've taken up all your reading time," she says apologetically. "I'll send Felix out with a lantern. You can keep it out here. The nights will be getting longer from now on."

"Thank you. Good night, Mrs. Claxton."

"Goodnight, Judah," she says quietly. Then she heads back to the house.

I don't much feel like reading tonight, which is good because it turns out Felix feels like talking. Within a few minutes he crashes out the back door, making sure to slam it nice and loud so all the chickens in the coop wake up. With the lantern swinging precariously on his index finger, Felix whistles his way through the dark and over to the shed.

"Hey-ah, Judah. Ma said you needed some light." Felix tosses the lantern up in the air, and only just catches it before it crashes to the ground.

"You trying to burn the place down?" Felix takes a look at my face and wipes the grin off his own. I take the lantern from him and set it on the ground by my bed. I turn the flame down low, so I won't waste the expensive kerosene. "You know what a loose cannon is, Felix?"

"'Course, everyone knows what that is."

"You really think the Union Army wants a loose cannon in its ranks?"

These days the only way to get through to Felix is to talk about the Union Army. At fourteen, Felix is too young to enlist but he's tall like his father and if things keep going badly for the North, they just might be willing to sign up an eager teenager. Of course, right now in New York State Black men aren't even allowed to enlist. But there are rumors in Weeksville that that might be about to change.

Felix doesn't answer my question. He just sulks and kicks at the curly wood shavings scattered on the floor of the shed. "Aw, Judah. You sound just like Pa. How come you got to be so serious all the time? You act like an old man."

"And you act like a young fool. Why are you in such a hurry to get your head blown off? Why can't you just finish up your last year of school and help your father out in his shop? It would mean a lot to your mother, you know."

Felix kicks another shaving out of the way and squats down next to my bed. "I ain't got time to be sitting around some stupid classroom with a bunch of little kids. I already know how to read and write. I can do sums, and I know all I need to know about geography. They're making history out there, Judah! Colored soldiers are *fighting*—with guns and bayonets! They're killing White men, instead of waiting for the crackers to come and kill them."

I roll up the extra blanket Mrs. Claxton gave me and tuck it under my head. We're still in the middle of 1863. The Civil War won't be over until 1865. I look at Felix with his glossy brown curls, his freckles, and his babysoft skin. He has the faintest trace of a moustache above his upper lip, but Felix is still a boy. I sigh and roll over on my side, hoping Felix will take the hint and leave me alone. "Wars go on for years, Felix. Trust me—the army will wait for you."

Felix doesn't respond, but after a while I can hear him unfolding some kind of paper. "Psst, hey Judah. Judah—you want some of this?"

I know I shouldn't, but I look over my shoulder at the crumpled piece of paper Felix is holding out to me. On it are several green buds that look a lot like marijuana. I sit up quickly and inspect the paper in Felix's hand. "Where'd you get that?"

Felix laughs and offers it to me once again. I look up to see if any lights are on in the house, then I pick up a bud and sniff it. The stuff is genuine. Felix watches me, his eyes shining with anticipation. "Let's go out to the field and smoke it. I got a pipe we can use."

"You grew this?"

"Naw, man. That old Indian woman who lives out in the woods. She grows all kinds of wild stuff."

"You bought it from her? What did it cost?"

Felix laughs again and looks smug. "Didn't cost me a penny. You coming?"

Felix stands up and waits for me. I haven't smoked ganja in a real long time, and I could really use something right now to help me see my way forward in this world. But something about Felix's story doesn't sound right.

"How'd you find out about this woman?"

Felix sighs impatiently. "Everyone knows about old Hetty. She's crazy as a loon, but folks go see her sometimes if they get sick and can't afford to call for the doctor."

"So if she grew it and you've got it, but it didn't cost you a penny— how'd you get it? You *steal* it?"

"Man, why you so uptight? All *I* asked was, you want some? Why you got to ask me all these stupid questions? She ain't gonna miss it, alright?"

I look at Felix and hope he can see the disgust I feel right now. "Get out of here, Felix. And take this stuff with you." I turn out the lamp, and turn over on my side. Felix curses under his breath as he stumbles out of the dark shed. He makes sure to slam the back door real loud when he goes inside the house.

I close my eyes and make a list in my mind of the things I need to do. I figure I have a few options. I could stay here in Weeksville, or I could try to get to Africa. The African Civilization Society is still looking for volunteers to go to Liberia. I could be like Felix, and wait for my chance to fight in the Union army. I could head north to Canada, or I could try to find a ship that would take me back to Jamaica. But until the war is over, it won't be safe to try to head south. And I don't know anyone in Canada or Jamaica.

I like the Claxtons, and I wouldn't mind staying here for a little while longer. But if I do stay here, they'll expect me to be a role model for Felix. He thinks I act like an old man, and around here maybe I do. Maybe everything I've been through has made me forget what it's like to have fun, to just kick back and relax. My birthday's at the end of October—I would turn eighteen if I were back in my own world. But I feel a whole lot older here.

It was hard turning down that herb tonight, and I have to admit that finding Hetty is also on my list of things to do. But I have to be careful what I do around here. It's hard to keep secrets in a small place like Weeksville. Everybody's on edge because of the riot, and folks are keeping their eyes peeled for any sign of trouble. And even though there aren't any telephones yet, news—good or bad—spreads like wildfire just by word of mouth. I don't want to do anything that might make trouble for the Claxtons. They've got enough to worry about with their own son. Felix isn't a bad kid, and I know what it's like when you're trying to act like a man and everyone still treats you like a boy. Every Black man in this world knows just how bad that feels.

Genna

31.

Peter meets me after school and takes me over to his uncle's place. My insides are twisting a bit, but Peter seems even more nervous than me. He's talking nonstop, which isn't like him at all. I just nod so he thinks I'm listening, but mostly I'm thinking about Judah and how happy he'll be when I come back to him.

"My uncle's pretty cool—I mean, he's a doctor and everything, but he's really down to earth and easy to talk to. Plus he's traveled a lot— he even studied at the Sorbonne! Lots of Haitians go to France for their education—well, those who can afford it. We won our independence two hundred years ago, but that colonial tie is still strong. I've got an aunt who lives in Paris, and a few cousins in Montreal. Most Haitians speak Kreyol, but some also speak French. I'm not fluent, but I can get by. Right now I'm taking Spanish—Mrs. Freeman says foreign languages strengthen your college applications. What about you?"

This time a nod won't do so I stammer out a real response. "Yeah—I mean, no. She told me that, too, but..."

"I guess you speak Spanish at home, huh?"

I shake my head and hope Peter won't ask me to explain why. Fortunately, just at that moment we arrive at his uncle's place. It's one of about five brownstones tucked in between two apartment buildings. A small white marble sign hangs from a post announcing the office of Dr. S. Celestin. Peter opens the black iron gate for me, and I follow the stone path that leads to a door under the front stoop. Peter comes up behind me and presses a buzzer on the wall. The intercom crackles with static, and Peter says loudly, "Se mwen." He puts his hand on the knob and waits for the buzz that unlocks the door.

I let Peter go in first. Now that we're here, my stomach's starting to do back flips. I'm not sure what to expect. I'm already surprised to find a Voduo priest working out of a brownstone. I'd never admit it to Peter, but I did think there might be some chickens on the scene. That's what it's like in the movies.

Peter leads me down a short dim hallway and into a softly lit waiting room. Tiny lights hang like stars from two tracks that run along the ceiling. Half a dozen older women are seated on chairs that line the exposed brick walls. Peter greets them, then leans in and says something to the young receptionist. I can't tell if he's speaking Kreyol or French. She keeps her eyes focused on the computer screen then nods once and picks up the phone to call her boss.

I look around for an empty chair. The women here look like the same ones I see doing their shopping on Nostrand Avenue on Saturday morning. Flipping through popular magazines, they look bored and impatient, not crazed or possessed. Inside I admit to myself that I'm a little disappointed to find nothing out of the ordinary here.

Before I can sit down, Peter says, "Come on." The receptionist lets us into Dr. Celestin's office then closes the door behind us. I follow Peter's lead and sit in one of the empty chairs facing a large glass desk. Everything on the desk's tidy surface is chrome. I see my distorted reflection everywhere.

"Where's your uncle?" I ask Peter.

"He's just finishing up with a client. He'll be in soon."

Peter sits back and gets comfortable in the black leather chair. I sit back, too, and wonder why Peter said "client" instead of "patient." I lean forward and take one of the business cards stacked neatly in a chrome holder: Dr. Serge Celestin.

There is a door in one corner of the room. Just as I am wondering where it leads, a small, chocolate-colored man in a white coat opens the door and enters the office. He smiles first at Peter, then at me. "Bonjou, Ti Piè," he says to Peter before sitting in the black leather chair behind his desk.

"Bonjou, tonton," Peter replies. "This is my friend, Genna."

"Hello, Genna." Dr. Celestin's accent doesn't disappear the way Peter's does when he speaks English.

I try to say hello but only a squeaky sound comes out of my mouth, so I just smile and nod instead. Dr. Celestin folds his hands together and smiles warmly at me. "How may I assist you today?"

I glance at Peter and wonder what he's told his uncle about "my problem." But Peter's looking at the chrome clock on the wall like it's more interesting than anything I have to say. I take a deep breath and begin. "I have a friend."

Dr. Celestin nods. "Not my nephew."

I shake my head. "No, but Peter knows him, too. His name's Judah."

Peter looks at me now, daring me to tell his uncle the same bizarre story I have told him. "Judah is...gone. And I need to find a way to get him back. To get back to him, I mean."

Dr. Celestin frowns and looks confused. "I'm sorry, Genna, but I don't see how I can help you. I am a chiropractor."

He points to the model spine dangling near his desk and my face flushes with heat. Is this some kind of joke? The doctor and I turn to Peter. Dr. Celestin's voice loses some of its warmth as he switches from English to Kreyol.

"Sak fè ou di'l?"

Peter drops his eyes and mumbles at the floor. "I told her you might be able to help her."

Dr. Celestin turns his eyes on me even though he's still talking to Peter. "Li pa yonn nan nou."

"Mwen konnen, men...li diferan," Peter says. "She's different."

Dr. Celestin looks at me, his eyes searching my face for the difference his nephew claims to see in me.

I self-consciously reach for the scratches that hold his gaze. "I had an accident," I explain. He makes a strange sideways nod and I rush on to fill the uncomfortable space that has opened between us. "I'm here because Peter said you might be able to help me. I know this will sound crazy, but last summer I—I went back in time. And Judah did, too. Then I came back and left Judah behind—I didn't mean to, but that's what happened. And now I'm trying to get back to him. I need to be *there*, not here."

Peter's uncle stares at me without blinking or saying a word. With his eyes still fixed on my face he asks Peter, "Ou kwè l?"

Peter sighs, then runs his hand over his face as if to wipe away his own doubts. "They both went missing in June. Now she's back and he's not." Peter pauses then adds, "I believe her."

Dr. Celestin unlocks his graceful fingers and picks up a silver pen. He turns it between his hands for a moment. "You say you went back in time."

"Yes, sir."

"Where did you go exactly?"

"I was still in Brooklyn, but it was 1863."

"And how did this…journey come about?"

"I was in the botanic garden—it was late at night, and I wasn't supposed to be there, but I'd had a fight with my mother. She hit me, and I walked out."

"And this fight was about your friend, Judah?"

I nod and look at my hands twisting nervously in my lap. "I snuck into the garden and went to my favorite fountain. I was alone, but then I heard voices…" I stop and wait to see how Dr. Celestin will react, but the expression on his face doesn't change.

"What did they say, these voices?"

I frown and try to remember. That moment feels like it happened a lifetime ago. "They told me to run, to hide, to be careful. To keep going." I pause, wondering if I should tell him about the ghosts.

Dr. Celestin must know I'm holding back because he asks, "And as these voices spoke to you, what did you see?"

"Just a little boy, at first. He said, 'Don't leave me.'" I clear my throat and try to blink back the tears gathering in my eyes. "Then I saw a woman. She was dressed in old-fashioned clothes. They all were."

"These ghosts—did they touch you?"

I start to shake my head then stop. "I don't know. They vanished and then I saw a penny on the ground. I wanted to make a wish in the fountain but something wasn't right—the penny was too heavy, and the air was cold and...thick. And then security showed up and the voices returned and I could feel hands tugging at my body. Then someone fired a gun. I felt a flash of pain..." I shrug. None of it makes any sense. "Then everything went dark."

Dr. Celestin watches me for a moment, then hands me a box of tissues. I take one and whisper "thank you" before wiping away the salty tears that are stinging my scratched face.

"Had you indeed been shot?"

"No. When I woke up I was in an ash dump—that's what the garden used to be. I was on my stomach and it was snowing but my back was on fire. I'd been beaten by someone...but I couldn't remember what had happened to me, or why. All I felt was the pain." I shudder at the memory of being tied to the bed at the orphanage, my dress cut away from my bloody, blistered skin. "I still have the scars on my back." I will show them to him if he asks me to. He's a doctor—he knows my body can't lie.

But Dr. Celestin doesn't ask for proof. He simply sets the silver pen down on the desk, folds his hands once more, and looks at me. "It is possible the ancestors summoned you."

"The ancestors?"

"Yes."

"You mean those ghosts were—they were related to me?"

"It is possible, yes."

"But...then how did I come back? And why didn't Judah come, too?

"Perhaps his work there is not yet done."

A hundred other questions flood my mind but I keep my mouth shut. Work? It's hard to believe Judah and I were "on assignment" in the past. If our ancestors needed something, why didn't they tell us what it was? And why did they make us suffer so much?

Dr. Celestin glances at the clock on the wall. "I do not wish to be rude, but I'm afraid I have other patients to see."

Peter stands up but I'm not ready to leave yet. I haven't got what I came here for. "So how do I get back to Judah? I mean, is there a way to contact my ancestors — to make them pull me back in time again?"

"The ancestors inhabit the spirit world, Genna. You cannot *make* them do anything."

Desperation loosens my tongue. "I know — I read that online. You have to make an offering first, right? Peter says that's what you do." I reach down and force my trembling hands to unzip my book bag. "You probably think I don't know anything about Vodou. But I've been doing some research," I say as I pull the books out one by one and set them on the edge of his desk.

Dr. Celestin only glances at the different covers, but his disdain is obvious — *A Beginner's Guide to Black Magic*, *The Book of Vodoo Rituals*, and *Doktor John's Book of Spells & Curses*. Peter looks like he wishes he could sink through the floor. For a moment I wish I could, too. But I don't have time to be embarrassed by my own ignorance. I am here because I need information.

Dr. Celestin seems to read my mind because he clears his throat and says, "The answers you seek cannot be found in any book, Genna."

I will myself not to cry as I pull the books onto my lap. "But…I don't know where else to look."

For just a moment, Dr. Celestin looks at me the way my father used to when I was a child. There is tenderness in his eyes, but I don't want him to pity me. I want him to tell me how to reach Judah. Instead Dr. Celestin softens his voice and says, "Sometimes we search outside ourselves for what is already within."

What's that supposed to mean? It sounds like something you'd find inside a fortune cookie. Anger starts bubbling up my throat. I look at Peter but he is steadily watching the floor.

"I'm sorry," Dr. Celestin says as he pushes his chair back from the desk and stands. "I'm afraid I cannot help you."

"But...I can pay you—I have money!"

"Genna—"

Peter tries to shut me up but my mouth fills with more and more words. Don't turn me away. Please don't turn me away...

"You help people—I know you do. Why won't you help me? Is it because I'm American?"

A sad smile crosses his face as Dr. Celestin prepares to show us the door. "No, Genna. I cannot help you because you lack the proper konesans."

"Connay—what? What's that? I'll get it—whatever it is, I'll get it!"

Peter scowls but accepts his role as translator. "Konesans means knowledge, Genna. It's not something you can buy at the botánica."

Dr. Celestin looks sad and sympathetic at the same time. "The Power you seek is reserved for those who truly believe and are willing to serve. There are tools you must use, and it takes time to learn how to handle them with respect. Initiation is required, and only a few are chosen."

Suddenly I am on my feet. The books tumble to the floor and my voice hits the roof. "I don't have time! And I've already been chosen—you said so yourself. The ghosts in the garden that night—they spoke to *me*, they picked *me*!"

Peter snatches up the books I just dropped and then grabs me by the arm. "Let's go—*now*."

He tries to drag me toward the door but I yank my arm away and stoop down to grab my book bag. I want to say something sharp that will hurt Dr. Celestin the way he has hurt me, but all I can manage is a sullen, "Thanks for nothing."

The women in the waiting area look up as I stumble out of the doctor's office and make my way toward the front door. My eyes are almost blind with tears, but my ears are clear. Behind me I hear Dr. Celestin giving instructions in English to Peter: Help her to understand.

Judah

32.

The next morning Mrs. Claxton comes out to the workshop and gives me a small, thin book. "This was written by a great man, Judah. He'll be coming to Weeksville soon to speak at the next meeting of the African Civilization Society. I don't think he's one of your people, but he spent some years of his life in Jamaica. I thought it might interest you."

I take the book from Mrs. Claxton and quickly glance at the name of the author: Henry Highland Garnet. I thank her for it, then tuck it away with the rest of my belongings. It is mid-morning, and I am helping Mr. Claxton finish a dining table and six chairs. The order has to be delivered by noon, so I don't have time to talk. Mr. Claxton's so focused he doesn't even look up to acknowledge his wife.

An hour later, Mr. Claxton puts his large, calloused hand on my shoulder. "You're a good worker, Judah." We stand before the loaded wagon, admiring the table and chairs. Then Mr. Claxton looks up at the sky. The large white clouds overhead have grey underbellies. "Better get these delivered before the rain comes."

Mr. Claxton doesn't invite me to go with him. Instead, I do as I am expected and grab the broom that stands in the corner. I begin sweeping up the shavings and sawdust while Mr. Claxton gets up on the wagon and slaps the reins lightly to urge his horse on.

When I can no longer hear the tread of hooves on the road, I set the broom aside and reach for the book Mrs. Claxton gave me. I open the cover and look at the portrait of Henry Highland Garnet.

"You work here?"

Startled, I quickly close the book and put it behind me on the worktable. I reach for the broom once more and try to look like I really do work for Mr. Claxton. "The boss won't be back for an hour or so. You here about an order?"

I ask this because it seems like the right thing to say. I can't think of another reason for this girl and her little brother to be here. I know they're siblings because they look exactly alike. The girl looks about fourteen or fifteen, and though he looks like he's about ten years old, the boy burrows shyly against his sister. His eyes are frightened, but curious as well. While his sister talks to me, the boy's eyes roam all over the workshop.

"Name's Mattie. This here's my brother, Money. Genna tell you 'bout me?"

I stop sweeping and stare at my strange visitors. Mattie glances around the workshop with disdain. Her arms are folded tight across her chest. *Mattie.* The girl Genna met at the orphanage here in Weeksville. I nod at her, and Mattie smiles like she's proud. Like she knew Genna wouldn't keep their friendship a secret.

"Folks say you're here looking for your sister. Say you lost her in the riot."

I nod again and continue sweeping. There is something unnerving about Mattie's bright black eyes. I keep my own eyes on the pile of sawdust forming before my broom.

"I know Genna ain't your sister."

Mattie waits a moment for me to respond. She is trying to threaten me with the truth, but I won't be intimidated by this girl. I keep on sweeping like she's not even there.

Mattie waits a bit longer, then walks past me and begins inspecting the workshop. Her brother stays by her side, saying nothing but drinking in everything with his eyes. When Mattie picks up the book I laid upon the table, Money stoops down and snatches up a curly wood shaving before I can reach it with my broom. He holds it tenderly between his palms as if it were a butterfly.

Mattie is struggling to read the title of the book. She knows the letters, but she can't put together all the words. Mattie looks up and sees me watching her. She tosses the book aside like it doesn't really matter. Then she checks the yard to make sure that no one else is around.

"She ain't dead, is she." Mattie says her words with confidence, like she doesn't need me to confirm what she already knows to be true.

I stop sweeping this time and look at Mattie long and hard. I wonder what Genna told her about our journey into the past. I wonder if she can be trusted with the truth.

"She gone back to where she come from?"

I nod and scan Mattie's face for some kind of sign.

"That's where you from, too?"

I nod once more, not sure it is safe to be admitting this to anyone. But Mattie knew Genna when she first arrived in this world. Mattie was there to help Genna when I couldn't even help myself. In a strange way, I feel like I owe her the truth.

Mattie turns away suddenly and goes over to a rocking chair that's waiting to be repaired. "Your hair ain't neat like hers. Esther seen you around. Say you look a mess. She say you could look more civilized if you just comb your hair and wipe the evil out your eye."

Mattie looks over at me and waits to see how I'll respond. I don't know who this Esther is, but she needs to mind her business. That's one thing about living in such a small community—everybody feels like they got a right to talk about everybody else. And with White eyes always watching us, waiting for us to mess up, we end up feeling like we have to be perfect all the time. At least, some Black folks feel that way—not me.

When her comments fail to get a rise out of me, Mattie comes close again and changes her tone. "You gon' find her?"

"I can't."

"Why not?"

"I don't know how."

"Well—you gon' *try*?"

Mattie practically spits those words at me. I don't appreciate being grilled by a complete stranger, but I keep my anger in check. This ignorant girl doesn't understand what we're dealing with. But there is a part of me that feels like I deserve her contempt. Just then the back door to the house opens and Megda heads toward the workshop with my lunch. She smiles warmly at my visitors, but receives only a shy grin from the boy and a cold stare from Mattie in return. Megda sets the covered plate on the table, nods quickly at me, then leaves without saying a word. Mattie watches her go, hands on hips, her eyes slit like blades.

"I guess maybe you too *busy* to look for Genna."

I wait until Megda has gone back inside the house. Then I take a deep breath and press flat the spike of anger on my tongue. "Mattie, you don't understand. Genna's not *lost*—she's not hiding someplace around here. She's *gone*, Mattie—to a place where I can't go."

"You try?"

Again Mattie's eyes condemn me. I look down at her brother, holding that thin curl of wood like it's the most precious thing in the world. "You know how we make those, Money?"

The boy looks up at his sister, and she nods to let him know it's okay to respond. "No, suh," he says quietly.

"My name's Judah, not sir. Come over here and I'll show you how."

Money looks at his sister and waits for her nod before coming and standing next to me. I put a block of wood on the table and take the drill off the wall. I place the boy's hands under mine and show him how to turn the crank and sink the drill bit into the wood.

Mattie watches me working with her little brother, and her eyes soften somewhat. One of her hands leaves her hip and creeps up around her mouth. Finally she folds her arms across her chest and blurts out, "I can help."

I let Money's hands turn the drill and stare at her. When she sees my confusion, Mattie goes on.

"Not with that. I can help you find a way to get Genna back. I know somebody—a African. You can ask him what to do. Some o' them Africans, they knows how to fly. Esther calls it black magic, but Genna always used to say black ain't bad, it's just different. Seems to me like you need a different kinda magic if you gon' find her again."

I look at Mattie and realize I was wrong. She's not ignorant at all. "This African—he lives here in Weeksville?"

"Outside—'bout a mile past the Henson farm. He got a drum and a three-legged dog. You can hear him beatin' on it most nights. The drum, not the dog."

Mattie waits to see my smile, then reaches out and touches her brother's arm. "C'mon, Money. We gotta go."

Mattie waits for her brother to join her and they both head out of the workshop. Before she passes through the door Mattie turns and looks at me. Her eyes flicker from my face to the plate Megda left for me.

"I be back."

Mattie's words sound like both a promise and a threat. I smile in spite of myself, glad Genna has such a devoted friend in this world.

Judah

33.

"Why you standing there gawking at us? Can't you see we're busy? Get back inside the house where you belong, you stupid heifer."

Megda flushes and drops her eyes before slinking away.

I set down my fishing gear and glare at Felix. "Why you talk to her like that, man? That's your sister."

"So?"

"SO?" My voice is louder than I mean it to be. "Our women get disrespected every day in this world. The least we can do is show them respect—and call them by their proper names."

Felix stares at me for a moment, then bursts out laughing. "Aw, man, don't tell me you're sweet on Megda! Nigger, you ain't *never* gonna get no sugar out of *that* jar. Now if sugar's what you're looking for, Mary Johnson's the girl you should be talking to—"

Felix doesn't see my hand until it has tightened around his throat. I bring my lips close to his face even though he disgusts me right now.

"Don't you EVER call me that. And if I hear you call your sister out of her name again, I'll knock your rotten teeth down your throat. Understand?"

Felix tries to smile even as his face turns pink. "Hey, ease up. I was just f-fooling around."

Felix squirms and sputters but my hand won't let go. "Judah, I c-can't breathe—"

I wait until Felix's cork-colored face is almost purple. Then I loosen my grip and watch him stagger over to the water pump, coughing and holding his throat. When I turn to leave the yard, Megda is there by the door, watching me. In her eyes is a tangle of gratitude and fear. I look down at my hand and wonder why it didn't let go sooner. When I look up again, Megda is gone.

The truth is, Megda's sweet on *me*. Her mother encourages her, I think, even though she's more like a kid sister to me. She's eager to please — too eager — but she's got a good heart. Megda thought I didn't like her cooking, but when I told her about Ital, she convinced her mother to start cooking without salt. Megda tells me when they're going to have pork for dinner, and if I catch fish, she cleans and cooks it for me. Megda even knitted me a cap to cover my hair — it's not red, gold, and green, but it fits and makes me look a bit more "civilized."

Except for locking my hair, living in the past isn't so hard for a Rastafarian. Here in Weeksville we mostly eat what we grow. Everybody's got a little garden out back, and the Claxtons don't use canned food, though it's available. Canned food helps keep the soldiers alive. But in 1863 most people still live off the land, even in a city like Brooklyn. You leave Weeksville and it's mostly farmland around here. About a mile away there's a creek I visit sometimes. Megda follows me once in a while. Sometimes she keeps me company in silence. Other times she picks my brain. Today is one of those days.

"Was she pretty, your sister?"

I don't feel like talking right now, but the words spill out of my mouth before I can think to swallow them. "Genna was beautiful." I wonder why I used the past tense. I should have said "is." *Genna is beautiful.*

Megda smiles quietly and dips her toes into the water. Her boots and stockings are beside her on the rock. "Tommy Werther once told me I was pretty," she says shyly.

"He's right."

Megda blushes and tucks her feet under her skirt. "Felix doesn't think so. He says I'm uglier than a warthog."

I sigh. "Felix is an idiot — he's probably never even *seen* a warthog. He just says stuff like that to hurt your feelings. You two are twins — if you're a warthog, so is he." I glance at Megda and we both laugh, knowing how vain Felix is.

"Lots of girls think Felix is handsome, but I think that's just because he's so bright."

I look at Megda like I must have heard her wrong. "Bright? Felix?"

She laughs her quiet laugh and glances over her shoulder before answering. "Not *smart* — bright. His color, I mean, because he's so fair."

"Oh."

Megda rushes on, worried I'll get the wrong idea. "Mama says we shouldn't pay no mind to folks who are colorstruck. *I* don't. Mama married Papa *because* he's dark, and he didn't care that her daddy was a White man. Mama says she prayed and prayed that God would give her beautiful Black babies, but He gave her me and Felix instead."

I set down my fishing pole and look at Megda. "Beauty comes from inside, Megda. There's nothing wrong with the way you look."

Megda tries to hide her smile, but her cheeks turn bright red anyway. She's a sweet kid, I think to myself, but she better toughen up or Felix will walk all over her.

Megda seems to read my mind. She stops blushing and holds her head up high. Megda takes a deep breath, and then looks straight at me. "She wasn't really your sister, was she?"

I pick up my pole and look out over the water. There's no such thing as a secret in Weeksville.

"Don't be mad. I don't care what other people say. You loved her a whole lot, I can tell." Megda glances at me to make sure I'm not angry, then goes on. "What color was she?"

"Black."

"Like you?"

I nod but keep my eyes in the middle of the creek. "Like me."

Megda tucks her hands under her knees to make her honey-colored skin disappear. "Mama says it would be better if everyone looked the same. She says that way light-skinned folks wouldn't put on airs and think they're better than anyone else. Mama says we should try to go back to the way we were before slavery. She says being fair is like having a stain on your skin that just won't go away."

My head is starting to ache and I don't think I can stand to hear Megda say "Mama says" one more time. I get up off my rock and wade over to where Medga is sitting. I reach into the shallow water and scoop up a handful of pebbles.

"What you do think about these rocks, Megda?" The wet stones glisten in the sunlight and Megda's eyes light up as if I am holding diamonds in the palm of my hand.

"They're pretty. I used to collect stones when I was little."

"Really? If you still collected stones, which one of these would you choose?"

Megda peers into my palm and points to a pink stone with gray flecks. I put it in her hand and throw all the others away.

"What if all the stones in the river looked like that one, Medga? Would you still like it as much?"

Megda looks up at me then down at the stone in her hand. She nods uncertainly.

"There wouldn't be much point collecting stones if they all looked the same. You collect only certain stones because they're special in some way — they stand out, right?

Megda nods more confidently this time.

"We're like the stones in this river, Megda. We come in all different shapes and sizes — and colors, too. Being different is what makes us special. It'd be pretty boring if everyone looked the same. And no disrespect to your mother, but Black people didn't all look the same before slavery. The people in Africa are diverse, just like the stones in this river."

Megda sucks in her bottom lip and blushes as I wade back to my fishing rock. When she thinks I'm not looking, she slips the small pink stone into her pocket.

"Is that what you liked about her—your sweetheart?"

I don't feel like talking about Genna with this girl, but her old-fashioned word makes me smile to myself. "That's exactly what I liked about her. She stood out."

"'Cause she was dark?"

I sigh and wonder if Megda has understood anything I've said. "She stood out because she wasn't trying to be somebody else. Genna was just herself, and that's what made her beautiful. Even when I wanted her to change, to think more like me, she kept on being who she was."

"Do you think you could ever like a girl who wasn't...quite so dark?"

I keep my eyes glued on the feather bait bobbing in the river and try to remember the boy Megda mentioned before. I knew Megda had a crush on me, but this is starting to get serious.

"Timmy Warner thinks you're pretty."

"Tommy Werther. But he's just a boy, and he's nearly as light as me. Besides, Mama says—"

I don't mean to, but I lose it. "Megda! One of these days you're going to have to make up your own mind instead of doing whatever your mother tells you to do, or think, or say, or feel." I didn't mean to raise my voice, but I can tell I have hurt her just the same.

Megda stands up, her mouth open with surprise. She blinks at me, then shuts her mouth and tries hard to act much older than she is. "I know exactly how I feel, Judah. I'm not a child, you know!"

As soon as she says this, Megda bursts into tears. Shamed by her uncontrollable emotions, Megda stamps her foot in the shallow water, scoops up her boots, and then rushes up the path that leads back to Weeksville.

I hold in my laughter until I'm sure Megda can't hear me. Then I let it out, laugh long and hard, and get quiet again so I won't scare away the fish.

Genna

34.

I am through asking others for help. From now on, I vow, I will handle my business myself. No one understands what it's like to live this way, with my body in one world and my heart in another. I hurry away from Dr. Celestin's brownstone and make my way up to the parkway. By the time Peter finds me, my eyes are dry. I've decided I will not shed any more tears. Like Nannie, from now on, I'm keeping my salt.

Peter sits down at the far end of the bench and sets the books I dropped in the space between us. Without speaking or looking at him, I grab the books and shove them inside my bag. I will take them back to the library just as soon as Peter curses me out for embarrassing him in front of his uncle.

"You okay?"

The concern in his voice surprises me. I nod but keep my gaze fixed on the traffic whizzing by. Out of the corner of my eye, I see Peter lean forward and prop his elbows on his knees. He doesn't seem angry, so I decide to speak first. "Sorry I freaked out like that." Peter just shrugs, so I go on. "Your uncle must think I'm crazy."

Peter laughs a bit. "My uncle's a Vodou priest, Genna. Trust me— he's seen it all."

Somehow that makes me feel a bit better. I shift on the bench and stare at the interlocking paving stones under Peter's feet. He turns a bit toward me, too, but there's still an empty block of space between us.

"Listen," Peter says, "I love my uncle and I respect what he does, but..."

"But what?"

"He's basically a really good interpreter. Maybe you weren't 'summoned' by your ancestors. Maybe it was something else — some kind of pattern. Like a formula or something."

"A formula?"

"Well, look at it this way. You've moved through time twice. Maybe there's something about the first trip and the second trip that's the same. If you figure out what happened in both of those moments, maybe you'll find out how to do it again."

Peter asks me for something to write with. I take my notebook out of my book bag and hand him a pen. Peter opens up to a blank page and then waits for me to begin.

"What do you want me to do?" I ask him.

"Just break it down for me one more time. What happened that night in the garden?"

I sigh, but force myself to tell the story one more time. "I snuck in after dark..."

Peter starts to write. I look down and see the words "garden" and "night."

He looks up at me. "And the second time — were you in a garden late at night?"

I shake my head. "I wasn't in a garden, but it was pretty late — and I was standing by the fountain at Borough Hall because I'd just made another wish."

Peter starts scribbling again. This time he writes "fountain" and "wish." He scratches out the word "garden."

"If you were making a wish, you must have had a penny or something, right?" I nod, and Peter writes down "coin." I slide closer to him on the bench and wonder why I never thought of doing this myself.

"Keep going," Peter says. "What else can you think of?"

"Pain," I say softly. "Both times there was pain."

"Because you were shot, right?"

"I think so. The second time it was a knife."

Peter thinks for a moment, then writes "weapon/violence" at the bottom of our list. "Anything else? How were you feeling before you got…sent back?"

"The first time I was upset—my mother slapped me, I couldn't find Judah."

"Were you crying?"

"Probably."

Peter writes down "tears."

"Then those ghosts showed up and scared the hell out of me."

"And the second time?"

"I was terrified—we were running from a mob! But then the police beat them back, and all I felt was relief."

Peter points his pen toward the paper, but no new words appear on the page. "So the first time you were feeling—what? Angry? Lonely? Scared?"

"I guess."

"Maybe it's adrenaline. Maybe that's one of the ingredients."

I think about what happened when I went to the Hunterfly Road houses—the remnants of Weeksville. I wasn't scared or angry then, but my heart was pounding pretty fast. There was no fountain there, no weapon. But I did scratch my face on that fence…

I take the pen from Peter, scratch out "fountain" and "weapon/violence," and then add "blood" to our list. I tell him about that afternoon and how I was able to hear Judah and Mattie for just a moment.

"You're sure it was them talking—not somebody else on the block?"

"There was no one else around, which sort of creeped me out. I mean, how often does it get totally quiet in Brooklyn in the middle of the day?"

Peter nods and considers scratching "night" off the list. "You really think it almost happened again?"

"I don't know. I never felt that way before. Not really scared, but—strong. And hot! This heat started in my back and then spread all over. I pulled on that fence and part of me felt like if I pulled on it again, it'd give. Like I could tear down whatever stood between me and Judah with just my bare hands."

Without meaning to, I suddenly recall Dr. Celestin's words: Sometimes we search outside ourselves for what is already within. Could there be something inside of me?

For the first time, Peter looks at me like he's not sure I'm all there. Yet he knows all too well that my blood really can start to boil.

"I'm not crazy," I say with a bit too much attitude.

"Never said you were," he replies but without looking me in the eye.

"Those other times it felt like something was happening *to* me. But this last time—I felt like I was part of it. Not in control, but not out of control, either."

Peter takes a moment to let my words sink in. Then he asks me to tell him more about that day. "Can you think of anything it had in common with the other two...trips?"

I force my mind to recall all the details, but can only come up with one. "The air changed."

Peter sits up, intrigued. "Changed how?"

"It got all wavy, blurry-like. When I went back the first time, the air was different, too. I felt like I was wading through water."

"What about the second time?"

"I don't know—everything happened so quickly that night. It was a heat wave, so the air was warm—even at night—but I remember shivering because my dress was soaked with sweat. I never ran so hard in all my life..."

Peter clears his throat to bring me back to 2001. I shake off the memory and focus on the list. He has added "sweat." I cross it out along with "tears" and add "salt" instead.

"So. Now what?"

Peter takes a deep breath and tries to look more confident than he sounds. "Now...you try to recreate the conditions that made you travel through time. This must be the formula."

~~garden~~
~~night~~
~~fountain~~
wish
coin
~~weapon/violence~~
~~tears~~
adrenaline
blood
~~sweat~~
salt

He hands me back my notebook, but I don't see a formula. I see a list of random words, half of which are scratched out.

"Thanks," I say. I suck my lips up against my teeth, afraid the next words out of my mouth will reveal just how worried I am about this "experiment." What if I can't pull it off on my own?

"Sometimes I feel as if the whole world's upside down. It's like watching those planes flying into the Twin Towers—even when you see it happen over and over again on TV, it still doesn't seem real."

"There's a huge crater in lower Manhattan. Ground Zero's real. Thousands of people murdered or missing...all that's real, Genna."

"I know. It's beyond real."

"Surreal."

"Yeah."

We sit without speaking for a minute, the sounds of the busy parkway taking up the space where our words ought to be. Peter and I aren't really friends—we've just been thrown together by this bizarre situation. All we have in common is our concern for Judah.

Peter's hard, flat voice surprises me. "I know there are two worlds, Genna. I've always known that. Sometimes they exist side by side. And sometimes the world you know comes to an end. It comes crashing down around you and a new world takes its place. Not better or worse—just different."

Peter opens his mouth to say something more, then changes his mind and looks off into the distance. I can't see his face that well. He talks to the ground, pushing out one word after another as if he were turning a screw.

"I live between two worlds, Genna. I'm Haitian but I live here, in America. I've had to learn how to be two things at once."

In the pause that follows I search for a way to contribute something just as meaningful. But all I can think to say is, "My father came from Panama."

Peter nods, but still doesn't turn to look at me. I sink down a bit further on the bench and wait for him to go on.

Finally Peter says, "I asked my uncle to help me once—just once. I needed help and I didn't know where else to go."

"What did he do?"

Peter shakes his head and practically spits the word at me. "Nothing. I was so mad...my uncle helps dozens of people every day. I couldn't understand why he wouldn't help me."

"He didn't say why?"

Peter just barely nods. "He said it wasn't his place to change God's work. God made me, and no ritual or prayer or potion can change what God made."

I'm confused, but I stay quiet for a moment and try to straighten things out in my mind. Didn't Peter tell me his uncle believed in the lwa? Just as I open my mouth to ask for an explanation, Peter goes on.

"I don't live with my uncle so I can help him with his practice." Suddenly he turns to face me. "I live with my uncle because my parents threw me out."

"They threw you out? Why?"

Peter's mouth twists with contempt. "They're Seventh Day Adventists. Deep into the church. To them, the Bible really is the word of God. And my uncle—they call him 'an instrument of the devil.'"

I nod as though I get what Peter's talking about, but really I don't. I'm not about to admit that, though. I don't want him to call me "a stupid American," so I just wait for Peter to go on.

"My folks—they don't understand that there are two worlds. For them, there's only heaven or hell." Peter gives a short, sad laugh. "They said I was a bad influence on my younger brothers."

He's not my type, but Peter is a good-looking guy. He stays out of trouble and gets good grades at school. I look at him and I don't see a "bad influence." Then I think of Mama kicking Toshi to the curb and wonder how parents can be so cruel.

Peter looks as if he's trying to say something but can't find the right words. "I'm just saying..." He stops then tries again. "Sometimes you can't count on other people. Sometimes the only person you can count on is you." He looks at me, hard. There are other words trapped by his clenched jaw, so Peter tries to send me a soundless message with his eyes.

"You really think I can do this—send myself back in time?"

"It's not like it'd be the first time, right? Plus I know you'd do anything for Judah."

I nod and brush away the doubts that have been gathering in my mind. I trust my heart. I have to trust what's inside of me.

Somehow we both understand that it's time to go and so we get up from the bench. The sky's growing dark and I don't want Mama to worry about me.

"You going to school tomorrow?"

I roll my eyes and heave my book bag onto my shoulder. "Have to. If I skip too much, my mother freaks out."

Peter nods like he remembers what that kind of motherly concern feels like. "When are you going to...test the formula?"

I don't honestly know, so I just shrug and say, "Soon. Time moves more quickly in their world than in ours. If I make it, I'll send you a postcard."

My corny joke gets a smile out of Peter, but his eyes are still serious. "Do you remember what you wished for?" When I hesitate, Peter goes on. "It's a major part of the formula, you know. What you asked for—how you asked for it—all that matters, Genna."

I have told Peter everything but for some reason, I don't want him to know that I can't remember the two most important wishes I've ever made. I can remember every other detail—the chilly trickle of sweat that ran down my spine a moment before the blade pierced my skin. But the words I whispered inside my mind are gone, like a vivid dream that vanishes the moment you wake up.

"Not many people can make their own wishes come true."

This time I look at Peter and see the envy in his eyes. "Maybe my uncle's right, maybe you really were 'summoned.' But if he's wrong, and we're right—if you really do play a role in all this, then that means…"

"I better be careful what I wish for?"

"You better know what it is you really want." Peter turns and heads down the parkway before I can say goodbye.

Judah

35.

We don't normally eat this late in the evening, but Mrs. Claxton wouldn't dream of sending her guest to bed on an empty stomach. Reverend Garnet is spending the night with us in Brooklyn and even after delivering a three-hour lecture at tonight's meeting of the African Civilization Society, he still has a lot more to say. Megda is supposed to be clearing the table, but she can't stop thinking about Reverend Garnet's narrow escape during the draft riots.

"The mob came right to your door?" she asks, her eyes open wide.

Reverend Garnet sits at the head of the table, as solemn and stately as he had been in the pulpit earlier this evening. "They would have, my dear — they marched right up the block calling for me by name. I shudder to think what the blood-thirsty fiends might have done had my family and I been discovered."

Mrs. Claxton stops pouring the coffee and sinks into her seat. "Had you already fled? Where did you go?"

"Not far — there wasn't time. Were it not for the consideration and compassion of our White neighbors, we might have shared the fate of the other martyrs. And our home would surely have been plundered had my daughter not had the forethought to take an axe to the brass plate on the front door."

Mrs. Claxton's pale face flushes with rage. "It's not enough that they hunt us like animals. The brutes must also take the fruit of our labor — the proof of our striving! Hardly a month off the boat and they feel entitled to all that we have paid for with our blood, sweat, and tears!"

"Cora—"

Mr. Claxton softly checks his wife's rage. Embarrassed, she rises and goes into the kitchen. Megda hesitates then decides her proper place is not at the table with the men, but with her mother.

Reverend Garnet puts a hand on Mr. Claxton's arm, but speaks loud enough for Mrs. Claxton to hear. "It's alright, Lionel. Her indignation is fully warranted. Even the angels in heaven beat their breasts over the suffering of our people. Why, I saw with my own eyes the mutilation of a colored man whose only crime was the color of his skin. A fiend in human form took a knife and cut his prey's flesh into shreds, asking 'Who wants some nigger meat?' And the shameless rowdies, they clamored for it, even coming to blows as if a dead man's flesh were worth more than gold."

I look up and see Megda standing in the doorway, horrified but transfixed by the terrible tale. Mr. Claxton follows my gaze and clears his throat to stop Reverend Garnet from going on.

"Megda, why don't you go on up to bed," he suggests, but it is really a command.

Mrs. Claxton comes up and puts an arm around her daughter's shoulders. Megda jumps, startled by her mother's touch, then allows herself to be led upstairs.

Reverend Garnet tucks his thumbs into the front pockets of his silk vest. "You've made good use of the funds set aside for the victims, Lionel."

Mr. Claxton only gives a grim nod. "We've built temporary housing for almost all of the refugees. Cora and the other church ladies have supplied warm blankets, clothes, and victuals, of course. Those who choose to remain here in Weeksville will receive all the assistance they need in finding work, shelter, and schooling for their children. Your White merchants were more than generous."

"Indeed they were. Most were appalled by the riots—ashamed, even. Our beleaguered race could not ask for better allies."

I open my mouth to speak, then change my mind. Reverend Garnet smiles, sensing a challenge. "You have a different opinion of our White benefactors?"

I was not raised to challenge my elders and don't want to offend the Claxtons' guest, so I hold my tongue.

Felix snickers and says, "Judah's *shy*." A stern look from his father wipes the smirk off Felix's face.

Mr. Claxton looks straight at me. "Humility has its place, Judah. But you're free to speak your mind here."

I clear my throat and try to make sure my logic is sound. "Sir," I say to Reverend Garnet, "wasn't it the wealth of our White sympathizers that infuriated the Irish? Rich Republicans used money to buy their way out of the war. Seems to me money's just a substitute for real action and true conviction."

Reverend Garnet looks at me for a moment, then glances at Mr. Claxton and says, "You were right, Lionel. Your new apprentice has surprising depth."

"Still waters run deep." Mr. Claxton looks at Felix. "Judah may not run his mouth all the time, but his mind is always working. He reads a great deal also."

Reverend Garnet now takes an interest in me. "You think we ought not to accept the aid of our friends?"

"The constitution of the African Civilization Society stresses the importance of *self-reliance*, sir."

"Indeed it does, Judah. But the colored race cannot afford to refuse the generosity of like-minded citizens. Four million of our people still toil under the lash without hope of just compensation for their labor. The financial support of our White sympathizers is, I'm afraid, indispensable. Once this war ends and slavery is abolished, then we can focus on generating our own wealth."

But the war won't end until 1865, and most freed slaves will never get their forty acres and a mule. I want to say this out loud but know I can't. Instead

I ask, "Do you think the war will end soon?"

"Now that colored troops have joined the fray, I'm sure victory will be swift. If I could, I'd shoulder a rifle and march off to war myself!" Reverend Garnet adopts a loud, patriotic voice and thrusts his fist into the air. "*Give me liberty or give me death!*"

"Who first said that, Felix?" Mr. Claxton drills his eyes into his son's reddening face.

Felix darts his eyes at me as Reverend Garnet frowns with disappointment. "Uh—I guess it was...uh..."

Finally I put Felix out of his misery. "Patrick Henry said it in 1775."

Both Mr. Claxton and Reverend Garnet give me looks of approval. Felix seethes silently.

"All patriots know the full price of freedom," Revered Garnet continues. "And true Christians know, as did our Lord and Savior Jesus Christ, that there is no hope for redemption without the shedding of blood."

Felix clasps his hands behind his head and tips his chair back from the table. "I'm ready to spill some blood."

"Your own, no doubt, the way you handle a gun."

Mr. Claxton's contempt for his son has never been more obvious. I glance at Felix and realize for the first time how much he hates his father. Reverend Garnet tries to change the subject.

"I pray the war will end before you reach the age of enlistment, son. For now, you should focus on your studies. When I was your age, there were many obstacles to an education that we have since fought to clear from your path."

Felix slumps sullenly. "It's hard to focus on facts and figures when there's a war going on. I want to fight!"

"A well-developed mind is as dangerous as a loaded gun, Felix. Why do you think Whites have fought so mightily to withhold knowledge from colored people? Why, thirty years ago I could hardly find a school that would accept colored students. I went to New Hampshire, to the Noyes

Academy, and the local Whites hitched a team of oxen to the school building and dragged it off its foundation. Then they set it on fire and threatened to turn their cannons on us!"

"What did you do?" asks Felix.

Reverend Garnet winks and makes his hand into a gun. "I fired a warning shot into the mob, and we fled the town once night fell. Eventually I went upstate and graduated from Oneida Institute."

I think of my classmates in 2001. Many of them would cheer if their school burned down. "Have things really changed since then?" I ask Reverend Garnet.

"We're fighting to create change, Judah. The Negro has made great strides, but there is still a long way to go."

"Do you really think they'll allow colored men from these parts to take up arms?" Mr. Claxton asks.

"They must if the Union is to be preserved," Reverend Garnet replies.

Felix perks up now that we're talking about the war again. "Look at the 54th—even President Lincoln praised them for their courage in battle down in South Carolina."

"They lost, Felix," I remind him.

"Yeah, but I bet they took a whole lotta Rebs with 'em!"

I'm so busy rolling my eyes at Felix I don't see Reverend Garnet turn to me. "What about you, son?" he asks.

"Sir?"

"You're a smart, sturdy young man. Are you ready to stand up and fight for the cause of freedom?"

All eyes are on me, but there are so many words crowding my brain that I can hardly see. I blink and try to focus on something simple, *yes* or *no*, but not a single word comes out. I want to ask Reverend Garnet a hundred different questions, but I'm afraid to say them out loud. I also don't want to lose the approval I so often see in Mr. Claxton's eyes.

"I...I should check on the horses. Excuse me." I push my chair back from the table and flee to the barn, my face burning with shame.

Judah

36.

I check on the horses and then go behind the shed to search for answers among the stars. It is hard to believe this is the same night sky that guided me north just a few months ago. North to freedom. North to Genna.

I wonder how many stars she can see at night. New York's bright city lights make them vanish almost. Here in Weeksville, the stars have no competition yet somehow, standing beneath a million of them, I feel more alone than ever. Does Genna even think about me? Or did she slip back into the future and back into her old life? Maybe all she thinks about now is going to college and building a new life without me.

Reverend Garnet's voice breaks up my pity party. "Mind if I smoke?"

My heart speeds up a bit, but I shake my head and watch as the Reverend lights the tobacco in the bowl of his pipe. He takes a few puffs to get it going, then takes a long draw and blows the smoke up into the sky. "Lionel tells me you were born in Jamaica."

"Yes, sir."

"You're far from home, then."

"Yes, sir." I look up and try to remember the way the stars looked when I lived on the mountain with my mother.

"I take it you don't believe we can win this war."

Until the philosophy
which holds one race superior

and another
inferior
is finally
and permanently
discredited
and abandoned,
everywhere is war...

I close my eyes and say a quick prayer of thanks to His Imperial Majesty for these words of wisdom. I should be able to defend my position, but I can't let the Reverend know that I have seen the future—a world that includes a Black king, the Emperor of Ethiopia, Haile Selassie I, who will speak these words before the United Nations one hundred years from now.

"It's just that...I'm not sure this war *has* an end, sir. We're caught in a long, bloody battle, but I think there will be more to come. Even if all the slaves are eventually set free, that won't change the way we're treated in this country. Prejudice will still exist—bigotry, hatred. And some slaves will remain slaves even after their chains are gone."

The Reverend nods but says, "The process of education has already begun, Judah. The American Missionary Association is sending teachers into the South to uplift our degraded brethren."

Once again I hear the voice of a prophet in my ears, but I say only some of the words out loud. "'None but ourselves can free our minds.' My countryman wrote that." I wonder what Reverend Garnet would think of a man like Marcus Garvey.

Reverend Garnet nods but only to show respect. "No man can see the future, Judah. Only the Almighty knows what lies ahead. But He expects us to rise up and meet our destiny. And the destiny of our people is to be free."

"In *Africa*—not here."

Reverend Garnet clamps his lips down on his pipe and scrutinizes me. "Emigration is only part of the solution, Judah. We cannot plan a future overseas when so many of our brethren are still enslaved here. Africa is our ancestral home, but many of us remember no home other than this land."

I don't want to sound defiant so I keep my voice low. "And the missionaries you spoke of a minute ago, will they teach the freedmen the truth about Africa? Or will they teach our people to be ashamed of 'the Dark Continent'?"

"The truth is not as simple as black and white, Judah. The soul-thieves must be forced out of our homeland, and only the best men of our race can ensure that Africa takes its rightful place in the world. But *this* country was built on our backs. We cannot walk away from the land that shaped us and which we have helped to shape. To stake our claim we must be recognized as *citizens* — civilized, educated, industrious citizens."

I say nothing but think of the three amendments to the Constitution that will follow the end of the Civil War. Slavery will end, Black people will be granted citizenship, and Black men will gain the right to vote. Then I think of the KKK, Jim Crow laws, and facilities that are separate but not equal. I think of Martin Luther King and Malcolm X—what would *they* say at this moment? Reverend Garnet mistakes my silence for confusion. "It is a complex situation, Judah, and even men of my age cannot agree on the remedy."

I pause. It would be easy to let Reverend Garnet think that I am just a confused teenager. But I am not confused. I feel like I know too much. Yet there is one question that's been weighing on my mind. "Why do you want to be part of a country that doesn't want you?" I ask him.

Reverend Garnet ponders the question for a moment and then replies, "Because I am a Christian, Judah. I believe in forgiveness and redemption. Slavery has not only cursed the colored race—it has left its mark on our enslavers as well. But those who emerge from the furnace of affliction shall be purified by the refiner's fire. It could be that God's plan is unfolding as intended. It must be so! We have spent our time in the wilderness but we will emerge triumphant. And America will be a better place for our suffering. It will not have been in vain."

I fight the urge to suck my teeth, but Reverend Garnet still sees the scornful twist of my lips.

He pulls the pipe from his mouth and frowns. "Do you think I have never felt a murderous rage against Whites burning inside my soul? I once walked up and down Broadway with a knife clasped in my hand, hoping to meet the slave catchers who had torn my family apart. If friends hadn't persuaded me to go into hiding...only God knows what I might have done. My leg may be made of wood, but my heart is made of pulsing flesh and blood—just like yours, Judah. It has been bruised and battered, but it beats within me still. And where there's life..."

"There's hope?" I ask, not bothering to hide my doubt.

He nods and takes another draw from his pipe. "I can tell you've been hurt, son. You've lost someone you love, and you don't believe justice will ever be served."

He looks at me for confirmation but I keep my eyes pointed up at the stars so my tears can't fall.

"I see in you the same restlessness I felt as a youth. You feel stifled here—even a country this vast is too small for your ambition."

I come back to earth and look at the Reverend. "You felt that way, too?"

He pulls the pipe from his mouth and chuckles. "I'm a man of the world, Judah. I've been to England, Scotland, Jamaica, and I was heading to Liberia when war broke out here. I was thirteen when I went to Cuba."

"Cuba!"

"I was just a cabin boy, but I realized then that the world was much bigger than I had ever imagined. And I knew then that my life could serve a greater purpose if I had the courage to cross the sea. We are a global people, Judah. We tend to lose sight of that, consumed as we are by internal strife here at home."

"This isn't home. Not for me."

"You could return to Jamaica one day. God's work awaits us everywhere." He pauses, then turns to me. "I'm sure you think you know your own heart, son, but I wonder if you've truly examined the source of your discontent."

I take a moment to consider Reverend Garnet's words, but they feel like a riddle I can't quite solve. "What do you mean?" I ask.

"You say you have nothing to fight for, yet if that were true, you'd be on a ship already bound for Africa or the West Indies. Instead, you're here in Weeksville. Why is that, Judah?"

I tilt my head up to the stars again. Why *am* I here? Because I still have hope that Genna will return? Or because I'm too afraid to strike out on my own?

The Reverend comes closer and puts his hand on my shoulder. I look down at the scuffs on my shoes, then remember I no longer have a heavy curtain of hair to shield my face. My tears fall softly into the grass at my feet.

"Son, we are bound to this country and this righteous battle not because of the soil or the flag. We are bound by blood to those who yearn to be free. We stay and we fight *for them*."

I lift my head and wipe my face with the back of my arm. "I've already been to war," I tell him. "I've walked through a Union camp and been called 'nigger' by the very men who are supposed to be fighting to set us free. They don't care about us."

"Does it matter? Will you stand by and let the Confederate scoundrels win this war?"

"You don't understand." I shrug hopelessly and turn away but Reverend Garnet grabs my shoulder and pulls me back.

"You think you are alone, Judah, but you're not. You're part of something much larger than yourself, son. Together we can shape the future! We can prove, once and for all, that we are MEN!"

"Men — or killers?"

The Reverend's hand falls away from my shoulder. He looks at me intently and somehow I manage to hold his gaze. I decide in that moment that I will tell him the truth, no matter what the consequences may be.

"Have you killed before, Judah?"

I start to nod then realize I need to say the words out loud. "Yes, sir. I have."

I don't know what I expected Reverend Garnet to do, but the pride in his eyes unnerves me. A slight smile lifts his lips, and he nods with understanding. Then he turns to the vast night sky and quietly sucks on his pipe.

I want to make a full confession. I want at least one person in this world to know *why* I took another life. But part of me is still ashamed — too ashamed to try and claim that I had no choice. I *did* have a choice. But I didn't think I could live another day as a slave, and so I took a life to save my own.

At last the Reverend turns to me and says, "It is no sin to take up arms in defense of liberty."

I frown. "But the Bible says, 'Thou shalt not kill.'"

"A slave cannot obey God's commandments. His desire to be virtuous and true is thwarted at every turn by demons who masquerade as Christians. It is the duty of every child of God to clear the path that leads to the cross, to redemption, to Christ. He who would impede the progress of any freedom-seeker must be struck down. God commands it."

These are almost the exact words I read in the pamphlet Mrs. Claxton gave to me. Reverend Garnet spoke them twenty years ago in an address to the enslaved. *Let your motto be resistance…*

"Our cause is a righteous one, Judah. You will not be condemned for what you have done. Is that what you fear?"

I look up at the countless stars, knowing more than six hundred thousand men will die before this war ends two years from now. I remember hearing the final, breathless gasp that told me Morgan was dead.

"I thought it would be harder, taking a man's life. I thought I would have to fight against myself, against all I believe—all I was taught." I look down at my hands—the same hands that crushed Morgan's throat, showing no mercy. "Soldiers kill. They follow orders and do as they're told without thinking twice. They can't afford to waver or feel regret. On the battlefield it's kill or be killed. I can't go back to that. I don't want to know—"

I stop. Reverend Garnet waits a moment, then prompts me to go on. "Know what, son?"

I don't want to tell Reverend Garnet about my father. And I can't tell him about my 'hood back in Brooklyn where some kids pick up a gun and go wild in the street like they're playing a video game. I can't tell him about those cops—trained to serve and protect—who pump lead into Black men who've done nothing wrong.

So I just say, "I don't want to know that side of myself, sir."

Maybe it's something inside all men. Maybe the urge to kill is always there, just waiting for a chance to come out. Or maybe it's just that there's something wrong with *me*. And what better way to find out than to wage a war against Whites?

Reverend Garnet says nothing for a very long time. I tell myself that if he had lost all respect for me, he would have walked away. But he just puffs on his pipe and after a while I grow comfortable with the silence between us. Finally, Reverend Garnet pulls the pipe from his mouth and turns to me. "You know, Judah, there are many different ways to serve."

I hope he's not talking about the military. I already know how Black folks "serve" White soldiers by washing their clothes, digging their latrines, cooking their food, and burying the dead. I wait for Reverend Garnet to explain what he means.

"There is a circuit—it's less active now than before the war began, but I'm sure I could find you a sympathetic audience."

This time I really am confused. Circuit? And why would I need an audience? Reverend Garnet realizes he's getting ahead of himself and leaving me far behind. He backs up and tries again.

"Public testimonials are one of the most effective tools in the anti-slavery struggle," he explains. "No one can sway hearts and minds better than an actual slave—a woman or man who knows from experience the horrors of slavery. You want to contribute to the cause of freedom, but you don't want to take up arms. Perhaps God has another plan for you, Judah."

I think quickly, trying to assemble the pieces of this puzzle. "You want me to—to tell people what I did?" I can't imagine telling a room full of White folks that I killed one of them with my bare hands.

Reverend Garnet offers something between a shrug and a nod. "Your story will have to be...*tailored*, shall we say, so as not to offend the delicate sensibilities of our White friends. But your story neither began nor ended with that encounter. Did it."

I shake my head. *My story.* I hardly know where it began, and I have no idea how it will end. I look at Reverend Garnet and say, "I was born free."

Reverend Garnet's eyes begin to sparkle like the stars overhead. He pulls the pipe from his mouth and taps it lightly against the side of the shed. The ashes glow for just a moment before the Reverend grinds them into the ground with his heel.

"I'll see that you get a journal. Take some time, recall and record as much as you can of your descent into slavery and your eventual escape. I'll make some inquiries and see about setting up a tour with two or three other speakers."

This is all so new to me, I'm not sure how I feel. Excited, but also afraid. I think of the court scenes I have seen on TV: a witness puts his hand on the Bible and swears to tell the truth, the whole truth, and nothing but the truth.

"Sir, if I am going to testify...I have to tell the truth."

Reverend Garnet becomes stern. "I fully expect you to be honest, Judah. Misleading the public does not help our cause in the least."

"But you said my story would have to be—"

"Tailored, not falsified. That is a significant distinction. For now, focus on writing everything down. Once I've read your story, I'll help you decide how best to relate your experience to an anti-slavery audience."

Reverend Garnet holds out his hand. I grasp it within my own and after one firm shake, let the Reverend go back inside. I bow my head and say a silent prayer of thanks to Jah. Perhaps *this* is my destiny. Already my head is as full of words as the night sky is full of stars.

Genna

37.

By the time I reach the library and drop off those useless books, my stomach has turned to lead. No more somersaults, no twisting inside. All I feel is the heavy, sick weight of my own guilt, which I couldn't heave up if I tried. *You better know what it is you really want.*

That night…that night when we ran for our lives through the streets of Brooklyn, I gave up on America. I said I'd go with Judah to Liberia, but what I really wanted — deep in my heart — was to go home. Is that what I wished for? Did I wish I could see Mama and Toshi and Tyjuan one more time?

My only consolation is that if I don't know the answer, then Judah can't know either. Yet somehow I still feel like I've been unfaithful to him. Disloyal. Dishonest. I said I would build a life with him in Africa, but I couldn't let go of this world. So I abandoned him, left him behind. If I go back, will Judah forgive me? Will he trust me when I say it's forever this time?

I walk home slowly, testing myself. I try to focus on Judah and not think of anything or anyone else. Instead of going straight home from the library, I make myself walk down Flatbush Avenue. The wild tangle of the garden calls to me over the spiky black fence, but I keep my eyes on the other side of the street. I look at the sky and think of Judah. I look at my feet and think of Judah running beside me as we fled from the mob. I look up at the trees getting ready to shed their leaves and think of Judah losing his locks as he was sold into slavery.

I love the garden, but I could leave it behind. I want to become a psychiatrist someday, but I could surrender that dream. For Judah, I'd do just about anything. That thought stops me in the street. *Just about?* Love is supposed to be unconditional. But how can you know what's buried deep inside your heart?

The lead in my stomach keeps me from eating much at dinner. Mama watches me, concerned, but she's got her hands full with Tyjuan. He's eating solid food now, but most of it ends up on the wall or the floor instead of in his mouth. I tell Mama I'll clean up while she gives Tyjuan his bath. I wash the dishes but try to keep Judah at the front of my mind. I force myself to tune out my baby brother's sweet squeals of laughter as he splashes in the bathtub. I can't let myself love him too much, because that will just make it harder to leave him behind.

Normally I would wipe the kitchen table and sit there to do my homework, but tonight I can't be bothered. The formulas we're learning in Algebra don't matter as much to me as the formula that will send me back to Judah. Mama comes out of the bedroom, quietly closing the door behind her. Now that Tyjuan's fast asleep, it's time for Mama to go to work. I'm stretched out on the sofa even though it's not even close to my bedtime. Mama slips her coat on over her blue medical scrubs. "What you working on?"

"Just some homework," I say, turning my notebook over so she can't see the formula. When I got home, all I wanted was to be alone. But now that Mama's about to leave, I feel a desperate desire for her to stay. I think of my actual homework and an idea pops into my head. "Mama, tell me a story."

Mama laughs at first, but then realizes I'm serious. "What kind of story?"

I shrug. "Something your mother told you when you were little—a fairy tale."

Mama makes that sound that's like a laugh without any joy in it. "My mother didn't believe in fairy tales."

"She never read to you before you went to bed?"

Mama shakes her head but looks away so I can't see her face. "She wasn't home. My mother worked the night shift in a factory. Gram talked to us sometimes."

"She was your father's mother?"

Mama smiles for real this time. "Uh huh. He left, she stayed."

"Like Abuela."

Mama nods but her smile fades. "Like your abuela. Gram could tell a story like nobody else! When she was cooking, she'd tell us tall tales to keep us from getting under her feet. Or she'd set us to peeling potatoes, and then tell us a story to make the time go by. It worked, too! We could listen to Gram for hours on end."

"Did your grandma ever tell you a story about black magic?"

Mama looks at me like I'm crazy. "Gram was Pentecostal! She wouldn't dare tell us a story about anything like that. Devilry—that's what she called it. Even horoscopes were off limits." Mama smoothes out the bedspread, then frowns and looks at me. "Why are you so interested in black magic?"

This time I don't have to lie. "We're doing a unit on folktales in English class. Everyone's supposed to bring in a story about how magic works in their culture. I don't know any stories from Panama, but thought you might know some stories from down south."

Mama thinks for a moment. "We used to have a collection of African American folktales around here somewhere." She gets up and starts moving picture frames and tacky chachkas off our one bookcase so she can see what books we have. I already know what's on those shelves: an old encyclopedia that's missing half its volumes, and second-hand books about Frederick Douglass and Sojourner Truth. That's why I practically live at the library.

Finally Mama finds what she's looking for and slides it out. I catch a glimpse of the cover as it falls off the book and drifts to the floor. Mama leaves it for me to pick up, her eyes busily scanning the table of contents. I reach for the tattered cover: *The People Could Fly*. A chain of dreamy-eyed Black folks drifts across a pale blue sky. I finger the old yellow tape that once held the cover together. It has long since lost its stickiness. "I remember that book," I say, surprised to know there are books on that shelf I have overlooked.

Mama carefully unfolds the creased pages. "I wonder who ripped the cover off."

Only one person in our family has zero respect for books, but neither of us wants to say Rico's name out loud.

Looking at the slaves in tattered clothes rising above the clouds suddenly reminds me of Mattie and something she once told me about flying Africans. "Do you think our people really could fly?"

Mama glances at the cover I'm holding in my hands. "Maybe," she says in a soft voice. "Once upon a time..." She hands me the book and jangles the keys in her coat pocket.

I know Mama needs to leave for work, but I try to get her to stay a bit longer. "Did your grandmother ever tell you that story?"

Mama nods and perches on the arm of the sofa. "But it was such a long time ago, I hardly remember how it goes. Gram's stories were always changing—one time the people did a little dance and flew away, another time they had to say something in African."

"African?"

Mama tries not to roll her eyes. I know she doesn't want another lecture from me about how Africa's a continent—not a country. There are more than a thousand different languages spoken in Africa. Judah told me that once when I said I was thinking about learning Spanish. He said that was the colonizer's language and I ought to learn an African language instead. I hope I'm not as annoying to Mama as Judah sometimes is to me.

"Well, whatever language they spoke before they were brought here to work as slaves. Not all of them could remember—that part I do recall. Gram said the rest of the slaves had to stay here because they couldn't remember the words they'd been taught back in Africa." Mama smiles. "I guess that was her way of teaching us to mind our elders and never forget what she told us."

I snuggle up close to Mama and rest my head against her thigh. "What do you want me to remember, Mama?"

I feel my mother's fingers sifting through my locks, but it's a while before she speaks. "I want you to remember that I love you, Genna. We all do. We're your family and this is your home."

Mama comes around and kneels on the floor so her eyes are level with mine. "This is where you belong — with us."

I don't trust myself to speak, so I just give Mama a quick peck on the cheek. Then I open the book and hold it real close to my face so she can't see the tears pooling in my eyes.

"Don't stay up too late," Mama says as she heads for the door.

"I love you," I whisper, but Mama's already gone. Next time I will say it to her face. I have to say everything that's in my heart while I still have time.

I let myself shed a few more tears and then turn my attention back to the book of folktales. The story about the flying Africans is at the very end so that's where I start. "They say the people could fly. Say that long ago in Africa, some of the people knew magic…"

I read the story three times, then set the book aside and reach up to turn off the lamp. I settle into the couch as the room settles into darkness. The warm glow of Tyjuan's nightlight seeps from under the closed bedroom door. Alone in the dark, I mouth the words spoken by the old slave, Toby: kum yali, kum buba tambe. In the story, this was enough to send a weary slave up into the clouds and back to Africa. Of course, it doesn't have that effect on me. I'm still laid out on the couch.

Why did they wait so long to leave? If they knew they could fly, why did they let themselves be whipped and beaten and starved for so long? My heart answers: because leaving is hard. Even when you're miserable, it's hard to let go.

Kum yali, kum buba tambe. The lights are out and no one's around to hear me, but I still feel foolish with those words on my tongue.

"Sounds like a bunch of mumbo jumbo," I say to the empty room. Then I feel ashamed. What do I know about African languages? I don't even know what the words mean, but I do know that magic won't work unless you believe in it. And doubt is something I can't afford right now.

I say the words a few more times until I know them by heart. I didn't use a magic spell from Africa to move through time before, but I'm all out of ideas. It's time to try something new.

Judah

38.

A strange whimpering comes from behind the stable. It sounds like a frightened, wounded animal, and I wonder if Felix has been setting traps in the yard again. Angered by his recklessness, I hold the lantern up high and turn the corner. The first thing I see is Megda's pale face distorted by fear and the hand roughly clamped over her mouth. Then I see Felix's other hand rifling through his sister's skirt. In an instant my mind goes blank and I see nothing as the velvet sheet from my slavery days twines around me once more. Then, before I know what I am doing, the lantern crashes to the ground and I grab Felix by the shoulders, spin him around, and pound my fist into his face.

He's stunned, but after the second blow Felix starts trying to defend himself. Now the terror is stamped on *his* face, but I don't stop swinging. When the blood starts flowing down her brother's face, Megda finally lets out the scream she'd been holding inside. I hardly notice as she dashes toward the house, calling for her mother. My hands circle Felix's scrawny neck and squeeze as if he is the source of all the noise.

The back door slams as the house empties and all three Claxtons rush to the work shed.

"No!"

Mrs. Claxton tries to pull me off her son, but Mr. Claxton holds her back. A few seconds more and I will be a murderer—again—but I don't let go until I feel Mr. Claxton's strong hand on my back. He rests his other hand on my rigid arm, and somehow his gentle touch makes my muscles relax. I blink and feel the velvety sheet sliding off my taut body. Slowly I loosen my hold on Felix. He sinks to the ground, sputtering and wiping at the blood gushing from his nose.

"He—he tried to kill me!"

Felix barely manages to point at me, huddled like a coward on the ground. Mrs. Claxton again tries to reach him, but Mr. Claxton bars her way with his outstretched arm. Megda is sobbing and so Mrs. Claxton instead turns her attention to her distraught daughter.

"Get up, boy."

Mr. Claxton is incredibly calm, and to my surprise, so am I. The murderous rage that flowed through me just a moment ago is gone. I pick up the lantern and stand by the shed as though I am a mere witness and not a participant in this ugly scene.

Felix looks to his mother but Mrs. Claxton can no longer face her son. Megda's dress is torn, and her parents know that I am not to blame.

"I said, GET UP, BOY!"

Mr. Claxton's thunderous voice knocks Felix back against the shed. Trembling, he slides up the wall until he is almost standing upright. Mr. Claxton surveys his son with obvious contempt. Blood has stained the front of Felix's shirt and his clothes are rumpled—but not from the scuffle with me. Felix hangs his head and fumbles to button up his pants. His pale face flushes with shame as Mr. Claxton glares at his son, turning away just long enough to spit out his disgust.

"Cora, take the girl inside."

"Lionel—"

"Do as I say, Cora."

Mr. Claxton calmly unbuckles his belt and slides the thick band of leather out of its loops. Keeping his eyes fixed on Felix, Mr. Claxton nods in the direction of the stable. "Get," he says softly, as if talking to his horse.

Mrs. Claxton has only taken a few reluctant steps toward the house. Megda clings to her, still sobbing and shaking. They both stop when Felix calls out in a puny, desperate voice. "Ma—"

The tapered end of the leather belt catches Felix across the face. I stagger back, stunned by the blow even though it didn't touch my skin. Felix howls, clutches his burning cheek, and once again huddles close to the ground. I think of Morgan flaying the skin off my back and for just a moment feel sorry for this boy.

Felix holds his other arm up as a shield against his father's rage. "Papa, please! I'm sorry—I'm sorry!"

Mrs. Claxton puts her hand over her mouth and rushes Megda into the house. Mr. Claxton steps forward and lightly kicks his son.

"Sorry? You will be before this night's done. Now get up."

Felix begins to cry, but doesn't move. Mr. Claxton kicks him again, harder this time. "GET!"

Somehow Felix manages to pull himself to his feet. The soaked front of his pants proves his fear, yet Felix still casts a defiant glance at me before slowly shuffling toward the stable. Mr. Claxton waits until Felix is a few feet ahead of him before raising his arm and bringing down the belt once more. This time, the tip of the belt connects with the pale skin at the base of Felix's neck. The boy cries out and falls on his knees.

Mr. Claxton takes a few steps forward and gives the same order as before: *get up*. Felix hauls himself up, his shoulders shaking with pain and stifled sobs. I can tell that he is torn: afraid to move forward, knowing just what awaits him out in the stable, yet afraid to disobey his father by standing still. Felix takes two tentative steps, then glances over his shoulder in time to see his father's unforgiving arm raise the belt once more.

"NO!"

Felix shouts at the night sky before suddenly bolting toward the field. Mr. Claxton, arm still raised, watches his son dart away. Felix runs as if he knows just where he's heading. He dives into the sea of tall grass and wades into the night.

I watch the tall grass until it stops swaying, knowing that Felix is heading from one battle to another. "He's probably going to try to enlist," I tell Mr. Claxton.

The leather belt softly slaps the ground as Mr. Claxton's arm falls to his side. Keeping his eyes away from mine, Mr. Claxton slowly winds the belt around his hand. "Any army that wants that boy can have him," he says with disdain. "He's already dead to me."

In the darkness it is hard to read the emotions stamped on his face. But Mr. Claxton's shoulders are sunken in a way I have never seen before. His tall, strong body is burdened not by fatigue, but by defeat.

I want to say, "Whatever's wrong with Felix, it's not your fault." But nothing I say will convince this father that he has not failed. Without saying another word, Mr. Claxton turns away from me and slowly walks back to the house.

Judah

39.

Everything changes after that night. Megda creeps around the place like a frightened rabbit, bursting into tears at the drop of a hat. I don't blame her. I've heard about stuff like this happening, but I never imagined I would be the one to stop it from happening in this family. We don't talk about it but that doesn't undo what's been done.

Mrs. Claxton has basically gone into mourning for her lost son and Mr. Claxton fumes silently at Felix — or himself. They're grateful that I stopped Felix before he could go any further, but they're also ashamed that an outsider witnessed the entire scene and exposed their son as a would-be rapist. More than ever I feel like an outsider — no matter how kind these people have been to me, the Claxtons aren't my family. Still, because I live and work here I'm pretty much caught in the middle of it all, which makes me wish I could disappear, too.

So when Reverend Garnet asks me to speak at his church the following week, I accept the invitation despite the queasy feeling in the pit of my belly. How can I stand in that pulpit, face the congregation, and admit that I'm a murderer? Reverend Garnet says to trust in the Lord and the compassionate hearts of true Christians. I want to believe I can be redeemed but in my experience, lots of Christians are quick to judge and slow to forgive.

Still, all through the week I pull my pencil out of my pocket and scribble down notes in the journal Reverend Garnet gave to me. Then at night I piece the fragments together until a story starts to form in my mind. I say the words over and over in the dark and by the end of the week I've memorized a story that starts and ends with freedom. It's what's in the middle that troubles me.

I can't say anything about being from the future, of course. If anyone asks me where I'm from I'll just say I was born in Jamaica, which is the truth. I *want* to tell the truth. I want to testify, confess, wipe my soul clean with words. Reverend Garnet says this is the first step on the road to redemption. Some prominent abolitionists from the Anti-Slavery Society will be there and if they like my presentation, they may invite me to tour other churches upstate and in Ohio.

I don't want to disappoint Reverend Garnet or his influential friends, but I've never really spoken in public before. And I've never opened up my heart and shown others what's inside. I did it with Genna once, but that was before I wound up in chains having to fight to survive in this crazy world. But if that church really is filled with love, then maybe—just maybe—this is the chance I've been waiting for. I need to know that this journey through time has not been in vain.

I don't advertise my invitation to speak at Reverend Garnet's church but somehow the Claxtons still find out. Mrs. Claxton decides we'll all go over to Manhattan together even though I tell her this is something I'd rather do alone.

"Nonsense," she says in a way that tells me her mind's made up. "I can't tell you how proud we are, Judah. Half of Weeksville will be there to support you."

I think Mrs. Claxton's happy to have something other than Felix to think about. It would be a lot easier to tell my story if I didn't actually know anyone in the congregation. Now I lie awake at night wondering what the Claxtons will think of me once they know they've been sheltering a murderer. And Esther—that woman is just the kind of two-faced Christian I'm worried about. But when Sunday morning rolls around and I walk over to the wagon where everyone's waiting, Esther almost smiles at me.

At least she makes it clear that she approves of the clean clothes I have on and the way I've combed my hair.

I've decided not to lock my hair again until I reach Liberia. I'm still not cutting it, but I do make a part and comb it out so it has some kind of shape. Today I looked in the mirror in Mrs. Claxton's sitting room and felt like a young Frederick Douglass. It was here in New York that Frederick Douglass claimed his freedom after escaping by boat from his owners in Baltimore.

There is no Brooklyn Bridge. It hasn't been built yet. There are all kinds of people on the ferry but we stand out—a group of Black people wearing their Sunday best. My stomach churns a bit as the ferry takes us from Brooklyn to Manhattan. I keep an eye out for signs of hostility, but the poor White folks most likely to start something with us are probably at home sleeping off their hangovers. We pass a few White men lolling in the gutter on our way to the church.

Shiloh Presbyterian Church is already full when we arrive but people get up to greet us warmly. Reverend Garnet leads me up to the front and tells me to take a seat just behind the pulpit. I look out at the congregation and see how the men have given up their seats in the pews so the women and children from Weeksville can sit down. They have moved to the back of the church and stand along the wall like soldiers at attention—armed with bibles instead of guns.

Everyone is wearing their Sunday best but the finest clothes belong to the White men from the Anti-Slavery Society. I see their pink faces hovering above the ruffled white linen at their necks. They are smiling and shaking hands with people regardless of their race. I wonder if they will shake my hand once they hear what I have to say.

Before Reverend Garnet even reaches the pulpit the sanctuary grows quiet. He greets the congregation and they obey his request for them to rise and sing. I stand as well and open my mouth to sing, but my voice is drowned out by the loud buzzing in my ears. I stand on the dais and watch the members of the congregation raise their voices in song but I can barely hear them. The organ to my left sends vibrations through my body but the tune escapes me. My own voice thins to a whisper and then vanishes altogether as my throat closes. I shut my mouth and wait for the buzzing to stop but it only grows louder. Finally the hymn ends and the congregation follows Reverend Garnet's lead. While their heads are bowed in prayer I scan the church for the fastest escape route. I could jump off the dais, sprint up the center aisle, and reach the door in less than ten seconds.

Suddenly the buzzing stops and I am immediately aware of the silence in the sanctuary. I sense hundreds of eyes staring at me but my limbs feel wooden—I am a tree, rooted to this spot. I look over and see Reverend Garnet smiling at me, his arm extended as he steps aside to make room for me at the pulpit. I try to shake my head but my body no longer obeys my commands. The congregation is seated now and they look up at me with expectant eyes. I try to open my mouth but my lips are sealed shut. Reverend Garnet comes over to me and places a hand on my shoulder.

"We're ready for you, Judah."

I try to open my mouth to apologize. I try to think of some excuse, a way to explain what panic is doing to my body. But Reverend Garnet simply steers me into the pulpit and then takes my seat on the dais.

I try to swallow but my mouth is like a desert. The congregation waits patiently for me to begin. Voices call out assurances:

"Take your time."

"Go ahead, son."

"Don't be afraid."

"God is with you."

Their encouraging words turn my body from wood to flesh, and the first thing I feel are the tears streaming down my face. Before I can wipe my eyes with my sleeve, an old woman in the front row stands up and waves at me. I come around the pulpit and take the handkerchief from her wrinkled brown hand.

I clear my throat and find my voice again. "Thank you, ma'am." I look into her face and see that her cheeks are wet with tears, too.

"Open your heart, son," she says in her wavering voice, "Let God in."

Her words give me strength. I decide not to return to the pulpit. I stay where I am at the edge of the dais, close to the congregation. They will catch me if I fall.

All the words I memorized during the week have disappeared. I have no script to read from but I know this story by heart because it is my life. The proof is written in the scars on my body and the wounds in my heart. I open my mouth and say, "My name is Judah. I was born free, in Jamaica, but when I came to this land I was kidnapped and put in chains. I killed a man in order to regain my freedom. This is my story."

The desert inside my mouth is flooded with words. They flow from my mouth like water down a mountain. At times I falter but every time I hesitate, members of the congregation urge me on again. I look up and see women dabbing at their eyes with white handkerchiefs. The White men in the fancy linen are no longer smiling but even they nod as if they understand everything I am saying. When I finally stop talking there is a moment of total silence and then the congregation fills the sanctuary with thunderous, endless applause. Reverend Garnet comes up and places his arm around my shoulder.

"Our brothers and sisters in chains wage battle every day for their freedom. Will we leave them to fight the evil of slavery alone?"

"NO!"

"Will we condemn our brother for using his God-given strength to repel the brutal arm of the slave breaker?"

"NO!"

"Will we, as true Christians, do everything in our power to enable our brother to testify so that unbelievers may be converted to the cause of liberty?"

"YES!"

Reverend Garnet folds me in a warm embrace. "You're on your way, son," he whispers in my ear. Then he nods at the organist who begins to play "Am I Not a Man and Brother."

I stand beside the Reverend and sing along with the congregation. And for the first time since I landed in this century, I feel truly and fully free. The love from the congregation washes over me like a wave, and my heart finally lets go of the anchor that has bound me to the distant future—to my past—to Genna.

Genna

40.

The first thing I do is call Toshi. "I need you to watch Tyjuan for a while," I tell her then hang up before she can ask me why. I dress my beautiful baby brother and then settle his sleeping body in the stroller.

"Don't do nothing stupid, Genna," Toshi warns when I show up at her door. Then she leans in and adds, "Not for some boy."

I tell Toshi not to worry. "I've thought this through—really. If it doesn't work out, I'll be back in a few hours to pick up Tyjuan."

"For real?"

"For real."

"What if it does work out—what then?"

I bite my lip. *Don't talk, just move.* I grab Toshi in a tight embrace that catches her off guard, and stoop to kiss Tyjuan one last time. Then I dash down the stairs before my big sister can ask me anything else.

When Mama gets home from work, she'll find the note I left for her on the kitchen table. Or—if this experiment fails—I'll get home first and Mama will never know that I tried to leave her again. I've got everything I need in my book bag, including the prayer card from Abuela and the picture of the Black Madonna that I got from the botánica. I tried to call Peter to say goodbye but he didn't pick up, so I left a message on his voicemail: *Hey, Peter. It's Genna. I'm going now. Thanks for being such a good friend to Judah—and to me.*

I've never been out on the street this late before—not by myself. The sidewalks are mostly empty, but even at 2am there are still plenty of cars racing along the parkway. I walk slowly but deliberately, focusing on my destination—and my destiny. I have to believe I can make this happen. I have to know what's in my heart. The moon isn't quite full, but its bright light comforts me as I weave through the city on my way back to Weeksville. Back to Judah.

Only bodegas are open at this hour. Their doors are locked so people crowd around the pass-through window on the side of the store. Then they drink their drinks and smoke their smokes under the brightly lit awning, laughing, fighting, dancing, and acting in outrageous ways that only the night allows. I feel a strange freedom myself as I walk through the city in the middle of the night. I am anonymous, invisible, insignificant.

I weave my way through the streets, alternating between the wide avenues and the dark side streets. I am calm but alert, and find myself looking for clues from the past—engraved cornerstones that reveal a church's age, scrolled molding at the top of row houses that now have metal siding instead of wood shingles. Brooklyn's history is buried, but you can still find traces of the past if you know where to look.

Once I turn onto Bergen Street I finally slow down. In the middle of the block, the historic houses stand, silent and dark, but the projects across the street still show signs of life. I cast a quick glance over my shoulder but keep my gaze focused on the buildings beyond the chain link fence. They are from another Brooklyn, another world. That is where I truly belong, but I can only get there by opening a door between past and present. I slip my arms out of my book bag and set it down on the sidewalk. It's time to test the formula.

I kneel and begin removing items from my bag but stop when I sense someone coming up the street. I see a figure out of the corner of my eye. It's seems like a young man and he's walking toward me with purpose in his stride. I feel my heart speed up but refuse to turn my head and make direct eye contact. I'm not looking for trouble and anyone out at this time of night is probably doing something shady that I'd rather not know about.

"Genna!"

I look up when I recognize Peter's voice. "What are you doing here?" I hiss at him. "You scared me half to death!"

"I got your message. Here—take this." Peter reaches inside his coat and thrusts a small, strange object at me. It looks like half a pretzel with some feathers on top and a rolled sock on the bottom. All the parts are bound together with white ribbon, and there are tiny mirrors that flash in the moonlight as I turn it over in my hands.

I am about to thank Peter when I realize I don't know what I'm thanking him for. "What is it?"

Peter twists his lips the way he always does when he has to translate something for me. Finally he finds a word my small American brain can understand. "It's…a paket."

"What's inside?"

Peter gives me his usual hard look. "You really want to know?"

I take a quick sniff of the paket and shake my head. Peter gives me a half-grin. "It's for luck. And…protection."

I shift things around in my bag to make room for the paket. "Thanks." I don't ask Peter what he thinks I need protection from.

"You ready?" he asks.

I nod but can't seem to stop myself from trembling. I'm kind of glad to see Peter, but I can't do this while he's watching me. I need to be alone. Peter shifts from foot to foot. His eyes are alert, looking around for unwanted witnesses. When his eyes lock on something in the distance, I follow his gaze to the church at the end of the block. Above the doors, a large ivory cross stands out against the red brick façade.

"You should stand down there," he says suddenly. Peter nods toward the intersection at the end of the block where the church is. "If you want it to work, you should stand on the corner."

I look down the block and frown. The streetlights are brighter over there, and I don't want any cars pulling up at a red light while I'm trying to move through time. I know what men think about a girl like me who's standing out on the corner in the middle of the night.

"I'd rather stay—"

"Come on."

I barely have time to scoop up my bag before Peter grabs hold of my arm and drags me toward the intersection.

"Trust me," he mutters, "it's better if you stand at the crossroads."

I was in the middle of the block the last time I was here and heard Mattie's voice, but I let Peter push me ahead of him until we reach the corner. The streetlight overhead is flickering off and on. I already said goodbye on the phone, but Peter doesn't seem ready to go. I can tell he's nervous but he doesn't want to leave me alone.

I can't quite manage to smile but I appreciate his concern and try to reassure him. "I'm alright, you know. You don't have to stay." Peter nods but doesn't look at me so he can't tell what I'm trying to say. I spell it out for him. "Actually, Peter, I don't think I can do it if anyone else is around."

He reaches into his pocket and nods. "I'm not staying." Then he glances around, squats close to the ground, and starts dribbling some kind of grain onto the sidewalk.

I don't mean to freak out but I'm already nervous and I don't need Peter making a scene. "Peter! What are you doing?"

Peter ignores me and uses the trail of grain to draw a cross. He reaches into his pocket and pulls out another handful. He adds curlicues and stars to make the cross look fancier. I have seen signs like these in the books I checked out from the library. Each lwa has a symbol, a vévé.

At any other time, I probably would have been impressed. But this is too much. First he pushes me from the shadows into the light, and now Peter's making a weird drawing on the ground that the rats will happily devour.

"Who's that for?" I ask testily.

"You," Peter replies without looking up.

"No—I mean, which lwa does it belong to?"

Peter finally finishes and stands up to examine his work. "Papa Legba." Then he wipes his hands on his jeans and finally looks at me. "Good luck, Genna."

I want to ask him what special powers Papa Legba has, but I know Peter doesn't want to explain. And I don't have any more time to waste. "Goodbye, Peter. Thanks for—" I glance at the intricate cross on the sidewalk. "Uh—thanks for your help. Now get out of here!"

Peter nods and backs away from the corner. As soon as he steps outside the ring of light, the flickering streetlight above us goes out, leaving me in shadow once more. I wait until Peter's about a third of the way up the block, then I open my book bag and prepare to open the door in time that will lead me back to Judah.

First I take out Mama's stainless steel mixing bowl. I open a bottle of water and pour the contents into the bowl. It's not a fountain, but it's fresh water and it will have to do. I set a penny on the ground next to the bowl. My heart is pounding hard and fast. If adrenaline is part of this magic formula, then I should have everything I need. I take one last item out of the bag, then zip it up and slip my arms through the straps. I don't know if my bag will make the journey with me, but I hope it does.

I take a deep breath. I have rehearsed this moment over and over in my mind, but it feels different now that I am here. With trembling fingers I open Rico's pocketknife. The small blade glints in the moonlight, and for just a moment I let myself think about my brother. No doubt he has fashioned other weapons out of whatever they allow him to have in prison.

I never got along with my big brother, but a small part of me still wishes I could reach into his cell and take him with me. Would Rico be freer as a Black boy in 1863? Judah learned how to survive but Rico isn't like Judah. My brother's toughness was just an act. Rico never meant for me to have his knife, but I found it wedged between the sofa cushions and claimed it for myself. I say a silent prayer of thanks to my brother and focus once more.

The blade is sharpest at the tip and so I squeeze my eyes shut and press the point into my left palm. A small bulb of blood appears and I hope that will be enough because I doubt I could cut any deeper. I reach down for the penny with my other hand and press it into my palm, making sure to smear both sides of the coin with blood. Then I close my eyes, make a wish, and drop the penny into the bowl of water.

Nothing happens.

I open my eyes and take a step closer to the fence that encloses the original houses of Weeksville. With my bloody left hand I reach for the steel pole that connects the two sides of the chain link fence. A quick pulse of electricity runs through my fingers and up my arm, causing me to gasp and pull back my hand. On the far side of the intersection, a second streetlight flickers and then goes out. My heart sinks in my chest but I am not ready to give up. Not yet.

I glance down at the cross Peter drew on the ground. Despite the shadows, it seems to glow. I can feel the paket pressing through my book bag and weighing against the base of my spine. I close my eyes and summon from memory the magic words from Mama's book about enslaved Africans. Softly I chant the words that once helped my ancestors to fly.

> *Kum yali kum buba tambe*
> *Kum yali kum buba tambe*
> *Kum yali kum buba tambe*

Nothing happens.

Salty tears slip through my closed lids and slide down my cheeks. I don't want to open my eyes. I don't want to see my feet still planted on the concrete sidewalk, but the distant blare of sirens insists that I have not moved. I plead with God to let me go back where I belong, but my sobs choke the desperate prayer before it can leave my lips. My fingers wrap around the chain link fence and I press my face into the cold steel. I force myself to stand, though defeat has turned my limbs to jelly. What have

I done wrong? My mind flashes back to the last two times I opened the door. What has changed? I've never been clearer about what I want.

My clothes are still damp from walking over here so quickly. I feel their weight against my skin and fight a sudden urge to strip myself bare. My back itches, twitches, and then lights up with zigzagging sparks of pain. I bite down on my lip and pull against the fence with all my might. It billows but doesn't budge. My back prickles with pain as I alternate between tugging at the fence with my hands and kicking at it with my feet. Just as I fit the toe of my shoe inside a link and start to climb the fence, something strikes me from behind. The skin on my back sizzles and then tears, and before I know it, I am screaming at the top of my voice. Only Peter's hand clamping down on my mouth silences me.

"Genna, stop—stop!"

I blink at him through my terror and tears. I want to sink to the ground and bawl like a baby but my fingers—curved like claws—won't let go of the fence.

Peter takes his hand away from my face and tugs at my arm. "Come on, Genna," he says gently. "Let's go home."

Home. There is no home without Judah. I shake my head and peer through the fence at the row of wooden houses in the distance. I stare in the window of the 1860s house until I see a faint glimmer in the dark window.

"Did you see that?"

Peter glances over his shoulder at the houses but quickly turns back to face me. "See what? Genna, I think you've had enough for one night..."

Peter's voice buzzes in my ear like a mosquito. Irritated, I try to swat him away so that I can focus on the scene beyond the fence but Peter won't leave me alone. His hand tugs at me, more forcefully this time, but my eyes find the tiny flame wavering in the distant window. It's a candle. Someone has lit a candle!

"There! There!" I cry and my excitement persuades Peter to look one more time.

"I don't see anything. Listen—you tried, Genna. You did everything you could, but it's not working. Let's get out of here before somebody calls the cops."

I ignore Peter and keep my gaze fixed on the flame in the window. Someone has lit it for me. I'm sure of it, though I can't see just who's inside the house. Could it be Mattie? A smile creeps across my face as hope solidifies my limbs. I close my eyes and envision the candle burning in the window, guiding me home. My smile deepens as the air around me starts to change. I shiver as the cool air gels around me.

It's happening—at last!

Peter watches me and no doubt sees a girl who is losing her mind. When he pulls on my arm once more, I angrily hiss, "Go away!"

I can't sustain my focus on the flame and explain what I'm feeling to Peter. He can't tell, but something is about to happen—I can feel it. Whatever magic I have summoned is working, but it is just for me. There is only enough *for me*. I feel a surging wave of ecstasy bubbling up my throat. Laughter spills from my mouth and floats on the thickening air.

Peter shifts his hand from my arm to the fence. I feel him trying to peel my hooked fingers off the chain link fence. "We're leaving—*now*," he says in a low, menacing voice.

My body tenses again as every part of me rejects his command. "Get off me!" I yell. "GET OFF ME!"

Peter freezes and I see the panic in his eyes. He glances across the street at the projects to make sure no one thinks—or cares—that I'm a damsel in distress. "Genna—what's wrong with you?"

"You should have left. I have to do this alone!"

Peter just shakes his head and grips my wrist. "I'm not leaving you here."

We struggle for several seconds. Peter pulls at the fingers of my right hand, forcing me to let go of the fence and claw at him with my left hand. I can tell he's losing his patience but I will not back down. This is a battle I must win.

Peter grabs hold of my left hand and uses his shoulder to knock me back-first into the fence. My body sinks into the woven steel but then the fence launches me back at Peter. My fingers reach for his face and my nails connect with the soft flesh of his cheek.

"Ow!" Peter pushes me away and puts his hand up to his face. When he looks at his fingers, I see that I have drawn blood. I don't feel any satisfaction, but for some reason I smile. And then he hits me.

The body that carried me back in time endured things I can only imagine. I woke up in 1863 with a bloody back and it took several days—and several doses of morphine—in order for me to heal. But in this world—in 2001—I have never been struck by a man. The back of Peter's hand knocks the crazed smile off my face, but the look of fury that replaces it makes him take a step back.

The candle in the window of the house behind me flickers and then flares. I see it even though my eyes are fixed on Peter. I feel its heat spreading through my body, filling me with a light so bright that Peter has to shield his eyes from the glare. I take advantage of his blindness. I step forward, press my palms into Peter's chest, and push him as hard as I can. I see his body fly through the air. I watch as he lands awkwardly on top of a parked car on the other side of the street, triggering the alarm. I see the windshield shatter from the force of his landing. Satisfied, I turn away from the sound of Peter moaning in pain and prepare to leave this world.

I dip my hands into the bowl of water and scrub the blood from my left palm. I want to be clean for this journey. For Judah. After wiping my hands dry on my jeans, I step closer to the fence and rest my fingertips on the cold steel links. This time I don't grab hold and try to pull the fence free from the ground. Instead I simply turn my palms outward and push the fence apart as if I am opening drawn curtains. I chant two words over and over in a soundless whisper:

I believe I believe I believe

Sweat slides down my face. The heat surging through my body is almost more than I can bear, but I know that it's worth it. I know that I am close. I am doing this. I am making this happen.

I close my eyes and shift my focus from the candle in the window to Judah. Moments after the fence parts, the sky rips wide open, sunlight pours into the dark street, and I see my destination clearly. I hear voices and know that they are coming from the other side. I am standing at the threshold, teetering on the brink of the past. The scene beyond the fence brightens as if it is noon and not the middle of the night. "I'm coming, Judah," I whisper. A stab of excruciating pain sucks the air from my lungs, and then I am gone.

Genna

41.

I did it. *I did it*! I'm here—in Weeksville. In the past.

A small boy is standing a few feet away in the center of the dirt road. The hoop he has been pushing along with a stick rolls past me and wobbles onto its side on the ground. I smile at him but the boy's mouth is as round as his hoop. He must have seen me arrive.

I reach for the fallen hoop so I can return it to him, but instead drop to my knees and double over with pain. The journey through time has left me with blisters again, but this time they're on my hands and not on my back. With some effort I pull myself up and stagger over to the barrel full of rainwater next to what I assume is the boy's house. I splash a little on my hands but that doesn't really help.

I know I can't linger here because the little boy is gone, and his urgent cries for his mother will bring the kind of attention I don't want right now. I'm not dressed like a nineteenth-century girl. There are painkillers in my book bag—which is still strapped to my back—but I'm not sure I can dig them out. My hands are curled into claws, the singed skin pulled taut by fresh pink blisters.

"Can I help you?"

I came back in my own clothes this time: jeans and one of Rico's old hoodies. I knew it would be cold at this time of year and I thought these clothes would keep me warm and conceal my gender. I look at the brown-skinned woman standing in the open door of the small wooden house—the same house I saw in Brooklyn in 2001 when I stumbled upon the surviving acre of Weeksville. She is wiping her hands on a cloth, and her eyes look wary but not unkind.

"Thank you, I—I just got turned around. I'm heading for the orphanage."

"Been traveling?"

"Yes, ma'am."

She narrows her eyes and scans me from head to toe. I realize too late that I should have deepened my voice.

"There's a church on your way. They got clothes for those who need them. Clean, free."

I nod and know this woman hasn't mistaken me for a boy, as I'd hoped. No proper young lady would be seen in public like this—not in 1863. Her eyes show curiosity but no judgment.

"Thank you, ma'am," I say. "I'll be sure to stop in on my way. Just safer to travel as a boy."

Sympathy softens the stern lines in her face. "Thirsty? A cup of coffee might warm you up."

I realize for the first time that I am trembling. It's adrenaline, though, and not the cold. "No, thank you, ma'am. The orphanage—it's up this street?" I try to point but can't unfurl my index finger without wincing.

She leaves her front step and comes closer to me. "You sure you're alright?"

I back away from the picket fence that separates her tidy yard from the dusty road. "I will be once I get to the orphanage. I have people there waiting for me."

That stops her advance. "Well, if you've got folks expecting you, you best be on your way."

I nod once more and walk away wondering which neighbor this woman will talk to first. Weeksville's a small community and newcomers are always interesting to the residents—especially a girl like me who appeared out of nowhere wearing pants instead of a dress. Telephones haven't been invented yet, but the grapevine in Weeksville is just as efficient.

Once I've left the woman and her son behind, I pull the hood up over my head wrap and try not to walk in a way that will attract attention. I want to run—to race toward the one person who can tell me whether Judah is still here: Mattie. The last time I saw her she was helping out in the kitchen while her younger brother Money went to class with the other orphans. Mattie and Money were fugitive slaves from the South. They lost their mother and two siblings on their journey north but were finally freed when President Lincoln issued the Emancipation Proclamation. I can still remember the shine in Mattie's eyes when she snuck into my room on New Year's Day to tell me the good news. Back then she thought—as everyone here did—that I was also a fugitive slave. Once we became friends and I knew she could be trusted, I told Mattie the truth.

As I walk through Weeksville I'm surprised by how familiar everything seems despite being dramatically different from the city where I grew up. In Brooklyn 1863 everything is smaller and more spread out. There are wide, open fields and a lot more space between buildings, which are mostly made of wood. The church, however, is built with bricks. I pause on the roadside and consider whether it's safe to go in and ask for some clothes. Mattie may be able to find me something to wear at the orphanage, but I'm also going to need a place to stay and don't want to ask for too much at once. A man in a black suit with a white collar around his neck comes out the front door of the church and then locks it behind him. I'm too late. As I turn to go, he calls out to me.

"Hello there! Were you coming to see me?"

I shake my head. "No, sir. I just—I heard you have clothes for those in need."

"Why yes, we do. Come around the back. My sister will help you find something suitable. I'm just heading over to see Reverend Macklin."

I smile in spite of myself and the minister's eyebrows go up. "Do you know Reverend Macklin?"

"Not very well," I tell him, "but he helped me find a job once. He's a good man."

"Tell me your name and I'll be sure to give him your regards."

"Genna," I say and the minister gives me another look of surprise. I pull down my hood so he can see that I really am a girl. I decide not to share the story of how I once impersonated Reverend Macklin's niece in order to prove I was free and not a runaway slave with a price on her head.

"Well, Genna, my sister Mildred will find you some proper clothes." The minister leads me to a wooden door around the side of the church. He knocks loudly and within seconds a coffee-colored woman with grey hair appears. "Just tell her what you need." He nods at me and his sister, then dons his hat and heads down the street.

I follow Mildred down a short staircase and into the basement of the church. A small room probably used for Sunday school is now full of donated clothes that hang on hooks lining the walls. Mildred sizes me up and then takes a plain cotton blouse and a long skirt off the wall. "These should fit you," she says with a smile.

I look around to see where I'm supposed to change. Then I realize that Mildred is waiting for me to undress. I clear my throat and clutch the clothes to my chest. Mildred takes the hint and moves toward the door. "I'll give you some privacy."

Before I can thank her, she's gone. I set my book bag on a nearby chair and try to wriggle out of my modern clothes. It takes a while to get my jeans off since I use only my fingertips in order to protect my damaged hands. Just as I pull the hoodie over my head, Mildred walks back into the room. I hear her gasp and wonder if she is shocked by my underwear— purple bikini briefs and a black sports bra. I decided before I came back that I wasn't going to wear a corset again if I could help it. But Mildred isn't shocked by my underwear—she's shocked by the scars on my back.

Mildred comes over and unbuttons the beige blouse. Without saying a word, she helps me slip my arms into the sleeves. I can manage the skirt without her help. I appreciate the silence between us. Mildred has stifled whatever curiosity she might have about my scars.

"Thank you, Miss Mildred," I say once I'm dressed. I hope the look in my eyes conveys how grateful I am for her help.

With some effort I manage to fold my old clothes and pack them inside my book bag. I sling the strap over my shoulder and head for the door.

"Where you heading?" Mildred asks.

"To the orphanage," I reply.

"Put some butter on those burns. You can wrap your hands with these." Mildred reaches into the pocket of her skirt and hands me a roll of linen. Strips of cloth are what people here use to bandage wounds. I have adhesive bandages in my bag but it's probably best to fit in whenever I can. When I get to the orphanage I can apply some antibiotic ointment before wrapping my hands.

Mildred walks me to the door. For a moment we stand together awkwardly, unsure how to part. I can't shake hands so I put my arms around Mildred and give her a quick hug. "Thanks again," I say before heading out the door and into the street as a nineteenth-century girl.

I walk purposefully now, feeling like I belong. I smile to myself as I compare this arrival to the first time I landed in the past. The amazing thing about Weeksville, this free Black community, is that everyone is willing to help whether they know you or not. It's not like that in the neighborhood where I was born and raised. I wonder when Black people stopped caring about each other.

Before long the orphanage comes into view. I unlatch the gate and let myself into the yard. No children are playing outside so class must be in session. I used to teach the smaller children before I got a job babysitting for the Brants. I wonder who's teaching the kids now.

The kitchen is at the back so I head in that direction. I hear a door open and close and then a woman with a shawl wrapped around her head and shoulders hurries to the pump in the corner of the backyard. I watch as she pushes the handle down several times and waits for water to pour into the wooden bucket on the ground.

"Mattie?"

The figure spins and looks in my direction. Mattie used to dress like a girl but now she wears a dress that shows she's a young woman. One thing hasn't changed: Mattie's eyes still shine like silver.

The hand that had been cranking the pump flies up to her mouth but cannot hide her smile.

"I always knew you wasn't gone for good," she says with satisfaction. Then Mattie drops the bucket and flies into my outstretched arms.

Mattie was my first friend — and for a long time my only friend — in the past. We used to stay up late sharing our secrets and before that Mattie nursed me back to health. I was in rough shape when I first arrived at the orphanage. This time it's just my hands that need attention.

Mattie scoops up her bucket and links her free arm through mine. "Let's get outta the cold. I got a pot boilin' on the stove. It's nice 'n warm in the kitchen."

"Esther lets you cook now?"

Mattie laughs. "Shoot. I been cookin' all my life. Esther jus' stopped fussin' over me all the time."

"She must trust you."

Mattie points her eyes at me and I laugh. We both know how much Esther likes being the boss.

"She jus' needed another pair o' hands. We got a lot mo' mouths to feed since the riots."

With my fingertips I manage to turn the knob and open the back door that leads to the kitchen. Mattie follows me in and sets down the heavy bucket of water. The kitchen is warm and fragrant, and the pot boiling on the cast iron stove has misted the windowpanes with steam.

"You hungry? This soup be ready 'fore long."

"I'm ok. I just need to fix my hands up."

I unzip my bag and take out a small bottle of hand sanitizer and a tube of ointment. Mattie slices a loaf of bread over at the table but keeps an eye on me.

"Butter's good for burns. Want some?"

I wince as the alcohol sinks in and shake my head. "I brought medicine with me this time."

Mattie puts down her knife and helps me wind the linen strips around my hands. Unlike Mildred, Mattie doesn't try to hide her curiosity. She takes up the bottle of hand sanitizer and sniffs the contents.

"Alcohol," I say as she wrinkles up her nose. "You can use just a dab of this to clean your hands instead of using soap and water."

I see Mattie's amazement and then look around the kitchen. It's clean but there are things folks don't yet know about hygiene in 1863.

"Keep it," I tell Mattie, pressing the bottle into her hands. "I've got more, and you need to have clean hands if you're cooking for all these kids."

Mattie snaps the top on the bottle, then flips it open and snaps it shut again. "Thanks, Genna," she says softly before slipping the bottle in her skirt pocket.

I grab hold of her hand before she can go back to the vegetables waiting on the kitchen table. "Mattie, is Judah here in Weeksville?"

Mattie grunts and turns away but not before giving my hand a gentle squeeze. She saws into the loaf of bread and says, "Naw. He's long gone."

I gasp and stagger back to lean against the kitchen wall. I feel as if someone has reached inside my chest and crushed my heart. "Gone?"

Mattie nods and stacks the sliced bread on a serving platter. "He come to Weeksville after the riots. Esther say he ain't had nowhere else to go. She don't like him."

I push myself off the wall and force my legs to bring me back to Mattie's side. "So Judah *was* here."

"Yeah, but he been gone 'bout a month now."

My blistered hands are bandaged but I ball them into fists and press my knuckles into the hard tabletop. My knees feel like they're about to give out. "He left for Africa?"

Mattie shakes her head. "Naw, he went off with some White folks from the capital. *Abolitionists*." She says this last word carefully, wanting to get it right.

Air rushes back into my lungs. "Judah's in D.C.?"

Mattie finally looks at me. "Albany. He's talkin' in churches upstate. Least that's what Esther said. She don't know why any Christian in they right mind would pay to sit and listen to a heathen like him."

"Judah's not a heathen."

Mattie shrugs and checks on the pot of boiling broth. "Look like one to me. Don't comb his hair, don't never smile at nobody. 'Cept that yella gal he was livin' with. Seen her cookin' and cleanin' for him, followin' him 'round like a puppy."

"'*Yella*?'"

"Fair. One of them Claxton twins. Their ma's near white but their pa's dark like us. He's a carpenter and Judah helps out. Least he did 'fore he took off."

"You don't like Judah, do you, Mattie?"

"I know you love him. But he didn't try like you tried. Seem to me you missed him more 'n he missed you."

"He can't do what I can do, Mattie."

"You didn't know what all you could do 'til you *tried*. But him? He jus' went 'bout his business like you wasn't worth rememberin'. I kept my eye on him while you was gone."

"Thanks, Mattie. You're a good friend." I put my arm around her shoulders and pull her close. "I missed you."

Mattie smiles shyly. "I know I ain't special. I'm a decent cook but I can't do the magic things you do. But a true friend's s'posed to be loyal and stand by you when times is tough. You left but I never did forget about you, Genna."

"Judah's loyal too, Mattie."

"Then why ain't he here?"

I don't have an answer for that. I didn't expect Judah to just sit around and wait for me. How could he have known I would find my way back? Mostly I'm just glad that he's still in the country and not on a ship heading to Liberia. Albany isn't that far away—I could even take a train up there and surprise him. But right now I need to find a place to stay and a way to earn some money.

I never got to say goodbye to any of my friends before I got sent back to the future, and I want to make sure they know I'm okay. So much has changed—New York was being torn apart by rioters when I left in July. Mattie wasn't hard to find here in Weeksville. I don't know if the Brants will take me back, but Nannie should still be working as their housekeeper over in Brooklyn Heights. Martha may be harder to find but her family lives in Five Points and hopefully they'll help me figure out how to track her down. These people are the closest thing to a family that I have here in the past. And until Judah returns, they're all I've got.

Genna

42.

"Need a hand?"

The bright, midday sun is behind me. Nannie holds a hand up to shield her eyes. My mouth turns up in a smile as hers turns downward in a frown.

"Who's there?" she asks in a voice full of distrust.

"It's me, Nannie. I've come back." My voice alone does not reassure her so I circle the small, elderly woman and let the sun shine full on my face.

Nannie drops her hand but continues to glare at me. "You real?"

I take the heavy, damp sheet from Nannie's hand and pin it to the clothesline that extends across the Brants' backyard. "Of course, I'm real. I look like a ghost to you?"

Nannie reaches out and pinches my arm just to be safe.

"Ow!" I rub my arm but laugh at Nannie's need to prove that I haven't come back from the dead.

The sound of my laughter seems to make Nannie relax. "You ain't come back to haunt me then?"

"No, ma'am. I just thought maybe you could use some help with this laundry. Haven't you missed me, Nannie?"

"On wash day, sure." Nannie grabs the other end of the sheet to keep it from dragging on the ground. "You ran outta here that night and I didn't know what to think. Figured those animals must 'o strung you up or thrown you in the river. Never thought you'd just run off without sayin' goodbye."

"I didn't run off, Nannie. I—I..."

How can I explain what happened that night? The last time I saw Nannie there was a mob of drunken, angry White men outside the Brants' front door. When they tried to force their way in, I took the pistol Dr. Brant gave me and fired into the crowd. Then I saw Judah coming up the street and I raced out to save him from the mob. We ran for our lives that night and when it was over, I made a careless wish in the fountain and woke up in the botanic garden—more than a hundred years later.

"I didn't expect to leave so suddenly," I tell her. "I'm sorry."

Nannie watches me for a moment. I bend down and sift through the items in her wicker basket, extracting a pair of pillowcases.

Finally she says, "Well, you're back now. That's what matters." Nannie picks up a towel and forces herself to sound nonchalant. "How long you plannin' to stay this time?"

I hand Nannie a clothespin but avoid her eyes. "I'm waiting for Judah to come back from Albany."

Nannie grunts. "If you waitin' on *that* boy, you might be waitin' a mighty long time. You got somewhere to stay till then?"

"I stayed at the orphanage in Weeksville last night but they've hardly got room for all the children left homeless by the riots."

"You could have a room to yourself here. Your old room's jus' the way you left it."

"Dr. Brant didn't hire someone to take my place?"

"What for? The missus took Henry and moved out to Long Island after the riots. She been stayin' with her aunt the past few months. 'Fore the doctor left this mornin' he told me they be comin' back the start o' next week. Missus sho' be glad to see you."

"Me? Why?" Mrs. Brant is without question the worst boss I ever had. She lost her mind and tried to hit me once but I slapped her down first.

"You know how fussy lil Henry can be. He didn't take to the gal who works for his auntie, and you know that boy loves you more than his own mama."

"You really think they'd take me back? Even if I can't stay long?"

"Only one way to find out. I'll put in a good word for you." Nannie takes the last towel out of the basket and hands it to me. "I sure could use some help gettin' the house ready for Her Majesty. Just look—we got the laundry hung up to dry in no time. Come inside and I'll make us some lunch."

Nannie's kitchen is as clean as Esther's, but the Brants are wealthy so there's more of everything. "I got some pork chops leftover from last night. Just take me a minute to whip up some biscuits. You still like biscuits?" Nannie winks at me and doesn't even wait for my reply. Nannie's the best cook in Brooklyn.

I pull out a chair and sit down at the kitchen table. Being here with Nannie makes me feel like I never left. But I did leave and things have changed since I've been gone. I take a deep breath and ask, "Nannie, where's Martha?"

Nannie sniffs and screws her lips up into a knot. "Gone."

"Gone where?"

Nannie shrugs and turns her attention back to the lump of dough. She mashes her knuckles into it and squeezes out bits of information. "The missus tried to keep her on—for your sake, I think. But that gal was a mess! Give her somethin' to do and she'd make a start, but she couldn't finish nothin'. You ask her a question and she just stood there like she was deaf—starin' at the wall, her face blank as a slate. Other times she'd start to shake so bad she couldn't hold nothin' in her hands. She broke three pieces of the good china, but Missus still wouldn't let her go. She's a changed woman, you know. Ever since that night..."

Nannie pauses and examines the dough. "She gave that gal more than a fair chance. It's the drink did her in."

I wait to see if Nannie will say something bad about the Irish. Instead, she shrugs once more and launches herself back into kneading the dough.

"She wanted to stay, I know that much. But her head weren't right since the riots. More than once she woke the house with her screamin' — nightmares, I reckon. She was scared to go outside, and I can't say as I blame her. I sure made myself scarce after that night! But you can't hide forever."

I squirm in my seat and try to get Nannie to hurry up and finish her story about Martha. All I need is a clue, something to point me in the right direction.

"Where did she go, Nannie?"

"Told you already, I don't know. She drank just a little at first, to keep her hands from shakin' so bad. Then she started to drink at night. To help with the nightmares, I 'spect. She polished off the bottles of wine I keep here in the kitchen, then started helpin' herself to the doctor's sherry. Missus said she couldn't keep a drunkard in the house. She didn't want to put her out, but there weren't nothin' more she could do for that gal."

"Martha didn't—I mean, she wouldn't have gone back...there," I say, hoping Nannie will stamp out my worst fear. I want to find Martha, but I definitely don't want to go into Manhattan.

Nannie snorts. "Where else she gonna go?" Then she sees the look on my face and tries to reassure me. "They say Five Points was spared during the riots. I guess even a dog knows better than to chew up his own bed." Nannie clears her throat and spits into the fire. I flinch as her spit sizzles against the inside of the black iron stove.

"What you gonna do if you find her?"

I haven't thought that far ahead. "I don't know, but it sounds like Martha needs help."

"You can't help her if she don't wanna help herself."

I nod and we sit in silence for a moment.

"You ain't asked 'bout Paul yet."

I feel my cheeks warming up but fight to keep myself from grinning like a little girl.

Nannie chuckles. "Now, seems to me, if you gon' wait on a boy, you be better off waitin' on a boy like Paul. You know he was sweet on you."

"He was sweet on *you*, Nannie, and your cooking. Paul was your favorite, not mine. He and I were just friends."

"Hmph. Coulda been more 'n friends if you wasn't wastin' your time tryin' to change that wild-eyed boy." Before I can open my mouth to defend Judah, Nannie pulls a letter out of her skirt pocket. "Had a letter from Paul not too long ago. My pastor read it to me. He asked after you."

I have two thoughts at once: I never finished teaching Nannie how to read, and Paul still thinks about me! Nannie hands me the letter and I force my fingers not to shake as I open the envelope.

I never learned how to write with a quill and ink but Paul's penmanship is impressive. It only takes me a minute to scan the few lines he's penned to Nannie. "He's coming back to New York!"

Nannie smiles like her heart's about to burst with joy. "Be here in a day or two. Says he'll join up here now that they're takin' colored soldiers. I 'spect they'll make him an officer."

"An officer? Paul's too young to lead a regiment."

"He be eighteen soon. War will make a man of him."

If he lives. Would Paul believe me if I told him the war will end in less than two years? Nannie takes the letter back and slips it in her pocket. "Doesn't it scare you, Nannie—the fact that he could die in battle?"

"Death ain't nothin' but a doorway to heaven, Genna. If that boy wants to take up arms to free our people, then I ain't about to stop him."

I will—if I can.

Genna

43.

Martha's back in Five Points. Nannie insists she's a lost cause, but Martha's my friend and I'm not giving up on her. Five Points is the last place I want to go, but Nannie assures me there hasn't been any trouble since the riots last summer. African Americans and Irish immigrants live side by side in Five Points, but that didn't stop a mostly Irish mob from going on a killing rampage in July.

When Nannie sees how determined I am, she lends me a dollar and sends me on my way. I take a ferry over to Manhattan and then walk the rest of the way. Everybody knows everybody in Five Points so it doesn't take me long to find Martha's home. Problem is, she's not there. One of her brothers says Martha's working for a woman named Sal.

He gives me pretty good directions, and before long I find myself in front of a dilapidated, three-story wood building. It looks like a rowdy kind of place, but the street's not so calm, either, and I'm tired of picking my way through the mud and trash and horseshit. The hem of my skirt's already heavy with filth and I've been holding it up all this time. Five Points is worse than any ghetto I've ever seen in 2001.

"Come for a job, have you, love?"

The White woman with rouged cheeks winks at me so I won't take offense. She's perched on the porch railing, her large breasts rolling loosely beneath a camisole that probably used to be white.

I shake my head and smile a bit so I don't look as disgusted as I feel. "I'm looking for my friend, Martha. I was told she works for Sal."

"Martha? We ain't got no Martha here, far's I know."

A White man staggers past me, then falls to his knees and pukes in the street. Two stray dogs scamper over and begin licking up the vomit. I grab hold of the wooden banister to steady my nerves.

"Are you sure? Her brother told me she works here."

"He did, eh? Well, there's lotsa girls workin' here. You can try askin' upstairs, if you like. Or out back."

I look in the direction of her thumb, and thank her before climbing the six steps that lift me out of the street and onto the porch. The front door is wide open and it's clear there's a party going on inside. Men and women — Black and White — are singing and drinking and grabbing at each other.

I step over the threshold and weave my way through the smoky, crowded room to a half-open door that leads to the kitchen. The bottom half of the door is closed, but through the open top half I can see a dirty, bustling kitchen. Another door in the far wall leads out to the back alley, and through that door I see a Black girl tossing a pail of scraps onto the mucky ground. As she turns to re-enter the kitchen, she sees me at the door and stops short.

The cook hollers at her to hurry up, so the girl drops the empty pail, and takes up a tray with several small glasses and a bottle of gin. I can see the girl is heading my way, so I reach inside and undo the latch on the lower half of the door. I swing it open and hold it for her. The girl nods a silent thanks at me, and passes by, expertly dodging the rowdy men whose greedy hands are hungrily groping every female body within reach.

I follow the silent girl as closely as I can, swatting away the filthy, clawing hands. The girl seems strangely indifferent to the chaos and within seconds we have reached the stairs that lead up to the second floor.

It is only after we climb the stairs and reach the landing that she stops and turns to me.

"Why are you here?"

The harsh tone of her voice surprises me, and I find myself wanting to ask her the very same question. Instead I say, "I'm looking for my friend. Her name's Martha." I pause then think to add, "She's Irish—about our age."

The girl drops her eyes and nods once. "She's here." Then she turns and leads me down the dimly lit hallway. Most of the doors are closed, but the walls are thin and we can hear everything that's going on inside those rooms. Part of me wants to turn around and bolt out of that whorehouse as fast as I can, but I can't leave Martha behind. I need to understand why she chose this life over working for the Brants.

The girl leads me toward another narrow flight of stairs, but we have to wait in order to avoid contact with the half-dressed man who is staggering down the stairs. His drunken, sweaty body looms above us and I back away in fear and disgust. When he tries to swipe a shot glass off the girl's tray, she pulls it back.

"Drinks cost extra," she says in that same flat voice, and to my surprise, the drunk actually flips a coin onto her tray before tossing back the shot and staggering down the hall. I turn and press my face into the wall but still smell his sour breath as he squeezes past me, grabbing my ass and then nearly crashing down the stairs when my elbow connects with his ribs.

The girl looks at me with her blank, unfeeling eyes. "You alright?"

I nod, but realize I am shaking, my heart pounding fast within my chest. I fight the urge to tear off my dress and rid myself of the john's stench. But I know that what's coming is worse—much worse. The girl leads me up the stairs and points to the room the john just left. "She's in there."

I take a deep breath and move towards the open door. Before I see her, I hear Martha mumbling incoherently. I blink quickly to clear the tears from my eyes, but I am still not ready for what I see when I finally stand in the doorway. Martha is sprawled on the floor of the tiny room, trying without much success to pull herself back onto the bed. With the back of her bare arm she wipes the slime dripping from her mouth and off her chin. She is wearing a loose, soiled white shift and as she tugs at the bed covers, the unwashed linen slides off the bed and pools around her on the floor. Martha — my friend — is drowning in filth.

"Martha?"

At first I don't recognize the sound of my own voice, but then I realize I have not spoken yet. It is the girl, now standing behind me in the doorway. "Martha, get up. You got company."

Martha tries to lift her head, but seems unable to see us. Her greasy hair falls forward and she swats at it with her hand. "What? So soon? Give us a minute, love." Martha's words slur together as her hand reaches out and gropes blindly at the air between us. "Better yet, give us a drink, hey?"

I look at Martha and feel a sudden urge to vomit. Just as I begin to gag, the girl presses her tray into my back, forcing me inside the room. She sets her tray on the bed and closes the door behind us. I fold myself into a corner, my eyes shut tight, my hand clamped over my mouth to keep my disgust inside.

"Give us a drink, Nell. Just a nip — that's all I need..."

"You need to get up, Martha. Come on. That's it — up, up."

I hear a grunt and then the sound of bed springs creaking as the girl called Nell heaves Martha onto the bed. I want to be strong. I want to be the friend I came here to be. But the stench of the full chamber pot under the bed is making me ill, and through the thin walls I can hear the john next door grunting and groaning. I sense Nell's blank eyes focused on my back.

"Thought you came to see your friend," she says and I suspect that if I turn, I will find a sneer on her face.

I edge myself over to the window and, with some effort, force it open.

The air out back is hardly fresh, the alley being lined with privies. But a slight breeze makes its way into the room, and I take a deep breath to steady myself. Finally I turn and take a long, hard look at Martha. "How long has she been this way?"

Nell glances at Martha and shrugs. "For as long as I've known her."

"She wasn't like this before. The Martha I knew never would let—" I stop myself when I see the total indifference in Nell's face. "Where are her clothes?" I ask.

Nell shrugs again and folds her arms across her chest. "She ain't got none."

I am mad about a lot of things right now, but Nell's attitude is really starting to piss me off. I want to say, "What the fuck are you talking about?" But instead I say, "What do you mean? She must have a dress or something."

I look around the room but there's no closet, no chest of drawers. Just the raggedy old bed and a small washstand, which is a joke because nothing in this room is clean.

Nell looks at Martha's pitiful form sprawled out on the bed. "What's she need clothes for? She's a whore."

I want to reach out and smack this girl, but I may need her help to get Martha out of here. So I push aside my ghetto self and try to act right. "She's not a whore—she's my friend, and I'm getting her out of here."

Nell fixes her eyes on mine and for the first time I see a flicker of emotion. Maybe even respect. I look around the room again and spot a wine-colored robe hanging on a hook on the back of the door. I cross the cramped room and snatch the robe off the door. Then I lean over the bed and try to get Martha to wake up. Problem is, Martha isn't sleeping. She's drunk, half-naked, and about to pass out.

"Martha? Martha, come on. It's time to go." I push the stringy hair out of Martha's face and gently pat her cheek a few times. To my surprise, Martha's skin is clammy and hot.

Martha flinches, squints at me, and tries to lift her head off the bed.

"Who're you?" she mumbles.

"I'm Genna. Remember me? I used to work for the Brants. We were friends — remember?"

Martha blinks and peers into my face. "Genna?"

"That's right. You remember. Come on now, sit up. That a girl."

With Nell's help I manage to get Martha into a sitting position. I slip one of her arms through the sleeve of the robe and Nell does the same with the other.

"You got a plan?"

Nell's voice surprises me almost as much as the interest suddenly brightening her eyes. My ghetto self would say, "What's it to you?" But I don't have time to cop attitude right now. I decide instead to tell her the truth.

"Not really. I guess we can't just go down the way we came up, huh?"

"Not with her you can't." Nell follows my gaze over to the window. "You could take her down the fire escape."

"Fire escape?"

Nell nods and I rush over to the window. Sure enough, a rickety wooden death trap leads down to the ground. I turn back to Nell. "You ever been out there?"

Nell shakes her head. "We ain't had a fire since I been here." She pauses and almost smiles at me. "Not yet, anyway."

Nell locks her eyes on mine and just when I think I understand her meaning, Martha lurches forward and pukes all over the floor. Nell somehow manages to get out of the way in time, but my boots are now covered in slime along with the hem of my dress. I'm about to start cursing when the door opens and a Black man suddenly appears. He has one hand on the doorknob and the other is already unfastening his fly. Nell steps forward and blocks his way.

"She's sick, sir. We'll need a few minutes to get her cleaned up."

The Black man's eyes sweep over me, then linger on Martha's flushed face and soiled clothes. "Don't bother," he says. "Plenty more fish in the sea."

Nell nods and begins closing the door. "Tell my aunt you need another girl. She'll take care of you."

He chuckles and zips up his pants. "Sure 'nough. Sal knows just what a fella needs."

Nell closes the door, then takes a bunch of keys from her pocket and locks it. She presses her lips together and darts her eyes at me.

"Black Sal's your aunt?" I ask, amazed.

"By marriage," she mumbles, "not by blood." For a moment, Nell's eyes linger on the puke-covered floor. Then something in Nell stiffens and she lifts her chin. "Where you taking her?"

"Back to Weeksville," I say, without conviction. Martha's in no condition to climb down a rickety fire escape, walk back to the ferry, and cross the river over to Brooklyn. I look at Nell and for the first time realize that she, too, is desperate to get away from this place. "You could come with us," I tell her, hoping she'll agree.

Turns out that's all I need to say. Nell takes control of everything from that moment on.

"Splash some water on her face and get her over to the window," she says, and I do my best to get Martha off the bed and over to the far side of the room.

Nell takes up the soiled sheet and starts tearing it into shreds. She dumps out the bottle of liquor she was meant to sell, making sure the shredded linen is soaked with gin. Then she reaches into her pocket and pulls out her bundle of keys and a small box of matches. Nell turns the key in the lock and opens the door just a crack. She looks at me over her shoulder. "Ready?" she asks in that flat, hard voice.

I take a deep breath and nod. From where I'm standing by the window, the ground looks real far away. With Martha in the state she's in, Brooklyn might as well be on another planet. But if Nell's willing to help us, I can't back down now.

"I'm ready," I say, with the surest voice I can manage.

Nell looks at me, hard. "Whatever happens, don't run. You run, they'll follow. Got it? Whatever happens, just walk away."

I nod but think I won't be walking if there's a mob of angry White folks coming after me. Yet with Martha in the state she's in, I probably won't have much choice.

Nell strikes a match and holds it to a strip of gin-soaked bed sheet. "You first. I'll wait 'til you're both out. Then I'll sound the alarm."

I do as I'm told and climb out the window. Then I lean back in to coax Martha outside. "Come on, Martha. We're going now."

I hold out my hands and am relieved when Martha readily grasps my fingers in her clammy palms.

"Out the window?" she asks, hesitantly putting one knee on the window ledge.

I catch a whiff of smoke and try to pull Martha out onto the fire escape. "Hurry, Martha. We have to go now!"

Smoke and heat blow full into my face as Nell opens the bedroom door and yells, "FIRE!" Then in an instant Martha tumbles into my arms, shoved from behind by Nell. "Let's go," she says in a sure, steady voice.

What about the others? I want to say. There are White and Black women trapped in those rooms, never mind their johns. What if someone dies because of what we've done?

Nell turns and sees me frozen, my hands gripping the wooden railing. She hisses impatiently, "Let's go! A little fire can make a whole lotta smoke. It'll burn itself out before we reach the ground."

I push Martha before me, and she follows Nell like an obedient child. I bang on every window we pass on the way down, and before long the weight of at least twenty other people tests the strength of the creaking wooden fire escape. There are moments when I'm not sure it's actually attached to the brick building, but it holds up long enough for all of us to get down to the ground.

When I say "ground," what I really mean is muck. There are wooden planks laid down in a path to the privy and back alley, but with each step, thick greenish slime oozes up between the boards. I can't even describe the stench. Of course, Nell isn't fazed at all, and Martha's staggering between us like a wide-eyed child who's never been outside before—everything's new and interesting, even if it's filthy and disgusting.

When we reach the alley, we stop and turn back to check on the progress of the fire. The early shrieks of panic have been replaced by bawdy laughter as half-dressed men and women catch their breath or keep on doing what they were doing before the fire broke out. I glance at Nell and see her eyes are fixed on the third-floor room from which we escaped. Leaning out of the window now is an older Black woman who also seems to be taking the emergency in stride. Her eyes find Nell despite the chaotic swirl of bodies in the backyard, and for a moment Sal almost smiles. Nell pulls up all the bitterness she has swallowed over the years and spits it on the ground. Then, without looking at me or Martha, she says, "Let's go."

Nell says the ferry's too far away. "We'll hire a boat at the water's edge," she says, so I just nod and keep doing as I'm told. If Nell says, "Turn left," I turn left. If she tells me to speed up, I move as fast as I can without breaking into a run. I think Nell's worried somebody might be following us, but I don't stop to ask questions. I just do as I'm told. This is her 'hood, not mine.

"Let's go down here," Nell says.

We're on either side of Martha, half-carrying and half-dragging her along. The alley is full of what smells like raw sewage, but I figure it must be a shortcut so I follow Nell's lead. Before we get halfway through, a hefty White guy swings around the corner and heads our way, all casual-like.

Nell narrows her eyes and whispers to me, "Remember, don't run."

"Well, well," he says in a cheerful voice. "Fancy meetin' you lovely ladies in a place like this."

He loops his thumbs behind his suspenders and plants his feet far apart, blocking our way. I glance over my shoulder to see if anyone's behind us. The coast is clear, but Nell said not to run and she seems to know what she's doing. At least, I hope she does.

"Where might you be headin' on such a fine day?"

I glance at Nell but her eyes are on the ground so I answer instead. "We're going to Brooklyn."

"Brooklyn? A fine city, to be sure. But your friend there doesn't have her travelin' clothes on."

He nods at Martha and I wrap my arm tight around her waist. After all she's been through, there's no way I'm letting this creep get his hands on her. "She's...sick, so we're taking her home."

"Ah, but she's not yours to take," he says, sliding his eyes from my face to Nell's. "Now, is she?"

I'm waiting for Nell to say or do something, but she's still got her eyes glued to the ground. Over the White man's shoulder I see a Black man in a beat-up top hat peering at us from the far end of the alley. Will he help us? I'm just about to call out to him when Nell suddenly speaks up.

"Please, sir," she says in a soft, girlish voice I've never heard her use before. "I've got money. I'll give it to you if you leave us be."

The White man folds his arms across his broad chest and grins. "Rich like your aunty, are ya? Sal does pay handsomely." He considers the offer, then nods in the direction of Nell's pocketed hand. "Let's see what you got," he says with a wink. "Maybe we can strike a deal."

Nell shifts Martha's weight onto me and tries to send a silent message with her eyes. Problem is, I don't know what she's trying to say. Nell waits for the guy to take a step closer, then turns her shoulder and pretends to gather coins that are buried deep in her skirt pocket. Instead, she wraps her fingers around the bundle of hard iron keys and gives this jerk what he least expects: a swift fist to the crotch! He groans, doubles over, and slowly slides down the alley wall.

"Let's go," says Nell in her regular voice. Then she steps over the guy's body like she does this kind of thing every day.

The raggedy Black man who had been loitering at the end of the alley comes toward us with a crazy smile on his face. I hold my breath and wait to see what Nell will do now, but she only nods at him as he removes his hat and bows before her like she's royalty. As soon as we get past him, he goes over to the White guy, slams his fist into his face, and then takes all of Sal's money out of the guy's pockets.

"Five Points," I mutter under my breath once we reach the end of the alley.

Nell gives a short, harsh laugh. "I've lived here all my life. You wouldn't believe the things I've seen. If I never set foot on these filthy streets again, it'll be too soon," she says bitterly.

"That makes two of us," I reply. We don't say much else after that and focus instead on getting Martha down to the river.

Genna

44.

We use the rest of Nannie's money to hire a man to row us across the East River.

"Now what?" Nell asks once we reach Brooklyn.

I look around and try to come up with a plan. I can't take Martha to the Brants' — not in this condition. There's a reason Martha's so heavy — she's pregnant! At first I thought she'd just gained a little weight, but she's probably drunk more than she's eaten for the past few months, which only makes matters worse. We watched a movie about birth defects in health class once so I know what drinking alcohol can do to an unborn baby.

It's cold outside but Martha's face is flushed and her hair is damp with sweat. I need to get her to a doctor but I'm out of money and I don't know who to turn to. Should I try to find someone Irish who might agree to help her? We're getting plenty of funny looks from people of both races and if Nell splits, I don't know what I'll do.

Suddenly I hear someone call my name. I frantically search the crowded docks, hoping to find a friendly face. Finally I spot Sam Jenkins standing up in his wagon just a few yards away.

"Thank God," I whisper. I hoist Martha up and half drag, half carry her over to Sam's wagon.

"You headin' back to Weeksville?" he asks.

Only Sam could see two Black girls carrying a drunk, pregnant, half-dressed White girl and not miss a beat.

"I'm so happy to see you, Sam. We have to get Martha to a doctor—fast."

Sam hops down from the wagon and comes around to open up the back. "I come down here to pick up some lumber. Just got it loaded up. Few more minutes and you'd a missed me."

"Must be the luck of the Irish," Nell says with a wry grin.

Sam rearranges the lumber so that there's room for me and Martha. I climb in first and prop myself up against the backboard. Sam delicately boosts Martha up and Nell helps me maneuver her into the wagon. I put my arm around her and Martha's head lolls on my shoulder. I assure her that we'll be home soon, but she only mutters incoherently. Sam tosses me a scratchy wool blanket and I gratefully drape it over both of us.

Nell accepts Sam's hand and pulls herself up so she can take a seat on the bench. I've ridden in this wagon before. Sam rescued me when I first arrived in this world and two White men took me to the police station hoping to claim a reward. Back then it was me who couldn't move or speak, but I eventually recovered with the help of folks in Weeksville.

Sam talks over his shoulder as the wagon bumps along the cobblestone street. "If we hurry we may catch the doc while he's still on his rounds."

It feels like forever but within an hour Sam pulls the wagon up in front of the orphanage. "Esther ain't gon' like us bringin' a sick gal into her kitchen."

"We won't stay," I assure him. "We'll just ask Dr. Brant to examine Martha."

It's a long shot, but I'm hoping Martha can come back to Brooklyn Heights. During the ride out to Weeksville I managed to give her a couple of ibuprofen from the bottle I carry in my pocket. Martha's still burning up but she's at least she's sleeping soundly, one hand cradling her swollen belly.

Dr. Brant's carriage is parked at the front entrance and we find

Adams, his driver, sitting at the kitchen table drinking a cup of coffee. Adams' eyes widen when he sees me but he says nothing. Martha's the focus of everyone's attention. Mattie knows she'll get in trouble once Esther finds out, but she still guides us into the small bedroom just off the kitchen. Nell helps me get Martha into bed and then I make myself scarce. I haven't seen Dr. Brant yet and don't know if Nannie had a chance to ask him about taking me back.

I linger on the back step until I'm sure Dr. Brant has been led into the back room. Then I slip back inside.

Esther looks up from the stove and scowls at me. "Hmph. You again. Shoulda known you brung that gal here. Just the kinda company I'd 'spect you to keep."

I decide not to take the bait. Instead I look around the kitchen and search for a way to make myself useful. "What can I do to help?"

"Can't cook without water," she says in her usual brusque tone.

I take up the bucket next to the stove and head out to the pump in the yard. When I return, Esther puts me to work peeling potatoes. I take a seat at the table in the center of the kitchen and pick up the knife Esther sets before me. Adams sits across from me, his head buried in the newspaper. He reads things out to Esther who adds her usual colorful commentary.

I keep an eye on the door to the bedroom and wonder what's taking so long. Martha must be worse off than I thought. Finally the door opens and Mattie exits carrying a basin full of pink water. Oh God. I hope Dr. Brant didn't "bleed" Martha. I hold the kitchen door open so that Mattie can toss the water into the yard. When I turn around Dr. Brant is standing in the kitchen staring at me.

"Genna? Is that you?"

I nearly curtsy but stop myself in time. "Good evening, Dr. Brant."

I've never seen Dr. Brant at a loss for words. He's a wealthy, educated, sometimes arrogant White man but for several seconds he just stands before me with his mouth open, unable to speak. Then a flood of questions comes at me.

"What does this mean? We thought you were—that you'd been... have you come back to us?"

I can feel everyone's eyes on me as I nod. "For now. I—I'm sorry that I left so abruptly last summer. I had a family emergency."

Mattie coughs behind me but doesn't expose my lie.

"And yet your brother stayed behind, I believe. What is his name?"

"Judah, sir."

"That's right. He's made a name for himself as of late. I haven't heard him myself, but I hear he's quite a compelling orator."

This time Esther coughs, no doubt unhappy to hear the esteemed doctor praising Judah.

"How's Martha?" I ask, eager to change the subject.

Dr. Brant frowns and nods at the bedroom door. I understand his silent command and follow him into Mattie's room. Martha lies beneath the cover, flushed and listless.

"Will she be ok?"

"The fever should subside but that isn't my main concern."

"It's not?" I swallow hard but can't bring myself to ask, "What is?"

Dr. Brant glances over his shoulder and sees the small crowd gathered at the open door. Without being asked, Esther shoos the others away and closes the door.

Dr. Brant lays a heavy hand on my shoulder. "I'm afraid your friend is in trouble, Genna."

Trouble? I hope he's not thinking about calling the police. Prostitution may be against the law, but so is keeping a teenage girl in a brothel against her will. I scramble to piece together a defense for my friend. "Martha's been through a lot, Dr. Brant."

"Well, she'll need all the strength she can muster to make it through the trial that lies ahead."

Trial? My mind starts to race. "Martha didn't choose to work at that brothel, Dr. Brant—I'm sure of it. I think she was sold to Black Sal. She didn't have any clothes and after we helped her escape, a man tried to force her to go back."

"Your unfortunate friend chose to drink, Genna. And I'm afraid that with her kind, one vice leads to another."

I search my mind for the term I heard on the news back in 2001. It was also in the psychology textbooks my old boss Hannah gave to me. "Martha was self-medicating," I tell Dr. Brant. "She used alcohol to block out her memory of the riots. Martha saw her friend killed, Dr. Brant—and she was nearly killed herself."

"That may be true. But your friend is now with child, Genna. And I'm sure I don't have to tell you that the child's paternity will be impossible to determine, considering her unsavory profession."

Dr. Brant is trying to be delicate, but I know what he's getting at. Martha's a poor Irish girl—a whore—who's about to have a baby out of wedlock. Her baby, fathered by some stinking john, will be illegitimate. A bastard. A nobody in this society.

"It's not her fault."

Dr. Brant watches Martha as she sleeps but his face doesn't soften. "Nonetheless," he says, turning back to me, "she's gotten herself into a rather unenviable situation. You would do well to sever your association with her for the sake of your own reputation."

If we were back in *my* Brooklyn, I'd tell this arrogant White man just where he could shove his stupid advice. But in this Brooklyn I can't do that. If I want to work for Dr. Brant—if I expect him to trust me with his infant son—then I have to go along to get along.

I nod without saying a word and Dr. Brant seems satisfied.

"Are you staying here in Weeksville?"

"I was but Nannie said she could use some help getting the house ready for Mrs. Brant's return."

"That's an excellent idea. Henry's missed you terribly, of course, and I'm sure Mrs. Brant would be delighted to see you again. Why don't you come with me this evening? I just have a few other children to see here. Adams will see that your things are loaded onto the carriage."

"Thank you, Dr. Brant."

Mattie slips inside the room as soon as Dr. Brant exits. I know what she's going to say before the words even leave her mouth.

"They not gon' let that White gal stay here, Genna. Not when she's... like that."

"Like what—sick with fever? They call themselves Christians and they're going to throw a sick girl out into the street?"

Mattie looks at me. She doesn't understand why I'm playing dumb, and neither do I. I sigh and sink into the only chair in the room. "Where else can I take her? No one around here's going to want to take in an Irish girl. Not when she's—*with child*."

"She know who the daddy is?" Mattie asks.

Esther's cruel voice catches us both by surprise. "'Course she don't. That gal's a whore and you got some nerve bringin' her here!"

Nell peeks around Esther who stands in the doorway with her arms folded defiantly across her chest. I spring up and push all of them out of the room, closing the door behind me. I glare at Nell. "What did you tell them?"

She just shrugs. "The truth—that you came looking for one of the girls and I helped you get her away from Sal. That I came to Weeksville to make a clean start. They're looking for a new teacher."

"And you're fit to teach? You were working in that brothel, too!"

"In the kitchen. I wasn't a whore."

Esther stomps around the kitchen, her face screwed up like she can just smell sin in the next room. "Nell went to the mission school. She knows the Lord and she ain't to blame for what her relations do. But that trash has got to go. Her kind o' dirt don't wash off with soap. Layin' up in that whorehouse, spreadin' her legs for every Tom, Dick, and Harry."

"There were colored men in there, you know!"

Esther just grunts and keeps on going. "I'm sure there were—the gutter's home to all kinds o' trash. That gal's been next to every kind of filth—the lowest of the low. And you didn't have enough sense to leave her there where she belongs—with her own kind! Woulda been more merciful and better 'n bringin' her here! I got enough mouths to feed— these children here plus all the folks we got to care for 'cause Paddies like her drove 'em out of the city!"

"Martha didn't do anything to you, or anyone else around here. The mob turned on her because she loved a colored boy—she had to run for her life!"

"Oh yeah? And where's that fool Negro now?

"Dead," I say quietly.

"That's right," Esther says smugly. "White folks like her don't bring nothin' but trouble. Lovin' some fool of a boy don't make her one of us. Let her turn to her own people for help 'cause we ain't got enough to go around."

"Well, that's mighty Christian of you."

Esther whirls around and flings out her finger to point at Sam. "Don't you lecture me on how to be a good Christian, Sam Jenkins! When's the last time you saw the inside of a church?"

"Ain't no room there for a poor soul like me. Too many high 'n mighty folks fillin' up the pews."

"I ain't ashamed to be a righteous woman," Esther says with a proud tilt of her chin.

"No—you just ashamed to stand too close to those who been brought low," Sam counters.

"If you lay down with dogs, you gonna get up with fleas. That gal got just what she asked for—nothin' less."

Sam strikes a match along the doorframe and lights his pipe. "How 'bout that other sayin'—how's it go? 'Judge not les' ye be judged'?"

"Don't you quote the Good Book at me! And don't you dare smoke that pipe in my kitchen, Sam. You so smart, figure out where to take that gal 'cause she can *not* stay here."

Esther turns on Mattie. "Why you sittin' there idle when supper ain't ready yet?"

Mattie jumps up and gets to work helping Esther. I slip outside to talk to Sam.

"Feelin's high 'gainst the Irish round here," he says.

I nod as humbly as I can. "I didn't mean to offend anybody. I just didn't know where else to go."

"They got a home for unwed mothers over in Clinton Hill. I doubt the Sisters of Mercy would turn away a sinner."

"You think they'd take Martha in? Dr. Brant said the fever would pass in a couple of days." Maybe sooner if I keep giving her ibuprofen.

"Might be worth payin' 'em a visit," Sam suggests. "I know some folks out that way. I'll ask around and see what's what."

"Oh, Sam!" I can't stop myself from throwing my arms around him. "You're the best," I say after planting a kiss on his stubbly cheek. "I wish there were more people like you in Weeksville."

"Well, now — Esther ain't so bad. She got a good heart to go with that quick tongue. She just worries too much 'bout being respectable. But ain't none of us clean all the time. This world's a mucky, murky place."

As Sam sucks on his pipe I think about the streets of Five Points and how hard it was to avoid the filth everywhere. The skirt Mildred gave me will have to be soaked and scrubbed, though soon I'll be wearing the drab black dress that all female house servants wear.

Bit by bit I am piecing together my old life. Martha's safe, Dr. Brant is willing to give me my job back, and my friends here in Weeksville haven't forgotten me. All that's missing is Judah.

Mattie helps me get clean so that I don't stink up the carriage. I give her a quick hug and promise to come back soon. Adams takes my bag before opening the carriage door so that I can climb inside. He gives my hand an extra squeeze and nods silently before closing the door.

The carriage rocks as Adams climbs back up to take his seat. I spread my damp skirt to help it dry and try to remember the last time I saw Adams — he was firing out the window of the Brant's house, trying to beat back the mob of drunken White man that had gathered outside. His last glimpse of me would have been when I burst through the front door and raced up the street, trying to warn Judah. I led the mob away from the house, but then Judah and I had to run for our lives.

I take a deep breath and push the memory of that terrifying night from my mind. I grip the plush velvet seat beneath my legs and think of the book I read about PTSD. *Anchor yourself in the present moment.* That's what it said to do to keep terror in the past where it belongs. The riots are over. I survived. Judah survived. Adams, Nannie, Martha, and the Brants all survived. The leader of the mob did not. Judah killed him—but only because he thought the man had killed me. But I wasn't dead. I was just gone. And now I'm back. *Anchor yourself.* I feel the soft velvet beneath my fingers and smell the faint scent of Sam's pipe lingering in the air.

My heart has returned to its normal pace by the time Dr. Brant finishes seeing the sick children at the orphanage. I hear him tell Adams not to bother climbing down from the driver's seat. He opens the door of the carriage for himself and I slide over so Dr. Brant can settle beside me. Instead he sits directly across from me and smiles. He's a kind man but I don't want to be examined by the doctor right now. I glance out the window and stifle a yawn as the carriage rolls away.

Dr. Brant leans forward and pats my knee. "No doubt you'll be glad to get home. It has been a rather long day."

I nod and lean back against the padded velvet seat as the carriage pulls away from the orphanage. If we're both tired, maybe the trip won't involve an interrogation. Even small talk is beyond me right now.

"I met an interesting young man earlier this week."

I silently groan as Dr. Brant begins what is sure to be a long anecdote.

"Not a patient, really, but an intriguing case nonetheless. A German couple found the poor Negro moaning in a ditch by the side of the road, and I stopped to offer my assistance. He was in a great deal of pain but couldn't communicate in English. He was practically delirious and uttered a steady stream of words that sounded like utter gibberish."

The rocking motion of the carriage is lulling me to sleep but Dr. Brant doesn't seem to notice or care.

"Later, once I'd given him something for the pain, he was able to tell us his name. He speaks fluent English and seems quite intelligent. I even considered making him my new assistant, but that was before I discovered you had returned. He said his uncle was a physician, I believe. The family's originally from Haiti."

Haiti? My eyes flash open and my weary body straightens as I get a queasy feeling in the pit of my stomach. It couldn't be. I couldn't have brought someone with me—again.

"What happened to him?" I ask anxiously.

Dr. Brant frowns, though I know he enjoys solving medical mysteries. "That remains unclear. After the riots I feared the worst, of course. But the boy had no recollection of being assaulted. His right shoulder was dislocated, which is usually the result of a fall. There were superficial cuts on the right side of his face, and his upper arm was badly bruised, possibly fractured. I extracted some fragments of glass from his cheek and offered to take him back to the surgery, but the German couple was determined to care for him themselves." Dr. Brant pulls out his gold watch and checks the time before replacing it in his vest pocket. "I hope Nannie has dinner ready. I'm quite famished this evening."

I'm impatient, too, but not for dinner. I need to know more about this Haitian boy. I clear my throat and ask, "What did you say his name was?"

Dr. Brant thinks for a moment and then says the one name I'm dreading to hear: "Peter, I believe. I offered to check on the patient in a week or so. The family lives in Williamsburg. You're welcome to attend me if the case interests you."

"It does," I say eagerly, wondering if I can stand not knowing *for sure* for seven more days. I made it to Five Points on my own today, which means I can make it to Williamsburg, too.

Dr. Brant silently gazes out the window as we enter downtown Brooklyn and bump along the cobbled streets that lead home. My heart races as I think of all the terrible things that could have happened to Peter if those kind Germans hadn't stopped to help him. I close my eyes and shove my hands under my knees so the doctor won't see me gripping the edge of the velvet seat.

Anchor yourself in the present moment. I am here. I am safe. I never meant to hurt Peter, but now he's here, too. I will find him and I will tell him how sorry I am for dragging him into the past. Peter probably hates me right now, but he and Judah were best friends in that other Brooklyn and they'll be glad to see each other again. I *can* fix this. I will make it right.

Genna

45.

Mrs. Brant won't return from her aunt's place until Tuesday, so that gives me a few more days of freedom. As my hands heal I'm able to help Nannie around the house, but I also go out to Weeksville whenever I can. I try to keep my mouth shut and my ears open in case anyone there has news I can use. Judah doesn't know that I'm back, and I don't want anyone else to tell him. I want to be there to welcome him when Judah comes home. I want to see the look on his face when he realizes that I've come home, too.

Judah doesn't seem to have any friends, but at church on Sunday Mattie points out the family that took him in after the riots.

"You know them?" I ask while sizing up the teenage daughter who's almost as pale as her grey-eyed mother. Mr. Claxton is dark-skinned and stern. I bet he and Judah get along just fine. I tell myself Judah wouldn't give the time of day to that freckle-faced girl. Mattie says don't be so sure.

"The Claxtons are good people," she tells me. "Used to be a boy, too—Felix—but he run off all of a sudden. He weren't worth much no how."

A cluster of White women exits Berean Baptist Church, special guests of the minister and his wife. Folks line up to thank them for coming out to Weeksville and the White women receive them like so many queens greeting their humble subjects.

"Couldn't pay me to go back down south," Mattie says with a shiver.

I put my arm around her to shield her from the cold breeze and cruel memories from her past.

"Pay's not bad," a voice behind us says.

Mattie and I turn to find Nell standing behind us, her eyes glued to the White visitors and the line of Weeksville ladies waiting to shake their gloved hands. I've only seen Nell a couple of times since our escape from Five Points. She hasn't seemed keen on becoming friends, which suits me just fine.

"You thinking about signing up?" I ask, hoping she'll say yes. Something about this girl rubs me the wrong way. And I'm not the only one. Mattie can't stand Nell, but she's got folks at the orphanage falling all over her—especially Esther.

"Don't be fooled by all that silk and lace," Nell says, keeping her eyes glued to the knot of well-dressed White ladies. "Their type's all over the city." She grunts softly and finally looks away. "And now they're heading south to 'save' the poor benighted Negroes."

I want to know how the niece of a brothel owner knows anything about a bunch of rich White ladies, but I'm not sure how to ask without offending Nell. The truth is, I feel kind of guilty about not liking this girl. She's probably had a rough life, and Nell did help me rescue Martha from that disgusting brothel. She looks straight at me—through me—and seems to read my mind.

"The two on the left are patrons of the House of Industry and the Five Points Mission," Nell says flatly.

"Mission? You mean they're missionaries?" I was too busy daydreaming about Judah to pay much attention to the long, dull church service. Several White women addressed the congregation but I assumed they were all from the American Missionary Association.

"The rich ladies come and go, but the real devout ones live at the mission. They run the school, the sewing classes, the soup kitchen. They ship the poor Irish kids out of the city—after they clean them up and convert them, of course. Heathens."

Nell's eyes are fastened on the chattering ladies once again. I can't tell who she's calling heathens — the Irish kids or the missionaries. I watch Nell eyeing those White women and remember how I used to feel around the "cute" girls at school. Most of the time I couldn't stand them, but if they'd asked me to sit at their table in the cafeteria…I probably wouldn't have said no. You hate the clique because you're on the outside, but deep down almost everybody wants to be "in." Even Nell.

Teaching is just about the only respectable job a colored girl can get in this world. You can cook and clean for White folks, take care of their kids, or roll cigars in a factory if your fingers are nimble enough. But teaching is the only job where you're in charge and everyone in the community shows you respect. You have to stop once you get married, but for a girl like Nell, teaching orphans in Weeksville or freed slaves in South Carolina is definitely a step up from serving drinks in the family brothel.

We all watch as Mrs. Claxton welcomes the White ladies to Weeksville before presenting her daughter. She seems happy to let her mother do all the talking, and the White women seem impressed with whatever skills Mrs. Claxton is describing. I wouldn't mind if this girl signed up for a job that's hundreds of miles away, though it's hard to imagine a mouse like that teaching anything to anyone.

When Mrs. Claxton finally turns away from the missionaries, I take a step toward her and smile.

"Good afternoon, Mrs. Claxton," I say in my most polite voice. "My name is Genna. I—I'm Judah's sister."

For just a second the girl's eyes leave the ground and fix on my face. Then she blushes and tightens her grip on her mother's arm.

"How wonderful!" Mrs. Claxton says with a smile that seems genuine. "Is Judah expecting you?"

I shake my head. "I was hoping to surprise him. Do you know when he'll be back from his speaking tour?"

"We're expecting him today," she says, reaching out to squeeze my arm. "Why don't you come home with us. You can join us for dinner and tell us all about yourself while you wait for your brother to arrive."

Nothing could stop me from going home with this woman, but I force myself to act less desperate than I really am. "I don't want to intrude..."

"Nonsense! Judah's like a son to us and if you're his sister," she puts just enough emphasis on the word "if" to make me blush, "then you're more than welcome in our home. Isn't that right, Megda?"

The girl looks up at her mother and forces herself to smile as she nods her head. Then her eyes find mine and in that instant I realize that she knows I am not Judah's sister. Why would he trust her with the truth?

I say a quick goodbye to Mattie and Nell before rejoining Mrs. Claxton and her daughter. As we walk toward their home, Megda surprises me by slipping her arm through mine. She smiles up at me like a child and for just a moment, I wonder what it would be like to have a little sister.

Mr. Claxton walks a few feet behind us, discussing the war with a neighbor. These people gave Judah a home when he had nowhere else to go, and now they've opened their home to me, too. Without them, Judah might have left for Liberia instead of settling in Weeksville. I turn to Medga and smile. I owe this family more than they'll ever know.

"Judah will be so happy to see you," Megda says in a voice that sounds sincere.

"I hope so," I reply and then wonder why I said that. Why wouldn't Judah be happy to see me? I look across the street to hide my eyes, but Mrs. Claxton sees the doubt in my weak smile and tries to reassure me.

"Judah has missed you terribly. He doesn't say much, that's not his way, but I can tell just the same. I haven't seen my own brother for almost twenty years, but I still think about him every day. I still hope that someday I'll open the front door and find him standing on my doorstep. Looks like you and Judah will have the happy ending I've always dreamed of."

I smile with more confidence than I actually feel. I hope Mrs. Claxton is right. Now that I'm just hours away from seeing Judah, the doubt I tried to uproot before is sprouting anew inside of me.

When Mr. Claxton's neighbor turns off at his own home, Mrs.

Claxton leaves Megda with me and falls back to join her husband. I glance at the couple over my shoulder and smile. They walk slowly, arms linked, sharing quiet words that make them smile. I don't remember ever seeing my own parents like that. All I have is an old yellow Polaroid taken at Coney Island. Mama's holding a puff of cotton candy and Papi's pretending to reach for it with his mouth, though his lips seem content just to rest on Mama's neck. I found the faded photo hidden in one of Mama's dresser drawers. I kept it as proof that my parents were happy when they were young and carefree—before they had kids. Before life got harder and filled them with regrets.

Megda giggles, pulling me back to her world. "My folks still act like sweethearts sometimes! Mama says if you take your time and choose the right man, you'll never fall out of love."

"Do you have anyone special?" I nudge Megda so she knows I'm teasing, but the smile vanishes from her face.

She blushes and shakes her head, avoiding my eyes.

"I don't have time to think about courting. I'm going to help teach our people down south."

"With the ladies who were in church today?" Medga nods but bites her bottom lip to stop it from trembling. I don't want to get in her business but something doesn't feel right, so I ask, "Is that what you really want?"

Megda looks up at me, surprised. And maybe a little bit scared. We aren't friends, after all. She doesn't question my sudden interest in her life, though. Trusting Judah must make it easy for her to trust me. She sighs and says in her kittenish voice, "It's better this way."

Next to Megda I feel like a Rottweiler—big, dark, and intimidating. I think of Dr. Fitzpatrick and try to do my best imitation of a shrink. "Better for you?" I ask in what I hope is a soothing voice. "Or somebody else?"

Megda blushes and then turns her face away, ashamed that I can track her changing emotions just by looking at her skin. "My brother...he ran away and my mother misses him terribly. Leaving will make it easier for him to come home."

"Did he enlist?"

Megda casts a nervous glance over her shoulder. "Papa says the army will never take a boy like Felix."

I laugh without meaning to and then hurry to explain. "Your brother sounds a lot like my brother. He broke my mother's heart when he left. Well, technically he got locked up."

Megda looks shocked so I stop talking about Rico. "You know, your mother will miss you, too, if you go down south."

Megda shakes her head, suddenly sure of herself. "I'm a girl. Mama always tells me it's my duty to look around and see what needs to be done. 'Don't wait to be asked,' she says. 'Just get to work.' The AMA needs teachers and I need—"

"A way out?"

For the first time, Megda speaks with confidence. "Peace. I feel like my family is at war. I'd do anything to make my mother happy again."

I nod, remembering how much it once meant to me to please my own mother. "You deserve to be happy, too, you know."

Megda just shrugs and says, "Being useful is enough."

Before I can respond she adds, "We're home," and our conversation comes to an end.

We stand at the gate and wait for her parents to join us. I pull my arm free from Megda's and politely decline Mrs. Claxton's invitation to join them for lunch.

She frowns at me and for a moment looks just like my own mother despite her pale skin. "But you must be hungry, Genna. The service was longer than usual today."

I am hungry but I also know that I can't sit and eat with a bunch of strangers right now. Walking helped, but now that we are standing still, it is taking all my strength to hide the fact that my legs are trembling. "I'm fine," I assure them, grabbing hold of the wooden fence rail to steady myself. "I'll just wait out here by the road."

"But it could be hours before he arrives!" Mrs. Claxton exclaims.

"The girl knows her own mind, Cora. Leave her be." Mr. Claxton takes his wife's arm and guides her toward the front porch.

Megda pipes up, saving me from thinking of a reasonable response. "She could wait in the work shed, Mama." Megda turns her freckled face back to me. "That's where Judah stays. I can bring you something to eat if you'd rather wait there."

I want to throw my arms around this slight girl and crush her with the force of my gratitude. Instead I smile and simply say, "Thank you." I feel a pang of guilt for wanting to banish Megda to the Sea Islands less than an hour ago. Now I know why Judah trusted her with the truth.

"Suit yourself," Mrs. Claxton says with a hint of disapproval before heading inside her home. Megda points me in the direction of the work shed and then hurries after her mother.

I go over to the shed, which is more like a small barn. Two horses are stabled at one end and the center door is wide enough to let in a wagon. When the wide door is closed, a smaller door allows people to enter the shed. I open this door and step inside the shed. A large work table fills takes up most of the room. Tools of every shape and size hang from nails on the wall and planks of wood are stacked in one corner.

In another corner there is a pallet on the floor. Someone has taken care to sweep away the hay and sawdust that covers the rest of the shed floor. A lantern sits on a wooden crate that serves as a makeshift nightstand. I think of Judah reading by its light at night—maybe even writing haiku for me—and smile to myself.

I go over and kneel beside the pallet. I lean forward and let my palms press into the scratchy wool blanket that is neatly spread over the lumpy mattress. I imagine Judah sleeping here night after night, dreaming about me, waiting for me to return. I glance over my shoulder before getting close enough to the pillow to inhale Judah's scent. Soon I won't have to imagine his arms around me. Our life together won't be on hold any more.

Suddenly the horses stir restlessly at the far end of the shed. I wipe the tears from my eyes and go over to the open door. A wagon is pulling away from the house and raising a cloud of dust as it heads down the dirt road. A lone man stands at the gate, a satchel slung over his shoulder. His clothes are rumpled from traveling and his long, thick hair—brushed, not locked—radiates from his head like a dark aureole. He is a Black angel—*my* angel. Judah has finally come home!

The work shed is behind the house, so Mrs. Claxton spots Judah at the same time and she reaches him first. I stand frozen in the doorway of the shed, watching as she skips down the porch steps and hurries up the path like a girl half her age. Their happy reunion unfolds before my eyes. Mrs. Claxton folds Judah in a long embrace that clearly makes him uncomfortable, though he patiently tolerates it for her sake. Megda joins her mother but stands a few feet away, smiling shyly and glancing over her shoulder in my direction. Her father finally steps forward and gently pulls his wife's arms away. He clamps a large hand on Judah's shoulder and pulls him toward the house.

I bite my lip to keep myself from shouting out, "No!" Panic and envy churn in my chest, and suddenly I resent this family for claiming Judah as their own. Then I remember that I have not been excluded. I chose to wait here, in Judah's space, away from the prying questions and appraising eyes of his new family. Judah means a lot to them, that's easy to see. But they don't know Judah like I do. *No one* loves Judah like I do. I tell myself that he can't have missed them as much as he has missed me.

I watch from the shadows as Medga tugs at Judah's sleeve and points at the shed with her other hand. I search Judah's face, hoping to find some trace of joy, but he merely squints at the open door. Mr. Claxton's arm falls away from Judah's shoulder and for a moment all four faces turn toward me. I hear Mrs. Claxton clear her throat before she herds her husband and daughter back inside the house. I'm sure they would like to witness our reunion but Mrs. Claxton can tell that something is wrong.

I know it, too. Judah has not dropped his bag and sprinted over to the shed. I am counting the seconds until I feel his arms wrapped around me, but Judah just glances in my general direction and then keeps on talking to Mrs. Claxton. She's already climbing the porch steps but he won't let her go. He insists on telling her the things he should be telling me.

While Judah's talking, Mrs. Claxton looks over his shoulder at the shed's open door. She knows I'm there in the shadows, waiting for Judah to come and claim me. Finally she squeezes his arm and goes back into the house, glancing over at the shed once more. She can't see me but still smiles in a way that feels like an apology.

Judah doesn't smile as he walks toward the shed — toward me. I don't know what to do with myself so I stand behind the worktable and grip its edge to keep my hands from betraying me. I don't want to be angry but I am. This isn't how this scene was supposed to unfold. I thought I would throw my arms around Judah, but right now I feel more like shaking him until he starts to act right.

When Judah finally reaches the shed and steps inside, it takes a moment for his eyes to adjust to the dim light. I watch the particles of dust twirling in the sunbeam let in by the open door. My heart pounds in my chest but I am afraid to breathe deeply. I was breathless the last time Judah saw me when we ran for our lives through the streets of Brooklyn. I want to be calm. I want to be perfect. I want to be the girl Judah has pictured in his dreams.

The silence between us is agonizing. I hold onto the table and will Judah to say something — anything — to me. But he won't look me in the eye so I can't reach him. He is just a few feet away, but the distance between us feels like far more than a century. I blink away my tears and remind myself that I have already traveled through time. I have opened a door between worlds. If Judah has closed his heart to me, I can make him open it again.

"Hey," I say softly. I silence the part of me that wants to hiss, "What's wrong with you?" I can't risk showing my anger. I don't want to push Judah farther away.

With the sun behind him, Judah's face is hard to see and impossible to read. His eyes scan the shadows that fill the back of the shed. When his gaze finally rests on me, I see a flicker of emotion and then his eyes become dull once more.

Judah drops his bag by the door. He doesn't go over to his pallet and he doesn't come over to me. He stays by the door like he's planning to leave again. Judah leans back against the doorframe and says, "Hey."

That's it. One word. I take a deep breath and tell myself that Judah is just playing it cool. It doesn't show, but inside he must be feeling hectic just like me. I search for the words that will draw Judah closer. "I hear you were up in Albany."

Judah simply nods. He had plenty to say to Mrs. Claxton. Why is he holding back with me? I try to make my voice sound cheerier than I feel. "How was it?"

Judah shrugs. "Alright. People upstate act like they don't know what slavery is, like it never happened here in New York. In their minds, slavery belongs way down there, in the South."

Toshi always said guys love to talk about themselves, but I never thought her rules applied to a guy like Judah. This is the most he has said so far, though, so I try to keep him talking. "So...what were you doing up there?"

Judah looks out the open door of the shed. Someone is in the yard. We can both hear the pump handle going up and down as water splashes into a bucket. Judah sighs like he's already bored with me and has someplace else he'd rather be.

I am losing patience with him. The Judah I know would never be this rude—this cold. I need to know what has changed. "Judah?"

He turns away from the yard and finally looks at me. "Hm?"

"I asked you a question. What were you doing upstate?"

"Telling my story."

What is your problem, Judah? Those are the words I want to say, but they would only push him away so I swallow them and try again. "It must take a lot of courage to tell a room full of strangers what it was like for you to live as a slave." I pause then add, "You never really told me what it was like."

If Judah hears the accusation in my voice, he shows no sign. Instead he looks me in the eye and says, "I wasn't ready to talk about it then. And when I was ready, you weren't here."

Judah is looking right at me but I still can't tell if he's angry, or hurt, or just stating a fact. It's like he's wearing some kind of mask. Is Judah waiting for an apology? After everything I've been through, I don't feel like I owe anything to anyone. But if those words will turn Judah into the boy I remember, I am willing to swallow my pride.

"I'm sorry," I say, knowing that my voice sounds strange because I'm on the brink of tears—again.

Judah doesn't respond so I say it again, louder. He looks out at the yard. My cheeks start to burn with shame. I never imagined I would let a boy humiliate me like this. I never imagined Judah would try to make me feel so small.

"I'll just go, I guess." I say the words more to myself than to Judah. I slowly circle the table, hoping he'll stop me and tell me to stay. But Judah doesn't budge. He keeps his eyes out in the yard, even when I am standing just inches away.

"Can I at least get a hug?"

I shouldn't have to ask him to touch me. I shouldn't have to beg for the smallest sign of affection after everything we've been through. But I am too close to despair to let my pride call the shots.

At first Judah doesn't move and I think he may deny me even this. Then he leans forward and presses his hands into my back—our bodies don't touch and neither do our cheeks. Before I can pull him closer, Judah coughs and backs away. He brushes my hands away and shoves his own deep into his pockets so he won't have to touch me again.

For a long moment we stand in the doorway with nothing but dust spinning in the space between us. I feel like I'm caught in a bad dream. How can this be happening? How can Judah treat me this way?

Maybe Judah sees the hurt in my eyes. He must still have a conscience because he coughs nervously and asks, "When did you get back?"

Suddenly I feel so tired that I'm not sure I can stand. I glance around and spot a stool tucked under the worktable. I pull it out and sink onto it before my legs give way. Judah's eyes are back in the yard, but he asked the question so he must care about the answer. "I got back about a few weeks ago," I tell him. "I was worried you wouldn't be here—that you'd have left for Liberia."

Judah shakes his head. "Reverend Garnet asked me to delay my departure. The people at the Anti-Slavery Society want me to write a book."

"A book?"

"A slave narrative—just like Frederick Douglass'. They'd print it and keep most of the money, but I'd still get a share. I could earn enough to pay my way to Africa—or Jamaica."

Tired as I am, I can't hide my amazement at this development. "Jamaica?"

Judah turns his head to look at me. I see defiance in his eyes. "Things have changed, Gen. I've changed. Living in this world does that to you."

I barely have the strength to nod. Judah goes on.

"So. How long you staying this time?"

A sudden current sizzles up my spine. I find the energy to sit up and spit one word at him. "What?"

Judah doesn't back down. "You heard me."

This time I see the rage flashing in Judah's dark eyes. How can he be mad at *me*? A second current zips up my spine, jolting me off the stool. My hands land on my hips and I stop worrying about sounding confrontational. In fact, I take two steps forward and get in Judah's face.

"What is your problem, Judah? I'm *here*. Do you know what I went through to get back to you?"

"So you *can* control it." Judah sucks his teeth. "That's what I thought."

That's what this is about? Part of me wants to burst into tears, fling myself at him, and beg Judah to forgive me. But another part of me wants to stand my ground. I haven't done anything wrong. Why should I apologize?

"I *learned* to control it, Judah! I did everything I could think of just so I could be with you again. And this is the thanks I get? You act like you wish I hadn't bothered!"

"I don't make wishes, Genna — I make *plans*. What did you think — I'd just be sitting around waiting for you to come back? I can't live like that. Like I said, I've got plans."

"I thought I was part of those plans."

"You were — but then you left."

"And then I came back."

Judah just shrugs again. I look around at all the tools in this work shed — tools that build and polish and repair things made of wood. I want to seize the tool that will fix whatever's wrong with Judah. Right now our relationship is a three-legged table on the verge of toppling over. "I can't believe you're blaming me for this!"

"You can control it — you just said so yourself."

"But I couldn't control it before. I didn't even understand how it worked! I'm here because I — I love you, Judah. And I thought you loved me."

Judah turns away and fingers a metal ruler on the table. "Like I said before, people change."

Suddenly I realize we're not alone. A shy voice draws our attention out into the yard.

"Judah?"

I spin and practically scream at Megda. "What do you want? Can't you see we're busy!"

Judah puts his finger in my face. "Don't you talk to her like that."

I slap his hand away and stare at Judah in disbelief. He's defending *her*?

Megda hurries back to the house without delivering the two plates of food in her hands. Judah's eyes soften as he watches her retreat but they harden once more when he turns to me. "She's been through a lot lately. Her brother…he used to mess with her."

I shrug impatiently. "That's what brothers do. Rico used to mess with me all the time."

"No he didn't—not like this." Judah looks at me and for a second I see the door behind his eyes open just a crack. "Maybe you could talk to her."

My cheeks start to burn and I look away, ashamed of my own envy. Why is he looking out for some girl he's only known a few weeks?

"I already talked to her," I tell him. "She just wants to move on and forget about whatever happened."

Judah looks directly into my eyes and says, "Sometimes people can't forget."

This is my chance. My heart starts pounding inside my chest, but I force myself to take a step closer to Judah. If I reach out my hand, I could touch his face. But I don't. Instead I ask softly, "Is that what it's like for you, Judah?"

The door closes behind Judah's dark eyes. He turns away and takes up the ruler once more. "I can handle my own business."

I step back and let disappointment slow my heart down again. "Right. You don't need anyone for anything."

"It's easier to talk to someone who knows where you're coming from."

"I know where you're coming from. We come from the same place, Judah."

"No, Gen. We don't."

I did not travel through time for this. I have had enough. "Whatever, Judah," I mutter and try to build up speed so I can get out of this shed and away from Judah as fast as possible. But Judah is faster than me. He grabs my arm and spins me around just as I step out of the shade and into the bright sunlight. I squint against the glare, but I can still see the tiny sliver of light in Judah's eyes. The door he has closed against me is opening once more.

"Megda needs a woman to talk to—someone her age who's been through the same kind of thing."

Judah's fingers dig painfully into my arm but I don't try to break free. This is the closest he has come to claiming me. "What makes you think I know anything about what she's been through?"

Judah presses his lips together. I like being this close to him, but wish it wasn't so hard for him to open up to me.

"You told me once that you had to look out for yourself because I wasn't...because I couldn't be there for you." Judah pauses and I search my jumbled memories, trying to pull up the conversation he's talking about.

I'm the one who's supposed to protect you.

That's what Judah said when I told him about how I met Paul. Is he still jealous? Could that be why Judah's acting this way?

Judah finally lets go of my arm and steps back into the shadowy shed. "Just talk to her. Megda doesn't have any close friends."

I don't really want to know, but I ask anyway. "What'd her brother do?"

Judah looks across the yard as if to make sure we are alone, but I know he just wants to avoid eye contact with me. "Same thing you said those men down on the docks tried to do to you once."

My whole body flushes with hot shame and for the first time I wonder if that's how Judah sees me—as a victim, someone who needs to be saved. Judah mistakenly thinks I am softening toward Medga and goes on.

"You always said you wanted to help people with their problems. Well, here's your chance." Judah picks up the bag he dropped by the door and carries it over to his pallet. He kneels and starts unpacking with his back turned to me.

I feel like I have been dismissed but I can't go without making one last attempt to reach him—the Judah I used to know. I step back inside the shed and ask in the most neutral voice I can muster, "What about us?"

Judah freezes for a moment before turning back toward me. He looks genuinely confused. "What about us?"

I try not to choke on my words but fail miserably as tears flood my eyes. "Before I got sent back you wanted to marry me. You said we could build a new life together in Liberia."

Judah just shrugs and keeps pulling items out of his bag. "Like I said, things change. I have other plans now."

Other plans? Fury gives my limbs the strength they need. I am *done* with begging and hoping this is just a bad dream. I walk up to Judah and loom over him until he turns to face me.

"You know what?" I let my voice sound as cruel as I feel. "Mattie was right. You never even *tried* to get back to me. You just found someone new and moved on. Well, forget you, Judah. Forget you!"

I storm out of the shed and up the gravel path knowing the Claxtons' eyes are on me. I don't look back. I don't need their pity, and now I know there's nothing for me in this place. I stride up the road with my head held high, my eyes full of tears that refuse to fall. "Forget you, Judah," I say over and over. *Forget you.*

Judah

46.

There are only a few things that I miss about the future, and cricket is one of them. I can't remember the last time I held a bat, but watching these men play baseball has me thinking about the weekly cricket matches held in Prospect Park. The batsmen with pads strapped to their shins; the bowler aiming to dismiss them by taking the wicket. Ordinary Black men from countries in Africa and the Caribbean put on white shirts and pants and then stepped onto the pitch like knights in shining armor. It wasn't just about winning the game — it was about playing with honor and dignity.

Here in Weeksville we've got our own baseball team — the Unknowns. With a name like that, you wouldn't expect them to play very well, but right now they're beating the Williamsburg Van Delkens 42-10! All of Weeksville has turned out for the game and lots of families have spread blankets near Yucatan Pond to share a picnic lunch. With young and old cheering on both teams beneath the warm autumn sun, it's easy to forget that we're in the middle of a war. The draft riots seem like a distant memory and with no Whites in sight, everyone seems relaxed.

I wander away from the crowd and settle on a grassy knoll shaded by a massive oak tree. From here I can still see the game, and to occupy my restless arms I pick acorns off the ground and hurl them into the long grass. I give myself a point every time I manage to hit a milkweed pod. When there are no more acorns within reach, I think about the herb Felix offered me a few weeks back and wish I had paid Hetty a visit. A spliff would settle my mind and help me see a clear path forward—a path I seem destined to walk alone.

If I stay in Weeksville, I could try out for the baseball team. *If* I stay. New York State has finally started to enlist Black men so this may be one of the last games we'll see for some time. I count the players on the field—men in their prime—and wonder how many will live to play "America's pastime" after the war.

On a day like today, when everyone's laughing and getting along, I am tempted to make this place my home. Sometimes it's hard to believe this is Brooklyn. There's so much open space, so many living things with room to grow. Weeksville serves as a sanctuary from the hostile White world, but at the end of the day, it's just a village. The faint whistle of the steam engine chugging along Atlantic Avenue reminds me of the time I spent on the speaker circuit upstate. This is a big state in an even bigger country, and there's a whole world beyond its borders. After everything I've been through, it's nice to live a quiet life in Weeksville. But I can't live like this forever. Something deep within me needs to keep moving.

A restless spirit's never satisfied. That's what Mrs. Claxton said to me the other day. I think she knows I won't be here much longer, and that's why she's stopped pushing Megda at me. Megda's been glued to her mother since that night in the yard. I scan the crowd and find Megda tucked under her mother's arm like a baby bird. I'm glad she came with us but I wish Megda would join the other girls her age who are waving their hankies at their favorite players as they round the bases and slide home. Instead Megda jumps like a shell-shocked soldier every time the ball cracks off the bat. She needs help, but where do Black girls go in 1863 when they're assaulted by their own brother? Church? The police? For just an instant, Genna's face floats across my mind but she only sees Megda as a rival. I laugh at the idea and then put Genna out of my mind so I can focus on the baseball game instead.

To my surprise, I see a couple of White faces in the crowd. One belongs to a middle-aged man with a handlebar mustache that does little to hide the sneer on his face. Every few minutes he scribbles something in a small notebook before reaching inside his coat for a silver flask. It glints in the sun every time he takes a swig, and it's clear from the smirk on his face that he finds us amusing. If he's taking notes, I can only assume he's some type of reporter.

I suck my teeth and imagine what he'll write about this glorious autumn afternoon. He can't see the love we have for one another, the freedom we feel to be ourselves here in Weeksville. It's all there on the faces of my people but this White man can't—or won't—see what's right in front of his eyes. He sees what he wants to see: a bunch of darkies whooping and hollering while pickaninnies turn cartwheels in the grass. We're savages to be mocked or menaced. Nothing more.

The other White face in the crowd belongs to a teenage boy. His long blond hair flashes in the sunlight as he tosses his head back and laughs along with a group of local boys. Not *at* them—*with* them. I'm so busy trying to get a good look at the White boy's face that I don't notice the Black boy wading through the grass. He's heading straight toward me, one arm cradled in a dingy cloth sling.

"I know you." I realize I've said those words out loud just before I realize that I'm no longer sitting down. Even before I can clearly see his face, a smile spreads across mine. I know that walk, that cocky swagger that boys from that other Brooklyn adopt in order to make their way safely through the streets. It's Peter! It can't be, but it is.

Peter starts laughing as he steps out of the tall grass and climbs the small hill. Burrs cling to his pants and he stops to pointlessly brush at them with his free hand. I head down the hill with my arms open. With his injury it's hard for us to embrace, but I make sure Peter knows just how happy I am to see him. Peter is the closest thing to a brother that I've ever had. My cousin Samuel's alright but he's more into partying than politics. Me and Peter—we could talk about anything.

"I can't believe you're here!" I say, slapping him on the back.

Peter winces but still manages to smile. "Trust me—no one's more shocked than I am! Though I bet Genna will be surprised when she finds out I'm here."

Just the mention of her name dims my joy. I feel my smile disappearing as I take a closer look at Peter, wondering where else he's been hurt. I shake my head and don't bother to hide my disgust. "So she did it to you, too, huh? That girl's dangerous. Just stay away from her, man."

Peter gives me a funny look. "It's not her fault, really. I was there when Genna tried to—when she opened the portal. I should have listened when she told me to leave her alone. But I was worried about her..."

I piece the rest together on my own. I hear the edge in my voice and I know Peter does, too. "So you stuck around and got sucked through the portal with her." I nod at his broken arm. "Hard landing?"

Peter avoids looking at me, which is how I know he's about to lie. Problem is, we've known each other so long that he *knows* I know.

Peter sighs and gives me a one-shoulder shrug. "It was an accident, Judah."

I shake my head and feel a strange urge to smile. "*She* did that to you?"

Peter reaches down to pluck a few burrs off his pants. Then he takes a deep breath and says, "We were struggling and I—I just wanted to take her home. I didn't mean to, Judah, but...I hit her."

There was a time when Peter would be right to be afraid of me after admitting he put his hands on my girl. But Genna's not my girl anymore so I'm not mad at him.

Peter shifts awkwardly from one foot to the other. "Aren't you going to say anything?" he asks anxiously.

It's my turn to shrug. "You're not that kind of guy. If you hit her, she must have—"

Peter holds up his free hand. "*Don't*, Judah. Don't say it."

"Say what?"

"That she must have asked for it. 'Cause she didn't. Things just got hectic that night. I've never seen anything like it, son, and you know I've seen some things."

I nod and reach out to give Peter's good shoulder a reassuring squeeze. "Don't worry about it. I'm just glad you're here in Weeksville. I wasn't so lucky when she dragged me into the past." I sit down on the hillside and motion for Peter to join me.

He eases himself onto the leaf-strewn grass. "Genna told me you went through a lot."

I grunt and fold my fingers around a crisp brown leaf. "She has no idea what I went through." I open my palm and examine what's left of the dead leaf. I tilt my hand and the dry brown fragments drift away on the breeze. "Genna only thinks about herself."

Peter looks genuinely shocked. "That's not true."

I don't want to fight with my brother so I swallow the rest of the words I want to say. He'll find out the truth about Genna soon enough. I decide to change the subject. "How's 1863 treating you so far? You living downtown?"

Peter shakes his head and looks out at the players on the field. "Williamsburg. This German family found me and took me in. They own a brewery out there. I help out as best I can."

Peter stops and I can tell he's weighing his words. I get the feeling he's about to tell me something important but then he changes his mind. "The Schaefers are good people," is all he says.

I scan the crowd for the blond-haired boy. He's rooting for the losing team but almost seems to be enjoying the game more than the Unknowns' fans. The White reporter must have emptied his flask because he's weaving his way through the crowd, unashamed of his drunkenness. I watch as he lurches into a cluster of teenage girls who scatter like frightened birds. My fingers instinctively curl into fists and only relax when I find Megda safely wedged between her parents.

I turn my attention back to Peter. "You don't have to stay with strangers," I tell him, leaving race out of it for now. "I could find you a place to stay here in Weeksville. The Claxtons got a full house and I'm sleeping out in the shed, but I'm sure someone else would take you in."

"I'm good," Peter insists. "Mr. and Mrs. Schaefer said I could stay as long as I want." Again Peter hesitates. This time he points at the blond boy and says, "They have a son—Fritz. I'm tutoring him in exchange for my room and board."

I nod and weigh my own words this time. "Well, think about it. If there's one thing I've learned since I've been here, it's not to trust White folks. Even the ones who seem decent can turn on a dime."

Peter nods like he understands but I can tell he doesn't agree with me. I smile and try to lighten my tone. "Wouldn't you rather stay with your own people? I know you must be hating that German food—sauerkraut and sausages day after day!"

Peter shakes his head and barely cracks a smile. "Nobody here is 'my people.' I feel like I've landed on Mars."

"I felt that way too when I first arrived. Don't worry—you get used to it after a while."

Peter picks up an acorn and lets it roll around the palm of his hand. "I don't know, Judah..."

I wait for Peter to go on but he just hurls the acorn into the tall grass without saying another word. "Talk to me, man."

Peter keeps his eyes on the waving sea of grass that separates us from the crowd. "I'm thinking about asking Genna to send me back. In fact, I was hoping she'd be here today. You seen her?"

I ignore Peter's question. "Send you back? Look at you, man—all banged up. You're telling me you'd put your life in *her* hands again?"

A loud cheer goes up from the crowd. The Unknowns have been declared the winners and the crowd is starting to disperse. Peter finally looks at me. "We're teenagers, Judah. We don't belong here."

"There's no such thing as a teenager in this world. There are kids and adults, and the kids grow up fast. That's one of the things I like about living here—everything's black and white. Makes it easy to take sides."

"You talking about the war?" Peter asks.

"Nah. I'm talking about community. Look around you, Peter. All this land? It's owned by Black folks. The school, the churches, the farms, the stores—all of it belongs to us. Few months ago shit got hectic in Manhattan. Mobs of drunk White folks took over the city, lynching and burning. And Black folks came *here*, Peter. Here. Weeksville is our sanctuary."

To my surprise, Peter scoffs at that idea. "Sure—until the next mob gathers. You know how this story ends, Judah. Back in 2001, nobody knows or cares about Weeksville because it no longer exists."

"We can change that. We can shape the future, Peter."

Peter opens his mouth to laugh but then realizes I'm dead serious. "What are you talking about, Judah?"

I grab Peter's good arm and hope my excitement will be contagious. "Think about it. Once the war's over, we could go to Liberia—or Haiti. Lincoln has opened up trade so now it's easier to travel back and forth."

"Judah—do you know what a sixty-year embargo does to a small country like Haiti? Just because the US has finally decided to admit we're an independent nation doesn't mean life in Haiti will be easy. What would we even *do* there?"

"There's a colony on Île-à-Vache. They're trying to grow cotton."

Peter sucks his teeth. "That colony failed miserably, man. What else you got planned?"

"I don't know. We'll just get there and see what needs to be done. We'll live with our people—really *live*!"

Peter scoffs at me. "Die young, you mean. People board a ship these days and half of them don't even survive the journey. And I'm not talking about slaves—I mean first-class passengers. And aren't you forgetting someone?"

Peter stares at me but I haven't forgotten anyone. I'm already talking about the people that matter—me and him.

He finally asks, "What about Genna?"

Peter is asking all the wrong questions. "What about her?"

I keep my eyes locked on Peter's. He waits for me to blink but I keep my gaze steady so he knows I'm serious. "She made her choice," I tell him.

The dry leaves crackle as Peter shifts a few inches away from me.

"You don't know what Genna went through. What she did to get back to you."

"We've all been through a lot. But what doesn't kill you, makes you stronger. We have knowledge that can help our people, Peter. We have a duty to do whatever we can while we're here." This is the voice I used when I was speaking upstate. It worked on sympathetic Whites but it has no effect on Peter.

He just looks at me and says, "She loves you, man."

I laugh and Peter sucks his teeth. "What's love got to do with anything? I'm talking about destiny, Peter."

"Genna *loves you*. She came back for you."

"Oh yeah? So where is she now? Probably out with that light-skinned dude she was messing around with the last time she was here. You think Genna came back for me, but she has a lot of friends here in Weeksville. And then there's her great White doctor—I'm sure she was missing him, too."

"Do you hear yourself, man? This is *Genna* we're talking about. She's not even about that and you know it."

"You never saw the way she looked at him—like he was some kind of god. And she told him I was her brother—*her brother*. The truth is, Peter, I don't know Genna and neither do you. She's got everybody fooled but I'm nobody's fool. Not anymore. Look what she did to you!"

Peter glances at his arm and shakes his head. "That was an accident. Genna wasn't herself that night. She was—"

"Out of control! You better stay away from her if you know what's good for you."

Peter frowns but can't hide the fact that Genna does scare him at least a little. "What Genna did...it's a gift, Judah. My uncle said maybe the ancestors have chosen her."

I mean no disrespect to the ancestors, but I can't stop myself from laughing again. Peter goes on.

"You used the say the same thing all the time back in Brooklyn—*our* Brooklyn. 'Genna's special.' That's what you used to say."

"I used to say a lot of things—until she changed."

"Seems like you've changed, too."

For a moment we stare at one another without words. This time I'm the first to look away. "I can't trust her, man. I went through hell to get back to Genna and she left me. *She* left *me*. Now she's back and she expects us to just pick up where we left off? I don't think so."

Peter takes a moment to think. That's what I like about him—he listens to me. He gets me in a way no one else does.

Finally he says, "I hear you, man. I do. But it takes time to learn how to handle that kind of power. You know that. I've been an initiate for a while now and there are still so many things about Vodou that I don't know and can't do—and won't be able to do until my uncle thinks I'm ready. Genna's had no training for this, no instruction. You can't blame her for making it up as she goes along."

I shrug and try to think of something I can say that will satisfy Peter. He thinks I'm being too hard on her. "I have to think about the future, Peter. Genna…she's part of the past." To my surprise, Peter laughs.

"Well, if there's one thing I've learned from this crazy experience, it's that time doesn't stand still. You can't put Genna in a box and think she's just going to stay there. She can move through time!"

"Give her a few more weeks living here in 1863. She'll get tired of country living or she'll start to miss her family and she'll be gone," I snap my fingers for effect. "Just like that. Watch."

Peter's voice gets low, which means he wants me to hear what he's saying. "She gave up a lot to be with you, Judah."

"I never asked Genna to do anything for me. She does whatever *she* wants. You think you can make her take you back to the future? Good luck with that."

"She doesn't have to go with me," Peter says sullenly.

"Sure she does. You said yourself she doesn't know what she's doing. Far as I can tell, she makes up her mind about where *she* wants to be, and any poor sucker who's dumb enough to get close to her ends up getting dragged along."

"You just said you belonged here. Now you're mad at Genna for 'dragging' you into the past. Make up your mind, Judah."

I turn away and stop the anger from sharpening my tongue into a blade. I don't really have any friends in this world. I can't afford to push Peter away. "It's complicated," I say finally.

Peter sighs and puts a sympathetic hand on my shoulder. "It sure is."

I feel like a sea has opened up between us. I search for a way to remind Peter of how things used to be. "You still drumming in the park?" I ask.

Peter smiles but shakes his head. "Not really."

"Why not? That's where we met, remember?"

Peter's eyes darken and the smile fades from his face. "I remember," he says quietly.

I beat my palms against my thighs and start one of the chants we used to sing at the drumming circle. Peter nods his head to the beat but doesn't join in.

I must trod home to that land
I must trod home to that land
I must trod home to that land where I am from
For there is love in that land
Joy and happiness in that land
I must trod home to that land where I am from

When I finish, Peter seems even farther away from me than before. "Why'd you stop going?" I ask. Peter shrugs and gives me what feels like half an answer.

"I got tired of people asking about you, man. When you vanished your aunt took it hard, Judah. You were like a son to her."

I grow solemn, too, as I think about Aunt Marcia. "If you do go back — if Genna really can send you back — tell my aunt I'm okay. Tell her not to worry about me."

"Tell her yourself," Peter says in a voice that sounds like a dare. "It's time to go home, man."

I shake my head and miss the weight of my locks sweeping across my back. "That world will never be home. Not for me."

Peter pushes himself off the ground with his good arm. We've just found each other again but I can tell he's ready to go.

"Well, *this* world will never be home to me," he says. "So I guess this is goodbye."

"When are you planning to leave?" I ask.

Peter gives me a one-armred shrug. "As soon as I can convince Genna to open another portal. If you really don't want her anymore...maybe it won't be that hard to convince her to go back to 2001."

"That's where she belongs."

Peter shakes his head. "Whatever you say, man."

I'm not sure why Peter's acting like I'm the one who has let him down. As he turns to go, I glimpse Megda clutching her mother's hand as the family walks toward their wagon. Mrs. Claxton is scanning the crowd, no doubt looking for me. I fight the urge to stand up and wave so she knows where I am. I want to stay longer and talk with Peter but it's clear he's done listening to me.

Peter leaves me as he found me — alone. I watch him wade through the tall grass, his healthy arm swinging more to compensate for the injured one. As my only friend disappears from view, for the first time I feel something break inside of me. What Morgan couldn't do with his whip, Peter has done simply by walking away.

Genna

47.

I hardly have a moment to myself once Mrs. Brant returns from Long Island. She doesn't ask where I've been or why I've come back. Mrs. Brant just heaves Henry into my arms and says, "How wonderfully providential! I need nothing more right now than an extra pair of hands."

Which is what I am to Mrs. Brant—an extra pair of hands to lift, and carry, and clean all the things she's never had to lift, or carry, or clean herself. Mrs. Brant squeezes my arm with her dainty little hand and then she whisks Nannie away to listen to endless tales about how her aunt's country home in Long Island is quaint but inferior to her own modern home. I press a kiss into Henry's soft cheek and carry him upstairs to the nursery. He sits quietly in my arms, eyeing me with mild suspicion. He seems to remember me but I don't think he trusts me. Why should he? I left him once and can't promise I won't leave him again.

I settle into my old life like a stone thrown from the shore into the sea. I surrender to this era and let myself sink into the familiar routines of the Brant household. After the chaos of 9/11, I welcome the quiet of this smaller city—the sirenless nights, the stars clear enough to count, the scent of wax as I blow out the candle that burns next to my bed. I didn't miss dusting the fancy crystal chandelier or lugging heavy buckets of coal up and down the narrow flight of stairs reserved for servants. But Nannie's too old to do that kind of work by herself, so I help out when

Henry's asleep in his crib.

Like most house servants, I have the afternoon to myself on Sunday. I waste hours going out to Williamsburg only to find that Peter has gone to Weeksville to watch a baseball game! The Schaefers assure me he is well and a great help to them and their son Fritz. They welcome me into their home and urge me to wait until the boys return, but I have wasted enough time. I get back on the ferry and then make my way to Weeksville.

The whole village has turned out for the game, though it's almost over by the time I arrive. Mattie and Money are there, and even Esther is hollering from the sidelines as her nephew hits the ball out of reach of the opposing team. I stand with them and smile to myself as I realize this is the first baseball game I've ever seen. I've heard old timers talk about Ebbets Field and the good old days when Jackie Robinson played for the Brooklyn Dodgers, but I've never been to Yankee Stadium up in the Bronx or to Shea Stadium out in Queens. If Papi had stayed, maybe he would have taken us to see the Yankees or the Mets. But he didn't, and Ebbets Field is now an apartment complex at the end of my block in Crown Heights. Rico used to wear a Yankees cap but I don't actually know anyone who plays baseball. Seems like Little League is for the White kids with fathers over in Park Slope, not poor Black kids in the 'hood.

I'm relieved not to see Judah at the game, but Peter is easy to spot in the crowd. He's got one arm in a sling and the other around the shoulders of a flushed White boy. They're laughing and falling over each other like they've been friends forever. I take a few steps toward them and wait for Peter to notice me. Maybe he won't be angry after all. Maybe he will understand that I never meant to hurt him. Maybe we can still be friends.

Then Peter's eyes find mine and in an instant his laughter dissolves. His arm slides off his friend's shoulder and Peter's lips settle into a grim line. He walks toward me and I open my mouth to blurt out a sincere apology but Peter doesn't stop to hear what I have to say. He stalks past me and I have to rush to catch up with him.

"Peter! Peter wait!"

He keeps walking until we are far away from the crowd. I trail after Peter as he weaves through the maze of parked wagons and gigs. Finally he spins and points an accusing finger at me.

"You did this. You did this to me!"

Even though we are alone, I lower my voice. "Peter—I didn't know! I never meant to bring you with me."

Peter points his finger at his injured arm instead of my face. "No—you did this *before* you opened the portal. Don't you even remember? You threw me into a car, Genna!"

I search my mind and pull up a hazy memory of Peter backhanding me. "You hit me," I say softly. My voice gets louder as my memory clears. "You hit me and I fought back. I was only defending myself!"

Peter looks away, ashamed. "I'm sorry—I didn't mean to hurt you. But you were...wild that night, Genna! You turned into someone else."

"No I didn't. I've never pretended to be something—or someone—I'm not. *You* were the one who encouraged me, Peter. *You* were the one who believed I could do it!"

"Yeah, but I didn't expect you to nearly kill me in the process. Do you have any idea what I've been through the past few days?"

I look at the ground as guilt replaces my indignation. "Dr. Brant told me what happened."

Peter suddenly raises his voice, forcing my eyes back up to his face. "No—he told you what happened *once he found me*. I landed in the middle of a field, Genna. It took me an entire agonizing day just to drag myself to the side of that road. Then I had to watch people passing by like I was road kill instead of a human being in need of help. If it weren't for the Schaefers..."

Peter has every right to be angry but I can't take much more of this. "Peter, *I'm sorry*, okay? If I'd known you were out there, if I'd known you needed help..."

I stop pleading because I'm not sure Peter's actually listening to me. His gaze has moved past me and for an instant I think maybe Judah's standing behind me. But when I glance over my shoulder, I see the Schaefers' son. There's a concerned, confused look on his face. Peter waves to reassure his friend that everything's okay.

I turn back to face Peter. "What have you told him?"

"Fritz? Nothing," Peter says bitterly. "They all think I got jumped and lost my memory."

I nod. "That works. Listen, I know you probably don't want any advice from me right now, but the less you tell people about your other life, the better. And you should probably act like we just met."

"Why?"

"Because it gets complicated once you start to lie and you can't afford to tell them the truth."

"Lying comes easily to some people," Peter says archly, "but not to me. I'll just tell Fritz we used to go school together. What's wrong with that?"

"Which school? Where did you live—Weeksville? Where's your family now? How did you get here from Haiti? Are you going to explain how you flew here on an airplane?"

Peter shakes his head but I know he knows I'm right.

"Haitians have been in this country a long time," he says defensively.

"But *you* haven't, Peter. You told Dr. Brant your uncle's a doctor. How many Haitian doctors do you think there are in Brooklyn in 1863? This world is smaller than the one we come from, Peter."

"So what am I supposed to do? Ignore them whenever they ask me a question? The Schaefers pretty much saved my life, Genna. I don't want to deceive them. I don't want to live a lie."

I get that Peter's mad at me but I don't appreciate his suggestion that I'm a master liar. I do what I have to do to survive and he'll do the same if he knows what's good for him. "Just say you can't remember and let them come to their own conclusions. You have to try to blend in, Peter. It's like being in a play and you have to choose a role. Dr. Brant thinks you'd make a good assistant. I help him on his rounds sometimes. It's not a bad job."

Peter looks at me like I've lost my mind. "I don't want a *job*, Genna. I want to go home!" Peter leans toward me and then groans in pain.

"What are you taking for the pain?" I ask.

"The Schaefers gave me a few swigs of whiskey. Then the doctor gave me opium, I think."

I reach into my pocket and pull out my bottle of ibuprofen. "Here. I brought painkillers with me this time. If you need more or they don't work, just let me know. I can probably steal a little morphine without Dr. Brant noticing."

"So you're a liar *and* a thief."

I look Peter dead in the eye and say, "I'm a survivor."

Peter leans his back against the wooden side of a nearby wagon. His runs his good hand over his face and seems to wipe away some of his anger. In a quiet voice he says, "I need you to send me back."

"What?" I take a step closer to Peter and wait for him to repeat himself. He couldn't have said what I think he said.

Peter turns so that his good shoulder presses into the wagon instead of his back. He looks at me with eyes full of desperation. "Open another portal and send me back to 2001. Please."

This is not what I expected. I genuinely want to help Peter but he's asking for too much. "I—I can't."

"Why not? You owe me, Genna. You ripped my arm out of its socket. You brought me here against my will. When you told me about this world, I believed you. I tried to help you. But I didn't sign up for this, Genna."

I try to gather my thoughts and defend myself but there are too many different emotions battling inside me. "You shouldn't have come that night. I told you to leave me alone…"

"You didn't know what you were doing. I didn't want you to get hurt."

I look down at my scarred hands and Peter follows my gaze. "I burned them holding onto the chain link fence." I cast a guilty glance at Peter's right arm and hand him the bottle of painkillers. "Take it—I've got more."

Peter accepts the bottle and shoves it in his pants pocket. "All I need you to do is send me home, Genna. Where I belong."

"I can't..."

"Can't—or won't?" Peter barely gives me a chance to respond before blurting out, "I just talked to Judah."

The noise inside my mind quiets immediately. I feel my face harden into a mask that Peter can't see beyond. "And?"

"And...he's different. He's changed—or this world changed him."

I wait for Peter to go on. He thinks he can use Judah as leverage, but he's wrong.

Peter tries to be gentle. "I don't think he's going to change his mind, Genna."

I am not fragile. Fragile things don't last long in this world. "About what?"

"About you."

I refuse to react even though Peter's words sink into my heart like a knife. I turn my head and search for Mattie and Money in the crowd. I nod in their direction so Peter knows I'm talking about real people. "I have friends here in Weeksville—people who need my help. I can't leave them just because you're homesick."

"So stay. Open the portal and send me back—alone."

My mask slips a bit and Peter sees my surprise. "Alone? I don't know how to do that. I wish I could help you, Peter, but I can't."

Peter scowls but takes a moment to think of another approach. "How much time do you need?"

"What?"

"You say people here *need* you. How long before your friends can manage on their own?"

I shrug but try to meet Peter halfway. "I don't know. A month, maybe two." Peter shakes his head like I've just given him a life sentence. "Listen, Peter, hardly any time has passed since we left 2001. You have a home here, and people who'll take care of you. Dr. Brant says your arm will heal if you just give it time...." Peter looks at me but I have nothing more to say. I shrug again and wait to see what he will do next.

"I'm not spending Christmas in this world, Genna. You've got two months—two months to figure out how to fix this."

I try to do the math in my head. Will Martha's baby be born by then? Peter's waiting for me to respond so I nod and say, "I will, Peter. I promise."

He nods and turns to leave but then hesitates and looks back at me. His eyes soften and I know he's about to say something cruel in the kindest way he can. This time I brace myself for the blow.

"He won't change, Genna. I've known Judah a long time—longer than you. He doesn't believe in compromise and he doesn't really 'do' forgiveness. I hope you don't think you can change his mind because once it's made up—"

I push past Peter without saying a word and search for Mattie's face in the crowd. As soon as she sees me, Mattie smiles and waves me over. I let the mask slide off my face so Mattie can see how grateful I am to have at least one true friend in this world.

Genna

48.

When I suggest to Mrs. Brant that she hire some extra help, she agrees to let Mattie come out from Weeksville and stay over two nights a week. All Mrs. Brant can talk about these days is the Sanitary Fair and the various committees she's on over at the Woman's Relief Association. They raised $100,000 at the fair in Chicago and Mrs. Brant is determined to raise at least twice as much here in Brooklyn by holding a dance, an auction, and even a cattle show! Some of her friends think they ought to just hold one fair in New York, but Brooklyn is its own city and Mrs. Brant wants to prove we can do our part for the war.

Of course, when I say "we," what I really mean is that Mrs. Brant gives the orders and Nannie and I do our best to keep up. Having Mattie around lightens the load—and our spirits. She and Nannie take to one another straight away, and Mattie's work habits and Southern manners impress Mrs. Brant. Even fussy Henry smiles for Mattie, and I feel a weight lift from my heart knowing she will be here for him if anything happens to me.

What *will* happen to me now that Judah has decided he has "other plans?" For a week I cry myself to sleep in my lonely bed, and in the daytime I fume silently while Nannie talks about "no count niggers" without ever mentioning Judah's name. Then Mattie comes and I remember that my world is much larger than one stupid boy. The faces she pulls to make

Henry smile make me smile, too. And her imitation of Mrs. Brant leaves me and Nannie doubled over with laughter.

Judah may not need me anymore, but I still have something to offer my friends. I borrow some of Henry's books and in the evenings we hold class in the kitchen. Mattie can already read a little and together we help Nannie sound out simple nursery rhymes. It's harder to smile when Mattie goes back to Weeksville, but while she's here the days fly by, and at night we curl up in bed and giggle under the covers until Nannie throws her shoe at the wall and tells us to "hush up" and go to sleep.

One weekend when Mattie's back at the orphanage, we have another visitor. I wake up Saturday morning and the smell of fresh-baked biscuits greets me before I even get all the way downstairs to the kitchen. Nannie is humming to herself and flitting about the kitchen like there's no place else she'd rather be. I know the Brants plan to be out for the evening but that doesn't usually put Nannie in such a good mood. Before I can ask she beams at me and says, "Today's the day—he's comin'! He's comin' home at last!"

"Who's coming?" I ask as her excitement spreads and puts a smile on my face, too.

Nannie makes an impatient sound with her mouth and waves her hand dismissively. "Paul, of course! My precious boy is comin' home. So you just fix up your face and act like you got some sense. You pretty enough when you ain't moanin' and mopin' over that fool. Don't let the right one get away this time!"

My smile vanishes and panic makes me think about risking some backtalk. "Why didn't you tell me Paul was coming?" I ask with a hint of attitude, but Nannie just smiles knowingly and flits away to tend to the pots simmering on the stove.

I stumble through the rest of the day in a daze. My feelings flash by like channels turned by remote control: anticipation follows dread, which is replaced by hope and then fear. What if Paul doesn't like me any more? With everything I've been through lately, I don't think I can stand being rejected again. If Mattie were here, we could just have dinner like a family. But with Nannie playing matchmaker, there's no way to see Paul as anything other than my "beau."

The Brants leave around seven. Twenty minutes later the sound of Nannie's laughter bubbling up from downstairs lets me know that Paul has finally arrived. I check on Henry, sleeping soundly in his crib, and then glance at my reflection in the large mirror above his dresser. I only have a small broken mirror on the wall of my tiny room, so I take a moment now to fix myself up.

I brought a little makeup with me in my knapsack, but I just dab a bit of gloss on my lips. Women don't really wear makeup in this world. The women at Sal's had their faces painted, but respectable ladies don't. I packed the makeup because I wanted to look my best for Judah, but when I look at my face in the mirror now, I know that I don't have to change myself for Paul.

I take a deep breath, walk down the carpeted hallway that leads to the servants quarters, and head down the back stairs that end at the kitchen. Another deep breath and I leave the dark, winding staircase and join the happy reunion.

Nannie has thrown her arms around Paul and is holding on for dear life. Although Paul is much taller, he happily tolerates Nannie's long, tight embrace. I will my heart to slow down and hope my voice doesn't betray my nervousness. I didn't expect to feel this way, but now that Paul is just a few feet away, I feel tears welling up in my eyes. Was he always this beautiful? Maybe my heart is fluttering because of the joy that's so evident in his eyes as Paul looks at me. This is the welcome I hoped to get from Judah.

I force my trembling lips into a wide grin and say, "So it's true! The prodigal son has returned."

Paul winks at me and I feel my spine tingle.

"We have been deceived, Nannie," he says in a teasing voice. "The girl before us is not a nurse at all—she's a magician, able to vanish at will."

Nannie laughs and turns her head to look at me, but she keeps her arms locked around Paul's waist. "When she turned up in the yard I thought she were a haint!"

I need something to do with my face besides smile. Eating would be a good option, but Nannie runs the kitchen and I know better than to try to take charge down here. I place a hand on my belly and appeal directly to Nannie's pride as a cook. "I'm very real and I'm *very* hungry. Can we eat now?"

Nannie immediately lets go of Paul and busies herself at the stove. Relieved, I drop the fake smile and reach for the closest chair at the kitchen table. Paul reaches for the same chair at the same time and for a moment his hand rests on mine. I don't know what's wrong with me. My cheeks are burning up even though Nannie's the one standing over the steaming pots of food.

Paul pulls the chair out and waits for me to sit down before leaning in to whisper, "Promise you won't disappear before supper's over?"

Paul's lips brush my earlobe and I giggle like an idiot in spite of myself. I squeak out "I promise" before looking up to find Nannie's eyes on me.

"Don't you worry none," Nannie says as she places a plate piled high with food in front of Paul. "That gal ain't goin' nowhere now that she done laid eyes on you."

I nervously tap my fingernails on the tabletop and wait for my own plate to arrive. "How was Boston?" I ask Paul.

Nannie returns with my plate, which has almost as much food on it. Before I can object, she turns her attention back to Paul. "Plenty of work on the docks up there, I 'spect."

Paul shakes his head. "Actually, I'm done with the shipping business. A friend of my father found me a temporary position at a colored school in the city, but I found teaching wasn't my calling either."

Nannie finally brings a plate for herself over to the table. She clamps a hand on Paul's shoulder before taking a seat. "Well, don't you worry none. A bright boy like you is sure to find work."

I wonder if Nannie's talking about Paul's color or his intelligence when she calls him "bright." Both can be an advantage in this world, though Paul's fair skin and blue eyes haven't protected him from racism. His father may be a wealthy White merchant but in this world, Paul's still on the wrong side of the color line.

I really am hungry and so I decide to hurry things along. "Why don't you say grace, Nannie?"

Paul nods and reaches for both of our hands. "You've prepared a sumptuous feast, Nannie. The cook ought to bless the meal."

Nannie looks flattered but shakes her head. "The man of the house ought to say grace."

I wait until my head is bowed before rolling my eyes. Paul gives my hand a playful squeeze and keeps his prayer short and sweet. After we all say "amen," Paul lets go of Nannie's hand but holds onto mine for a moment longer. Then he lets go, picks up his fork, and digs in. I watch him close his eyes as he savors his food loudly so that Nannie starts to beam again.

The last time I saw Paul he was determined to join the army. I couldn't change his mind before but I figure it can't hurt to try again now. "They say if you find a job you love, you'll never work a day in your life."

Nannie sucks her teeth. "What kind o' foolishness is that? Colored folks can't wait to find work they love! Good jobs are hard to come by. Honest work is God's work—you two just remember that."

Paul and I smother our smiles and say in unison, "Yes, ma'am."

Watching Nannie and Paul across the table, I suddenly feel overcome with emotion. I look down at my plate so no one can see the tears filling my eyes. Then I fill my mouth with food so I don't have to say anything right now. Together like this, we are a family. I mostly missed Judah while I was gone, but I don't know if I've ever felt this safe—this loved—with Judah. With him it was always the two of us against the world. Here, with Paul and Nannie, I don't have to fight anyone.

Paul glances at me and senses that something's wrong. I smile so he's knows I'm okay and he picks up where he left off. "Another friend of my father is an attorney. He said I could serve as his clerk after the war."

"Why wait? Why not start now?" I suggest, eager to see Paul do anything other than enlist.

After swallowing another mouthful of food, Paul lets his fork dangle idly from his fingers. "The country's at war, Genna," Paul says solemnly. Then he lifts his eyes from his plate and looks straight at me. "Some things have to wait."

My cheeks burn again and I happily let Nannie steer the conversation for the rest of the meal. Somehow Paul manages to eat seconds, which Nannie heaps onto his plate before it's even been cleared. Nannie's delicious food turns to dust in my mouth as I think about Paul heading off to war. It's almost over—just two more years—and Gettysburg, the bloodiest battle of the Civil War, is behind us. But there are still so many deadly battles yet to be fought. I can't let Paul throw away his life.

I offer to wash the dishes so that Nannie can have Paul's undivided attention. Nannie had four kids of her own but they were sold away while she was still enslaved. Her master fathered all her kids, but that didn't stop him from selling them when his wife wanted to redecorate the big house. Paul's father was different—he fell in love with a Black woman and would have married her if it were legal. Instead he freed her and so his son was born free.

I think Nannie sees her own kids when she looks at Paul. Nannie's more like a grandmother to me. When I first started working for the Brants, Nannie showed me the ropes and taught me to let go of the past so I could stop crying myself to sleep every night. Nannie won't say it out loud, but I can tell she doesn't want Paul to enlist either. She admires his courage and his loyalty to the Union, but I bet she'd be happier if he took a safe job sweeping streets here in Brooklyn.

I stare into the cloudy, soapy water and try to see what the future holds. Nannie will probably work for the Brants as long as she's able. She won't have a pension but she's been a loyal servant to this family and I hope the Brants will do right by her. After the war there will be a Home for the Aged in Weeksville—maybe Nannie will live out her days there. If Paul survives the war, maybe he'll follow his old dream about heading west.

And what about me? What will my life look like if I stay here in the past? Dr. Brant once promised to help me get into medical school, even though he thinks my "small brain" will keep me from achieving the same success as a big-headed White man like him. Susan Smith grew up in Weeksville and she went on to become the first African American woman doctor in New York State. Maybe I could try to find her and follow in her footsteps.

Or...

I plunge my hands into the murky water and search for cutlery on the bottom of the sink.

What if...

I grasp a spoon and use the sodden rag to wipe it clean of the slick grease that floats on the water's surface. What if...I didn't stay here? What if I did what Peter asked and opened a portal leading back to the future? I really don't think I could send Peter back on his own. But what if I went with him—and brought along a few of my friends? Would Mattie agree to come with me? Only if she could bring Money, too. And what about Martha—could she travel through time in her condition? What if I waited until after she had the baby? I search the scummy water for something solid to grasp and find one last piece of cutlery. What if...I asked Paul? He craves adventure—but would he travel through time with me?

I'm so deep in my thoughts that I don't hear Nannie calling my name or the scraping of chairs against the floor as she and Paul stand and say goodnight. I jump when I feel his fingers gently pressing into my back. The knife slips from my fingers and clatters to the floor. We stoop for it at the same time and knock heads, which makes Nannie laugh. She hands me a towel so I can dry my hands and then throws a woolen shawl around my shoulders before telling me to walk Paul out to the street.

It's a crisp autumn night. I wish I could take Paul's hand in mine but know I can't do that now. Not yet.

We follow the paving stones that lead to the front gate used by deliverymen and servants like me. Paul and I stand there together for a moment, saying nothing. Earlier this evening I was a bundle of nerves, but right now I feel totally at ease. I look up at the stars in the night sky and enjoy the comfortable silence between us.

Paul's voice pulls my gaze back to earth. "Do you remember the day we met?" he asks.

I laugh at the memory, though the experience was terrifying at the time. I went for a stroll along the docks and got cornered by a couple of creeps. "How could I forget? You were my knight in shining armor."

Paul shakes his head and winks at me. "You didn't need me to save you. I'd never seen a girl fight like that. You made quite an impression on me, Miss Colon." He pauses and I see the mischievous glint in his eyes. "I have to say, there were some fine young ladies in Boston."

"Oh, really?"

I know he's messing with me but I decide to play along. And the truth is, I actually do feel a way about Paul checking out other girls. I chose Judah over him, but that doesn't mean I'm ready to see Paul with some other girl.

Paul stands a bit taller, satisfied with the hint of jealousy in my voice. "I never knew there were so many accomplished colored girls in Boston. All deeply devoted to the Union, all doing their part by knitting socks for soldiers. I do find, however, that most of the young ladies I meet suffer when I compare them to you."

I arch an eyebrow and act coy. "*Most* of them?"

Paul laughs. "All of them, really. You're one of a kind, Genna."

Now it's my turn to feel satisfied. I don't want things to get too serious between us, though, so I keep on teasing him. "You led Nannie to believe you were pounding the pavement in Boston, searching high and low for a job."

"I was!"

"And you just happened to meet plenty of 'fine young ladies' while job hunting, huh? They must have been throwing themselves at your feet."

Paul straightens his cap and pretends to brush dust off his coat. "Believe it or not, I'm considered quite a catch in certain circles."

I look at Paul's smiling face and know he's telling the truth. He's good-looking, kind, intelligent, and a perfect gentleman. And because his father's rich, he's got "prospects." Other girls probably do throw themselves at his feet. But when I had my chance, I blew it.

Paul's wearing a scarf that Nannie knitted for him. I don't know if he wears it everyday, or if he wore it tonight just to make her happy. It's almost the same shade of blue as his eyes, though Paul doesn't try to draw attention to the way he looks. He's not ashamed of being mixed race, but he doesn't want special treatment because of it either.

I reach out my hand and fix his scarf so that it's wrapped more tightly around his pale throat. He swallows nervously and I feel his Adam's apple pulse against my fingers. I take a step back so I won't be tempted to touch him again. "You *are* a catch, Paul. Any girl would be lucky to have you."

For a moment we say nothing, but the silence between us isn't as comfortable as before. Once again my thoughts turn to Judah. I wonder what he would think if he saw me and Paul together like this. Would he even care? Probably not. Judah is nothing like Paul, and yet he's the one I wanted to spend the rest of my life with. I never thought Judah was perfect but I did think he was beautiful with his untamed locks, and onyx eyes, and poems written just for me. Judah was the first boy who told me I was beautiful and like a fool, I thought that meant he would love me as much as I loved him.

I feel a stab of pain in my heart and blink back the tears before they can fall. Paul seems to read my mind.

"You came back for him, didn't you?"

"For *him* – not *me*." Those are the words Paul is too polite to say out loud. I sigh and try to find a way to apologize. "I never got to say goodbye to anyone that night. It was total chaos. One second I was here and the next...I was gone." The words stop coming but I force myself to go on. "I hoped Judah would be waiting for me when I got back." I glance at Paul and hope he'll understand my meaning when I add, "But I was wrong. Judah has moved on."

Paul doesn't look at me so he doesn't understand what I'm trying to say. He just nods and says, "I hear he's touring the country, speaking out against slavery. You must be proud of him."

Proud? That idea never even crossed my mind. These days when I think about Judah I just feel angry, hurt, and confused. Paul has never made me feel that way. Why is love so complicated? I sigh and close my eyes against the whipping wind. Suddenly in my mind's eye I see a candle flickering in the window of a dark house. I gasp and my eyes fly open to see Paul watching me with concern.

"What is it?" he asks.

What if *this* is why I came back to this world—to be with Paul, not Judah? I thought I knew what my future looked like, but what if I was wrong—again? I take a deep breath and decide to risk telling Paul the truth—the whole truth. What have I got to lose?

"There's something I need to tell you, Paul."

This time he hears the seriousness in my voice. I open my mouth but no words come out. Paul patiently waits for me to go on but I can't figure out how to start.

He gently asks, "What is it, Genna?"

I clear my throat and grasp for something—anything—that will help me open this door. "You said before—at dinner—that I was a magician. Well, in a way, you're right. I—I can...I figured out a way to—" I try to finish my thought but just can't bring myself to say, "travel through time."

Paul tries to draw the truth out of me. "Where did you go, Genna? Nannie says you just vanished the night of the riots, but you must have gone somewhere."

I nod quickly and blurt out "I did!" I stare at Paul and try to figure out if there's any fear in his eyes. "I don't want you to think I'm crazy. And you know I wouldn't lie to you."

He reaches out a hand and squeezes my arm. "I know that. We're friends, right? I trust you and you can trust me."

I don't know whether it's the wind or his tenderness that makes a lone tear roll down my cheek. I brush it away and surprise myself by saying, "I don't want you to join the army, Paul. I don't want you to die."

Paul squeezes my arm once more before putting his hand back in his pocket. "I appreciate your concern, Genna, I really do. But I feel strongly about this. I want to do my part."

"But you don't have to, Paul—really."

Paul frowns. "I know I don't have to, but I *want* to, Genna. I was born free—I don't know what it's like to be owned by someone else. But I have to do this. For my people."

I take a deep breath and decide to start with the simplest confession. "I've never been a slave either, Paul."

His eyebrows go up in surprise and then scrunch together as he tries to make sense of what I've just said. "What do you mean? You told me you were—"

I interrupt him so I can take control of the conversation and steer us both toward the truth. "I know what I told you. But everything I know about slavery I learned in a book. That's how I know that the North will win the Civil War. Lee will surrender in April 1865—two years from now—and slavery will be abolished."

Paul looks at me but I can't tell whether he's confused or amazed. "How can you know that?"

I hold Paul's gaze as I answer his question. "I know because I'm not from this world. I'm from the future, Paul. I was born in Brooklyn—but in 1985."

Paul tips his head back and laughs. "1985?" His smile disappears when he sees that I'm serious. "But...that's more than a hundred years from now!"

I nod and wait for Paul to process what I've said. I watch as he struggles to make sense of my story. He trusts me but nothing I'm saying makes sense right now.

"How is that possible? How could you—how did you get here?"

"I don't know why it happened. The first time I was in a garden late at night and I made a wish in a fountain. Somehow I opened a portal—a door in time. Judah showed up a few minutes later and got sucked into the past too, but I wound up in Weeksville and he got sold down South." I pause and wait for Paul to blink. His mouth is hanging open in amazement but through his eyes I see the wheels of his mind turning. He's trying to believe me.

"And during the riots?"

"The same thing happened except that time I went back to the future alone. Judah stayed here."

Paul nods. That much of my story rings true. "So...what's the world like in the future?"

I take a moment and think about what to say. Should I tell Paul that in 2001 our country is at war again? I don't want to lie to him but I also don't want to take away his hope. Right now Black people need to believe in the future.

"A lot of things are different...but some things are the same. Judah doesn't think we've made much progress."

"What do you think?" Paul asks.

"There are things I can do in the twenty-first century that I could never do here and now. When the war ends, Black men will be given the right to vote but women won't get that right for another fifty years—even longer for Negro women in the South. But in 2001 we can do just about anything—run corporations, become politicians. Wear pants!"

Paul raises an eyebrow. "I'd love to see that!" He winks at me and then grows serious. "I always knew you were a special kind of girl, Genna, but I never imagined you could travel through time."

I allow myself to inch a bit closer to Paul. "So you believe me?"

He shrugs helplessly. "I guess so. It certainly is...strange, but the world is full of wonders." Paul looks up at the stars. "One day you'll have to tell me more about your world—this world—the world this world becomes." Paul glances over his shoulder. "Nannie doesn't know, does she?"

I shake my head and draw my shawl more tightly around me as an icy wind whips at my thin dress. "She wouldn't understand. I've only told one other friend in Weeksville."

"Well, thank you for trusting me."

"Thank you for believing me. Or at least for not thinking I ought to be committed!"

For a moment we look into each other's eyes and this time my heart doesn't speed up. Instead I feel a sense of calm that I haven't known in months. Why is it so easy to be with Paul? It's because he accepts me. I don't have to prove anything with Paul the way I always had to with Judah. So why does Judah still have such a hold over my heart?

I'm the first to look away. I can feel Paul's eyes on my face and this time my heart does start to speed up. I know what will happen if I linger so I step back from the gate to release Paul and send him on his way. "I'd better go check on Henry," I say quietly.

Paul nods and opens the gate. He steps into the street and closes the gate behind him. He rests his hands on the wrought iron fence between us and says, "It's nice having you around again, Genna."

I smile and try to make things feel normal between us once more. "Well, don't be a stranger. Nannie's missed you a lot."

"I missed her, too." Paul pauses and playfully pats his full belly. "And her cooking."

We both laugh and then fall into that uncomfortable silence once more. I look at the flickering streetlamps, the stars above—everywhere except Paul's face. I know he's watching me and I know he wants to kiss me goodnight. My cheeks start to burn and so I take a few steps toward the house. Then I change my mind, dart forward, and press my cold lips against Paul's.

"Good night," I call over my shoulder as I rush up the path that leads back to the kitchen.

"I'll be seeing you, Genna," he calls after me.

I don't turn around but I hear the promise in his voice. I don't let Paul see the silly grin on my face, but Nannie sees it as soon as I open the back door. She usually turns in early, but it's clear Nannie's been waiting for me. She stands in the middle of the kitchen, her hands planted on her hips.

"If you done chasin' after that wild-haired fool, you might think twice 'fore you let *that* sweet boy head off to war with a broken heart."

Before I have time to figure out what Nannie's talking about, she goes on. "You could do a whole lot worse than Paul, and he'd make a better husband than that Judah."

My mouth falls open. "Husband? Nannie, I'm sixteen!"

"That's right, and it's high time you started thinkin' 'bout settlin' down. I already had two babies when I was your age, and no decent man willin' and able to put a ring on my finger. Now, I'm not one to meddle, but the good Lord laid this on my heart and I just had to speak my mind. I done said my piece, and now I'm goin' to bed."

Nannie heads upstairs, leaving me alone with my thoughts in the empty kitchen. I pull a chair over to the stove and remember to grab a rag before opening the small cast iron door to let some of the heat out. The fire inside is going down but Nannie's left a plate of food to warm on the stovetop in case Dr. Brant's hungry when he gets home. A fancy chef probably prepared a five-course meal for the Brants and their rich friends, but Dr. Brant always comes home craving Nannie's hearty home cooking. He's the last person I want to see right now, but I can't bring myself to leave the warmth and quiet of the kitchen. If I go to bed now, I'll just lie awake in bed with Nannie snoring peacefully in the next room.

I gaze at the dwindling flames and mull over what Nannie said about Paul. He still cares about me, I know that for sure. But *marriage*? In this world, there'd be nothing wrong with a couple of teenagers getting married. It might not even be illegal in that other Brooklyn. Toshi's engaged to Troy with a baby on the way and she's just a few years older than me. But if I went back to that Brooklyn with a handsome young husband in tow, Mama would pitch a fit. If Toshi meant what she said and let us move in with her, I guess I could go back to school. But what about Paul? Would he be willing to leave his world in order to start a new life in mine? He did say he wanted to learn more about the future. But could I really go back — open the portal one more time — and safely bring Paul with me?

I hold out my hands and warm them before the fire. What would it be like to have a ring on my finger? To have another person bound to me for the rest of my life? It's not like I never thought about marrying Judah. In this world, I could pretend to be his sister or I could become his wife — those were pretty much our only respectable options. Martha never cared what people thought about her and Willem, but I care. I used to, anyway. But Judah's not my brother or my husband — and now he's not even a friend. He doesn't want me but Paul does. Would Paul really marry me? I know one thing for sure: the only way to keep him out of *this* war is to take him back to the future.

The sound of the front door slamming shut upstairs jolts me out of my seat. I grab the rag and close the door to the stove. Then I replace my chair at the kitchen table and scurry up the back stairs before Dr. Brant comes into the kitchen in search of his second supper.

I undress without the help of a candle and slip under the covers before I let go of my silly dream. I squint in the darkness until I can make out the familiar water stains on the ceiling. Dr. Brant always promised he would get the roof fixed but I guess he figured there was no need once I disappeared. When Martha left, this room remained empty for months, though Nannie kept the place clean just in case I ever returned. Nannie's like that — she always holds onto hope. But sometimes hope feels like a curse. I needed it back in 2001 — hope was the anchor that kept me linked to the past and to Judah. But now...

I want to be done with Judah but there's still a tiny bud of hope in my heart. I know I ought to starve it until it shrivels and dies, but what if Judah just needs more time? He's been through so much—maybe I just need to be patient with him. Maybe he's not as strong as he pretends to be. Maybe I just have to prove to him that he can trust me again. Part of me needs to believe I can make things right between us.

Then there's the part of me that burns with shame whenever I think about what a fool I've been. I was so sure Judah would be waiting for me, but I couldn't have been more wrong. And deep down I know that Peter's right about his best friend. Judah doesn't need more time. He won't change his mind and he won't have a change of heart—if he has a heart at all. I totally misread Judah's feelings for me, so why should I trust what I feel about Paul—or what I think he feels about me?

I told you so. I hear my sister's voice creeping into my thoughts like the icy draft that slips into my room through the attic window. If Toshi were here, she'd probably sneer and say, "Like I told you, Genna—a man's just a man." Even Nannie told me that once. Toshi would probably also tell me not to do anything stupid when I'm still nursing a broken heart. I think about my sister's round belly and the baby that's on the way. Toshi's got a ring on her finger and a place of her own, but no diploma. If Troy ever does walk out on her, what's she going to do?

Suddenly taking advice from Toshi doesn't seem like such a good idea. I never listened to my big sister in the past because I knew I was on a different path—and Mama never let me forget it. But I don't know what path I'm on now. Everything around me looks familiar but I have never felt so lost.

I shut my eyes and try to fall asleep before the tears start flowing again. *Sometimes you got to roll the dice.* That's what Toshi said. I risked my life to come back to this war-torn world only to find out that the boy who convinced me I was special doesn't think I'm so special anymore. Sweet as he is, I'm not sure I'm ready to take a chance on Paul—not when I can't even trust myself.

Genna

49.

Nannie and I see a lot more of Paul after that night, which puts both of us in a good mood. I've celebrated Thanksgiving all my life, but this is the first year it will be a federal holiday in honor of the Union Army. Mrs. Brant decides to host a lavish dinner for those friends who share her admiration for President Lincoln.

It's not easy to prepare a feast with war-time rations, but Mrs. Brant insists we spare no expense and Nannie works her usual magic in the kitchen. Mattie comes out for the whole week, and together we polish all the silver until it shines and iron out the wrinkles in Mrs. Brant's finest table linen. Nannie shows us how to set the table after Adams inserts three boards that make it big enough to hold all the guests — and all the food! I recognize the roast turkey and cranberry sauce, but there's also oysters and duck and a whole lot of dishes I've never had before, like pumpkin pudding instead of pumpkin pie. Nannie stays up late cooking and baking way more food than twelve adults could ever hope to eat — which leaves plenty of leftovers for a late servants' dinner.

When the last guest rolls away in her carriage and the last crystal goblet has been washed and stored away, Paul arrives and joins Mattie, Money, Nannie, and me in the kitchen. Tired but happy, we gather around the humble wooden table and when Nannie tells "the man of the house" to say grace, Paul suggests that we each say one thing we're thankful for instead. Money, who came out from the orphanage to help us serve dinner to the Brants and their guests, smiles shyly and softly says he's thankful for the money he earned at his first job. Mattie beams at her little brother and says she's thankful for family and true friends. I give Mattie's hand a squeeze and open my mouth to go next, but Nannie beats me to it.

She clears her throat and holds her head up high as if that will stop the tears shining in her eyes from falling. "I pray for my four babies every day, even though I know the good Lord may never see fit to let me lay eyes on 'em again." Tears spill down Nannie's cheeks but she doesn't let go of our hands to wipe her eyes. She just clears her throat once more and goes on.

"I ain't got my babies and I ain't got a whole lotta friends. But I still got a mother's heart, and a mother's heart is always full o' love even if it ain't got no place to go. I love the Lord," Nannie pauses and then nods at the table laden with food, "and I put a little love into everythin' I cook. But tonight I'm thankin' my Heavenly Father for the four beautiful children gathered round this table. I didn't birth none 'o you, but you all is my babies tonight."

Nannie is standing at the head of the table with her head bowed. Paul holds one of her hands and I'm holding the other. But it's Money who breaks the chain and runs past us to throw his arms around Nannie's waist. The rest of us follow suit and within seconds we dissolve into a heaving mass of sobs and tears. Together we weep for all those we have lost.

"Alright now, that's enough," Nannie says after a long moment. I feel her soft, worn palm on the back of my bowed head but can't bring myself to pull away.

To our surprise, Nannie starts to laugh. "Enough!" she cries as she pries loose our arms and wipes the tears from her eyes with the hem of her apron. "You all sit down and eat this good food 'fore it gets cold!"

We laugh as well and do as we're told. Money scrambles back to his seat and watches with wide eyes as Nannie spoons more and more food onto his plate. He doesn't go hungry at the orphanage but I don't think he's ever seen so much food. We're old enough to help ourselves and waste no time digging in, but Nannie doesn't touch her food right away. For a moment she just folds her hand together and watches us devouring the food she lovingly prepared. Then she picks up her own fork and reminds us to save room for the three different kinds of pie she's made for dessert.

It's not until we've eaten our fill and pushed back from the table that Paul looks over at me and says, "You never told us what you're thankful for, Genna."

I say nothing but look at Paul long enough to make him blush and shift his own gaze to the fragment of pie crust left on his plate. All week I've been thinking about my family in the future. It isn't Thanksgiving yet in 2001 — I think Columbus Day is coming up — but I hope Mama and Toshi have made up by now so that they can spend the holidays together the way families should. I look around the table and wonder how I could be so blessed to have found a home in two different worlds.

"I'm thankful for sanctuary — for always finding a safe place to land."

"God is good," Nannie says with a solemn nod.

"What are you thankful for?" I ask Paul.

He sits up and rolls his lips together. Then he smiles and looks from Nannie, to Mattie, to Money, and lastly at me. "I've got a lot to be thankful for this year. I don't think I've ever been in a place like this — "

"A kitchen?" Money asks innocently.

Mattie shushes her brother but Paul just reaches out and playfully taps the boy's head.

"I've been in plenty of kitchens, Money. But I've never been in a place where I don't have to prove myself. Where people accept me as I am. Where I feel like I belong."

Before any of us can respond, Nannie suddenly gets up from the table and starts loudly gathering up our empty plates. She turns toward the sink with a stack of plates balanced in one hand, and with the other she squeezes Paul's shoulder. But then she quickly removes her hand and walks away before he can place his own hand over hers.

Paul looks at me and my smile makes him blush again. But the moment is ruined when Money suddenly blurts out, "When are you and Genna gonna get married?"

I gasp and stare at Mattie. She and I have talked about the idea during our late night chats, but I never thought she'd tell her little brother!

Money's not done. He looks from Paul to me and asks, "Can I be in the wedding? I never been in a wedding before."

Mattie jumps up and slaps her little brother on the back of his head to shut him up. But the opposite happens—Money starts to cry and so Mattie twists his ear to make him shut up. That just makes Money wail even louder, of course, and Nannie has to rush over to separate the two siblings before their squabbling wakes up the Brants.

Nannie thrusts her wet rag into Mattie's hand and makes her take over the job of washing the dishes. She tells Money to stop crying and puts a broom in his hand. Then she turns to us. "We got too many bodies in here. Take Paul outside, Genna. He can sleep in the carriage house since Adams is stayin' by his sister tonight."

I do as I'm told and welcome the feel of the crisp night air against my burning cheeks. Paul grins mischievously but says nothing about Money's impertinent questions as we walk along the paved path that leads to the carriage house. Judah used to stay here, too. One night last summer I walked this same path and offered myself to him, but Judah pushed me away. I glance over at Paul and silently vow that I'll find a way to stop these memories from invading my mind. *Anchor yourself.* I am here—with Paul—in the present. Judah belongs in the past.

When we reach the door to the small brick building, Paul pulls a small red box from his pocket. "I bought you some chocolates but I guess I should have gotten you a ring…"

I swat his arm playfully and snatch the box of candy from his hand. There are four chocolates inside. To stop his teasing, I shove one of the chocolates into Paul's mouth and then pop another in my own mouth. For a few seconds we just stand there in the dark, savoring the creamy chocolate and the unexpected intimacy of this moment. I look up at the stars and wonder what would happen if I followed Paul inside the carriage house and offered to give him what Judah didn't want from me. Would he push me away, too?

Paul presses something cold into my palm. I look down and find a shiny copper penny.

"For your thoughts," Paul says.

He is close enough for me to smell the sugar on his breath. I fold the penny inside my palm. "Pennies are for wishes," I tell him.

"Then make a wish," Paul replies.

I think about what I want most in that moment, and then I lean into Paul until his lips find mine. Paul tenses when my tongue slips between his lips but then he grabs me by the arms and pulls me close. We're both breathless when the back door of the house creaks open and Nannie hisses, "That's enough, you two!"

We pull apart but before I return to the house I say, "I need to ask you something."

"Are you going to propose?" he asks with a grin.

I shrug coyly and hold his gaze until Paul's smile disappears.

"Genna—are you serious about getting married?"

The yearning in Paul's voice excites and frightens me, but Nannie hisses at us again and so I let myself be drawn like a moth toward the candle she's holding up against the dark. "Let's talk about it next week. Okay?"

Paul nods and says goodnight. I hurry back to the house and slip inside the open door without making eye contact with Nannie. Not because I'm ashamed of kissing Paul, but because the penny in my palm will soon help me open another door that will take her beloved boy away for good.

Genna

50.

"What happened today, Paul?" I loosely lace my fingers between his so he knows I'm not trying to pry. This isn't the question I had planned to ask, but when Paul arrives at the back door looking glum, I set my own agenda aside for a moment.

Paul squeezes my hand, then holds it between his own and examines it for a moment. He strokes my dark skin and smiles ruefully. "I've tried, Gen, I really have. I've done everything I was supposed to do—I've got a certificate from two doctors, both attesting that I'm fit for service. But this fellow at the recruiting station—Grambling's his name. He keeps telling them to turn me away. All I want is to serve my country! I'm not looking for glory and I'm not asking for special treatment. I'm willing to do whatever they need me to do—I'll dig latrines, I'll mop floors. I'm not asking to be put in charge, and I can follow orders just as well as the next man. But they don't want me, Gen. And I'm starting to think there's nothing I can do that will change their minds."

New York's first Colored Troops began recruiting in September. I didn't want him to enlist but Paul was determined to try, and I've learned to hold my tongue whenever he comes around feeling frustrated.

"They *need* men like you," I tell him. At this point in the war, the Union army is taking any and every soldier it can get, but Paul isn't just any recruit. He's young, fit, educated, and fairly well off, which makes him officer material. This recruiter doesn't see Paul's potential, though.

All he sees is Paul's light skin, blue eyes, and wavy blond hair. I don't say anything but deep down I know Paul's right—nothing he can do will change this man Grambling's mind. Of course, I'm secretly hoping Paul will become so discouraged that he gives up on the idea of joining the army. I have other plans for him—for us.

I cover Paul's pale hand with my own and tilt his chin up so that his eyes meet mine. "It isn't fair. You'd make an amazing solider." I lean my head against his and wait a beat before adding. "But maybe it's just not meant to be."

Paul pulls away from me and gently sets my hand back in my lap. "They're worried I'll ruin their experiment."

"Experiment?"

"They want to prove that the Negro has just as much courage on the battlefield as White men."

"Well, if it's courage they're looking for, they won't find anyone braver than you."

Paul smiles to let me know he appreciates my vote of confidence. Then his eyes cloud over and he looks out over the Brants' garden. It's lush and filled with roses in the summertime, but right now the stone statues and bare branches make the yard feel more like a cemetery.

"Thanks, Gen. But you know what I'm getting at. They don't want me in the Colored Troops because I'm tainted." Bitterness thins Paul's lips. "Because my father's White."

"They shouldn't hold that against you. You can't choose who your parents are. And plenty of colored folks have White folks in their family tree." I don't point out the fact that most of them are White men who raped enslaved women.

"Grambling took one look at my face and made up his mind," Paul says with uncharacteristic bitterness. Then he sighs and seems to regret his tone. "I can't say that I blame him. I mean, look at how they treat Frederick Douglass. He's a brilliant orator and a self-made man, but those who despise the colored race attribute all his achievements to his White father."

We read Frederick Douglass' narrative in the ninth grade. Douglass' father was his owner and he never acknowledged his Black son. Instead he left Douglass to live as a slave on his plantation, eating out of a trough like an animal until he was old enough to be put to work. When I look at photographs of Frederick Douglass, I don't see any signs of his White father. But I guess people see what they want to see.

If you want to believe Blacks are inferior to Whites, then you'll blame Blacks for everything bad and praise Whites for everything good. And when a genius like Frederick Douglass breaks his chains so he can be free, those same people will say slavery made him great. They'll say slavery turns the "savage" African into a "civilized" man. Like they know anything about what it means to be civil. This bloody, five-year war is what they call "civil."

Paul laughs ruefully and says, "If I were Judah's color, they'd have signed me up in a flash." Paul looks at his hands and then shoves them into his pockets to make his handicap disappear.

I watch his ears burn red with shame. It's wrong for me to feel glad inside, but I don't want Paul to die just to prove a bunch of racists wrong. "So…what will you do now?" I ask innocently.

Paul shrugs. "I don't know. Buy some land—settle somewhere far away from here."

"How far away?"

Paul looks past the garden to the city across the river. "Canada— Kansas. What does it matter?"

I take a deep breath to steady my nerves. "What if—what if we went away…together?" Paul looks at me and for a moment hope brightens his eyes. "The army may not want you, but I do," I assure him.

Paul stares at me for what feels like an eternity. I blush but manage not to look away. I need him to know that I'm serious. It's time to make the strongest sales pitch I can.

"Do you really mean that, Genna?" he asks. "You'd go out west with me?"

I reach out and stroke Paul's face. "Actually...I was thinking you could come home with me."

Paul frowns but doesn't pull away. "Where—back there?" He nods at some invisible place off in the distance.

"I came back here, to Weeksville. If you come with me next time, we won't be going back—we'll go forward. To 2001."

This time Paul does pull back, but his hands reappear and catch hold of mine to keep me close. "You're serious then. You really think you can do it?"

"I know I can," I answer without any hesitation. I can tell by the way Paul's looking at me that he believes me. "All you have to do is hold onto me. Hold on and don't let go."

Paul kisses me and my heart trips. "Sounds easy enough."

I take a few deep breaths and let my heart rate even itself out. I can't convince Paul without specifics. I want him to know this isn't just a whim, but a legitimate plan that I've thought through.

"We'll have to live with my mother when we arrive, but in time we can get a place of our own. We can go to college—an Ivy League college. We can both apply to Harvard!"

Paul tips his head back and laughs. "We can't go to Harvard!"

"Why not?"

"They don't admit Negroes, Genna."

"In my world, segregation is illegal, Paul. Everything's integrated—Congress, the police, schools." I think about the schools I've attended in Brooklyn—with not a single White student—and decide I better correct myself. "Well, almost everything. The world has changed in so many ways, Paul. You could go to law school, become a lawyer. More things are possible for us there."

Paul thinks for a moment and I dare to hope that my pitch is working. "I have saved up some money. My half-brother James bought out my share of our father's shipping business."

Paul has never mentioned having a half-brother before. I guess they're not close but decide not to bring up any emotional ties that might stop Paul from leaving this world. "Your savings—are they in paper bills?" When Paul nods I tell him, "Dollars won't work. Can you get gold?"

Paul frowns. "I guess so. People only use gold in your world?"

"No—they use paper money and coins." I decide not to tell him about credit cards. I think about the penny Paul gave me on Thanksgiving. "Actually, we should take some coins back with us—they might be valuable to a collector. There's this show on TV, *Antiques Roadshow*, and someone brought in an old nickel that was worth thousands of dollars!"

"TV?"

How do you explain television to someone who doesn't yet know about electricity? "TV is short for television. It's a box you buy and keep in your home. In this world, you go to a theater to see a show performed on a stage. But a TV has hundreds of channels and lots of shows are on all the time."

"Inside the box?" Paul asks incredulously.

I nod and smile wide so he knows there's nothing to fear. "The future's going to blow your mind, Paul! But don't worry—I'll be there to help you make sense of it all." I stop and think for a moment. "Would it bother you if you had to change your name?"

"Why would I have to do that? I can't be Paul Easterly in the future?"

"I'm not sure. When I came back in time, people here took me in. They didn't ask a whole lot of questions—they just did whatever they could to help me. The Brants hired me without knowing much more than my name. But in my world, it's not like that. You need certain documents—a social security card, a driver's license, a birth certificate. People who don't have those things are treated like second-class citizens. I don't want that to happen to you."

"But I have a birth certificate."

"From *this* century. No one would believe it was real if you showed it to them. And we can't exactly tell them that you traveled through time."

"So what will I have to do?"

"My sister's fiancé—Troy—he's a bit shady but he's got connections. I'm sure Troy knows someone who could get you a fake birth certificate and social security card. That way you could work." Paul looks at me warily and so I rush on. "It's not legal but people do it all the time—they have to. We'll probably have to pay a lot of money to get you a new identity…but it'd be like starting a new life. You'll be brand new to everyone else, but you'll still be Paul Easterly when you're with me."

For a long time Paul doesn't say anything. "I'd understand if you didn't want to come with me," I tell him, surprised at the depth of my own disappointment.

"I never said that." Paul reaches over and takes my hand. He looks at me tenderly and with total seriousness asks, "Can we get married in your world?"

The last thing I want to do is hurt Paul but I can't hide how surprised I am. We joked about it before but the look on Paul's face tells me he's not joking now.

"Married?" I practically choke on the word.

"I want *something* to be official. I can change my name and use someone else's identity if I have to. But I need something between us to be real. I need one thing I can hold onto."

"I honestly don't know if teenagers can get married in my world," I tell him.

"We could do it here," Paul says, "before we go. It was always my plan—well, my hope—that you would agree to become my wife. How else could we go out west together? I respect you too much to ask for anything less."

Paul's thoughtfulness melts me but I try to think practically. "If we get married in this world, it won't be legal in that other world. We won't have proof, I mean."

"We won't need proof," Paul says simply. "We'll just know."

Whenever I dreamt about someone proposing to me, it was always

Judah I saw before me, down on one knee with a ring in his hand. But I know now that that's never going to happen. And that was just a dream — this is real. Paul's love for me is *real*.

Paul squeezes my hand. "Will you at least think about it?"

"I won't be able to think about anything else!" I exclaim and my laughter seems to put Paul at ease. I lean against him and tuck my head beneath his chin. Maybe we do belong together. "I'll think about your proposal and you think about mine. Okay?"

Paul kisses my forehead and wraps his arms around me. "Okay."

Genna

51.

I wait for Paul on Sunday but he doesn't arrive at his usual time. I've gotten used to spending my afternoons off with him, and I thought he'd show up for sure after he proposed last week. But apparently I was wrong to think he'd be eager to see me. After waiting for Paul for well over an hour, I decide I have better things to do. I've been meaning to visit Martha and so I wrap myself in my warmest shawl and pull on a pair of mittens that Nannie knitted for me. We don't have any snow yet but it's definitely starting to feel like winter.

As I walk from Brooklyn Heights over to Clinton Hill, I realize that in some ways this Brooklyn isn't so different from the borough it will become. It's like the seeds planted in this era just need time before they blossom in my own century. Fulton Street is still a busy shopping district like it is in 1863, and Ft. Greene still has stately brownstones that line the streets surrounding the park. It's named after George Washington right now, but one thing that won't change over time is the number of Black people living on the north side of the park. There are no housing projects in 1863, but there are enough Black folks around here that they opened their own school. It's called Colored School No. 1 but it used to be called the African Free School, and just a few blocks away is the park where the Black folks from my era hold the African Street Festival. So some things have changed, but some things have stayed the same.

In Clinton Hill there are mansions for the wealthy, but also modest, wood-frame row houses painted in bright colors. Some of them look familiar, with shutters at the windows and wide front porches. I'm pretty sure at least a few of these buildings have survived to the twenty-first century. This Brooklyn is less crowded than the borough I used to call home but today, but as I walk through the streets on my way to visit my friend, it doesn't feel all that foreign. For just a moment I think about what it would be like to have a home in both eras. Once I got the hang of opening the portal, I could become a commuter and travel between worlds once a week—or once a day! It wouldn't be like choosing between Judah and Paul. I could have a life in *both* worlds. Two families. Two realities.

It's not hard to spot the convent. It looms above the street, an imposing red brick building with three storeys, a spire, and brittle ivy creeping up the facade. Nothing else could scale those walls—the convent is surrounded by a tall cast-iron fence with spikes sharp enough to deter any burglar. I stand on the sidewalk staring up at the curtained windows, hoping to catch a glimpse of Martha or any friendly face. The ornate cast-iron gate is closed and the words, "Convent of Srs. of Mercy" is spelled out in silver letters across the top. I'm not sure I should use the front entrance but a White man exiting the building holds the gate open for me and so I pass through, climb the steep stairs, and knock on the wide wooden door.

A fresh-faced nun appears, looks me up and down, and asks, "Are you here for a ticket?"

"A ticket?" I repeat, confused.

She explains that tickets are given to the poor at the other entrance on the side of the building. "Someone there will help you, my child."

"I'm not poor."

I don't mean to say it with attitude, but the young nun steps back just the same. Suddenly self-conscious, I reach back and finger the stray coils of hair at the nape of my neck. I try to make sure they're tucked inside the tam Nannie knitted for me. Why would she think I'm poor? Just because I'm Black? I fight the urge to rub my forehead and erase the tattoo there that tells the world I'm from the 'hood—even in 1863.

"How can I help you then?" the nun asks with an embarrassed smile.

Her blue eyes and rosy cheeks remind me of Maria in that corny movie *The Sound of Music*, which Mama used to watch whenever it came on TV. I hope she's the sort of nun who tries to fit in but isn't really cut out for a life behind walls—I'd like Martha to have someone like that taking care of her.

I ask to see Martha and notice that the nun hesitates for just a moment before opening the door and inviting me inside. Her Irish accent is thicker than Martha's so I'm guessing she was born there instead of here. The nun closes the door and tells me to wait while she checks to see if Martha is available. She seems kind of young to already be a nun, but she has the same slow, solemn movements as the older veiled women who glide up and down the hallway with a strange mixture of peace and purpose.

The convent is not at all what I expected. It's not as grand as the entrance to the Brant home, but there are gleaming wood panels running along the walls, perfectly polished mosaic tiles on the floor, and a modest chandelier hanging overhead. A portrait of a modest, smiling nun hangs on one wall encased in a hard-to-dust gold frame, and on the opposite walls hangs an ornately carved wooden crucifix—probably also hard to clean. But everything in the convent that I can see is spotless. I wonder what poor woman has to clean up around here and then realize it's probably the job of the unwed mothers like Martha.

I take a few steps forward and peek around the corner. The hallway is empty and so I take a few steps more, making sure to walk on my toes in order to make less noise. There are rooms on either side of the hall, most with closed doors. Through one partially opened door I catch a glimpse of two young White women seated at a table doing needlepoint. One wears the shapeless shift reserved for pregnant women but the other wears a dress that's a lot like mine—not fancy but well made and respectable. I try to imagine Martha spending her days in this quiet, orderly place that's nothing like the wild world of Five Points. Maybe the change suits her, but how does she pass the time? If Martha could read, I'd bring her some books from Dr. Brant's library, but she can't. Martha went to work instead of going to school because her ever-expanding family needed the money she could earn scrubbing floors.

Suddenly the silence of the convent is broken by an eerie moaning. I freeze in the empty hallway and try to locate the sound. Somewhere upstairs, behind a closed door, a young woman begins groaning and then screaming in agony as she struggles to give birth. That's what it's like in the nineteenth century—women have babies without the help of painkillers or an epidural, which Toshi swears she's going to have. Here in 1863 women don't even go to the hospital, and they only call for a doctor if there are complications. Most women, rich or poor, White or Black, give birth at home with only other women to help them. Sometimes they bleed to death. Sometimes the baby dies, too.

When the screams suddenly stop, I strain my ears to hear what's going on. Has the baby been born, or have they stuffed something into the girl's mouth to stifle her screams? I listen with a pounding heart and hope that the mother-to-be isn't Martha. If my math is right, it's too soon for her to be delivering her baby. Impatient, I creep down the hall in search of the stairs that might take me to my friend. I pass a grandfather clock that tells me it's almost half past three. The church bell tolled three just as I arrived at the convent, which means I have been waiting for almost half an hour.

I find the stairwell at the end of the hallway and weigh my options. I don't want to disobey the nice young nun, but thirty minutes is a long time to wait. I try to think of the worst thing that could happen if I get caught upstairs. The older nuns could ask me to leave—or they might refuse to let me see Martha. But what if she's the one in labor? I place a hand on the polished wooden banister and put one foot on the staircase but quickly step back into the hallway when I hear the young nun calling me.

She stands near the front door where she left me and for a second time calls out, "Miss?"

I hurry back and the sound of my hard heels on the tile floor makes her turn and frown at me. I offer an apologetic smile and hope she'll take me to see Martha now, but the look on her face tells me that's probably not going to happen.

The nun clasps my hand to soften the bad news. "I'm so sorry to have kept you waiting, but I'm afraid Martha isn't able to have visitors today."

"Why not?" I ask. The nun takes back her cold fingers and frowns at me. I wonder if all nuns are as strict as the ones I've seen on TV. She doesn't look that much older than me, but something tells me she's not used to being questioned by girls my age. I hurry on and try to sound less defiant. "Is Martha okay? I mean—there's nothing wrong with the baby, is there?"

"Both are doing fine, but Martha is busy in the chapel."

"Busy?" I'm not sure what this means but I can tell this nun wants to get rid of me and that makes me all the more determined to stick around. "Is she tidying up or something? Because I'm not in any rush—I can wait. Or I could help her..."

The nun lowers her eyes and smiles in a way that makes me feel like she pities me for being so ignorant. "No, dear, Martha isn't cleaning the chapel. She's purifying her soul." The look on my face must prompt her to go on because the next thing she says is, "Martha's praying to atone for her sins. I'm afraid the Reverend Mother said she cannot be disturbed."

Five things almost fly out of my mouth at once, but somehow I manage to keep every unholy word inside my sealed lips. Martha *is* Catholic so I guess she might have chosen to pray instead of seeing her only friend, but something tells me these nuns probably didn't give Martha much of a choice. In my head I can see my pregnant friend forced to kneel on the hard tile floor, her clasped hands held against her big belly as she pleads with God for forgiveness. But Martha doesn't need to be forgiven because she hasn't done anything wrong. Plenty of wrong things were done *to* her, and maybe these nuns need to focus on saving *those* sinners instead. Martha has already spent too much of her young life on her knees.

These are some of the things I *want* to say, but all I manage to do is look sullen and mutter, "Martha's not a sinner."

The nun smiles and places a surprisingly gentle hand on my arm. "We're all sinners, my child." Then she takes her hand away and opens the front door, "Good day to you."

I know that I am being dismissed and so I take a step over the threshold, but I'm not ready to leave yet. "Could you—I mean, would you please tell Martha that I came by? My name's Genna."

The nun presses her lips into an impatient smile. "I will, child," she says, closing the door behind me.

I press my palm against the door to stop her from shutting me out. "When is the baby due?"

"Only the Lord knows for certain," she says, no longer trying to hide her exasperation.

I manage to stop myself from going off on this nun. "Could someone send me a message when the baby's on its way? I can write down my address." I tack on a "please" and the nun's face softens.

She glances over her shoulder and then leans forward and asks, "You're a friend?"

I lie. "Family, actually." The nun's eyes open wide with surprise so I quickly add, "The baby's father. He's my—I mean, he was..."

She casts her eyes down and nods, letting me know I don't have to go on. I wonder what Martha has told them about Willem. I wonder what "sins" she has confessed. I look at the white cloth wound so tightly around the young nun's face and neck and find myself randomly wondering what color her hair is. Knowing that would make her seem more human and less holy, which is why nuns wear the wimple, I guess.

The nun opens the door once more to let me back inside the convent. She sits on the narrow bench and pulls from her pocket a small black notebook with an even smaller pencil tucked inside its cover. I give her the Brants' address and then watch as she tucks the pencil inside the notebook and makes both vanish within the folds of her habit.

"Thank you," I say sincerely with my hand on the doorknob.

The nun holds the door open and watches as I go down the steep front steps. "God bless you and keep you, my child," she says before closing the door between us.

I close the heavy iron gate behind me and look up at the fortress-like building. There's no way Martha could break out of this place. I hope somehow Martha knows that I haven't abandoned her.

To my surprise, I find Paul waiting for me at the corner. He holds out a box and offers an apologetic grin. "Sorry I was late today—there was a long line at the store."

I take the box but look back over my shoulder at the convent. The curtained windows show no sign of Martha. "I just lied to a nun," I tell Paul.

"Guess you're going to hell then," he says. We both laugh and then he points to the box. "Open it."

I loosen the string and tear away the plain brown paper to find a pair of brown leather ice skates inside. I make another confession: "I don't know how to skate."

"Not yet," he says, holding up his own worn skates so that the metal blades clank together.

I glance over my shoulder once more at the convent. "I think those nuns are holding my friend hostage."

Paul frowns. "Why would they do that?"

"Because she's a sinner."

Paul laughs and quips, "We're all sinners."

I punch him playfully in the chest. "You sound just like that nun!"

"Well, she's right—none of us is perfect."

"I know. But sometimes people call you a sinner just to make you feel ashamed of who you are." I frown and scan the convent windows once more.

Paul gently takes my chin in his hand and turns my head away from the convent. Once he's got my undivided attention he says, "Why don't we check on your friend next Sunday—and every Sunday—until you're sure that she's alright."

"You'll come with me?" I ask, touched by his offer.

"Of course! *If* you allow me to take you skating when the rink opens next week."

I agree and the following week we head for the town of Williamsburg in a gig Paul borrowed from a friend. It's not always easy for us to go out together in public because people mistake Paul for a White man and then despise him for "consorting with a negress." Having our own ride means we can avoid potential harassment from people taking the trolley.

There's no snow on the ground yet but there's a real chill in the air, and the rink is clearly a popular destination. For a moment I worry that the rink won't admit Black people, but then I squeeze Paul's hand and know he wouldn't take me any place where I wouldn't feel welcome. When we reach the entrance, Paul pays for two tickets and we prepare ourselves to join the dozens of other skaters out on the ice. A few months ago they were playing baseball on this fenced-in field, but now Union Pond has frozen over and the rink is packed with courting couples, rowdy packs of teenage boys, and families enjoying the brisk afternoon.

I've been on rollerblades before but this is my first time on ice — and my first time skating in a dress! I watch the wealthy ladies gracefully circling the rink in stylish skating ensembles trimmed with fur and know I won't attract any admiration with my anxious, awkward movements. Paul holds one of my hands and wraps his other arm firmly around my waist. That's the only way I'm able to stay upright, but Paul doesn't laugh as I wobble along on my new skates, clinging to him for dear life.

As the sun sets, lights blaze from the three-storey pagoda in the center of the field. It's a strange, small building with a pointy roof that seems to serve no purpose other than to provide light for night skating. After a long hour with only one or two falls — set to music, because there's a live band! — Paul guides me over to the seating area where we rest and huddle together to keep warm. While waiting for the fireworks to begin, we take from our pockets the fat wedges of pound cake that Nannie packed for us and devour them while watching the remaining skaters.

Most families have gone home for the night, which leaves only a few love-struck couples and the wild, intoxicated boys who tear around the rink knocking each other down, or play crack the whip just to send one of their friends smashing into the fence.

I'm pulling on my mittens again after polishing off Nannie's rich cake when something on the ice rink catches my eye. There's a tall blond boy zipping across the ice like he was born on blades. His face is familiar but I don't remember where I've seen him before until I see the Black boy holding his hand. It's Peter.

"What's wrong?" Paul asks.

I open my mouth to respond but suddenly the sky explodes with color as the pyrotechnics begin. The band plays louder in order to be heard over the booming explosions, and the crowd gasps in awe and applauds as each glittering rocket flares in the darkness. Paul wraps his arm around me to pull me close. I want to enjoy the show but instead my eyes scan the rink for Peter.

Even with the pagoda's candles burning bright and the night sky lit with sulfur, it's hard to clearly see the faces of the skaters. Many have scarves wrapped around their faces so I search for the flash of gold until I find the German-American boy with his long blond hair whipping behind him. Peter's arm must have healed because he shows no sign of pain as he clutches the White boy's hand and whirls around the rink. Then I realize they aren't playing crack the whip, and they aren't drunk like the other young men at the rink. The blond boy doesn't want to free himself from Peter. And Peter doesn't want him to let go.

I tune out the blaring brass band and the blasts overhead as I struggle to recall something Peter said to me before we journeyed back in time. *I live between two worlds...I've had to learn how to be two things at once...I live with my uncle because my parents threw me out...*

I didn't understand then what he was trying to tell me, but now it's starting to make sense. Peter said he once asked his uncle to "fix" him, but his uncle couldn't—or wouldn't. *He said it wasn't his place to change God's work. God made me, and no ritual or prayer or potion can change what God made.*

There must have been a time when Peter hoped his uncle could use his priestly powers to make him straight. But watching Peter out on the rink, so alive and happy—truly happy—it's hard to believe he'd make that same wish now. Then panic seizes my heart, sucking the air from my lungs. Judah. He doesn't know. He *can't* know because in his mind, gay men *aren't* men. Peter would no longer be Judah's best friend—he'd be just a *batty bwoy* for "real" men to kick, curse, and shoot in the head. *Boom Bye Bye.*

My eyes fill with tears as my heart reminds me—once again—of Judah's betrayal. I know all too well how much it hurts when Judah turns his back on you for no reason—or for something you can't control. Peter left a lot behind in 2001 and I know he didn't ask to be here. But in this other world Peter has found something precious: real friendship—maybe even love—with someone who accepts him for who he really is. I hope, for his sake, that it lasts as long as possible. I hope the joy Peter feels tonight is worth the risk.

"Genna?"

I jump and realize that the firework show has drawn to a close. One last rocket shoots up into the black sky and showers us with glittering silver light. Then the band finishes its last song with a flourish and those left at the rink applaud. I look at Paul and smile, hoping the darkness hides the tears shining in my eyes. Paul tugs at my hand until the mitten slides off my left hand.

"I've got an answer for you—and a question. You asked me to go back to your world with you, and I've given it a lot of thought. Have you thought about what I asked you?"

The rink suddenly feels quiet as the other skaters head toward the exit, leaving me and Paul alone on the bleachers. I try to answer but find my throat has closed so I simply nod instead.

Paul reaches into his pocket and pulls out a ring. "I hope it fits," he says anxiously. "It was my mother's." Then he takes my left hand in his own shaking hand and slides the ring onto my finger. In the darkness I can only see the gleam of a gemstone and two small white pearls set in gold.

"My father couldn't marry my mother, but he loved her and she always told me this ring was proof of his love for us both. It came to me when she died." When I still can't manage to utter a word, Paul nervously clearly his throat. "It's a green garnet. You can't really see in this light, but in the morning—" Paul's voice trails off and he waits in silence for me to respond.

"It's beautiful," I finally manage to whisper. The tears Judah brought to my eyes earlier spill down my cheeks and onto our cold, clasped hands.

Paul uses his thumb to gently brush my tears away. "Will you marry me, Genna? I'm willing to start a new life with you—in the future—if you'll be my wife."

I don't mean to look away but suddenly I want to see Peter and his friend one last time. I scan the rink but can't find them. The memory of their shared joy lingers in my mind, however, and when I look at Paul it's clear how much he cares for me. He has never asked me to be anything other than who and what I am. When I deceived him, he forgave me. When I abandoned him, he welcomed me back with open arms. I look at Paul and see the fear darkening his eyes. He's willing to risk everything for me. I squeeze his hand and then throw my arms around his neck. I don't know what our future together will be like. But Paul is loving, and loyal, and willing to spend the rest of his life with me. I owe him this much—and more.

"You haven't given me an answer," he reminds me.

I unwrap my arms and press my lips against his. "Yes."

Paul and I leave the rink with our skates slung over our shoulders and our mittened hands clasped between us. As we near the parked gig, a burst of male laughter draws our attention. I turn and see Peter staggering toward the road with the White boy's arm draped around his neck. Off the ice they are graceless but their bodies are still loose, and they lean comfortably against one another like lifelong friends.

For just an instant, Peter's eyes meet mine. I try to smile in a way that will let Peter know that I'm happy for him. Part of me wants to rush over and show him my ring, to let him to know that I've found someone, too. But I don't want to intrude. So I don't say a word and just hope Peter knows that he has nothing to fear—no reason to feel embarrassed or ashamed. But Peter doesn't smile back at me. He just looks away and then steers his friend across the street.

Genna

52.

Before Paul can take me back to the convent on Sunday, a breathless White boy knocks at the kitchen door and hands Nannie a note before dashing off once more. Nannie tries to read it but she struggles with cursive and so passes the folded piece of paper to me. She watches anxiously as my eyes scan the hastily written lines.

"It's not about Paul, is it?" she asks.

I shake my head. "It's Martha." I slump down in my chair and stare blankly at the potatoes I'd been peeling a moment ago. "She's had her baby. It's a boy."

"So soon?" Nannie asks with a concerned frown. When I don't respond, Nannie reaches for the woolen shawl that hangs by the back door. "Here," she says as she hands the shawl to me. "I can give Henry his supper tonight. You go on over there and see what you can do for the poor gal. She could use a friend right now."

I hurry over to the convent and along the way try not to think about the worst possible outcomes. I don't know what I'll find when I get there, but it's hard to imagine a happy ending to Martha's story.

Once again the young nun opens the door and this time her smile is reassuring.

"Thank you for sending that note," I say once I've caught my breath.

She pulls me inside the convent and tells me to follow her. We go down the hall and upstairs to a room that's not unlike the sleeping quarters in the orphanage at Weeksville. This room's not as large or drafty, and lacks the faint smell of urine and unwashed bodies. Instead of housing dozens of kids, this tidy room has only ten occupants. Nine of the beds are neatly made and only one bed is occupied at this time of day. The young nun lets me find my own way to Martha's bedside with a request for me not to tire her further by staying too long.

I slowly walk to the far end of the room, my heart pounding inside my chest. Martha doesn't seem to hear me approaching despite the sound of hardwood floors creaking beneath my weight. She is too absorbed in the bundle she's holding in her arms.

I stand at the foot of the bed and try to get a glimpse of the baby's face, but he's swaddled in a yellow blanket. "Martha?"

Martha makes a sound but doesn't tear her eyes away from the baby. It's not until I sit down on the edge of the bed that she looks up at me.

"He's so beautiful, Genna. Just like his da."

I lean forward and pull away the blanket that's covering the baby's face. A gasp escapes my lips just as tiny brown fingers curl around Martha's pinky finger. Martha's baby is Black. That doesn't mean Willem's the father—Martha had a lot of "customers" at the brothel. But whoever the father may be, the tiny brown baby *is* beautiful. I sit back and say, "Congratulations, Martha."

She smiles dreamily and keeps gazing down at her newborn boy. "He's a gift from God. An angel of my own. My very own..."

Martha looks much better than the last time I saw her. Her hair is pulled back in a loose braid, though damp tendrils curl around her temple. Her belly is still swollen but it's clear she's been fed well here at the convent. She obviously beat the fever but there's no telling what other challenges she'll face in the months and years to come. Sexually transmitted diseases like syphilis can't be treated in 1863, and often it isn't even diagnosed until the disease is too advanced to treat. I think of the illustrated books I've seen in Dr. Brant's office and pray that Martha and her son will never suffer those kinds of symptoms.

The young nun comes into the room and gently eases the baby out of Martha's arms.

"Try to get some rest, dear," she says as she walks away cradling the baby.

Martha looks heartbroken but she forces herself to smile and says, "I will, Sister Margaret."

"Where is she taking him?" I ask with my eyes on Sister Margaret's back. I've heard stories about babies being sold or given away without their mother's consent. I'm not even sure a White girl like Martha will be allowed to keep her Black baby. Yet the orphanage at Weeksville is full. No one's rushing to adopt Black babies in 1863.

Martha sinks back against her pillows, the exhaustion showing in her face now that the baby is gone. "To the nursery. All the babies are kept in there."

I wait until the nun turns a corner and disappears from sight before I ask, "Are you okay here, Martha?"

She sighs heavily but still manages to smile. "'Course I am. I never been treated so well in all my life! The holy sisters have been ever so kind."

"So they don't—I mean, do they make you do anything you don't want to do? Because I could get you out of here. You and the baby could come stay with me and Mattie at the Brants'."

Martha surprises me by laughing out loud. "Mrs. Brant won't ever take me back! Not after the way I carried on. I'm ashamed to think of the state I was in back then. 'Sides, I don't wanna go nowhere else. The nuns have taught me so many things, Gen—and they've promised they'll help me find a job once I'm on my feet again. Honest work in a respectable home—or a factory even! They teach us needlework 'n how to make wreaths out of flowers—fake ones, o' course, but they're ever so lovely! I can make shirts, too." Martha leans forward and whispers, "Teresa made the vestments for Father Michael! Her stitches are better 'n mine but I'm goin' to keep on practicin' till mine are just are fine as hers."

I smile and wonder if I should set my fears aside. If Martha's content, maybe the nuns really do have her best interest at heart. Then I remember that as Martha's friend, it's my job to see the things she can't see for herself. "When I came to visit you before, they told me you were praying." I stop and wait for Martha to say something but she just watches me with drowsy eyes. "They said you couldn't have any visitors because you were praying to atone for your sins."

Martha perks up and nods eagerly. "Have you seen the chapel, Genna? It's *gorgeous* — stained glass windows with more colors than a rainbow 'n fine paintings all 'round the altar. Sweet lil' babies everywhere — cherubs they're called. And the Holy Mother, o' course, cradlin' her own precious babe. I go there when I need to talk to God and sometimes just to sit 'n think."

"So you don't have to kneel?" I ask warily.

"Only when I'm prayin' — but there are stars on the floor! And marble steps leading up to the sacred altar. At first I didn't want to touch nothin' — I didn't feel worthy to be in such a holy place. But the Reverend Mother helped me to understand that we purify ourselves through prayer. Sometimes I lose track o' time when I'm in the chapel. It's where I feel close to God."

Martha's barely able to keep her eyes open, but she's smiling and squeezing my hand.

I squeeze back and find myself making an unexpected confession. "I feel terrible about what happened to you, Martha. If I'd known that you'd end up in that…awful place…I don't know what I could have done, but I want you to know that I'm sorry, Martha. I'm so sorry."

Martha reaches over and cups my face in the palm of her hand. Her tenderness surprises me and I wonder if motherhood has changed her already. "You saved me, Genna. You made sure my baby wasn't born in that house of sin. Now I'll have a piece of my Willem to hold onto. My poor love's dead but he's not gone."

Willem died — was killed by a White mob — during the draft riots back in July. And sometime in August Martha started working at the brothel. I do the math and realize Martha's right. Dr. Brant got it wrong—the baby didn't come early. Willem must be the father. "What will you call the baby?" I ask.

"Willem, of course."

Martha falls back against her pillows with a satisfied smile on her face.

I watch her for a moment and then lean forward and kiss her forehead. "Sweet dreams, Martha. You're going to have to be strong for your baby."

Martha nods and finally lets her eyes close. Just when I think she has fallen asleep, Martha squeezes my hand. "I'll be such a good mum, Genna. I'll do right by my baby, I will."

I hush Martha once more and sit with her until she's sound asleep. On my way out, I stop an older nun and ask if I can see the chapel. She gives me a strange look but nods wordlessly and leads me down the hall to a pair of double doors. Everything Martha said was true—the chapel is beautiful. Tall stained glass windows on either side of the pews show different saints performing acts of kindness. As I draw closer to the front of the chapel, I see that Martha's right—there are angels everywhere. Their winged faces appear in the stained glass windows that line the walls, in the colorful paintings that circle the altar, and it looks like there's even an angel in the domed ceiling. But not one of these cherubs looks like Martha's brown baby.

As I leave the chapel I turn the ring Paul placed on my finger. It's hard to believe that soon I will be walking down an aisle like this as his bride. I think of little Willem cradled in Martha's loving arms and know I don't want to wind up in her position. Babies aren't angels—I know from experience that they're a lot of work. I love Tyjuan and I love Henry but if I were responsible for taking care of either one, I'd have to kiss my dream of going to Harvard goodbye. A baby at sixteen would mean the end of all my dreams. I need to make sure Paul understands that. There are so many things we have to do before we even think about starting a family.

Despite the cold, I take my time walking back to the Brants'. If

Martha's happy at the convent, there's no point offering to take her with us when we travel into the future. And though my time-traveling skills are improving, it could still be a bumpy ride and I'm not ready to risk a newborn's life. I make a mental list of all the people I need to say goodbye to this time around. Should I bother telling Judah? Part of me wonders what he would say if he saw my ring and knew that I'd made other plans, too.

When I finally get home, I find Peter sitting on the back steps. He jumps up when he sees me and steps forward, tugging down the brim of his tweed cap.

"I need you to open the door, Genna. *Now.* I can't wait any longer. I need to get out of this world." Peter pauses and presses his lips together. Then he pulls me a bit farther away from the door where Nannie is no doubt listening to every word we say. In a weary voice he says, "Judah knows."

"Knows what?"

"About me...and Fritz." Peter takes the cap off his head, revealing a badly bruised left eye.

For a moment I say nothing. Peter watches me, waiting to see if I can understand his sense of urgency. I reach out to touch Peter's face but he steps back and puts the cap back on his head. I drop my hand and shiver as a cold thread of energy coils around my spine. If Judah were within reach right now, I'd make him pay for hurting Peter. But Judah isn't within reach, so I fold my arms across my chest and ask, "How did he find out?"

Peter looks over his shoulder at the lights burning on the other side of the river. "We went into the city. There's a beer cellar there, Pfaff's, that lets...it's a place where men can go to—socialize." My eyebrows go up and Peter sucks his teeth. "It's just a place I heard about. I wasn't even sure they'd let me in, but Walt Whitman used to go there so I wanted to check it out."

We read Walt Whitman's poetry in English class. I know that he was gay, and I know that there are plenty of gay bars in twenty-first century New York City. I've been to the Village a couple of times, and the annual Gay Pride Parade always makes the local news. When I babysat for Hannah I'd always see rainbow flags in some of the windows in her neighborhood. But I never thought there would be places like that in 1863. In this era, homosexuality is against the law. I know how hard it is to be Black and female in this world, so I can just imagine what it's like to be Black and gay. Part of me wants to tell Peter to hide that part of himself, even though I know he shouldn't have to. We run from so many things in this world. There ought to be at least one place where he can feel free.

Peter's eyeing me impatiently. "I don't know why Judah was in the city but he saw me—*us*—outside the saloon. We weren't doing anything, just talking to some of the regulars. Judah just walked up, spun Fritz around, and punched him in the face. Then he turned his fury on me. If the others hadn't pulled him off me...I want to go home, Genna—I can't wait any longer. You said you could do whatever you had to do before Christmas. Well, that's just a few days from now. You promised me, Genna."

"I know. I just have a few loose ends to tie up. Can you be ready at the end of the week?"

"I'm ready *now!*" Peter hisses.

"Well, I'm not! Just give me a few more days, Peter. You're not in danger, are you? Does anyone else know?" Peter shakes his head and looks away. "You don't think Judah would come looking for you, do you?"

Peter makes a sound of contempt. "Not a chance. Judah's done with me."

Peter tries to hide the pain of that fact but I see it just the same. I want to say, "I know what you're going through," but I'm not sure I do. Judah doesn't want me anymore, but I don't think he hates me. He doesn't believe I deserve to die.

"I could talk to him, if you want," I offer.

"NO!"

Peter's vehemence surprises me. "Why not? He owes you an apology, at the very least."

Peter just shakes his head. "You don't get it."

"No—I don't. Why should Judah even care? It's your life. You can love whoever you want."

"You know it's not that simple. Not for me—and not for Judah." Peter nervously tugs at his cap and says, "What do you know about Judah's mother?"

His question catches me off guard. "Nothing, really. I met his aunt a few times but he never really talked about his mother."

Peter nods but keeps his eyes on his feet. "You ever wonder why?"

I frown and consider both questions. Why *didn't* Judah talk about his mother? And why didn't I notice when we were together? Paul often talks about his mother even though she passed away when he was a boy. He loves to share his memories of her and I know it makes him proud to see me wearing her ring.

I look up and find Peter watching me. I think he takes some strange pleasure in treating this like a game. *He* has already solved this puzzle but he's waiting to see if I can figure it out, too. I wait for him to give me another clue.

"Judah's father killed himself," he says finally.

I nod. That much I knew. "His mother died when he was young, too, right?"

"She was murdered," Peter says flatly. "Judah's father hacked her to death with a machete."

"Oh, my God!"

My horror pleases Peter and so he gives me another clue. "Judah was there."

I know about domestic violence. I know couples argue and sometimes men lash out. It happened in my own home but Papi never went that far. He never should have hit Mama but once he did, he left.

"Why would he do that, Genna? Why would a man kill the mother of his child?"

I frown and try to spot the trap I know Peter is setting for me. "Maybe he was jealous. Maybe he thought there was another man."

Peter shakes his head. "There was no other man. But there was a woman. He killed her, too."

"What are you saying, Peter? His mother was — I mean, was she a…?"

Peter's lips twist with obvious disdain. "You can't even say it."

My cheeks burn as I struggle to make it clear that I'm not a bigot like Judah. "I'm just trying to figure this out! Are you saying Judah's mother was — that she turned into a…" I stumble over my words, which only makes Peter sneer at me. Finally I ask, "Did she love women?"

Peter shrugs. "People thought she was a lesbian."

"But she had Judah. Doesn't that mean she's…bi?"

"Whatever word you use, the bottom line is that the choices she made cost her her life. She lived with another woman. People talked. She died."

"Maybe they were just friends."

"Maybe they were more than friends," Peter counters.

"Well — which is it?" I ask impatiently.

"I don't know, Genna. I wasn't there."

"But Judah was."

"Yeah."

Nannie opens the back door and shakes a rug free of dust. I know that's my cue to come inside. Peter heads toward the street.

"I'll come back on Saturday," he says. "You can tell me then when we're leaving and where to meet you."

I nod and then surprise us both by saying, "You could bring Fritz, you know."

Peter just shakes his head and keeps walking. I follow him into the shadows and ask, "Why not? It's clear you care about each other."

"It's too soon and it's too much to ask. I'd be all he had in a totally foreign world. I'd have to explain everything to him on top of being his only friend — and maybe his first lover."

I don't mean to, but I flinch and then blush when Peter uses that word. His life in this world—and the world we left behind—is so different than mine. I'm only realizing now how brave Peter is.

"Maybe?" I ask, hoping I seem curious and not just nosy.

"Do you know what 'gay' means in this world, Genna? *Happy.* Gay people have been around forever, not that you'd know it from our history textbooks. But Fritz isn't part of a community or a movement. He doesn't even know what a homosexual is! *He likes me*—that's it. We like each other, and we spend time together, and maybe that could lead to something more. But his parents have already picked out a nice German girl for him to marry, and he's not about to let them down. He's curious about everything—that's what I like about him—but he's not ready to be 'out and proud' in 1863 or 2001. And neither am I. I'm getting there, but…it's hard. In Haiti, I'm masisi. In the US, I'm a nigger to some and a faggot to others. It wouldn't be fair to bring Fritz into all of that. I'd have to protect him *and* myself, and that's more than I can handle right now."

For a moment Peter and I stand silently in the safety of the shadows. He avoids my eyes and I look away to hide the guilt I feel because the whole time Peter was talking, I was thinking about my own situation. I've known Paul longer than Peter has known Fritz. It will be different for us—that's what I tell myself.

"Paul and I are getting married," I say defiantly with my left hand held up even though Peter can't see the ring in the dark. "He's coming back with us."

For several seconds Peter says nothing. He just watches me, a small smile playing on his lips. "You're willing to roll the dice, huh?" When I just shrug he asks, "Does Judah know?"

Peter's question catches me off guard but I try to act nonchalant. "He doesn't care what I do," I say. Then I worry that that sounded petulant so I quickly add, "And I don't care what Judah does—not anymore."

Peter just watches me for a moment. Then he sighs heavily and says, "You might as well do what makes you happy, Genna. As my uncle always says, 'Deye mon gen mon.' Behind one mountain is another mountain."

I watch Peter let himself out through the gate and head up the street. He didn't have to say he was happy for me, but he didn't have to share that depressing proverb either. I don't need Peter to remind me that life is full of obstacles. I've been climbing uphill all my life.

Judah

52.

I hear them arguing in hushed tones before they even knock on the shed door. Genna's telling Mattie she doesn't have to come in but Mattie doesn't want to leave Genna alone with me.

"If he punched his own best friend, ain't no tellin' what he might do to you."

I wince and wonder who else knows about what happened between me and Peter. I'm not proud of hitting him, but I'm also not about to apologize to a couple of gossiping girls. Deceit has consequences. Peter's bruises will heal but I don't know if I'll ever recover from his betrayal. I knocked his "friend" down and then Peter looked me dead in the eye with no shame. No shame! I wouldn't have hit him so hard if he hadn't looked at me that way.

When they finally find the courage to knock, I harden my voice and tell them to come in. Genna is the first to enter but Mattie is close behind her and, as always, Money's pressed up next to her. They tumble in all together and I turn away to hide the smile sneaking across my face.

I keep working at the table and wait for them to say whatever it is they've come to say. Out of the corner of my eye I can see Mattie elbowing Genna as a way of encouraging her to get it over with. Mattie never liked me and the look on her face assures me that nothing has changed. Money watches the curls of shaved wood spiraling off the plane and shyly smiles up at me.

Genna clears her throat and waits until I look at her. "I just came to say goodbye."

Mattie twists up her face and mutters, "Good riddance, too!"

This time Genna elbows her and they fuss for a few more seconds before Genna goes on. "We're leaving on New Year's Eve." When I say nothing, Genna balls her hands into fists and lifts her chin up in the air. "Peter's coming with us."

I don't know why I'm giving her such a hard time. I could give her my full attention, let her say her piece, and then leave. But I don't. I keep running the plane along the piece of wood, knowing their eyes are on me. I nod at Money. "Want to give it a try?"

Money nods and steps forward but Mattie grabs his shoulder and pulls him back.

"We ain't here to learn no woodworkin.'"

Money looks longingly at the pile of curly wood shavings on the ground and surrenders his desire to work alongside me.

I surprise myself by saying, "Why don't you just leave him be, Mattie."

It's more of a command than a question and for a moment she just looks at me, too stunned to speak. Then Mattie pushes Money behind her and steps forward, stopping only when Genna puts her hand on Mattie's arm. "What you say to me?"

"Money's a boy, not a little girl. He can't be up under you all the time. Money's got to learn to look out for himself if he's going to make it in this world."

Even with Genna holding her back, Mattie manages to get close to me. I'm at least a foot taller than her, but Mattie's like that scrappy little dog on the block that gets in the face of pit bulls twice its size.

She plants her free hand on her hip and says, "Me and Money ain't got nothin' in this world but each other. Our mama told me to take care of him, and that's what I aim to do, and I don't need *you* tellin' me different. What you know anyhow? You a mean, sad loner. Ain't got nobody and don't care 'bout nobody but yourself. Esther's right—you ain't even civilized. Don't matter where you come from or where you go—you won't never be right. Them Liberians can have you, 'cause we sure don't need you 'round here."

Genna inserts herself between Mattie and me and tries to usher her friend back out the door. Mattie backs up but makes it clear she's not leaving without Genna.

I could drop it but I don't. I stand to my full height and talk over Genna's head. "You're supposed to take care of Money yet you're willing to put his life in *her* hands?"

Genna spins around to face me. "Mattie's not coming with us—and neither is Money."

I look past Genna and address Mattie instead. "Guess you got some sense after all."

Before Mattie can fire back at me, Genna turns to her friend and softly says, "You *could* come with us, Mattie. You and Money have come so far already...travelling's in your blood."

Mattie laughs a bit as if to say, "Ain't that the truth!" But then she gets quiet and looks up at Mr. Claxton's tools hanging on the shed wall. "I did give it some thought. I'm sure gonna miss you, Genna. But if we go with you, Papa won't be able to find us."

I look away, suddenly embarrassed to be witnessing this intimate moment between two friends. I think of Peter and the way we parted— the way he'll always remember me—and feel my face burn with shame. I return to my work with unnecessary vigor, trying to drown out the tenderness in Genna's voice. That's how she tricks people into opening up to her. Yet here she is, offering to drag Mattie and Money into the future like she knows what's best for them. It probably never occurred to her that Mattie was waiting for her father. Like so many fugitives, Mattie's holding onto the slender hope that the few remaining members of her family will be together again someday.

Like me, Genna knows that even after the war ends, most Black people will never find the loved ones they lost to slavery. I listen as she tries to gently reason with Mattie. "But—didn't you say he was sold down south? How's your father going to find you, Mattie?"

She shrugs but seems to trust her own logic. "Papa told us to head north. I figure once the war's over, he'll head north, too. He don't know 'bout Mama or Jackie. And Sophie…" Mattie touches her lips, stopping herself from reciting the names of the dead. "Me 'n Money—we got to wait for him. We's all Papa's got left."

Genna nods and then seems to remember that I'm still there. She stiffens and all the tenderness leaves her voice. "Good luck, Judah— wherever you end up."

"It's not about luck. Some of us have a destiny to fulfill."

I can tell Genna wants to walk away but she can't resist the urge to clap back. "You really think a lot of yourself, don't you? You think you can just show up in a place—Liberia, or Jamaica, or Haiti—and change the course of history? *You*—a teenager with nothing but a chip on his shoulder."

"There's a difference between confidence and arrogance. Claiming you can move through time—and take other people with you. If that's not arrogance, I don't know what is. Look what you did to Peter!"

Genna's eyes flash with rage. "Me? Look at what YOU did to Peter! Smashed your fist into his face and for what? Finding a *true* friend, one who accepts him for who he really is!

"Did you see that little blond fag—"

Genna lunges at me like she's going to cram the word back down my throat. Mattie tugs on Genna's hand and says, "Let's go, Genna. He ain't worth the spit it takes to curse."

Genna nods but keeps her eyes locked on mine. Even with Mattie tugging on her she leans in and hisses, "So what if he's White—so what if they're gay. SO WHAT?! You think you're perfect—better than everyone else. Out here in a barn talking about "destiny" —I see your destiny, Judah. You're destined to be miserable and alone because you can't stand to see anyone else happy. I feel sorry for you, I really do."

She turns and follows Mattie and Money who are already going out the door. My heart aches suddenly but the words that come out of my mouth are too petty to bring her back. "Try not to hurt anyone this time."

With one hand on the doorframe, Genna turns and calmly says, "No one will get hurt if they follow the rules."

I laugh and make sure she hears my contempt. "What rules? There are no RULES!" My stomach sinks with shame as I search for a way to prolong this argument. I fight because I don't have the courage to admit that I don't want to let her go. "You don't even know what you're doing," I say.

The fire is gone from Genna's voice. She looks at me and asks in a tired voice, "And you do? At least I've got a plan for my future, Judah. What have you got?"

"I've got plans, too." I hear the defensiveness in my own voice and try to infuse it with confidence I don't really feel. "Whatever I do will be for my people, Genna. *Our* people."

"You call them 'your people' but what if the folks in Liberia don't see you that way, Judah? You won't be one of them. And you'll probably die of fever like the most of the other settlers."

I think I hear concern in her voice. Could she still care for me? I shrug and tell her the truth. "I'm not afraid to die. We all got to go sometime, and I'd rather die *there* than *here*." I pause and look at her with my real eyes, my true heart. "Is that why you changed your mind, Gen? Were you afraid?"

She just sighs and says, "Africa was always your dream, Judah. Not mine."

I want to hide the hurt her words inflict, but the mask is too heavy to hold. I let it fall and whisper, "You said you'd go with me."

A tear rolls down Genna's cheek, letting me know she sees my heart. "I did. But I only said that because I wanted to be with you."

I finally allow my eyes to rest on the brilliant green gem circled with gold that flashes in the candlelight. "And now you want to be with him."

Genna turns the ring on her finger and I find myself hoping she'll pull it off. But she doesn't. It sparkles against her dark skin, taunting me. Genna nods and says, "I do," as if she's practicing for her wedding day.

"And I want to go home, Judah. I want to go back where I belong. You expected me to cross the ocean with you, following your dream. But what about what *I* want—did that ever matter to you?"

I don't have an answer so I pick up the plane and go back to work. When the door bangs shut and I'm sure that Genna's gone, I sink to my knees and let my tears fall silently into the soft wood shavings on the floor.

Genna

53.

Paul and I are married in Nannie's church. Our small wedding party assembles at Bridge Street African Wesleyan Methodist Episcopal Church on the morning of December 31, 1863. Paul is totally calm with his half-brother James standing by his side. Mattie is my maid of honor and Sam Jenkins does me the honor of walking me down the aisle. The only way I manage to say my vows is by reminding myself that this marriage isn't real. I love Paul and I intend to be faithful to him, but I don't know what will happen once we get to the future. I'll tell Mama and Toshi that Paul and I are married, but I won't tell anyone else that I'm a teen bride. And there will be no proof other than my ring and Paul's word.

I tell myself that nothing is final. This is a big step for me and I do think I'm moving toward the life I want. I don't feel trapped—I feel free because I know I still hold the power to turn back time.

After the ceremony Mrs. Brant generously hosts a dinner for us in her elegant dining room. It feels strange sitting around the table with our guests—most of whom are also the Brants' servants. It's a buffet dinner but Nannie and Mattie still have to do double duty otherwise there'd be no one to wait on us.

It's hard to anchor myself in the moment when I know that I have to open the portal in just a few hours. I have done everything I can to make sure my departure won't inconvenience anyone. Mrs. Brant agrees to have Mattie and Money move into my room on New Year's Day. Mattie will take over my job as Henry's nurse, and Money will help around the house on weeknights and weekends. During the day he'll attend Colored School No. 1 in Ft. Greene.

Like the Brants, Nannie thinks Paul and I are heading to California. She has given us her blessing and now that she can read a little, Nannie urges us to write as soon as we're settled. I feel a stab of guilt when I promise to keep in touch, but then remind myself that this doesn't have to be a one-way trip. If the portal becomes easier to open, that "commuter life" I thought about just might become a reality.

When dinner is over, Paul and I retreat to the carriage house, which Nannie and Mattie have decorated in our honor. Adams kindly offered to spend New Year's Eve with his sister so that Paul and I can spend our wedding night in his living quarters. Paul wanted us to stay at a fancy hotel, but I knew they would only think I was a prostitute with a wealthy john. Besides, if all goes as planned, we'll be gone by midnight. No point wasting money on a room we'll only need for a few more hours.

Even with the door closed, we can still smell the horses down below, but we're too busy feverishly exploring each other's body to think too much about that. It takes forever for Paul to peel away my dress and endless underclothes, and he's so nervous that his fingers fumble with all the hooks, buttons, and strings he has to untie. When I'm half-undressed he says maybe we should wait until after the journey to consummate our marriage. But I don't want to wait. We'll be living with Mama for the next little while so we need to make the most of this moment because I don't know when we'll have a place of our own again.

Unlike the wedding ceremony, this part of our marriage feels real. I'm glad I brought a box of condoms with me when I returned, though at the time I imagined I'd be using them with Judah. It turns out Paul isn't as experienced as I thought he would be, so I take charge and help him put the condom on. He doesn't seem to mind following my lead, and so I make a few other suggestions. He comes faster than I do but Paul doesn't just pull out and fall asleep like (I've heard) some guys do. Paul wants to please me as much as I want to satisfy him, and so we take our time and let ourselves laugh when things don't work out as planned. He kisses me everywhere—I mean *everywhere*—and then twines his fingers in my locks—the locks I grew to please Judah. I don't let myself think about how it would feel to have Judah's hands touching me instead of Paul's.

When we wake up we sponge ourselves clean with the cold water in the basin. I leave my wedding dress behind and instead put on the clothes I traveled in before. Paul likes the way I look in jeans and I tell him to get used to it because I won't be wearing a corset and petticoat anymore. We strip the sheets from Adams' bed and fold them neatly. It's a little strange to think of Nannie washing the sheets we just had sex on, but we're married now so Nannie probably won't mind. She's probably hoping for grandkids but Paul and I have agreed that that won't happen anytime soon. I'm going to ask Toshi how to get on the Pill as soon as I get home.

Home.

We slip away from the Brants without any fanfare. Paul's brother has agreed to drive us out to Weeksville. He doesn't say much during the ride, and he doesn't ask any questions when we ask to be dropped off at the crossroads that Peter selected. Paul shakes his brother's hand and then James wishes us luck and drives away in the gig without looking back.

I kneel, unzip my bookbag, and begin unpacking the items I'll need to open the door. I'm emptying a plastic bottle of water into the stainless steel bowl when Peter arrives. He nods at Paul and from his own satchel pulls out another paket. I set it on the ground next to the bowl. In my pocket I've got the knife and the penny Paul gave me on Thanksgiving.

It's New Year's Eve but there are no revelers around—the crossroads are silent and dark. I think of the ball dropping in chaotic Times Square and for the hundredth time hope that Paul won't be overwhelmed by my world. I turn to him and hold out my hand. "Stay close," I tell him.

Peter steps forward as well. He has chosen a spot that's isolated but not too far from Weeksville. Hopefully that means we will "land" in the same part of Brooklyn. There is no traffic at this time of night and there is only a sliver of moon above. A stray dog is sniffing around and barks occasionally. When Paul picks up a stone to throw at the mangy dog, Peter grabs his arm.

"Don't," he says testily. "Dogs are sacred to Papa Legba."

Paul looks around and frowns. "Who's that?"

I give him a look that says, "Don't ask," but Peter answers just the same. "He's the guardian of the crossroads."

I hold my other hand out to Peter. "Ready?"

Peter doesn't reply and doesn't take my hand. He squints at the darkness beyond me and asks, "Who's that?"

I turn and look down the road that leads to Weeksville. Mattie is hurrying along with a lantern swinging in her hand. Money is close behind her. She rushes up to me, breathless.

"Did you change your mind?" I ask her, surprised by the hopefulness in my voice.

Mattie shakes her head and tries to catch her breath. "We just came to say goodbye."

"Again," says Money in a sleepy voice.

Mattie throws her arms around me. "You can come back, right?"

I nod and blink away the tears in my eyes. I said goodbye to Mattie and Money after our wedding dinner earlier today. I hoped to make a clean break but I am glad she came to see us off. "Make sure you two stand far back, okay?"

Mattie nods and leads her little brother back down the road. Peter watches her go but keeps peering into the darkness. "There's someone else on the road," he says nervously.

We wait to see if anyone else will emerge from the shadows but the lone figure stops moving.

"It's Judah," Peter says.

"He's not coming with us, is he?" Paul asks testily.

I shake my head and turn my back to Judah. "He's come to watch me fail."

Paul drops my hand and wraps his arm around me instead. He presses his lips to my temple and I try to still the quavering feeling within. I can't do this if I have any doubt. I have to *believe* I can open the door.

"You won't fail," Peter assures me. "Prann kouraj. Be strong."

I nod and pull the knife from my pocket. Paul looks anxious but I tell him I just need a bit of blood. I dig the blade tip into my scarred palm and smear the penny in my blood before dropping it into the bowl of water. Then I hold out my hands. Paul grabs hold of my bloody hand and Peter takes the other. I think I can hear Mattie crying softly in the distance. My own tears start to fall as I think about how blessed I have been to be so loved in this world.

I search the darkness of my mind for a light to guide me but the candle does not appear. I take deep breaths to steady my heart. I have to give the task at hand my total concentration, but Judah's eyes tug at me like a magnet. To break his spell, I remind myself that I have changed. I am not the same girl who so foolishly surrendered her heart. I am stronger now, wiser. I have a husband—a lover—who would do anything for me. I remember the sensation of Paul's lips exploring my body just a few hours ago. My skin tingles, tightens, and then hardens like a shield.

I can do this.

And yet—against my will—I look back over my shoulder. The sight of Judah rushing up the road sets something on fire inside of me. Does he want me to stay? Is he coming with us—or is he trying to stop me from doing what *I* want to do? My heart beats so fast I can barely breathe.

Then an invisible finger reaches out from the darkness and presses the button in my back. Pain streaks up my spine and I lift my head to the sky before letting out a scream that terrifies us all. Thunder suddenly booms above us and it feels as if the earth shudders beneath my feet. I am frightened. I am furious. I am searching for the open door but can only focus on my pain. Between the explosions of thunder and the crackle of lightning I hear other voices in distress. And then, amidst all the chaos, I see it—the beacon that will guide me back to my world. I crush the hands within my own and tuck my chin into my chest before charging toward the future.

Without opening my eyes, I see everything that is happening behind me. Money bolts across the field with Mattie several steps behind him. Money flees from the streaks of lightning shattering the sky. He swims through the blue night air and I see Judah reach out a hand to grab the frightened boy, but then my neck snaps back and a bolt of energy surges through my body. I grip the hands of my fellow travelers and command the door to open...

We tumble like dice along the pavement. My skin tears against the concrete and my head throbs with blinding pain. There are too many bodies feeling too many emotions, and I struggle to disentangle myself. It is a brisk autumn night in the city. It must be late because only a few people are walking along the parkway, but the roar of traffic makes me raise my hands to my ears. But I instantly wince in pain and look down to find my palms have been scraped bloody. I turn myself over and survey the damage: my jeans are torn and so is the skin on my knees. My body is tired and sore, but not broken.

Paul is sprawled nearby, too stunned to move, his eyes wide with alarm. A few feet away, Peter grabs hold of a bench and pulls himself up off the ground. He holds his head in his hands and takes several deep breaths before uttering in Kreyol what sounds like a prayer of thanks. Then his face changes and I follow his gaze farther down the parkway to see what has shocked Peter. I see a boy sobbing and a kneeling man cradling the child in his arms. I see the smear of blood on the man's dark skin and then realize what I have done. Judah is here. And the boy in his arms is Money.

My heart stops. "Mattie?" I call her name quietly at first but as my panic grows, I lift myself from the ground and scream as loud as I can. "MATTIE!"

What have I done?

Judah's eyes accuse me, though no words come from his mouth. He blames me. He hates me. If ever I hoped that Judah and I might one day reconcile, I know that will never happen now. Peter sinks onto the bench and holds his head in his hands. I have betrayed him, too. With Judah in this world, Peter's secret is no longer safe.

I look down at my bleeding hands and try to block out Money's frantic cries for his lost sister. I can fix this. I have opened the door between his time and ours more than once. I tell myself I can do it again. I can go back and find her—take Money back or bring Mattie here to this world. Unless...

What if she has landed somewhere else in Brooklyn? Or what if her arrival is merely delayed—will she appear on the parkway a day or week from now?

What have I done?

Paul stares at the streetlights and the cars zooming down the parkway with his mouth hanging open. I want him to hold me until the shaking stops. I want him to claim me the way Judah has claimed Money. But everything is alien to him right now. This Brooklyn must seem like another planet.

"Paul?"

My voice, faint as it is, carries enough pain and need to draw him— my husband—to my side.

"Are you hurt?" he asks. Paul immediately gathers my hands in his own and brushes the tears from my cheek with his lips. Then he wraps me in an embrace that nearly crushes the air from my lungs. I am all he has now. He needs me to be his anchor. I can feel his heart racing inside his chest. He wants to comfort me but this is *my* world. I have brought him here and in this world he is as helpless as Money.

With his arms around me I barely find enough air to sob quietly. "I didn't mean to...I would never do anything to hurt her...Money's all she had left!"

Paul is suffocating me and so I push against him to break his embrace. I've got to take charge. My eyes desperately scan the parkway for landmarks to help me situate myself. We aren't far from the museum. Maybe Mattie landed closer to Weeksville. The thought of her alone in this terrifying new world prompts me to act. I grab Paul's hand and call Peter over.

"We have to find Mattie," I tell them. "Peter, you cover the blocks south of the parkway and we'll search the ones to the north."

Peter gives me a hopeless look but agrees to help in the search. Then dread fills his face as he stares past me at someone approaching us from behind. I spin, hoping to find Mattie, but it's only Judah. Money clings to his leg the way he used to cling to his big sister.

Judah points at Money. "Look what you've done."

The shy boy has never looked more miserable. My heart aches for him but when I pull my gaze away, Judah barks at me. "LOOK AT HIM!"

Paul jumps between us and pushes Judah away. Judah grabs Paul under the arms and tries to throw him to the ground. But Paul stands firm and the two of them wrestle until Peter and I manage to pry them apart. Money wails pitifully, shaming us all.

I kneel and pull the frightened boy into my arms. His body trembles against mine, refusing to be soothed.

"Don't worry, Money," I tell him with false confidence. "Mattie will be here soon." I smile brightly but Money doesn't raise his eyes to look at me.

"I want to go home," he says softly.

Before I can think of a way to reassure him, Judah pulls the boy away from me.

"Come on, Money," he says, "I'll take you home."

I jump up, my body suddenly electrified. "You can't take him home— only *I* can open the portal!"

Judah's disdainful eyes sweep over me. "The only thing *you* know how to do is destroy people's lives." Judah scoops Money up in his arms and backs away, his finger pointing at me. "You stay the hell away from me—and Money. I'm taking him to my aunt's place. We'll take care of him until you find a way to make things right. And you *better* make things right."

Paul hears the threat in Judah's voice and leans in, ready for another fight. This time I put my body between them.

"YOU did this!" I shout at Judah even as he retreats in disgust. "You ruined everything. You should have just left us alone…" A wailing siren drowns out my voice and I feel Paul cringe behind me as the ambulance races past.

Once it's gone, the city sinks into an eerie silence. Peter goes in the opposite direction from Judah. Paul slips his arms around my waist and rests his chin on my shoulder. We watch Judah carrying Money away, the child's head resting forlornly against his shoulder.

"Don't worry, Gen," Paul whispers in my ear. "We'll find her."

I layer my arms over Paul's and hold myself in an even tighter embrace. Together we anchor ourselves in this moment, in this world. I make a silent, solemn promise to myself—and to Mattie, wherever she may be.

I *can* fix this. I will make it right.

The End

THE DOOR AT
THE CROSSROADS

DISCUSSION GUIDE

Discussion Guide

- Peter warns Genna to be clear about what her heart most desires. What *does* Genna truly want? In which world does she belong?

- Judah learns that love can be a form of enslavement. Does closing his heart make him truly free? Would women be more powerful if they didn't feel bound to anyone else?

- Peter rightly resents Genna's attempts to take only what she needs from his religion. Where would you look if you needed to find magic within your own culture(s)? What does *black magic* mean to you?

- The teens in this novel are aware of the limits of their education. Their school textbooks don't teach them about LGBT contributions to history, Native American involvement in the Underground Railroad, and free Black communities like Weeksville. Does learning about the injustices of the past empower or embitter young people?

- Paul commits to returning with Genna to the twenty-first century. Was she honest about the progress Blacks in the US have made since 1863? Will Paul's life be better, worse, or about the same?

- The importation of enslaved Africans continued long after the 1807 abolition of the trans-Atlantic slave trade, but only Captain Nathaniel Gordon paid the ultimate price for continuing to sell human beings. Genna rescues Martha from a brothel but teenage girls continue to be trafficked for sexual purposes in the 21st century. Can slavery ever be abolished? Why does it persist? How does the sale of certain bodies diminish the freedom of others?

- Genna knows she's not ready to become a mother, but what will her life be like as a married teen in 2001? Can she still achieve her goal of becoming a psychiatrist? How will her mother react?

- Peter tells Genna that he knows how it feels to "live between two worlds" as an immigrant and a closeted gay teen. Does a hybrid identity allow one to be more authentic or is it a necessary disguise for some?

- Genna faces racism and sexism because of her identity as a young Black woman, but she also learns about her friends' struggles against Islamophobia and homophobia. Do intersectional identities make us more or less compassionate? Why do people who have faced bigotry inflict pain on others?

- Weeksville once served as a sanctuary for African Americans, but self-sufficient, all-Black towns have largely disappeared. Why? In what ways does the spirit of Weeksville live on in contemporary US cities? Where do Black lives matter most?

Acknowledgments

I take full responsibility for this book. When I finished writing *A Wish After Midnight* in 2003, I immediately got to work on the sequel, *Judah's Tale*. But my father had cancer and I was responsible for managing his care, so ultimately that book had to wait. I went back to it every couple of years, but I couldn't give the sequel my full attention and over time it evolved into *The Door at the Crossroads*. I know that readers who loved *A Wish After Midnight* have waited a long time to discover what happened to Genna and Judah, and I know that this book will likely be a disappointment for some. When I finally made finishing this sequel a priority, I accepted the fact that *The Door at the Crossroads* was going to be a very different book than *Judah's Tale*. I don't recommend writing a novel off and on over twelve years, but sometimes it happens and you just have to find your way to the end as best you can.

Like *A Wish After Midnight*, this novel is a work of speculative fiction. I pulled together certain historical facts, which served as loose parameters for the story I wanted to tell. My imagination helped me "fill in the gaps," but it isn't always easy to write in the era of Black Lives Matter and the tone of this novel is grim at times. As an immigrant, I have spent many hours wondering whether I truly belong in this country. And as gentrification reshapes Brooklyn, I worry that I may be displaced before I choose to move on. When I teach children about Weeksville, we focus on three themes: home, community, and belonging. This novel shares those themes, asking readers to consider just how much progress Blacks in this nation have made. I have sketched an outline for Book #3 but don't know where my home will be when I finally sit down to write.

I am a solitary person, but I could not publish my books without the support of my community. I met many wonderful people over the past decade, and their expertise contributed to the completion of this novel. Executive Director Tia Powell-Harris invited me to serve two terms as writer-in-residence at Weeksville Heritage Center, which had long been a dream of mine. The months I spent teaching children and adults about Weeksville helped to anchor me in the past while providing much needed time for me to dream and write. Everyone on staff at the center made me feel welcome and supported, and I thank you all for adopting me into the Weeksville family. The Malka Foundation and the NYC Department of Cultural Affairs funded my two residencies at the Weeksville Heritage Center, and I am grateful for their investment in such a vital cultural institution.

From 2011-2014 I taught in the Center for Ethnic Studies at Borough of Manhattan Community College; in 2012 I received a Faculty Development Grant that enabled me to travel to South Carolina on two occasions to conduct research for this book. I thank the institution and my Chair for supporting creative writing in the academy. I am also grateful for my women of color colleagues at BMCC who showed me how to stay focused on my own work despite the stress of teaching. When I made the decision to quit my job and leave the academy, another group of women of color came into my life and our monthly meetings helped me stay connected to the "kid lit" world. My west coast "rad women" held my hand as we explored other paths to publication and I am grateful for their daring, which continues to inspire and embolden me. And I would be lost without those dear sister-friends who, for over twenty years, have walked with me through the botanic garden, mailed me dragons, shared pancakes on Sunday, and sent me words of encouragement when I needed them most.

I am responsible, of course, for any errors in this book but I would still like to thank those who graciously offered me their assistance. Several Haitian friends helped me with Kreyol phrases and details about Vodou; thank you Vladimir Cybil Charlier, Ibi Zoboi, Jerry Philogene, Bertin Louis, and Gabrielle Civil. Sayida Self and Rod Ptahsen-Shabazz helped me with information about Rastafarian cultural practices and philosophy. Marissa Jackson suggested appropriate curses for Judah to use when he reached his breaking point. Terry Boddie, Tony Carter, and my cousin

Clayton Huggins shared their insights on the game of cricket. When I began to search for magic in children's books by African American authors, I naturally turned to the work of Virginia Hamilton; she cast a spell over so many young readers and it lingers to this day. Mary Cronin and Maria McGarrity helped me avoid the mistakes I made with my Irish-American characters in *A Wish After Midnight*. When I walked over to Clinton Hill to see The Sisters of Mercy Convent (now Mercy Home), Jyoti Lakhani welcomed me inside, gave me a tour, and let me linger a while in the chapel. When the novel was complete, I had three beta readers who provided excellent feedback, including my high school English teacher! Thank you, Stefanie Dash, Kate Foster, and Nancy Vichert for making time to read this long book and for offering such valuable feedback.

Operating outside of the traditional publishing industry isn't easy. Self-published books generally aren't eligible for review or for major awards, which can make it challenging to reach readers. Without the support of allies who are committed to decolonizing kid lit, most of my manuscripts would still be on my hard drive. I'd like to thank those educators who have shared my work with their students, and the handful of open-minded bloggers who feel my books are worthy of review. I especially appreciate those bold librarians who push back against policies that prohibit self-published books from being added to youth collections. Last but not least, I want to thank all the readers who have given my books a chance. Stories are meant to circulate, and I am indebted to everyone who refuses to judge a story by its source.

About the Author

Born in Canada, Zetta Elliott grew up reading British fantasy fiction that forced her to "dream herself into existence" (there were no Black girls with Afros in Narnia). She moved to the US in 1994 and is the author of twenty books for young readers, including the award-winning picture book *Bird*. Her urban fantasy novel *Ship of Souls* was named a *Booklist* Top Ten Sci-fi/Fantasy Title for Youth, and three of her self-published books have made the Best Children's Books of the Year list compiled by the Bank Street Center for Children's Literature. Her own imprint, Rosetta Press, generates culturally relevant stories that center children who have been marginalized, misrepresented, and/or rendered invisible in traditional children's literature. Elliott is an advocate for greater diversity and equity in publishing, and her essays have appeared in *Publishers Weekly*, *School Library Journal*, and *The Huffington Post*. She has served two terms as writer-in-residence at Weeksville Heritage Center and currently lives in Brooklyn. Learn more about the author and her books at www.zettaelliott.com.

Made in the USA
San Bernardino, CA
09 February 2019